SORROW

Tiffanie DeBartolo

woodhall press

Library of Congress Cataloguing-in-Publication Data available
ISBN Paperback 978-1-949116-30-4
ISBN Ebook 978-1-949116-31-1

First Edition
"Sorrow"
written by Matt Berninger and Aaron Dessner
Lyrics reprinted by permission of The National

Cover design by: Jessica Dionne Abouelela
Formatting: Jessica Dionne Abouelela

Woodhall Press, 81 Old Saugatuck Road, Norwalk, CT 06855
WoodhallPress.com
Distributed by INGRAM

For my parents

*Whoever uses the spirit
that is in him creatively is an artist.
To make living itself an art,
that is the goal.*

—HENRY MILLER

Nothing in any life,
no matter how well or poorly lived,
is wiser than failure
and clearer than sorrow.

—GREGORY DAVID ROBERTS, SHANTARAM

FROM: THOMAS FRASIER GALLERY <infothomasfrasiergallery.com>
SENT: Thurs, June 1, 2017 at 8:12 AM
TO: Joseph Harper <harperjoseph620@gmail.com>
SUBJECT: OCTOBER DANKO Sorrow: This is Art

The Thomas Frasier Gallery
in collaboration with
the San Francisco Museum of Modern Art
is proud to announce the world premiere of:

SORROW: This Is Art
A Living Exhibit by October Danko

October Danko's work has been a favorite
of art lovers from around the globe, and we are
pleased to invite you to the monthlong performance of:

SORROW: This Is Art
September 28–October 24

The newest piece in October's Living Exhibit series will find her sitting at a table in SFMoMa's Roberts Family Gallery from 10 a.m. until 5 p.m. daily. One at a time, gallery visitors will be invited to sit across from her and take her hands, wherein she will "hold their sorrow."

Each visitor may spend up to five minutes with the artist. They will be permitted to speak to her if they wish, but she will remain silent.

October explains: "This exhibit was inspired by my belief that pain can be art, that connecting as humans is the greatest gift we can give each other, and that, for better or worse, sometimes it's our pain that connects us."

*Ms. Danko suffers from Mirror Touch Synesthesia, a condition that enables her to experience the sensations of others simply by observing them experiencing the particular sensation. In its more esoteric form, the artist can intuit the emotions of another person by touching them.

October says she was inspired to create this Living Exhibit after a difficult period in her life. "There's nothing like heartbreak to crack a person wide open. But the cracks can sometimes act as reservoirs too. Not only for pain, but for joy as well. Leonard Cohen once wrote that the cracks are where the light gets in, and this exhibit is about letting the light in. It's about healing my own sorrow by connecting to the sorrow of others. It's about letting go of my pain by holding on to someone else's. Ultimately, it's about the oneness of love and hope."

Advanced tickets are now available on the museum website and *HERE*.

©October Danko, courtesy of The THOMAS FRASIER GALLERY

SFMoMA is closed on Wednesdays.

ONE.

MY NAME IS JOSEPH HARPER and if there is one thing you should know about me, it is this: I am not a brave man.

Over the course of my thirty-seven living years I have been called a lot of respectable things: intelligent, sensitive, even good-looking and gifted. But not brave.

Never brave.

And now, a confession. One I'm not proud of. I was recently asked to leave the Whitefish Community Library in Whitefish, Montana, due to intoxication. It wasn't even lunchtime yet, and the three shots of tequila I'd had before I got there began to hit me in an obvious and somewhat disorderly way.

I am not brave, I said to no one. *I have never been brave.*

I was alone in a warm, light-filled corner of the Botany section, on a leather recliner where, to my left, outside the window, the leaves of an aspen tree were announcing the steadfastness of spring. That settled me for a moment. Spring. Rebirth. New beginnings. But then I noticed the aspen's eyes trained on mine with what I was certain was disappointment.

"Stop looking at me like that," I said to the tree, louder than what was considered polite in a library.

I had the footrest up so my feet were comfortably elevated, and there was a rectangular coffee-table book called *Remarkable Trees of the World* on my lap. I used the book as a desk for my laptop because I found that if I just set the laptop on my legs, it eventually heated up and burned my skin, even through my jeans.

"Mr. Harper, is everything all right?"

Patty, the librarian, had wandered over to check on me. She knew me by name because I had been going there for almost three years to read and write and check my e-mail. The little guest cabin I lived in on Sid's property didn't have an internet connection, and even though Sid said I could get one, I never bothered because I didn't think I'd be staying in Montana long enough to need it.

"Mr. Harper?" Patty said again.

She was wearing her usual camouflage pants, and I said, "Patty, where are your legs?" but she didn't get the joke.

"Are you all right?"

I wanted to shake my head and tell her that I was most definitely not all right, but I gathered she was aware of this fact, that her question was largely rhetorical. She'd seen me when I was there an hour earlier, and I had been fine then. Well, I'd been sober. We'd exchanged trite pleasantries about the weather, and I was as right as a guy like me can be, which, if right were the whole, is only a fraction. But then I opened my inbox and saw the e-mail from the Thomas Frasier Gallery announcing October's upcoming Living Exhibit entitled *Sorrow*, and the fraction halved.

I read the e-mail, even though I told myself not to. *What's it to me?* I thought. *Who cares?*

I did. I cared so much that I shut my computer, left the library, and walked straight to the Great Northern Bar & Grill, where in quick succession I had the aforementioned shots of Cuervo Gold.

After that I returned to the library, intent on writing October an e-mail.

How are you? I typed. *Long time no talk. Congratulations on SFMoMA.*

October had once told me that having a show at SFMoMA was one of her biggest dreams in life.

You did it, I wrote. *Hope you're well.*

Even in my inebriated state, I knew this was a pathetic attempt at communication, particularly since it had been 949 days since I'd last seen and/or spoken to her, and I deleted the whole thing. That's when I directed my attention to the tree, and then Patty came over.

The aspen knew I wasn't brave. I could see it in its eyes.

"Do you know why aspens have eyes?" I asked Patty, who was standing near my chair, looking either worried or fearful; I couldn't tell which.

"They're shade-intolerant," I explained. "They need light. Lots of it. They battle with their neighbors for sun, and the higher they grow, the shadier their lower branches get. So you know what they do? They basically cut off the blood supply to the lower branches so that the taller branches, the ones that get all the light, can thrive. They're smart trees. They don't want to expend any energy trying to save the branches in the dark. Not when the ones in the light can flourish. The lower branches eventually fall off, and that leaves a scar. That's what the eyes are. Scars."

"Mr. Harper," Patty said, "I think it might be time for you to go home."

"My home is in California," I told her.

"Some fresh air would do you good," she said, quietly but firmly. "Would you like me to call Sid to come and get you?"

Fucking small towns. Everybody knows everybody. Right away I started packing up my stuff because I didn't want her to call Sid. He didn't need to see me like that.

Sid had been my thesis adviser back at UC Berkeley more than fifteen years ago. He teaches at the Flathead Valley Community College now, twelve miles south of Whitefish. He and his teenage daughter, Maggie, had moved up to Montana after his wife died in 2009. We'd kept in touch over the years, and when I found myself wandering aimlessly around the Pacific Northwest, I called him and told him I was in a bad way. He invited me to come and stay in the little caretaker's cabin on his property while I figured things out.

I planned on hanging around for a month or so, until I got my head back on straight.

It's been almost three years.

Back in college, I'd written my thesis on Aristotle and his definition of happiness as it related to how well one has lived up to one's potential as a human being, and Sid had called it exemplary. He said I was a bright, insightful thinker, and he'd granted me my degree with a warm handshake and the kind of encouraging pat on the back that could only come from someone who had no idea what a gutless failure I was going to turn out to be. Or, rather, what a gutless failure I already was.

Because, if I'm being honest, getting that degree was another failure in a succession of failures. I know that sounds absurd, but it's true. Going to college wasn't a risky decision. It wasn't brave. It wasn't what I'd wanted to do. It was what my father expected of me. The one thing I'd wanted to do with my life—the big dream that would have given depth to my soul and confidence to my heart—I didn't have the guts to go after.

The last thing Sid said to me before he sent me off into my future was, "You've got tremendous potential, Joe. Promise me you'll do something with it."

Like I said, that was a long time ago. And for every step forward since, I've taken three steps back.

October called it doing the Hokey Pokey. The month before I abandoned her at the Greek Theater in Berkeley, disappearing without explanation, she said, "That's how you live your life, Joe." She leaned in close to my face and sang: *You put your left foot in, you take your left foot out, you put your right foot in then you freak the fuck about.*

It never ceased to amaze me, the way she seemed to perceive what I was feeling when I was feeling it. I've always been skilled at hiding my emotions, but October runs on intuition and empathy like cars run on gasoline. And when she addressed me in that voice of hers, full of love and compassion and other sanguine motivations few people possess with that kind of authenticity, I wavered between wanting to throw her off the Golden Gate Bridge and fuck her brains out. Not that I had the balls to do either.

Anyway, if you want to know what my big dream was, I can sum it up in one word: guitar.

I started playing when I was twelve, and by the time I was sixteen I was as good as a kid could be. And this wasn't according to me; it was according to just about everyone who saw me perform, including the guy who played guitar for Journey, who had been a child prodigy himself back in the 1970s and lived in my hometown of Mill Valley, a small, woody enclave north of San Francisco, across the Golden Gate Bridge, at the base of Mount Tamalpais, Marin County's highest peak. The Journey guy saw me and Cal perform at an open mic night in town; afterward he came over, shook my hand, and told me I was a genius.

Cal was my best friend all through high school, and to this day the best friend I've ever had. The summer we met he could already sing, play guitar and drums, and within days of our meeting, he informed me that as soon as we graduated we were going to move to Brooklyn, start a band, and become legends. We even cut the tips of our thumbs and sealed the deal with our blood so there could be no turning back. We were going to call the band Blood Brothers in honor of our commitment.

"Brooklyn or bust," Cal used to say.

And this was before every budding musician in the country was moving to Brooklyn to start a band. This was back in the mid-'90s, when people were still heading to Seattle for their musical fortunes and fame. But that pretty much sums Cal up in a nutshell. He was always ahead of the curve. He didn't follow trends, he set them.

Cal used to say, "Dreams aren't just ideas, Harp. They're maps."

If you want to know the truth, sometimes it feels stupid trying to put into words how important music was to me back then. But when I was a kid, music was all I had. It was my voice, my only real mode of communication. And until Cal Callahan came into my life, it was my only friend.

And what did I give music in return?

Nothing.

I betrayed it.

Like I betrayed Cal.

Like I betrayed October.

Here's the thing: I knew that reading the e-mail from the Thomas Fraser Gallery announcing October's upcoming Living Exhibit would get me to thinking. Or perhaps it's more accurate to say it got me to feeling.

Four times out of five, I deleted e-mails that had anything to do with October or the gallery, but for some reason I didn't delete this one.

Consequently, I knew about *Sorrow*.

I knew I could see her. I could talk to her. I could explain why I left that night, why I disappeared without saying goodbye, and she wouldn't be able to talk back, order me to leave, call me a coward, or tell me how badly I hurt her.

Or I could do what I'd spent my life doing: nothing.

I was at a crossroads. And while finding myself at a crossroads was not new to me, I'd gone the wrong way at almost every turn.

The road less traveled? That had never been the road on which I'd walked. And if it's true that fortune favors the brave, my life, up until that point, was a testament to the fact that the opposite is true as well.

Misfortune favors the spineless.

You know what October said to me once when I was feeling down on myself? We'd just hiked to Stinson Beach and were sitting on a piece of driftwood, eating vanilla soft-serve cones, and out of nowhere the feeling hit me—it's a feeling that overcomes me sometimes, a voice that tells me I'm not good enough, that I'll never be good enough—and as October's fingers played connect-the-dots with the freckles on my forearm, her perspicacity kicked in and she said, "You know, it's never too late to be the person you really are, Joe."

I didn't say anything, but what I thought was: *Yeah, well, who the fuck is that?*

As I zipped up my backpack and stumbled toward the library's exit, I thanked Patty for her patience. She said, "You're not going to drive, are you?"

I shook my head and promised her that I intended to sit in my truck and think for a while.

"I really need to think," I assured her.

But it was more specific than that. What I needed to do was decide whether I was going to go back to California.

October was the only reason I would ever go back.

She was the reason I left, and she was the only reason I would ever return.

TWO.

ALMOST THREE YEARS and twelve hundred miles between us, and there was still a pit in my stomach every time I thought about her. And I thought about her a lot. Though rarely in the present tense. What I mean is, I didn't often find myself wondering where October was or what she was doing. In my mind she existed almost exclusively in the past, in the memories I had of her, in the short time we had spent together.

For a while after I left, I chose to believe we were doomed from the start. That even if I'd stayed, everything would have eventually busted apart. I chose to believe I was doing us both a favor by taking off. I don't believe that anymore. Not deep down, anyway. The stomach pit wouldn't be there if I did.

Nevertheless, from day one there were obstacles, the most obvious one being that October Danko is a world-renowned artist. Granted, she's only renowned to people in the world that know art. It's not like she's a household name or a celebrity. Still, she was accomplished enough when we met that, in comparison, I felt lacking.

That being said, I had never heard of her until I called about the job. The post I'd seen was elusive anyway:

ARTIST/STUDIO ASSISTANT WANTED for film/art project(s)— beautiful redwood retreat setting (Mill Valley, CA)—salaried position w/potential to live on property—construction experience a must— call for details.

The location and the live/work situation caught my eye. I was still living in Berkeley and had been yearning to move back to Mill Valley, though I hadn't pursued that desire in earnest for a couple of reasons. First, I didn't want to deal with the emotional ramifications of living anywhere near my father. However, he had recently sold his company and retired to Vail, so I could check that excuse off my list.

Bob Harper's departure aside, I couldn't afford to live in Mill Valley on my own and probably would have taken the job at October's even if it had required me to shovel shit for eight hours a day, if for no other reason than it might allow me to live among the redwoods again.

When I called the number on the ad, I reached October's assistant, Rae. It was almost ten o'clock at night, but she answered right away, a Type-A sort of hello, sharp and no nonsense. She introduced herself and then launched into an explanation about how the position was not to replace her. She was the personal and administrative assistant, she said, and did not work on projects in the studio.

The tone of Rae's voice told me she took herself and her job very seriously. And I could tell she was protective of her boss. Though when I made reference to her boss—because at that point I still didn't know October's name—she said, "I'm more like the artist's friend who happens to organize her life, yeah?"

Rae, I would quickly come to learn, had a habit of ending the majority of her sentences with "yeah?" even if they were not questions. I can be easily annoyed, and this was a quirk that never ceased to get on my nerves.

I told Rae I was interested in the position, though I had no idea what it required.

"Like I said, you'd be the studio assistant. October needs someone to help her with a film project she's been working on, as well as various other art and technology projects. Someone who will not be intrusive. Someone who knows how to work cameras and lighting equipment, can build things, and has a general understanding of art. Is that you, Mister what-is-your-name?"

"Harper. Joe."

"What is your current occupation, Mr. Harper? You work in the film industry, yeah?"

"The ad didn't say anything about that being a requirement."

"You're an artist then?"

I explained to Rae that I was currently employed by an organic produce delivery service called FarmHouse. My job consisted of driving around to local farms, picking up fruits and vegetables, eggs, and jars of various pickled foods, and delivering them to people's homes. The pay was shit, but spending the day visiting farms in Northern California was more appealing than working for my dad's construction company, which was what I'd done for almost a decade after college.

"You deliver vegetables?" Rae exhaled with obvious irritation. "You have no experience with film or art?"

I thought about being honest and telling her I was applying for the job because of the trees mentioned in the ad, but she didn't sound like someone who would appreciate that. So I told her how I'd spent ten years working in construction, which seemed to soften her a bit, and then I added something stupid about how in high school my art teacher said I was good at drawing.

"I used to play guitar pretty well too. If you count that as art."

Rae did not make a sound to indicate if she did one way or the other.

"I've built entire houses, so I'm sure I can build anything an artist might need. And I'm a quick learner."

"That's something," Rae groaned. "The truth is we need someone ASAP. Our last assistant got a job on a feature film and left us in the lurch. Tell me you have an eye for composition and can decorate a set."

"Sure," I said, though I wasn't confident that was the case.

"And you can come in for an interview first thing in the morning, yeah?"

"Yeah."

"Are you familiar with October Danko's work?"

"Full disclosure? I've never heard of her. Do I lose points for that too?"

"No. October would prefer it, actually. You should know this before you come in. She's a very private person. Sensitive. Needs a lot of space. Her assistant has to be quiet and unobtrusive."

"Gotcha," I said. "I'm pretty introverted myself. Trust me, she won't even know I'm there."

"Also," Rae went on, "October is not into people who make a fuss about her, so don't come in and try to impress her with a bunch of stuff you think you know about her or you'll be out of luck."

"I just told you I don't know anything about her."

"I'll text you the address. Be there by nine, yeah?"

"Yeah."

The next morning I was heading west on the Richmond Bridge just after sunrise. There was an accident up ahead, and traffic was at such a standstill that I put my truck in park, reclined my seat, and scanned my brain for a positive thought on which to focus.

That day, like most days, I'd woken up with the sense that I was invisible, that I'd disappeared inside the heavy, cloudlike mass of my past, that I'd gone too far astray and was unable to get back on track no matter how hard I tried.

The city of San Francisco was to my left; to my right the fog was just starting to lift from a midpoint above the water like a big white circus tent being erected over the Bay.

I kept staring out to the north, and maybe a mile in that direction a tiny rock of a landmass off Port Richmond caught my eye. The rock was East Brother Island, a light station built in the late 1800s to guide sailors safely in and out of the Bay.

That morning I could see the light in the lighthouse blinking. Having grown up in the Bay Area, I'd driven across the Richmond Bridge more times than I could count, but I'd never noticed a light on in the tower, and for one surreal moment I wondered if I was the only person who could see it. I watched the flare trying to reach up toward the sky, barely making it through the fog, and all I could think was *That's me.*

As the traffic began to lurch forward, I put the truck back into drive and did something I do when I'm feeling lost: I talked to my dead brother. That day I asked him for a sign. I needed him to remind me that I wasn't as alone as I felt, and if he could let me know whether this job was the right move, that would be cool too.

I didn't necessarily think Sam could hear me, let alone respond, but I figured it was slightly possible, in as much as it was highly improbable, that his energy or spirit or whatever you want to call it was out there somewhere, probably rolling its spectral eyes at me but willing to help if he could.

"The sign needs to be something unmistakable," I said aloud, because as far as I'm concerned, interpretation is for the faithful—the skeptical and hopeless need to be hit over the head with certainty.

I asked Sam to deliver his message to me in the form of a song. The next song to come on the radio, to be exact.

Normally I listened to NPR in the morning, but I switched over to Live 105 to receive my brother's communiqué. It was the station he'd listened to when he was alive, so I figured it would be the music he could control best as a spirit. There was a commercial on when I tuned in, and this seemed fortuitous. It meant Sam had extra time to play a mind trick on the DJ and get him to put on a relevant song after the commercial was over.

I still remember the commercial playing that morning. It was an ad for a discount diamond store that I'd been hearing since I was a kid. *Now you have a friend in the diamond business.*

When the commercial was over, the DJ started jabbering about a contest the station was having: Starting tomorrow, if you were the fifth caller after you heard the next song, you would win a trip to a music festival in Southern California, where this band would be playing in a couple of months.

The DJ said Cal's name, along with something about the song being the first single off Callahan's new, critically acclaimed third album. I changed the station straightaway because I wasn't emotionally equipped to hear the song. And because I didn't need to hear it to understand the point Sam was trying to make.

It was the same point Sam always made.

And when I took the East Blithedale exit into Mill Valley a few minutes later, I was thinking about Cal, and Sam, and even Bob, and my heart felt so heavy I was afraid my chest was going to collapse in on itself and kill me. I would die on some artist's front doorstep, having never taken a real chance on anything.

I hadn't touched my guitar in years.

I'd just broken up with a glib acupuncturist named Meadow, a well-meaning woman for whom I'd often felt an emotion akin to disdain.

And I couldn't help but wonder what I'd be doing *right now* if I'd gone to Brooklyn with Cal.

THREE.

OCTOBER'S PROPERTY is up West Blithedale Canyon, just two miles past Mill Valley's small, quaint downtown, and only another few miles on foot to the top of Mount Tamalpais, one of my favorite spots in all of Marin County, where on a clear day you can see the whole Bay Area in a spectacular 360-degree view.

The gate at the bottom of October's driveway held a small, beautifully welded sign that read "CASA DIEZ." There was a keypad to open it, but since I didn't know the code, I pressed the call button and watched the mechanized gate slide open a few seconds later.

A long gravel road took me up a steep hill and around a hairpin turn, opening into a rustic compound completely hidden by an array of trees—redwoods, oaks, poplars, madrones, and even a couple of elegant California buckeyes, their rosy-white floral fireworks in full bloom.

I saw three buildings situated in a semicircle around the end of the driveway, all made of wood, painted farmhouse red but heavily faded from weather and age. The front of the building immediately to the right was a big wall of windows; I knew it was the studio, based on Rae's directions—and the fact that I could see a stack of canvases piled up against the wall.

The main house was straight ahead. It was much smaller than the studio, and even more run-down, in that charming old Mill Valley sort of way. The paint was chipped and I could see some dry rot in the window frames, but jasmine vines stretched and crawled up the front-facing wall, scenting the air wafting in through my open window.

A large garage sat to the left of the main house, and after I parked my truck I wandered over to check it out. The door was padlocked, the windows were all covered up and I couldn't see inside, but Rae had mentioned that the top floor was the apartment where I could live if I got the job. I walked up the staircase attached to the north side of the building and tried the door. It was locked, but the blinds were up. I cupped my hands around my eyes and peered in the window. The apartment was one big room, the size of the oversize garage beneath it. A wrought-iron bed covered in a striped camping blanket was pushed against the sidewall. A leather couch that looked as soft and worn as my brother's old baseball mitt sat below the front window, and a storage chest acting as a coffee table sat in front of that. The little kitchen looked to be in the back, on the other side of the bed, and there was a door I assumed led to a bathroom behind that. The lofty redwoods that surrounded the garage cast the whole space in shadow and reminded me of a cabin that Bob, Sam, and I had stayed in on a trip to Mount Shasta when I was a kid.

My immediate gut reaction was that I could be happy there. A moment later I heard Rae call my name. And I knew it was Rae because she said, "Joe, yeah?"

I turned around to see her walking from the house toward the garage. She stopped at the bottom of the steps and waited for me to come down, one hand on her hip, a bag of what looked like trail mix dangling from the other. She grabbed a couple of nuts, plopped them into her mouth, and pointed over her left shoulder. "October's studio is there."

Rae was younger than I'd imagined. Not a day over thirty, of what I guessed to be Japanese descent, with hair dyed a color that was either gray or lavender depending on how the light hit it. She was wearing a heavy black skirt that dragged on the ground when she walked, though the way she moved was more like a shuffle.

"You look too small to build houses," she said, and I couldn't tell if she was accusing me of something or trying to make a joke. She put another handful of what I could now see were almonds and raisins in her mouth and headed toward the studio, scuffling across the gravel as if she weren't lifting her feet at all.

I spun around to take in the property. Everything was damp from the morning fog still lingering on the ridge across the valley—incidentally, the ridge where I had grown up—and I saw a gap in the thick cluster of trees where I could just barely make out the roof of my old house. My mom, Ingrid, had sold the place back when I was in college, right before she remarried and relocated to Dallas. I hadn't laid eyes on it in years.

The woodsy, mossy smell of my childhood lingered in the air, and that, along with the quick glimpse of the house, caused me to experience a pang of Mill Valley *hiraeth* that was both crushing and comforting all at once.

"I forgot to ask you on the phone," Rae said as she opened the door. "Are you good with dogs?"

I didn't have time to answer her before the tallest, gangliest dog I'd ever seen came rushing in our direction. So enormous, it didn't even seem like a dog; it seemed like a furry, prehistoric creature. I stood still while it sniffed my fist and wagged its yardstick-long tail.

"This is Diego. He looks intimidating but he's a giant baby." Rae held her bag of snacks up over her head so the dog couldn't get to it.

The dog's head reached my ribcage, and I was certain it outweighed me, probably by twenty-five pounds. "I've never seen a dog this big."

"Irish wolfhound. Tallest breed in the world." The dog ran off as we walked into the studio and then trotted back with a thick piece of rope in its mouth.

I played a quick game of tug with Diego and glanced around the room, which smelled like turpentine, hot metal, and palo santo. The studio was a big, loftlike space—probably once a barn—with a high ceiling, the center of which held two large skylights that were littered with fallen branches, dead leaves, and other random forest detritus that I silently vowed to clean if I got the job. I could see a portioned-off film set in the back, decorated to look like an old suburban living room: lots of grandma patterns and textures, only with fake blood splattered on everything, like a crime scene. A camera sat on a tripod in front of the little alcove, and a small lighting rig was set up to the side.

Another prop I noticed in the makeshift room was a beautiful old Gibson Dove that sent a shockwave to my heart. It had been years since I'd taken my guitar out from under the bed, and seeing one without warning was like running into an old, unrequited love.

The canvases up against the wall were in various stages of being built and/or drawn, but not yet painted. They were clearly part of a series and had gigantic sketches of vintage boats on them, with ship-related phrases stenciled on top of the images. The first one I saw read, "I'LL SINK THIS SHIP IF I WANT TO." Another said, "SAILING ON A SHIP OF FOOLS." And another, the one that spoke to me with poignant and rather heartbreaking significance, even then, said, "BOY DID YOU MISS THE BOAT."

October's back was to us as Rae and I approached. She was sitting on a stool in front of a long steel table, clear safety goggles on her face, using a small blowtorch on a canvas.

The first thing I noticed about October was how small her hands were. Then I noticed everything about her was small. Her wrists, her ears, her shoulders. Coupled with what she was wearing—hickory-striped overalls streaked with dirt, paint, and grease, over a big, threadbare sweatshirt that reminded me of the one Cal wore all summer the year he and I met—she could have passed for a tomboyish teenager and wasn't at all what I had expected.

Rae tapped October on the back. October looked over her shoulder, and I caught her eye for half a second. She looked down to turn off the torch and then spun back around as if she'd been awakened by a hypnic jerk.

She stood and pulled the goggles off, causing her dark, sun-streaked hair to fall down over her shoulders. Soot and splotches of paint smeared her face, and half-moon indentations marked her cheeks where the goggles had been pressing into her skin. With her head tilted to the side, she pushed her fringy bangs away from her eyes and looked sideways at me.

"This is the guy who called about the job," Rae told her.

"Joe Harper," I said, extending my hand.

She took my hand and held it flat between both of hers.

"Joe Harper," she repeated. Her voice was low and soft. Then "Joe Harper" again, the second time with a more curious inflection. She was still holding my hand, now squinting hard at me, as if I were a spoon she was trying to bend with her mind, and my first thought was *This woman is a little odd*.

Finally, she let go of my hand. Then she took an elastic band from her wrist, wrapped her hair up in it and said, "Tell me about your relationship to art, Joe Harper."

That caught me off guard. It didn't seem like a topic I could address without a lot of thought. "Tell me what it means to you," she added.

It had been a long time since anyone had asked me what I thought or felt about art. I didn't live in a world where that was the norm. Cal and I used to talk about art all the time, but that was back when he had me convinced I was an artist.

I stood in silence, reflecting on what to say. Rae stepped impatiently from one foot to the other, snacking on her nuts and raisins, while October remained still, and seemed as though she could have waited all day for my response.

Bear in mind, I didn't yet know anything more than what I'd just seen about the kind of art October made, and that meant I had to think about the kind of art I knew—music—and offer her an honest reply.

I tried to remember how playing guitar used to make me feel and said, "I guess, for me, art is how to tell, not *the* truth, but *my* truth. It's a way to communicate who you are and what you feel. Some people think art is pretending, but to me it's the opposite. It's the one place where you can't pretend."

October was watching me closely as I spoke, her eyes soft but curious.

"The job is yours," she said. "If you want it."

Rae jumped to attention. "Wait. You want to ask him more questions, yeah?"

October was still studying me. "Rae said you used to work in construction?"

"I did. For years."

"On a scale from 1 to 10, how tech savvy are you?"

"About an 8," I said. I was probably closer to a 5, but, like I'd told Rae, I'm a quick learner.

October looked at Rae and nodded, and Rae said, "All right, then. How soon can you start?"

I figured I had to give FarmHouse some notice and said, "Two weeks?"

It was a Thursday. October's eyes widened and she said, "Monday would be better."

I nodded. I wanted the job. Or, more specifically, I wanted the apartment. I still didn't know what the job was. "I can probably make that work."

The three of us stood inside a lingering silence that was awkward for me and ostensibly for Rae, who was picking bits of almond skin from her teeth. But October seemed relaxed and content, her eyes moving back and forth across my face as if it were a page in a book she was reading.

"If you need a place to live, it makes sense to live on the property. My days start early."

Rae said, "Maybe wait and see if you like the job before you decide."

"No," I said quickly. The apartment was the main reason I'd come. I already had my heart set on living in it. "I'll take it."

"Great," October said. "Follow me."

I went with her to the back of the studio, to a tiny office with a desk, a computer, and an old futon. She picked up a bowl of keys, pilfered through them, found a keychain shaped like the Golden Gate Bridge, and gave it to me. "The blue key unlocks your apartment. The white one is to this building." She grabbed a Post-it note, wrote a series of numbers down on it, and handed that to me too.

I looked at it, chuckled, and said, "My birthday."

She looked taken aback. "That's the gate code."

I laughed and said, "Your gate code is my birthday." I gave the Post-it note back to her. "I probably don't need that."

"No, I guess you don't."

She walked me to the front door of the studio and told Rae to show me the apartment, discuss the salary with me, and, if everything was acceptable, have me fill out some paperwork.

"You can start moving in over the weekend. We'll hit the ground running on Monday."

As I followed Rae across the driveway, I glanced back toward the studio. October was standing in the doorway, leaning against the jamb with her arms crossed and her giant, mastodon dog beside her. They were both watching me.

FOUR.

MY LANDLORD SAID if I moved out on such short notice I would lose my deposit, but I left anyway. I was convinced this job was a sign of good things to come. A fresh start. I was going to show up on day one as a new and improved Joe Harper. Leaving my miserable years in Berkeley behind. Leaving the Mill Valley of my past behind. The Mill Valley of Bob, Sam, and even Cal behind.

Leaving my sorrow behind.

I didn't have much to pack—just clothes, books, some kitchen paraphernalia, a couple of lamps, my laptop, and my guitar.

I threw it all in my truck and headed back to Casa Diez on Saturday morning.

The studio was dark when I got there, and I went to the main house and knocked, figuring I should let October know I'd arrived. The furry dinosaur greeted me first, rushing out through a linebacker-size dog door on the east side of the house.

"Hey there, Diego." He walked underneath my hand and leaned into me, and I scratched his back without having to reach for it.

October opened the door seconds later, holding a pair of dirty sneakers.

"Hey," I said.

"Hey," she said back at me, a broad, thousand-watt smile immediately lighting up her face.

Only then did it hit me how pretty she was. I don't know why it hadn't been more obvious at our first meeting. Sometimes I can't see things when they're right in front of my face. But I saw it then. I saw how her eyes were like the forest that surrounded her house: mysterious but fresh, bright, and alive. And I saw how all of her features seemed kaleidoscopic: colorful and constantly changing, depending on the angles, the reflections, and the light.

However, it feels important to say this: It wasn't anything as superficial as the way October looked that eventually drew me to her. It was something else. Something deeper. An energy. A spirit. Her presence warmed my heart and terrified me at the same time.

She sat down right where she stood in the middle of the doorway and put on her shoes.

"We're about to head out for a hike." She nodded toward the dog. "He won't let me do anything unless I tire him out first. Walk with us. Then you can unpack."

We followed the path that wound around the back of the house, through deer ferns, sorrel, and ivy, and up a short hill to the property line, where a chain-link fence with a gate entangled in wild blackberry bushes opened onto the fire road that led to the top of the mountain. It was a trail that Bob, Sam, and I had spent a lot of time on when I was a kid and, later, Cal and I as teenagers. I knew it as well as I knew the five-string triad arpeggios I used to practice with my eyes closed.

Diego ran up ahead, zooming in circles around a big tree until we reached him. I knew that tree too. Bob and I had named it together. He'd claimed it was the tallest coast live oak on that part of the trail, and we'd called it Beanstalk, then, later, Bean for short.

After the quick sprint the dog calmed down, ambled back over to us, and walked beside me, as if he thought it was his job to usher us up the trail.

We walked for maybe a quarter of a mile in silence. Finally October said, "Did Rae warn you not to talk too much, or are you just generally quiet?"

"Both."

She chuckled. "Don't let Rae scare you. She the oldest of five kids. Thinks she has to mother everyone. Including me."

I didn't know what to say to that except "OK."

We were quiet again. Then October said, "Come on. Tell me about yourself. Besides your birthday, since I already know that."

I made it a point not to tell people the pitiful details of my life, and I didn't think I'd be working there longer than the project would last, so making shit up didn't seem to matter. When I'd moved to Berkeley as a college freshman, I'd gotten into the asinine habit of telling people the tale of Bob's childhood as my own, and I'd been doing it ever since.

"I grew up in Spokane. Moved here to go to Berkeley. How about you? Where are you from?"

"Rochester. New York, not Minnesota."

That surprised me. She seemed too interesting to be from Rochester. "Did you study art there?"

She shook her head. "RISD."

"How did you end up out here?"

"Got recruited to do graphic design for a tech company in the city."

"Which one?"

"Ribble."

"Wow. What did you do for them?"

She looked down and kicked at some rocks. "You know the little logo cartoons on the search engine homepage?"

"The Ribble scribbles?"

She squinted up her face and gave me a quick nod.

"You used to make those?"

She stopped walking, turned her head slightly in my direction, gave me a sharp side-eye, and whispered, "I still make those."

"Really?" I was genuinely impressed. "That's cool."

She nudged me playfully with her elbow, and I remember thinking the gesture felt weirdly intimate, like something you'd do with an old friend, not a virtual stranger.

"It is *not* cool. It's mortifyingly corporate. But it pays the bills, if you know what I mean."

I nodded. I'd heard even the interns made six figures at Ribble. "I liked the one you did for Bob Dylan's birthday last year, the one where his face was a cake, with the animated harmonica."

She halted, wide-eyed. "You remember that?"

"Yeah. And the April Fool's Day one with the spinning kangaroo. That was great."

She threw her head back and laughed so hard she had to wipe tears from her eyes.

"What?" I mumbled.

She nudged me again, this time a playful push with her palm. "That wasn't a kangaroo! It was Diego!"

"Ah. Shit." I laughed too, our eyes met, and right away I felt like I was doing something wrong. To change the subject, I asked her how long she'd been living in Mill Valley.

"About three years. I lived in the city first, but I didn't like it. Sensory overload. I moved over here as soon as I could afford it."

We continued hiking uphill, and October spoke mostly to the dog, telling him what a good boy he was, pointing out birds and squirrels for him to see, stopping to give him water every so often. She talked to him like he was a child, and he looked at her with rapt attention anytime she said his name or raised the pitch of her voice.

I remember thinking that perhaps she was testing me, to see if I could be unobtrusive, and I'd been trying not to speak too much unless she spoke to me. But I also didn't want her to think I wasn't interested in her work; eventually I got up the nerve to ask her what kind of artist she was.

She bent down to tie her shoelace, looked up at me and, with a chuckle, said, "You took this job without knowing that?"

I shrugged, gestured toward the mountain. "I like redwoods."

She smiled. "It's funny; when people ask me what I do for a living and I say, 'I'm an artist,' their next question is almost always 'What kind?' I suppose they imagine I'm a painter, sculptor, photographer, you know, one specific thing. And I work in all of those media. But if it were up to me, it would be enough to say, 'I'm an Artist of Life.'" She covered her face with her hands for a moment, as if anticipating a scoff. "I know that might seem vague or, worse, pretentious, but it's honestly the closest I can get to explaining my career."

She turned toward me and met my eyes, focused and serious, her hands moving enthusiastically as she spoke, as if my question had opened something up in her. She'd gone from awkwardly quiet to aflame in an instant. "At the core of my work is the belief that everything we do and every moment we live can be a work of art. Every experience can be a thing of beauty or love, sorrow or pain. We choose. We impart the moments with meaning. That's what art is to me. Imparting objects, sounds, creations and experiences with meaning. Making even the most mundane into something significant and extraordinary."

"I like that." Her words rang true inside of me. I didn't know how to articulate the idea like she did, or how to live it, for that matter, but I understood it, and I believed in it.

"Good. Because it's crucial to your role here that you do." She paused to gather the rest of her thoughts. It seemed important to her that I grasp what she was saying. "That's how I approach my work, and it's how I approach my existence. I feel things, and then I try to inspire other people to feel things. I want to connect my humanity to the humanity of others, and somehow I've been lucky enough to make this desire my life's work." We resumed walking, and October continued glancing at me as she spoke. "As if you can't tell, I like talking about art." Someone had discarded a plastic bottle on the trail; October picked it up and put it in the little backpack she wore to hold Diego's water. "But, to answer your question, society likes labels and our culture likes to put people in boxes, and because I'm mostly known for my performance pieces, Ribble and Google and Wikipedia and all the other cyber boxes tend to label me a performance artist. But, like I said, if it were up to me, it would be enough to simply say, 'I am an Artist of Life.'"

I didn't say anything in response to that, and she mistook my silence for something it wasn't.

"Told you it was going to sound pretentious."

"No," I said, too seriously. "I like the idea that a person can go about their daily life and be an artist simply by being. But that seems like the most difficult kind of artist to be. What do you think the key is? To making that work, I mean?"

She shrugged, a lopsided, contemplative look on her face. "I think that's a question I'll be trying to answer for the rest of my life. I certainly haven't figured it out yet. But my hunch is that just being here is a good start." She locked her eyes on mine, and again it felt too intimate. "Being present, I mean. Like we are now. I'm looking at you, you're looking at me. I'm listening to you, you're listening to me. We're engaged. Connected."

"This is art?" I asked.

She nodded, and her face shone. "This is art."

As we turned and headed back to her house, completely out of the blue she said, "Have you ever done mushrooms? You know, the magic kind?"

I laughed. "Why? Are you planning on drug-testing me?"

She laughed too. "Inquiring for research purposes."

"Yeah. Sure. A couple times in college."

She looked at me again. Diego looked at me too, with so much interest and clarity I contemplated the possibility that he was a person in a dog suit.

"What's it like?"

I wasn't sure I could describe doing mushrooms in a way that an artist would appreciate, but I said, "It's fun if you're in the right mood, I guess. However, things can get weird pretty quickly if you're not."

"I read an article this morning about psychedelic drugs and their effect on drawing. I want to do an experiment where I pick a subject and draw it naturally, and then draw the exact same thing after eating mushrooms, to see how differently they turn out."

There was a mischievous grin on her face that made me wonder how old she was. She could've been twenty-three or forty-five. It was impossible to tell.

"Don't worry, I'm not into drugs or anything," she assured me. "It's just that lately I've been feeling like I'm holding myself back. I'm stuck. I need to get out of my comfort zone, in the hopes that it will open me up and make me a better artist."

I nodded, wishing I could be more like her. Hoping I could become more like her through the osmosis of being around her. "How old are you?" I said, "if you don't mind me asking."

"Thirty-four."

She was only two years older than I, but she seemed so much farther ahead. "One of my old coworkers sells mushrooms," I told her. "He and I meet up for beers every so often. I could ask him for some next time I see him. If you want."

A little bashfully, she said, "If it's not too much trouble."

I told her it wasn't, and we were quiet again.

Once we got back to her property, she mentioned she was going out of town to visit her boyfriend, who was working in Denver. "I'll be back late Sunday night. Get yourself settled this weekend, and I'll see you Monday morning."

As I was walking toward my new apartment, she said, "Hey, Joe."

I turned around.

"I'm really looking forward to working with you."

FIVE.

ON PAPER, I WAS THE PROJECT COORDINATOR and studio assistant at Casa Diez, but the majority of my day was spent working on the specific Living Exhibit that October was focused on during that period.

October dubs her long-term performance pieces Living Exhibits because that's exactly what they are—life experiences she turns into performance art. The one she was working on when I started there was a film project called *365 Selfies*. My tasks included but were not limited to: set designer, camera and lighting crew, website and mailing list admin, general contractor, handyman, and occasional creative consultant.

365 Selfies was intended to be a statement on the "selfie" culture that was all the rage on social networks and in social lives at the time. However, as a contrast to the somewhat narcissistic nature of the trend, *365 Selfies* would only be available on a hidden website. October didn't intend to publicize the page, and when she finally announced the project, she didn't include a web address. Her fans and the art world found it eventually, though it took months, and I'm still not sure how it was discovered. However, I suspect it had something to do with the fact that the project was sponsored by Phil Pearlman, the art aficionado, entrepreneur, and founder of Ribble. Mr. P. was worth a couple billion dollars and chose to spend a miniscule chunk of his vast wealth supporting art and artists.

October told me she'd worked at Ribble for over a year before Phil knew she was anything other than one of his designers. But she'd invited him to her first Living Exhibit, *VooDo*, and he was so taken by her that he pledged to fund and promote her Living Exhibits for as long as she continued designing his Ribble scribbles.

"Basically, I'm a Ribble scribble whore," she sighed.

For *VooDo*, October had rented a small gallery in the Tenderloin. She wrapped her body in thick felt, crudely stitched it together at the beginning of the performance, and then stood on a pedestal while gallery visitors were invited to stab her arms and legs with extra-long, colored-ball pins she'd made especially for the exhibit.

"A human voodoo doll," she explained, as if that needed explaining.

The video footage she showed me was hard to watch. But what shocked me more than the performance itself was the way people reacted to it. I had assumed the visitors would be gentle with the pins or refrain from using them at all. Quite the reverse, they were overly aggressive, laughing and looking at one another as they stabbed October's limbs. She was a bloody mess by the end, and still has a few pinprick scars on her arms to show for it.

"Most people didn't understand," she said. "The audience seemed to think it was a game, some kind of S&M nonsense. They missed the point."

I didn't miss the point. As someone who has tried myriad ways to diminish and avert his own pain, I felt like I understood on an intuitive level what October had been attempting to do. It seemed similar to the reason I had liked working in construction. The physical struggle distracted from the emotional one.

The Living Exhibit I'd been hired to work on, *365 Selfies*, was October's fourth in the series, and despite its timely nature, she claimed it was, deep down, a tribute to one of her favorite artists, Frida Kahlo.

"Frida was the original selfie queen," October explained to me during my first day on the job. She pulled down one of the big art books from her shelf and showed me dozens of Frida's paintings, stopping to make sure I got a good look at each image. "Her portraits tell stories, see? Sometimes they tell true stories and sometimes they tell fictional stories. She shows us her dreams and her nightmares. Her joys and her sorrows. Her birth, her life, and her death. That's what I'm trying to do with *365 Selfies*, only I'm using video and photography instead of paint and canvas."

We typically filmed two to four days a week, depending on how involved her ideas were. Once a clip was edited, I cataloged it and uploaded it to the website. However, the website wouldn't go live until an entire year's worth of clips were ready, at which point October would post one selfie a day for 365 days; then they would live on the internet in perpetuity.

Some of the clips were simple: October would tell a story, share a dream, or talk about an experience she'd had. But often the selfies were weirder, like the time she dressed up in a giant pink bunny costume and tried to hitchhike on US 101 in the rain, screaming the word "flux" at passing cars. Or the time she dug a grave in her backyard, had me film her in the grave, and then had me film her covering the grave with dirt and flowers so that once it was cut together it looked like she was burying her own body. Occasionally she would say one word and tell me we were done for the day. Once she sat and stared into the camera for three hours without saying anything at all. One day she washed the dog. One day she shaved her legs with a straight razor. One day she had a phlebotomist come to the studio and take blood from her arm, and then she painted a self-portrait with the blood. Another day she spent twenty minutes making and eating a piece of toast, and trust me when I say it was the most compelling video of toast making and eating you could ever imagine.

I never knew what I was going to get with her, and in spite of how strange it sometimes seemed, I looked forward to going to work.

The shoots rarely took up more than a few hours, but October had numerous projects going on at once, including the Ribble cartoons, and the remainder of my time was spent helping her with whatever else she had coming up, plus more routine things like building and prepping canvases, mixing paint, running art-related errands, updating her website, sending out newsletters about upcoming exhibits and events to her mailing list, and researching other topics she wanted to explore in her work.

For the first time in a long time, I was doing something inspiring. But beyond completing my tasks to the best of my ability, I stayed out of October's way and didn't interact with her outside of work. I figured that was the way she wanted it. She was pretty reclusive. Not shy, per se. One-on-one in the studio, we talked often as we worked, and I found her to be open and warm. But out in the world she was easily overwhelmed. For example, we went to Hog Island to film a clip of her shucking oysters for a selfie she'd had all planned out, but it was absurdly crowded when we got there, filled with tourists, and she wouldn't even get out of the car. She just turned around and drove us home.

Like Rae had explained to me early on, October needed a lot of space. Occasionally we would film a selfie and afterward she would shut herself in her little office for a while, or she'd wander off with Diego for a hike, and they'd be gone for hours. Sometimes she would show up in the morning, give me my tasks, and ask if we could work in silence. Then she'd put on some music, and we wouldn't say another word to each other for the rest of the day.

None of that bothered me. The way I saw it, October put so much of herself into her work that she found it necessary to withdraw in order to come back recharged the next day. And being around more than a few people at a time made her uneasy. She had friends and associates who would stop at the house now and then, particularly Mr. P. and his husband, Thomas. They usually brought food and wine, or they would take October out for dinner. And she went to yoga class a few nights a week. But that was the extent of her social life that I could see, and Diego and Rae seemed to be her most trusted companions.

My first month at Casa Diez went by pretty routinely. I went to work and left work and minded my own business in the meantime. During my off hours I hiked and hung out at Equator Coffee, the little cafe in the town square.

That all changed one Friday morning when I showed up at the studio and noticed October seemed anxious. I assumed I'd done something to upset her, but before I could ask her what was up, she said, "I need to get out of here. I'll see you Monday."

She left the studio and then, not long after that, the property.

I spent the next few hours finally cleaning the skylights and then walked down to town for a beer.

When I returned home later that evening, I found a note taped to my front door, written in what looked like an architect's handwriting. It said:

Joe,

There's something I need to tell you. I haven't been able to stop thinking about you since we met, and I don't know what to do about it. Please text me when you get this so we can talk.

-Oct

Let's face it, a normal person would have responded immediately with the requested text. But I am not a normal person. I lack gumption. And as soon as I am aware that I need to do something, I do nothing.

October texted me the next morning: Can you talk?

At this point she and I had spent a considerable amount of time together, but we didn't know each other very well. Specifically, I didn't think she knew me very well, because if she did, I reasoned, she wouldn't have left me a note like that.

And if anyone had asked me back then, before she left the note, if I was attracted to her, I would have had a complicated, undoubtedly evasive answer. Obviously, she intrigued me. I thought she was beautiful, and unlike any woman I'd ever met. On top of that, she made me feel seen—she asked for my ideas, took my opinions to heart, and genuinely valued my contributions to her work.

But the truth is, it never occurred to me to be *interested* in her, or to allow myself to acknowledge any kind of real attraction, first and foremost because she was my boss, but also because, as far as I was concerned, she was so far out of my league that even fantasizing about her seemed like a joke, never mind entertaining the possibility that *she* could be attracted to *me*.

That's why I acted like a loser.

I was terrified.

Moreover, and not inconsequentially, I knew October had a long-term boyfriend. She'd only mentioned him to me in passing, but I'd heard her talking to Rae about him one day when the two of them were having lunch on the lawn outside the studio. What I'd gleaned about the guy was that his name was Chris, he was constantly out of town for work, she'd only spent two weekends with him in the last three months, and, interestingly enough, they had something of an open relationship.

October was expressing to Rae that she felt disconnected from the guy, was tired of having an absentee boyfriend, and wanted to date other men. Then she said, "I'm allowed to, remember? We give each other that freedom."

Rae scoffed. "Don't be ridiculous. Chris adores you, yeah? You've been together a long time. And trust me, dating in San Francisco is way worse than a boyfriend who's never home."

I remember being curious about the man October chose as her boyfriend. I remember wondering what "give each other that freedom" meant. But the idea that I had a chance with her never crossed my mind.

She texted again: Call me.

I'd quit FarmHouse as soon as October had hired me, but they hadn't found anyone who could work on weekends yet, so I filled in for them when they needed help. I'd been parked in a driveway in Petaluma that morning, about to pick up a dozen boxes of heirloom tomatoes, and I was so caught off guard by October's request for a call that I put my phone in airplane mode without writing back.

I couldn't keep avoiding her though. I lived fifteen yards from her front door, for Christ's sake. And as soon as I got back to Casa Diez that night and saw the light on in her house, I knew I had to respond. But before I did, I got out my blender and fixed myself a cocktail, adding considerably more tequila than necessary. I downed a glass, waited a couple of minutes for it to start kicking in, and then made the call.

"Hey," I mumbled.

"Hey." There was a pause. Then, "I'm sorry if I freaked you out with that note. I have this terrible habit of holding in my feelings for too long and then expressing them at really inopportune times."

"It's OK," I told her, hoping that would be the end of the conversation; that we would pretend it never happened.

"You're home," she said, as if she'd just looked out her window to check. "I'm coming over."

She knocked on my door five minutes later, barefoot, in threadbare sweats, a big gray hoodie around her shoulders, and carrying a pie.

"I bake when I'm anxious," she said, handing it to me.

She'd used all of the extra piecrust to make little clouds and lighting bolts, which she'd placed around the top of the pie before she baked it. It looked like an edible storm.

"Thanks."

"Blackberry. From the bushes in the yard. You should have some while it's still hot."

She followed me to the kitchen, and as I cut myself a piece of the pie, she eyed the frothy, mud-colored drink in the blender.

"I make cocktails when I'm anxious," I explained.

"That looks disgusting."

"Brown recluses are not disgusting."

I grabbed a clean glass from my dish rack and poured her one. She slipped her arms into her sweatshirt, took the glass from my hand and held it at arm's length, as if I'd given her shit, which, I admit, it did look like.

"I invented this cocktail," I said with pride. "Tequila, chocolate milk, cinnamon, a pinch of cayenne pepper, and ice."

"It sounds even worse than it looks." She smelled the drink and made a face.

"There's a word for that, you know."

"A word for what?" she said.

"For a person who makes a disgusted face when they're drinking liquor."

"Oh, yeah? What's the word?"

"'Paper-belly.' You're a paper-belly."

She tried to swat me with her hand, but her sweatshirt was too big and the sleeve kept sliding down so that not even the tips of her fingers were visible.

"Taste it," I prodded.

The cocktail was thick and sludgy, and she had to tilt her head back and sort of pour it into her mouth, but she was nodding and smiling as she swallowed.

"Wow. This is *way* better than it looks. Like a spicy, boozy milkshake."

"Exactly."

Her hands were so small she had to hold the glass with both of them. She took another drink, and I took a bite of the pie. To be honest, it looked better than it tasted, but I didn't tell her that.

"We should do a pie-making selfie," I suggested.

She gave me a funny smirk.

"What?"

"You said *we*."

"Sorry, I meant you."

"No. I like that you said *we*."

We stared at each other for a long, awkward instant. Then I refilled my glass and said, "I'm not good at this kind of thing. I don't know what I'm supposed to say."

"Neither do I." October took a long, deep breath, held it in, and then let it out as if she'd been underwater and had just resurfaced. She played with the zipper on her sweatshirt, up and down, up and down, the sound a feedback-like buzz. "Well, I mean, there are a lot of things I *want* to say, but they're not really appropriate. Because we work together. And I'm your boss. And—"

"—And you have a boyfriend."

"I was getting to that. But you should know things are complicated with me and Chris. And we're not exactly exclusive."

"Not exactly?"

"He's never here. And I don't believe in giving people rules or asking them to say no to experiences they may want to have. So, when we're apart, he can do what he wants, and I can too." She fingered the strings of her hoodie, pulling them back and forth like she was flossing her neck. "Don't get me wrong; Chris is an amazing person. But he's the exact opposite of me. He's social. Fun. Likes to be around people all the time. I think that was the reason I was originally drawn to him. I thought maybe he'd somehow break me out of my shell. But the longer we're together, the more I realize how incompatible we really are." She stopped, took another drink, thought before she spoke again. "The thing is, I don't think all relationships are meant to last forever. That doesn't mean they've failed; it just means we've learned all we can from them, they've run their course, and that's OK." She put her glass down, ran her finger around the rim. "Have you ever been in a relationship where, even though there's nothing obviously wrong, you just have a sense it's not where you're supposed to be?"

I nodded and couldn't remember the last time I'd been more nervous or excited by a woman.

"You know what else I think?" she said. "I think love is the ultimate art project. To me, there's nothing more beautiful, more powerful, or more meaningful than truly and purely loving another human. No expectations. No strings attached. Just the freedom to be who you are and to be loved in spite of that."

Sometimes the way October talked made my heart long for something I couldn't name. She had words for things I didn't. Space for things I'd shut out.

"But it's impossible to have that kind of relationship with someone who's gone all the time. And even when Chris is here, he's either working or thinking about work. And he's not remotely interested in mine. That's not what I want."

I nodded. It was the best I could do.

"Listen," she said, leaning on the counter. "I don't know what's going to happen when Chris gets home at the end of the month, but I know what *can* happen."

I put my hands in my pockets and fiddled with the change I could feel there. "What does that mean?"

She chose her words carefully. "I'd like to spend more time with you. Outside of work, I mean. If you're open to that."

I shook my head and sighed. "I don't think I'm an open relationship kind of guy. I don't want to get in the middle of something between you and your boyfriend. And more than that, I don't want to jeopardize my job."

"I understand. I do. But if you tell me you're interested in exploring this, I'll tell Chris. I'll break it off with him."

I nodded, though I can't say that made me feel any safer.

"The ball's in your court," October said.

That filled me with dread. I wasn't good at having the ball, especially with women. "Why me?"

"Because I can sense your apprehension, and I don't want to ask you for anything you don't want to give me."

I wanted to ask her more about Chris, but I knew the more I learned about him, the more insecure I would be, so instead I said, "What *do* you want?" However, I'd like to note the tone with which I asked the question. It wasn't bold, confrontational, or flirty—tequila could only help a guy like me so much—it was detached and wary. I was petrified of the answer I might get.

"I want some more boozy milkshake," she said, making the kind of eye contact that felt like a different and more dangerous conversation. But then she looked away, and I swore I saw her blush. "I feel nervous," she said. "I haven't been this nervous since *The Voyage*."

I handed her the blender. "What's *The Voyage*?"

She seemed relieved that I'd given her a topic of discussion, and as she refilled her glass, she began rambling on about her third Living Exhibit, which was, she said, ostensibly motivated by the aggressive anti-immigration rhetoric going on in the country at the time. But the specific details of the piece had been inspired by her great grandmother Rosa's real-life journey to America.

She pulled up a series of photos on her phone and showed them to me. The "boat" on which the exhibit took place was a massive hydraulic platform that resembled the side of an old ship, with a steep set of steel stairs that led down to the windowless steerage of the lower deck, where the poverty-stricken travelers like her grandmother spent their journeys.

October inhabited the small, makeshift living quarters for sixteen days with a dozen performance artists from all over the world—immigrants, if you will—who had volunteered to be the other travelers on the boat.

"Back in 1916, Rosa left Italy with what amounted to forty-nine dollars in her handbag, at the age of seventeen, after her nineteen-year-old husband was killed in one of the earliest battles Italy fought against Austria-Hungary in the war."

She showed me a photo of Rosa, taken a few months before her death at age ninety-nine. Rosa was even tinier than October, so tiny she looked as if she'd been folded in half, and her face was like pavement after a jackhammer.

"It was the most intense experience I've ever had during a performance, and the most challenging. I was living out this narrative that my great grandma had told me so many times, and it became so real to me that every night I would have nightmares about her dead husband and then wake up crying, full of grief and panic."

"Is that what you feel now? Grief and panic?"

October zoned out for a moment. Then she said, "The truth is, there's a part of me that knows I shouldn't be having this conversation with you. And another part of me that feels, I don't know, *compelled*. Like it's essential. An inevitability. Or maybe I'm just crazy. All I know is that the day you walked into my studio, I almost burned my hand off with that blowtorch when I saw you."

"Why?" I asked, baffled.

"Sometimes I meet people and I just know things about them."

"What did you know about me that day?"

She let her head fall back and stared at the ceiling. Then she looked at me again and said, "That you belong here."

I swallowed hard and felt the hair on my arms stand up.

She picked a blackberry out of the pie pan with her fingers and ate it. Then she wrinkled her nose like she knew it wasn't her best work. "Joe, I don't know how you ended up seeing that post and calling about the job and walking in that day, but you did, and here we are, and I refuse to believe there's not a reason for it."

I thought of Sam then, because if I believed in reasons and signs, then I had to believe they were from him. I had to consider the possibility that my brother had a hand in whatever *this* was.

I stood feebly in place, trying to figure out what to do. I wanted to be the kind of guy who could saunter around to the other side of the counter and kiss October right then and there, but I wasn't.

Two minutes or an hour went by with both of us standing there, the kitchen counter between us, sipping at our brown recluses.

October took her phone out again and said, "I want to play you a song."

I heard Sam's voice whisper: *Here's your stupid sign, you shithead.*

"I don't know why," October said, "but this song reminds me of you."

The song started out with this sprinkly high hat/kick drum combo that was fast but slowly brooding at the same time. Then the first two lines come in, and they aren't sung so much as they're murmured with an aloofness that felt too close to home.

> *Sorrow found me when I was young.*
> *Sorrow waited, sorrow won.*

A few seconds later the baritone singer starts repeating the line *I don't wanna get over you* in a way that seemed more like foreshadowing than a sign.

Listening to the song made me feel like October understood something crucial about me, something that lived deep inside my core, something she couldn't possibly know. That's when I knew I was in trouble. The fact that she played the song, and I understood why she played it, and perhaps she understood why she played it.

Still, it all seemed too fantastic. Too risky. And I didn't take risks.

Because where could this possibly go? And if I blew it, then what? I'd be out of a job and an apartment, not to mention potentially brokenhearted to the point of no return.

I don't wanna get over you.

I should have established boundaries right then. Refused to engage with her beyond our professional relationship. That's what I'd sworn to do before she came over. Nothing is going to happen between us, I told myself. I'm her employee. She has a boyfriend. She's successful and extraordinary and I hate myself. This could never work.

I don't wanna get over you.

She put her hand on top of mine, stared hard at me, and sighed. "This won't affect our work, I promise. I just had to get it off my chest. You can forget we had this conversation if that feels like what you need to do."

She came around to the other side of the counter and hugged me. It was a deliberate hug: sincere, innocent, full of heart. Then she put her hood back up and walked to the door.

The dialogue in my head went like this: *Don't say another word. Let her go.*

Then I remembered I was supposed to be a new and improved Joe Harper, and I tried to imagine what Cal would say if he were there to give me advice.

"Go for it, Harp."

Maybe it was the tequila. Maybe it was something else. A tiny burst of courage? My authentic self taking over? My truth? My destiny?

Even if I wanted to forget the conversation, I knew I never would.

"Hey," I said.

October turned around, one foot already out the door.

"Do you want to hang out tomorrow night?" I mumbled. "Maybe we could go for dinner or something?"

I could see a subtle smile like the crest of a wave trying to break across her face. She bit her lip to hold it back and nodded.

"Cool," I said.

"Cool."

SIX.

WHEN I Was a kid, I thought trees were gods. It's hard not to when the forests that surround your town are full of ancient redwoods that stretch like divine monuments so far into the sky you can't tell where the canopies of the trees end and the heavens begin.

The day I met Cal I was on one of my favorite trails near Muir Woods, having a conversation with a redwood I'd named Poseidon.

If you've never stood beside a redwood, this might not make sense, but trust me when I say they're immense, awe-inspiring, and majestic. Arboreal skyscrapers, they put you in your place and remind you how small and insignificant you are. They're living testaments to resilience, and proof that there is poetry in nature.

I'd named this particular tree Poseidon because its trunk was hollowed out at the base, so huge I could stand inside of it, and when I did I swore I could hear the ocean, even though the beach was another five miles away.

Given that I've already admitted to having conversations with my dead brother, and now I'm admitting that my closest living confidantes were trees, I feel the need to state, for the record, that I wasn't crazy. I just spent a lot of time alone. And trees, like music, have always been good at keeping me company.

If I'm trying to make a case for my sanity, I probably shouldn't admit this next part either, but on the particular day in question, I was discussing with Poseidon how I could kill Bob Harper and make it look like an accident.

Listen, my father issues are a long story, and I don't feel like getting too deep into them—there are enough sons in the world who blame their emotionally or physically unavailable dads for their problems. But I'm in my late thirties now, and that means I'm old enough to know I can only blame myself for where I am. Nevertheless, it's worth noting a few significant details that include Bob and Ingrid and their shortcomings as parents.

First, after my brother died, I stopped talking for two years. I can't explain why, except to say that it seemed too exhausting to use words after I lost Sam. It felt even more exhausting to use words that expressed what I was feeling. I tried, but nothing came out. And the longer I didn't talk, the easier it became to remain silent.

My silence was hard on Bob and Ingrid, and in the beginning they were sympathetic. I guess they figured that once I came to terms with what had happened to Sam, I would go back to being a normal kid. But months went by and I stayed mute and weird, and Bob's patience ran out.

He dragged me to a bunch of therapists, but none of them helped. After the therapists came a slew of medical doctors who assured Bob there was no physical reason I couldn't speak. That's when what was left of his sympathy turned to anger. I'm sure it was me he was mad at, but he took a lot of it out on Ingrid, and the following year they split up.

Ingrid and I stayed in the Mill Valley house, and Bob moved to a dark, three-story houseboat in Sausalito. He lived less than ten miles from us, and he and I were supposed to spend every other weekend together, but by the end of June I hadn't seen him once since school let out over a month earlier.

I don't think he liked being around me, and I couldn't blame him. Who wants to be around a sullen kid who doesn't talk? Bob would ask me questions and I would just stare at him. Then he would blow his top, grab me by the shoulders, and try to shake the words out of me, shaking so hard I could hear cracks and pops in my neck and back like I was being adjusted by some kind of lunatic chiropractor.

When that didn't get me to open up, Bob would shout about how hard he worked and ask me why I didn't understand that all of it was for me and Sam, and now that Sam was gone, I was all he had. *"Why can't you appreciate all I do for you, Joseph? I'm building you a business. Setting you up for life. And this is the thanks I get?"*

Bob owned and operated a successful construction company called Harper & Sons. He built McMansions all over the Bay Area and made shitloads of money, and because that was all he cared about, he assumed it was all the rest of us cared about too.

Even when Sam was alive, Bob wasn't an especially pleasant guy to be around. One of Bob's most prominent traits was that he didn't think he was ever wrong. Domineering and brusque, he was that guy at the table who would say a thing was black even if he knew it was white, just to start an argument.

I didn't have the nerve to challenge Bob, but Sam would spout off and call bullshit on him all the time, which you would think would piss Bob off, but it had the reverse effect. Bob believed it meant Sam knew how to be a leader. He used to tell his friends how Sam was a bull and was going to take over the business one day.

I was what a nice person might call a sensitive kid: shy, awkward, and generally nonconfrontational. Bob often referred to me as a pussy.

Taking all of these factors into consideration, I didn't care that Bob was avoiding me because I didn't want to be around him any more than he wanted to be around me. Except that I did. That's the rub for all kids with shitty parents, and don't let anyone tell you differently. You only hate them because you love them and you want them to love you back. And never was that truer than the Saturday in question, because it wasn't any old Saturday, it was my birthday, and Bob had promised to hike from Mill Valley to Muir Woods with me to celebrate.

When Bob was in college, before he started working in construction, he'd been obsessed with trees too. He'd moved to California from Spokane to study Forestry at UC Berkeley and could identify every tree and plant he saw, no matter where we were. Ingrid maintains it's the greatest gift my dad ever gave me: my love of trees. And it's why I loved hiking with him. When we were still a family, he and Sam and I would spend hours on the trails every weekend, exploring, foraging, and investigating the forest. Bob was a different person when he was in the woods. He was funny and patient, and all the good memories I have of him are from those times.

Bob and I hadn't hiked together once since Sam's death, and I'd been looking forward to it for weeks.

Twenty minutes before he was supposed to pick me up, the phone rang. The answering machine clicked on and I stood beside it, listening to Bob leave a message about how there was a running race happening on Bridgeway and a bunch of streets were blocked off and it was going to be a nightmare for him to make it over to Mill Valley and yadda yadda yadda, he was sorry but he wasn't coming.

"We'll go before the summer's over," he said. "I promise."

I picked up the receiver and slammed it down as hard as I could. The asshole never even wished me a happy birthday.

And he wasn't fooling me. He lived one measly town south of Mill Valley, and sitting in a little traffic in order to spend time with your kid on his birthday didn't seem like too much to ask.

Over the years, being lonely has become the standard for me. It feels normal now, like a bad leg wound that turned into a permanent limp, and I accept it. But back then loneliness was a new, excruciating state of being, and there were only two things that made me feel less alone. One was playing guitar and the other was being in the woods, and that day I opted to spend my time doing both. I was going to hike as planned, and I was going to take my guitar with me, Bob Harper be damned.

I had filled my backpack with what Bob told me to pack when he thought he would be coming: two turkey sandwiches, a couple cans of Dr Pepper, iced oatmeal cookies, and a canteen full of water.

When I realized Bob wouldn't be accompanying me, I added my portable CD player, a couple CDs, and a small notepad and pen, in case I got lost and had to ask for directions. Then I grabbed my guitar and headed out.

The beginning of the trail was a ten-minute walk from my house, and from there it was another mile to where I wanted to eat. When I finally got to the spot, my arm was sore and tired from lugging the guitar all the way there. I sat at an empty picnic table near Poseidon, took everything out of my pack, and set it up like I was having a party.

I was trying to pretend that it was fine for a kid to celebrate his birthday by himself, but my heart hurt like someone had hammered nails into it, and when I inhaled it felt like my breath had nowhere to go, like I could suffocate from all that solitude. That's when I started fantasizing about killing Bob. I figured if he died I could forgive him for ditching me on my birthday.

The best idea I could come up with—and by "best" I mean the idea that seemed least likely to look like foul play—was pushing Bob off the deck of his houseboat. It was built right over the water and had a simple wooden railing that was designed to let the view of the bay and city in but, if tampered with, would not be good at keeping an asshole father from falling out. And if he fell at low tide in only a couple inches of water, it would be like hitting cement.

The problem with my plan was that when I pictured what Bob's body would look like after they pulled it out of the water, it didn't satisfy my desire for revenge at all. Instead it made me think of Sam, and I forced myself to get off that train of thought before I felt even worse.

I drank some Dr Pepper to settle my stomach, took off my shoes and socks, and got out my guitar—I always play guitar barefoot, no matter where I am or what the temperature. I feel more connected to the earth when my feet are touching the ground. More deeply rooted. Like a redwood.

I started strumming an old Tom Petty tune that I'd just learned, and when I got to the chorus I heard a voice behind me singing the words.

I looked back and saw Cal on the trail down below. He was standing maybe ten yards away, his head raised toward the sky, and from where I sat it appeared as though he was staring directly into the sun.

I recognized Cal right away. Well, not by name, but I had seen him twice before, both times at the record store in Mill Valley.

It was hard not to notice Cal. He was extra tall for his age, reed thin and willowy, with fine, wispy yellow hair that made him look like a stalk of wheat blowing in the wind. He had a narrow face and these little round, crafty eyes that reminded me of the great gray owls Bob and I went looking for once in Yosemite. And that day he was wearing the only thing he wore the whole summer—a navy blue sweatshirt and a pair of cutoff denim shorts that his hipbones could barely hold up, with two drumsticks sticking out of his back pocket.

I quit strumming and he said, "That sounded rad." He slid onto the bench across from me. "I dig that song."

I reached into my backpack and pulled out the CD.

"You have the whole album?"

I nodded, though it actually belonged to my mom's boyfriend, Chuck, who was twenty-seven, had a perpetual tan, and worked as a trainer at the gym where she took exercise classes. Chuck was basically living at our house, and he called me Mutant Joe when my mom wasn't within earshot. I was pretty sure he was trying to make a joke about how I was mute, but he was too stupid to know that the word "mutant" wasn't some adjectival version of "mute," and if I hadn't actually been mute, not to mention timid beyond reason, I would have called him stupid to his face. Instead I wrote the word "rebound" on the notepad in the kitchen every morning, which made my mom laugh; back then, not much made Ingrid laugh, so I kept doing it.

I remember wanting to invite Cal to eat lunch with me, but I figured he was too cool to say yes. Even back then I had a sense that certain people were out of my league.

Luckily, Cal was sure of himself in a way kids that age rarely are, and he didn't need an invitation. He looked at all the food on the table and said, "What's with the spread?" Then he noticed the Dr Pepper and said, "Can I have one of those?"

He grabbed the can, opened it, and waited for the foam to fizz out over his hand. Then he drank the whole thing in seconds, an achievement that culminated in a long, loud burp, for which he took a bow.

I watched him, and that's when he began looking at me suspiciously, as if he were waiting for something—probably words—to come out of my mouth. The longer the quiet lingered between us, the more puzzled he seemed.

I swallowed hard and looked down at the table, embarrassed and now wishing he would go away.

But instead of laughing or calling me a freak or threatening to beat me up like most of the kids at school did, he leaned over and said, "You all right?"

That was a hard question to answer.

"Say something," he prodded.

I stared at him.

"*Can* you say something?"

I shrugged. That was an even harder question to answer.

Cal reached over and picked up my guitar, watching me carefully, as if I were a stray dog that might bite him.

After examining the guitar, he handed it back to me and said, "Play something else."

I looked down at the neck and started playing "Big Love" by Fleetwood Mac. It was a hard song and the one I often used to warm up because it required a lot of finger picking, plus some flamenco and classical stuff.

When I was done, I set the guitar on my lap and looked at Cal. His jaw was agape. "What are you, like, twelve? How is it possible you can play like that?"

I was small for my age, and people always thought I was younger than I was. I took out my notepad and wrote *I'm 14.*

"Me too," Cal said.

Wow woulda guessed 17, I wrote. *Thought u were older.*

"Everyone thinks that." He pointed to the guitar. "Seriously, though. Why are you so good?"

Practice, I wrote. I drew a smiley face next to that word, because it was such an understatement it made me laugh.

Cal gestured toward my Dr Pepper. "You gonna drink that?"

I took another sip. It was warm, and I handed it to Cal because it seemed like he wanted it more than I did. He was staring at the food and I handed him a sandwich too.

"What's your name? I go by my last one. Callahan. You can call me Cal." He ripped the crusts from the bread and stuffed them into his mouth. "I go to Tam High. Well, I mean, I'm starting there in September."

Me too! I wrote with an embarrassing amount of enthusiasm. Then I scribbled my name across the page. *Joseph Robert Harper.*

Cal asked me why I was there by myself and I added a couple of lines about how it was my birthday and my dad had ditched me; Cal said, "That sucks" in a way that made me feel better.

"At least you *have* a dad. Mine left before I was born. I've never even met him."

Cal grabbed the drumsticks from his back pocket and started playing a beat on the edge of the picnic table. Then he nodded toward my guitar and said, "Wanna jam?"

I wasn't sure how to do that, but I picked up the guitar and played the chord progression from an old Doug Blackman tune. Cal continued to play drums on the table, humming a melody over what I was doing, and pretty soon we had the makings of a song. Not a good song, but a song nevertheless.

That's when something started happening inside of me. It was as though the world was changing right in front of my eyes. *I* was changing. I know most of the time people describe monumental moments of their life as *taking* shape, but it's the exact opposite for me. I'd spent the last two years in a sharp and silent world, playing guitar by myself, and as Cal and I played together, I felt all the jagged edges inside of me start to soften and blur into something warm and ecstatic. My life suddenly seemed more bearable than it had in a long time, and I was glad Bob had bailed on me.

Cal and I stayed in the woods and made up songs all afternoon. When it started to get cold, I put my shoes back on, and we packed up and headed toward my house.

On our hike home, Cal asked me what I was up to for the rest of the weekend; I wrote that my mom was gone until Sunday night. She thought I was going to be with my dad, so she and Chuck had gone to Tahoe, and I hadn't bothered to tell her otherwise.

Cal suggested that he and I go back to my house, listen to Chuck's CDs, and learn more songs.

Cool, I wrote.

As we were crossing Panoramic Highway, Cal looked over at me and said, "Yo, what do you want to be when you grow up?"

I'd never given it much thought because Bob had already decided for me. I stopped and wrote, *My dad says I'm going to take over his company. U?*

"Duh," Cal said. "I'm going to be a musician."

Until Cal said that, it had never occurred to me that I could choose to play guitar as a profession, but it suddenly seemed like what I was born to do.

Me too, I wrote.

Cal spun around and walked backward, glaring at me with his little owl eyes as if he were a strigiform truth detector trying to measure how serious I was.

"For real?" he asked. "You swear?"

I wrote *I SWEAR* on my palm and held it up to him, nodding frantically at the same time.

He spun back around, once again took his place beside me, and we continued down my street.

So many new thoughts and dreams were rippling inside of me.

"Harp," Cal said. "I have another serious question."

I tried to curtail my smile because it didn't seem cool to smile as much as I could feel myself smiling, but no one had ever given me a nickname, at least not a nickname that wasn't an insult, and I felt as if Cal had just uncovered the real me. I stopped walking and tried to look serious, even though I suspected I was still smiling like a cartoon character.

"Do you want to be in my band?" Cal said.

It was as if all the stuff inside of me was about to gush out.

"I mean it's just me right now, but I need a guitar player, and not only are you the best guitar player I've ever met, but you're pretty decent looking too—girls like cute guitarists—and we're going to be in the same class, and that means we can practice all the time and grow up to be the Campbell and Petty of our generation. What do you say?"

I whipped out my notebook and was about to write *YES!* as big as I could fit it on the page, but that didn't seem emphatic enough. I wanted Cal to know I was more serious about this than I'd ever been about anything.

Cal was waiting for my answer. And I don't think he ever truly understood the significance of what happened next.

I looked him in the eye, took a deep breath, and said, "I definitely want to be in your band."

It was the first time I'd spoken in over two years.

"Cool," Cal said with a casual shrug.

He took my notebook from me and wrote up a contract stating that he and I were now best friends and bandmates for life. We both signed it, and then Cal folded up the paper, put it in his pocket, and followed me up my driveway.

SEVEN.

CAL AND I were inseparable all through high school. His mom, Terry, used to call us the Reese's Twins on account of an old commercial for Reese's Peanut Butter Cups that went *two great tastes that taste great together* or some such thing. She said that, much like chocolate and peanut butter, we were pretty awesome on our own, but that as a duo we were unstoppable. She actually used that word: "unstoppable." I'm sure she only said it because she was trying to be nice, because nothing about my personality screamed *unstoppable*, but she and Cal were both good at making me feel like I was worth something, and that meant a lot.

Every day after school, Cal and I would go back to my house and do our homework. Despite our obsession with music, we were both excellent students. I worked hard because Bob threatened to take away my guitar if I didn't maintain my GPA. Cal worked hard because he said slacker musicians were a cliché, and he refused to be a cliché. "Except with girls," he clarified. "One of the reasons I'm doing this is for the girls."

Once we finished our homework, I would fix us dinner, which varied between spaghetti, frozen pizza, mac and cheese, and canned chili. And by *us*, I mean I cooked for the whole house—myself, Cal, Ingrid, and, while he was around, Chuck.

51

I hope this doesn't give the impression that Ingrid was a bad mom. She wasn't. She was just heartbroken. That's what she used to say to me when I would find her fully dressed in her big, empty bathtub, staring out over the valley. I would ask her what was wrong, and she would say, "I'm heartbroken, Joey."

She'd lost a son and then a husband, and she didn't know how to heal from that. None of us did.

At any rate, if I hadn't cooked, we wouldn't have eaten, and that was that.

My mom and Chuck went out a lot after dinner, and Cal and I often had the house to ourselves. But even when Ingrid and Chuck were home, the house—a beige-hued Mediterranean-style monstrosity up on Edgewood Road that Bob had built himself—was big enough that we could do what we wanted and not bother anyone.

After dinner we would have band practice, which was just me and Cal working on songs in the garage. Then we'd watch movies or study guitar magazines until we fell asleep. We had a gigantic bulletin board on a wall in my bedroom—we called it our Wall of Dreams—where we tacked up pictures of all the guitars we fantasized about owning someday. Micawber, the Fender Telecaster made famous by Keith Richards, was the big one in the center, and all the other guitars—a Fender Esquire, a Gibson Les Paul Goldtop, a Martin D-18e, a Gibson Firebird, a 1961 Danelectro, to name a few—hung around it like moons orbiting Jupiter.

Once in a while Chuck would give us some pot, but Cal didn't like Chuck or pot, and he rarely smoked with me. "Pot is for boring, unambitious people," he'd decided early on. "I'm neither of those things. And anyone who can play guitar like you shouldn't be either."

Occasionally Cal and I switched it up and ate dinner with Terry when she had a rare night off, and she'd spend the whole meal asking us questions about what we'd been up to, what songs we were learning, and what we were studying in school.

Terry had been a teenager when she'd had Cal and was still young when Cal and I were in high school, but you wouldn't have known it by looking at her. Whereas even in her grief, Ingrid still looked like your typical, well-to-do Marin County mom—nice hair, good clothes, good shape—life had robbed Terry of her youth before its time. She lived paycheck to paycheck, smoked Marlboro Lights, and was always frazzled and exhausted. The blue shadows under her eyes never went away, and the corners of her mouth appeared to be trying to pull her whole face down to the ground.

Terry worked as a waitress at a steakhouse near US 101. She and Cal lived in a small apartment in Marin City, in a building that could have passed for a rundown motel. The place had a cinderblock half wall that divided the family room from the kitchen, there was an electric burner on the counter in place of a stove, and the room Cal slept in was the same size as the closet in my bedroom. The shitty kids in our school called Marin City the ghetto, and I felt bad for Cal when they said it, but that kind of stuff didn't faze Cal. He would peer down at them with his beady eyes—he was the tallest kid in our class and towered over everyone—and remind them that Tupac had once lived in Marin City. Cal never doubted that if Tupac could make it out of there, he could too.

Every other weekend I stayed with Bob on his houseboat in Sausalito. Bob didn't like commotion, so I wasn't allowed to bring my guitar. Never mind that he lived at the end of the dock where there were no trees and nothing to do except look at the water. Most of the time Bob did let me bring Cal, though, and for a while I thought this was a symbol that Bob cared about my happiness and was being a considerate father. Then Cal and I overheard Bob tell Debbie, the woman Bob was dating at the time, that he liked it when Cal tagged along because it meant he didn't have to babysit me.

"It's not called babysitting if you're the dad," Cal huffed to me, as if he were an expert on the subject. "It's called parenting."

Bob's take on music was even more appalling to Cal. As far as Bob was concerned, music was part of the background noise of the world, not an art form that deserved to play a major role in a person's life.

"Never trust a man who isn't moved by song," Cal reasoned. "It means he's dead inside."

One particular weekend, Cal talked Bob into taking us to the big Tower Records in the city on Friday night because Bob was having a party and we didn't want to have to sit around listening to his guests get drunk and babble about how much they'd spent on their houses. Bob had agreed, but he punctuated his consent by saying, "There's something wrong with two teenage boys who have nothing better to do on a Friday night than go to a record store."

"We don't think there's anything better to do," Cal replied on both our behalves, as he was wont to do.

"What are you, his lawyer?" Bob barked. "You know what I was doing on Friday nights at your age? Chasing girls."

"Harp and I don't have to chase girls. Girls chase us."

That was only marginally true. Girls chased Cal, he picked his favorites, and then he made sure whoever he was dating had a cute friend for me.

Back then, Cal wasn't what most people would call handsome. His face was too birdlike, all of his features too small to be considered traditionally attractive, and he was built like an I beam. But his confidence and charisma overshadowed all that. He was a player. And more often than not, he had the coolest girls in the room swooning.

On more than one occasion, Bob made it a point to tell me I was empirically better looking than Cal, as if this were something I should value or exploit. But I was one of the smallest kids in class, and I was shy and self-conscious around normal people, so you can imagine what I was like when I was in the vicinity of a girl I liked.

As the car pulled in to the Tower Records parking lot that night, Bob said, "You two better start putting as much energy into getting into college as you put into getting albums."

Cal caught my eye and I shook my head, silently begging him not to say a word. Early on in our friendship, I made Cal promise not to mention our Brooklyn plans to Bob until the time came for us to go. He had agreed, but I think he found it disappointing that I wouldn't tell Bob the truth.

When we got out of the car, Cal said, "Sometimes I question your commitment to our dreams, Harp."

"You don't understand. Bob would flip if I told him. He'd probably lock me in the house and homeschool me. And I know for sure he wouldn't let me hang out with you anymore."

That kept Cal quiet, but he was skeptical, and right to question my dedication. Unbeknownst to my best friend, I had already taken the SATs and ACTs and was working on applications to numerous California universities. I told myself I was just doing it to placate Bob, but there was a part of me that wondered if I was going to have the guts to go to Brooklyn with Cal.

I eventually applied to Stanford, Berkeley, UCLA, and UC Santa Cruz. Stanford rejected me, but I got into the others.

"You'll go to Berkeley, just like your old man," Bob declared during the winter of my senior year as he stood over me in his kitchen.

I knew it was now or never, and I told myself to come out with it. After pacing around the deck outside and then calling Cal for advice, I walked back into the kitchen and asked Bob if I could talk to him about something important.

He made direct eye contact with me, and I started glancing around the room, looking for something distracting on which to focus. Bob's kitchen looked like a dungeon. Everything was charcoal gray and blackened steel. The architecture of doom. Nothing calmed my nerves.

"Sit," Bob said.

I sat at one of the tall stools flanking the breakfast bar and knew immediately that I'd chosen the wrong location. My feet didn't touch the ground from there, and that made me feel already defeated.

I rested my arms on the cold countertop while Bob made himself an espresso. With his back to me, he said, "You're not about to tell me you're gay, are you? You and that Callahan?"

It was not the first time Bob had alluded to this possibility, and I suppose it wasn't so far-fetched from the outside looking in. Cal and I spent virtually every moment together, and kids at our school called us fags all the time. I didn't care. It was Bob's tone that hurt me. He sounded like he was already against whatever I was going to say, and how was a kid supposed to have a heart-to-heart with his dad if his dad came to the table with such a bad attitude?

"No," I sighed.

I was looking at the piece of art on the wall behind Bob's head. It was a painting of three jockeys on horses, all racing toward a finish line. The two horses in the lead were neck and neck and were both painted dark gray, the same color as everything else in the dungeon kitchen. The horse on the far left of the canvas, a couple of lengths back, was red. I wondered why the artist had chosen to paint that horse red, especially because it was losing. It was the only splash of color in the whole room.

"Go on, then," Bob said.

I hunched over the counter and mumbled, "It's about Berkeley."

"What about Berkeley?"

I can't remember what I said after that. Something about how I was thinking of deferring for a year so that I could move to New York and get a job and live in the real world before I spent four more years in school. I tried to make it sound like I wanted to get some life experience, and for a brief moment it seemed to be working.

"What kind of job?" Bob asked.

Graduation was still a few months off, but Cal already had a lot set up in New York. We were going to crash with Terry's brother Bill until we could afford an apartment, and Bill had promised us jobs at a bakery he ran in Williamsburg. In the meantime, Cal had been working part-time for a local landscaping company and had saved up enough money to buy a plane ticket.

Ingrid told me she'd buy me a plane ticket too. Her exact words were, "Follow your dreams, Joey, or you'll end up a bitter old asshole like your father."

"Well, what then?" Bob asked.

My stomach was a washing machine on spin. I couldn't think of any good lies, and I kept hearing Cal's voice in my head. When I'd told him on the phone that I was going to have the talk with Bob, he'd read me an inspirational quote about how a person's success and happiness in life was directly proportional to the amount of uncomfortable conversations he or she was willing to have.

"You can do it," Cal assured me. "He's not the boss of you. Not once you turn eighteen, anyway. Just tell him."

"Joseph," Bob said.

"It's like this. Cal got us jobs at this bakery, and we're going to—"

"*Cal?*" Bob shouted. "I should've known this had something to do with *Cal*. Forget it. Cal can work in a bakery all he wants. *You're* going to Berkeley."

"But Dad, we—"

"The answer is no. You're not going anywhere with *Cal*."

I hated the way he said Cal's name, as if Cal were a rapist or a pedophile.

"You're going to college, Joe."

"You won't even let me explain. We want to start a band. For real."

"You think *that's* going to convince me?"

"*Please*. Just *listen*." Tears blurred my vision and I wanted to punch something, but I tamped all my feelings down like trash in a compactor and stared at my hands while I spoke. "Just give me a year. That's all I'm asking. If nothing happens, I'll come back and go to Berkeley."

"You want a year to gallivant around New York like a bum, playing guitar and letting that kid mooch off you? On my dime? Not a chance. And why would you want to live like that? Don't you know how *lucky* you are? You get to go to school and study whatever the hell you want. And you'll have a *career* waiting for you when you're done. That's the deal. Otherwise, come June, you're on your own. And in a million years you couldn't make it on your own in New York City."

I heard Cal's voice in my head: *You don't need his stupid support. You're going to be a rock star.* But it wasn't as simple for me as it was for Cal.

First of all, Bob's words got stuck in my brain. I believed him when he said I didn't have what it took to make it in Brooklyn, and that gutted me. Second, and probably more significantly, for reasons I did not understand, Bob and I couldn't seem to get along, and I desperately wanted to change that. I wanted his love and approval, and I thought that if I stayed behind and did what he told me to do, I would get it.

I stared at the red horse again and noticed that the jockey on the back of it resembled my favorite guitar player at the time, Johnny Greenwood. I was sure that was a message from Sam, a message I didn't have the strength to heed.

"Joseph," Bob said, "are we clear?"

It's not that I knew all along I wasn't going to go with Cal. It was more like the idea of moving to Brooklyn and chasing some crazy dream didn't seem real to me. It's easy to fantasize about doing something and to talk about doing something and even to make plans to do something. It's a whole other thing to actually go and do it. It's idea versus action. And the difference between the two is guts, I suppose.

When I look back on that time now, it's clear that not going to Brooklyn was as much of a choice as going would have been. But it didn't seem like it then. At the time I saw the fact that I stayed behind as not making any choice at all.

And when August rolled around, Cal moved to New York just like he said he was going to do, and I went off to Berkeley, numb and full of regret.

To Cal's credit, he kept at me for a couple of years after he left, constantly begging me to drop out of school, move across the country, and be in his band.

"Nobody here plays like you, Harp. Blood Brothers, remember?"

I continually turned him down, and by my junior year at Berkeley, Cal and I had completely lost touch.

Though in the essence of truth telling, it's more accurate to say I stopped returning Cal's calls and e-mails. I purposely dropped off the face of his earth because whenever we talked, he would tell me stories about his life in New York—playing in dive bars, working as a dishwasher in a restaurant, sleeping in the restaurant's pantry when he couldn't afford rent—and I would hang up the phone feeling even worse about myself than

I already did.

I followed Cal's career from afar for a while. But the night Callahan appeared on *The Late Show with David Letterman* for the first time, I kicked the wall of my bedroom so hard I broke two toes.

After that I stopped paying attention to what Cal was doing. I stopped surfing the web for news of his life. I stopped listening to any radio station that might play his music. I never spoke of him again to anyone. In general, I tried to pretend Cal Callahan didn't exist.

It wasn't that I was jealous of Cal. I loved him, and I missed him. And I was prouder of him than I had ever been of anyone or anything. But it was impossible to feel that proud of everything Cal had accomplished without being reminded in the most painful way of all the things I would never do.

You know where I was the night Cal was making his national television debut on *The Late Show*? Before I went to the emergency room to have my toes X-rayed, that is? I was sitting in my shitty apartment in Berkeley, eating a shitty burrito from the shitty Mexican restaurant I lived above, wondering why I wasn't standing on that stage, playing guitar beside my best friend.

EIGHT.

I DIDN'T KNOW any nice places to eat in Mill Valley, so the night October and I went out to dinner for the first time, I let her pick the restaurant. She chose a tiny, farm-to-table spot off the main street in town and asked if we could go right when they opened, before it filled up, and for the first twenty minutes we had the place to ourselves.

The restaurant had an open kitchen, a wood-fired oven where they cooked everything in cast iron pans, and furry seat cushions that made the room feel cozy and romantic. There was a record player behind the bar, along with stacks of vinyl, and a playlist on the back of the menu, the albums selected by the chef to complement the food being served that night.

Rumors was playing when we walked in, and as October mouthed the words to "Go Your Own Way," my instinct was to tell her that the first songs I learned to play on guitar were Fleetwood Mac songs, but then I remembered she didn't know I could play guitar. As a matter of fact, she barely knew any veritable information about me at all.

October was wearing a loose-fitting, knee-length dress the color of Japanese maple leaves in the spring, a long, silky scarf tossed around her neck, and brown suede boots. She looked pretty and cool, and I contemplated telling her so, but that seemed like something you'd say on a date—and specifically not something you'd say to your boss over dinner—and since I wasn't sure which one of those scenarios we were in, I held back.

As soon as we sat down, the restaurant's young chef came out and greeted October by name. She introduced me as her friend Joe, and the chef shook my hand and asked me if I had any dietary restrictions. I told him I did not, and he took away our menus.

The waiter, whom October called Brad but whose shirt had the name "Al" stitched above the left pocket, asked if he should bring us some wine. October looked to me for the answer and I nodded without hesitation. I was nervous, and the restaurant didn't have a full bar, so tequila wasn't an option.

Brad/Al nodded in return, and then he turned to October and nonchalantly said, "How's Chris?" as he poured water into our glasses.

"Fine," she answered. "Out of town, as usual."

"Rough life that guy has."

October rolled her eyes and smiled politely, and I questioned what the hell I was doing there with her.

We were quiet then, the subject of Chris hanging between us like a spider that had just descended from the ceiling, neither one of us wanting to break the web and have to deal with the thing crawling around the table.

Once the waiter came back with the wine, October tucked a wavy chunk of hair behind her ear, looked around the empty room, and said, "Thanks for humoring me with the early-bird special."

I shrugged, not having given it much thought.

"It's this weird thing I have." She paused, picked at a seam on the edge of her scarf. "This condition . . ."

"You have a condition where you have to eat dinner before the sun goes down?"

She laughed, and I remember noticing how much I liked the sound. Her laugh was artless—probably the only artless thing about her—and contained absolutely no pretense.

"Anyway . . ." She took a sip of wine. She seemed nervous too, and I could tell she was really trying to think something through. A moment later, using a lot of medical jargon, she explained her condition to me.

I shook my head. "I'm not sure I understand."

Glancing obliquely at the ceiling, she thought for a few more seconds. Then she said, "In layman's terms, if I see someone being tickled, I'll feel as though I'm being tickled. And if I see someone get shot in the head, I'll feel as though I've been shot in the head. But it's not just physical sensations. I can often sense the emotional experience of another person by touching them."

I couldn't wrap my head around what she was saying, and I tried not to sound offensive when I mumbled, "This is an actual thing?"

She nodded and went on to explain that during her childhood, she couldn't watch much TV or go to movies because it caused her too much pain. Apparently this made her something of an outcast among her peers and, like me, she spent a tremendous amount of time alone. And, much like how I turned to guitar, she turned to drawing and painting to keep her company.

"I was a ferociously lonely kid," she said. "Art saved me."

Sounds familiar, I thought. But I didn't say it. "How old were you the first time it happened?"

"Eleven." There was a small vase of daisies in the middle of the table. October picked out a flower, spun it around in her fingers, and then, one-by-one, began gently petting the petals as she continued. "I was sitting on the floor in our living room. My mom and dad were on the couch behind me, watching a documentary about the Maasai tribe in Africa—my parents are both anthropology professors, and this was the kind of stuff they watched for fun. There was a scene in the film where a man slaughters a goat. I watched him draw the knife back and slit the animal's throat, and I started reeling on the floor, gasping for air, feeling like there was blood gushing from my neck."

"Jesus."

"My parents rushed me to the emergency room, but of course there was nothing wrong with me. Not physically, anyway. It took months for the doctors to figure out what was happening. After that, my parents didn't seem to know what to do. They were constantly walking on eggshells around me. They still do. Meanwhile, all my classmates mistook the sensory experiences I was having for some kind of clairvoyance, as if I could read minds or something. Obviously, I can't. I just have . . . how did one doctor put it? *A heightened ability to experience empathy.*" She stopped, put the daisy back in the vase. It seemed like she was waiting for me to say something, and when

I didn't, she added, in a tone that wasn't wholly convincing, "At the time, it felt like the end of the world. But as I've gotten older, I've chosen to see it as a gift."

"A gift?" It sounded like an unbearable affliction to me, but I can barely handle my own feelings, let alone suffer the feelings of others.

"I don't know why I'm telling you all this," she sighed. "It's not something I normally talk about on a first date. One day I'd like to get up the guts to use it in an exhibit."

I wanted to say something supportive. It seemed like she needed that. But I was caught up on the word "date." And besides, I was still skeptical. "So, you're telling me that if some random stranger walked in here right now and sat next to us, you could look at him and tell me what he's feeling?"

"Not necessarily. But maybe. Usually I have to touch the person. I have to open myself up to them. And it doesn't work with everyone. Rae, for instance. It's one of the reasons we work so well together. Energetically, she never gets in my way." Again, she waited for me to say something, and when I didn't she said, "You must think I'm a freak."

I shook my head. The truth was, whether her condition was real or not, it actually made me feel closer to her, not farther away. I had my own idiosyncratic issues to deal with, and limitations were aspects of her character that I could actually relate to.

"Movies and TV?" I said. "You still can't watch those?"

"Not much."

"What about live music?"

"I love live music, but concerts can be tough for me because when there's music involved, emotions are intensified, and the more intense they are, the easier it is to feel them. In general, I try to avoid crowds. You wouldn't believe how much sadness people carry around. In a large group that can be overwhelming."

"Hence the early-bird special."

"Hence."

The waiter brought over a dish of roasted vegetables sprinkled with local goat cheese and honey, and as I reached for a carrot, a question dawned on me, one that made me instantly uncomfortable.

"What about me?" I mumbled. "Can you feel what I feel?"

October took a bite of cheese, then caught my eyes, paused there for a moment, and nodded slowly. "Pretty sure I could if I tried."

I shook my head—I think I'd meant for that gesture to be imperceptible, but October saw it, and took it as a challenge.

"You don't believe me," she said, not a question but a declaration.

"It's not that I don't believe you, it's just that it sounds impossible."

"Give me your hand."

I wiped my fingers off on my napkin and slid my hand across the table. October reached over and rested her palm flat on my forearm. Then she scooted to the edge of her seat, extended her leg, and pressed her right calf into my left one.

She closed her eyes, and her breath stretched out like taffy on a long, slow inhale and an even longer, slower exhale. I watched her closely and could see her tiny ribcage and chest moving up and down rhythmically, six seconds in and eight seconds out.

There was an intense heat in her touch. I felt my heartbeat quicken, and I fought against becoming aroused. I hadn't had that kind of reaction to a woman in a long time, and as I looked across the table, I had this silly, adolescent vision of making a playlist of my favorite songs and playing it for October on a long drive up the coast.

After about a minute October lifted her hand, opened her eyes, and sat back in her chair. Then she took out her phone and showed me a short video of her second Living Exhibit, *Solitary*, in which she had aimed to exist without art. She'd spent two weeks locked in a tiny, gray studio apartment in an art gallery, where a two-way-mirrored wall allowed museum visitors to see what was going on inside the room and gave the viewer the impression of watching a human diorama come to life.

October lived alone and in silence inside that box for fourteen days. She had no music, no television, no books, no pencils, no paint, no color, no scents, and saw no other humans. She didn't even cook her own food, because she believes cooking is an art too. By the end of the video her big eyes were dull and her usually vibrant face was pallid and drawn. She looked like half a person.

"I felt like a ghost," she said, "like I didn't exist."

I got nauseous thinking about it. That was how I felt almost every day.

I looked away, drank the rest of the wine in my glass, and poured myself some more.

"Joe . . ." October said.

I shook my head. Shut down. Reverted to the lamest possible version of myself as I stabbed a piece of squash with my fork and wished I were somewhere else.

I could feel October staring at me, and after a while she said, "You know what hit me the hardest once I left that room? The smells. As soon as I walked outside, all these odors struck me—trash, gasoline, food, the Bay, the perfumes and scents of people walking by. I swore I could even smell the eucalyptus trees in the park, and they were over a mile away. It was like I'd developed some kind of superhuman sense of smell. When I got back to Mill Valley, it was even more intense. I'd only lived here for a couple of months at that point, and you know, this town smells like heaven anyway, but it *really* smells like heaven if you've been in limbo for two weeks. I remember getting out of the car and walking to the biggest redwood in the yard. You know the one between the house and the garage?"

I nodded. I could see that tree from my bed.

"I threw my arms around it and just inhaled." Her eyes filled with tears, and she used her napkin to dab at the corners. "Sorry. I haven't thought about that in a long time."

She took a sip of wine as Brad/Al dropped a mini loaf of bread off at our table, along with a ramekin filled with olive oil.

"I didn't mean to upset you," October finally said. "I was only trying to tell you that I understand."

I looked at her but didn't say anything. I felt all tied up inside, certain I was blowing it, certain this would be the first and last dinner we'd have together. But October held my look with soft eyes. Then she ripped off a piece of bread from the loaf, dipped it in the oil, and said, "It's OK. You'll tell me when you're ready."

She didn't seem at all annoyed with my emotional ineptitude, and that surprised me, mainly because it didn't jibe with the reaction I was used to getting from women, which was typically disappointment and frustration, not understanding.

Nevertheless, from my point of view, October might have been able to perceive emotions, but she couldn't perceive facts, and I believed it was the facts that counted. I believed that the more facts October learned, the easier it would be for her to see what a broken toy I was and discard me.

There were so many things trapped inside of me then. But they were things I didn't know how to express—not just to her, but to anyone.

I wanted to tell her the truth. I wanted to tell her that I'd grown up two miles from where we were sitting. I wanted to tell her about Bob and Ingrid, and Cal. I wanted to tell her how when I was in high school, Phil

Lesh saw me play at the Sweetwater and told me I was a better guitar player at sixteen than Jerry Garcia was at fifty. I even wanted to tell her about my brother, and I never told new people about Sam.

Something happened, I imagined I'd say. *I'm not supposed to be like this.*

To be clear, I don't blame my brother's death for who I am any more than I blame Bob or Ingrid, but it's hard not to wonder how differently I would have turned out had Sam lived. Of course the flip side is that Sam's death is what led me to the guitar, and to Cal, and without those two things, I'm not sure I would have survived my childhood.

Art saved me too, I wanted to confess.

I would have told October the story of how, exactly one month after Sam died, Bob came downstairs dressed for work, his eyes like two dead rats, and announced to Ingrid that he was getting rid of all of Sam's things— clothes, books, baseball and swim trophies, even the furniture in Sam's bedroom.

Ingrid had protested with shouts and tears—"*I'm not ready, Bob. Please.*"—but he told her he'd called the Salvation Army days earlier. "They're sending a truck over at noon. It's not up for discussion."

Ingrid was so upset that after Bob left for work, she told me to go into my brother's room and take whatever I wanted before the truck came.

What if Dad gets mad? I wrote in the notebook I'd taken to carrying around.

"Joey, I want you to have something to remember your brother by, and if your father says one word to you about that, you tell him I said he can shove it up his ass."

I wrote her exact words down just in case the opportunity to show it to Bob ever arose.

Even before I went into Sam's room, I knew what I wanted: the Martin acoustic dreadnought he'd gotten for his sixteenth birthday. The guitar was brand new, and when Sam was alive he wouldn't let me touch it because he said my hands were too grimy from petting trees all the time.

The guitar was the only thing I'd ever seen that was as beautiful as the redwoods I worshipped, and I started teaching myself how to play it by studying the Fleetwood Mac songbook Sam bought at a garage sale the same week he got the guitar.

Bob never did get mad about me keeping the guitar, but I figured it was because all I did was sit in my room and play it, and that meant Bob didn't have to see me or talk to me, or deal with me not talking to him. It was a win-win situation for all.

By the time I met Cal two years later, I knew how to play every song in that book and had moved on to the Eagles *Greatest Hits*. In fact, the first song Cal and I ever performed together in public, during our sophomore year, was "Take It Easy." We used the bleachers in the gym as a makeshift stage and played the song during the girls basketball practice because Cal insisted we needed to start getting some live show experience, and because he had a crush on a girl named Nell, who's family was moving to Frontier, North Dakota, at the end of the summer. Cal had been flirting with Nell for weeks. That day he changed the song's lyrics from "standing on a corner in Winslow, Arizona," to "standing on a corner in Frontier, North Dakota," and before Nell left town she gave Cal his first hand job, more than a year before I would get mine.

The second half of dinner went a lot smoother than the first. Brad/ Al continued to bring small plates of food to our table—Kennebec fries, braised short ribs, apple cake for dessert—all the while supplying us with the best red wine I'd had since back in high school, when I used to steal Silver Oak from Bob's fridge.

October didn't press or pry any further into my life, and that, along with the abundance of wine, put me at ease. I went on to spend a good portion of the meal giving her in-depth play-by-plays of movies she'd never seen—films that were too violent or disturbing for her, like *Reservoir Dogs*, *Goodfellas*, and a documentary about whales that I'd recently watched. I undertook the narratives with real commitment—"*Mr. Brown? That sounds too much like Mr. Shit. How about if I'm Mr. Purple? That sounds good to me. I'll be Mr. Purple*"—and October laughed at my sincere, theatrical portrayals, occasionally interrupting to tell me I was funny or cute, and pretty soon being with her began to feel warm and homey, to such a degree that my heart quailed whenever I wasn't talking.

The one personal question October did ask me before we left the restaurant was if I had any siblings. My simple, though not altogether accurate, answer was "No."

When we pulled up in front of October's house that night, I shut off the truck's engine but left the radio on low.

We sat in the dark for a while, listening to the quiet music. I didn't recognize the song that was on, but I imagined the guitarist was playing an old Taylor Milagro. The tone scraped at my insides and reminded me once again that despite the feelings of familiarity I was experiencing, the woman sitting beside me still had no idea who I really was.

Eventually October sighed and said, "I guess I should go." She paused, then turned toward me. "I had a really nice time tonight, Joe."

I nodded. "Me too."

She waited another long moment, the air in the truck suddenly becoming warm and stuffy. I got the sense she was waiting for me to make a move, but I didn't. Finally she wished me a good night and hopped out.

I watched her walk into her house and shut the door behind her. I watched Diego get up and spin in a circle around her. I watched October scratch the dog's neck and kiss the top of his head.

I sat there until the lights in the kitchen went off and the ones in the rear of the house went on. Then I went back to my apartment and, without turning on any of my own lights, lay on the bed, closed my eyes, and fell asleep wondering why I was already having the urge to bolt.

NINE.

CAL GAVE ME some sage advice once that I often call to mind whenever I'm attempting to step outside my comfort zone. During our junior year, a girl named Melissa asked him to ask me to ask her to Game Night at our school. Game Night was an event Tam High had once a year in the spring. They would set up tables in the gym and designate each one for a specific game: Monopoly, Trivial Pursuit, Scrabble, Boggle, stuff like that. They served pizza, there were prizes for winners, and kids took turns making out in the locker rooms.

"Melissa thinks you're cute," Cal said. "She wants to be your date. I promised her you'd call."

I told Cal there was no way I could call Melissa.

"Why not?"

"She's too pretty. I won't know what to say."

"But she's a sure thing," Cal argued, aghast at my insecurity. "She *asked* me to tell you this. She's not going to say no."

I told Cal I'd call Melissa if he smoked some pot with me first, and he said, "Fine, fine." He shook his head. "The things I do for you, Harp."

He put on a Tool album, which did not help my anxiety, and I lit the joint I'd found in Chuck's coat pocket. This was one of the few times Cal had agreed to get high with me, and despite all of his antidrug protests, he seemed to get a kick out of it. On the other hand, I felt more on edge with each inhale. Cal had to dial Melissa's number for me and then ask Melissa's mom if Melissa could come to the phone.

"I'm calling on behalf of Joseph Harper," he said formally.

I thought maybe Cal was going to do all the talking, but once Melissa got on the line, he tossed the phone at my chest. I don't know what the expression on my face was like, but he took one look at it and fell on the floor, pointing at me and laughing.

I put my hand over the receiver and asked Cal to turn the music down, but he was still on the ground, now playing air drums, and didn't hear me. I cupped my hand over my ear to block out the noise as best I could and managed to ask Melissa to go to Game Night with me, but after I hung up I knew it was going to be impossible for me to think about anything else until the date was over.

"See? That wasn't so hard." Instead of it mellowing him out, the pot made Cal extra verbose and too easily amused. "You know what I tell myself, Harp, whenever I get nervous about doing something?"

"You never get nervous about doing anything."

"But I do!" His eyes were glassy, and he was wobbly on his feet as he hopped onto my bed and began lip-syncing to the song.

"Cal, be serious for a sec." I was suddenly fascinated with the idea that Cal could feel insecure. "What do you get nervous about?"

"Ack." He rubbed his face with his palm like he was trying to rub off the high.

"*Cal*," I huffed, turning off the stereo with an irritated thud.

"Bro. Chill." He sat down and looked at me. "I'll tell you, even with this dumb Game Night, I worry that I'll sound stupid or lose every round to the biggest douchebags in our class."

"*Really?*" I said. "You *really* think like that?"

"Sometimes. Yeah." He laughed like a stoner. "But you know what I tell myself when I do?"

"What?"

"I tell myself that *everybody thinks like that*. And you know what else? Deep down, nobody gives a rat's ass what other people are doing, they're too concerned with themselves. You can't let that kind of shit stop you from doing your own shit. This is supposed to be *fun*. Games are *fun*. And *everything* in life is like that. Not all fun and games; I mean shit is *important*, obviously. Doing shit is *important*. Dreams are *important*."

"Cal."

"My point is—" He pointed his finger so close to my nose it made my eyes cross. "It's impossible to become *less* of yourself by doing something you really wanna do. You can only become less by *not* doing it. And becoming less means you shrivel up and die inside. That's why you have to *do* shit. Especially shit that scares the crap out of you. You know what I mean? You can only become *more* from that. More smart, more strong, more brave, more whatever. Even if you fail. That's the goal. To be *more*."

It was impressive how articulate he could be even when he was stoned out of his mind.

"More or less?" he asked in a prog metal voice.

I laughed. "You're so washed, dude."

"More or less, Harp?"

"More," I said. "For sure. More."

"*Way* more."

"Way."

That's what I was thinking about when I finally got up the nerve to kiss October. Cal and his concept of *more*.

It happened at work, at the beginning of what was supposed to be a long night shoot.

October and I had gone on one more dinner date that week, though it was to Super Duper for burgers and shakes, which we got to go and ate on the swings in Old Mill Park because October was in one of her moods where she didn't feel like being around people. We'd fallen into the habit of sending flirty texts back and forth before bed, but I hadn't touched her yet. I wanted to. And I could feel a tacit, palpable desire buzzing between us like a delay pedal on an endless feedback loop whenever I got within a two-foot radius of her. But she'd put the ball in my court, and that meant she had to wait for me to get my head out of my ass.

On Wednesday, October announced that Thursday's selfie would consist of me filming her entire night's sleep. She planned on condensing that into a four-minute video, on top of which she would overlay carefully selected words and phrases about time and death.

"And could you make the set look like a hospital room?"

She wanted it simple: just a bed, some medical equipment on the side, which I rented, and a working clock on the wall. "The biggest clock you can find so the numbers are visible above the bed."

She gave me the next day off to rest so that I wasn't too tired to man the camera for six hours that night, and she filmed and uploaded a selfie on her own that afternoon.

We reconvened late Thursday evening. October showed up in a hospital gown with a pair of white silk pajama pants underneath. Her hair was wet from a shower.

"Are you really going to be able to fall asleep with a camera running and a strange man staring at you?"

"I can fall asleep any place and under any circumstance." She sat up against the headboard and pulled the covers up to her chest like she was cold. "Last year, Chris and I took my parents to see Bruce Springsteen at Madison Square Garden. We had seats in the first row, and about two hours in I fell asleep." She bit her lip and chuckled. "To be fair, I was jetlagged. I'd flown in from an exhibit in London that morning. But the worst part of this story is that Bruce actually *saw* me sleeping, and in between songs he looked down at Chris and said, 'Am I boring your date?' to which Chris said, "Sorry, Boss. That appears to be the case."

"That's pretty funny," I said, though the ease with which she spoke to me about Chris made me uncomfortable.

"Mortifying is more like it." She shook her head as if clearing it of unnecessary debris. "OK. Less talking, more sleeping. Let's do this."

I checked the levels on the camera, gave her a thumbs-up, and pushed "Record."

She slid down into the bed, turned onto her side, and closed her eyes.

Less than a minute later she flipped onto her back, lay there for another few minutes, and sighed. "Remember when I said I could sleep anywhere? That only works if I'm actually tired."

As a joke I said, "Here, maybe this will help," and I played "Dancing in the Dark" on my phone. That cracked her up, which, in turn, cracked me up. After that we tried to right ourselves back into work mode, but we couldn't. October would settle back down, and I would stifle a laugh; then I would settle, and she would laugh. Finally she threw a pillow at me and said, "You're ruining this selfie!" But she wasn't mad, she was being playful.

And right then I had a sense I was going to remember the night in some meaningful way for a long time.

I handed her back the pillow and she said, "What time is it?"

I looked at the clock above her head—it was one of those big digital ones you'd imagine a fancy advertising agency or the NYSE might've had on the wall in the 1980s. I'd found it in a consignment shop in San Anselmo.
"11:09."

She sat up against the headboard again and said, "Tell me when it's 11:11 so I can make a wish."

I waited until it was 11:11 and said, "It's 11:11."

She closed her eyes, presumably made a wish, then opened them and looked at me in a way that tugged at my body.

I imagined Cal's voice in my head: *More or less, Harp?*

I asked her what she'd wished for and she said, "If I tell you it won't come true."

We looked at each other some more.

"Now what?" I said.

"Well, since you derailed the work, it's your responsibility to come up with something that makes up for it. This night can't be a total bust."

More or less, Harp?

I shut off the camera and the lights. The only illumination in the room was the soft glimmer coming from a floor lamp near the front of the studio and the weird red glow of the large digital clock above our heads.

I walked toward the bed, watching October's face for signs I was making the wrong move. I saw none. I felt daring. And since I didn't normally do daring things, the rush filled me with an audacity so foreign to my body it was as though I were watching a movie with Joe Harper as the star—only the Joe Harper in the movie was a hero.

I sat down on the edge of the bed, hands shaky, throat dry, wishing I had a shot of tequila. But I met October's gaze and held it.

"Tell me what you're thinking," she said softly.

"I was just thinking about my best friend from high school."

Her brow furrowed. "A *male* friend?"

I chuckled. "Yeah. Well, I was thinking about some advice he gave me once when I wanted to ask out a girl but was being shy and stupid."

"What was his advice?"

"He always told me to go for it."

"Sounds like good advice to me."

She stopped blinking, her gaze still locked on mine, little pilot lights burning in her redwood-colored eyes. She lifted my hand, pressed the tips of her fingers against mine and her palm into my palm, trying to figure out what I was feeling. And I tried to send her a message, tried to tell her through my skin what I couldn't say with words.

I'm pretty sure she heard me loud and clear, because a moment later she dropped my hand and took off the hospital gown. It tied in the back, but she didn't bother to untie it. She just lifted the whole thing over her head and tossed it onto the floor.

"Your turn," she said.

I took off my T-shirt, dropped it to the floor on top of her hospital gown, and got in bed.

We scooted down under the covers, facing each other on our sides, and she moved in close. Her breasts were warm against my chest, her palm cool on my back. She ran her thumb across my bottom lip, maneuvered her lower body so that my thigh was firmly between her legs.

"Remember, nothing has to happen if you don't want it to," she said.

"What if I want it to?"

I don't know who went first, but one of us—probably October—leaned in, and we kissed. It was clumsy at the start. My teeth banged into hers and my head was going in the wrong direction. She giggled at that; I righted myself, and then it was good and soft and warm. Her mouth tasted like tangerines and mint and her neck smelled like the jasmine that grew outside the house, and I didn't stop kissing her for a long time, so long that after a while it got to be too much—physically painful, I mean—and I knew I was going to have to either get the hell away from her or go all the way.

"The ball is in *your* court tonight," I said.

It wasn't just that I was scared. It was that she was my boss, and that meant she had to decide how far to take it. At least that was my assessment and my excuse.

She rolled over, climbed on top of me and began unbuttoning my jeans.

"Are you sure?" she said. "Because I can be kind of naughty when I'm in charge."

October did all the work that night, and afterward we were quiet; I held her close, our limbs entangled so that I didn't know where my body ended and hers began. And I remember thinking that holding her felt so much more right than my last girlfriend. Meadow was tall and strong, and holding her had been like trying to hold a mare. October was a fawn in my arms.

I was a moment from dozing off when October whispered, "You know what I like about you?"

I couldn't have answered that question if my life depended on it. "My dynamic, outgoing personality?"

She laughed and then said, "You understand how to exist inside silence. Most people don't know how to do that."

"I like silence."

"I like silence too."

Another long, quiet moment passed between us.

"Joe," she whispered again. "What's your favorite word?"

I told her I'd never thought about it and would have to get back to her on that. Then she asked if I'd ever heard the term "desiderium." She'd just discovered it, she said, and was trying to come up with a way to develop the concept into an exhibit.

"What does it mean?"

"An ardent longing," she said, "usually for something lost."

I had the feeling October was trying to tell me something specific with that word, to forewarn me about what would happen if I wasn't careful. Or, rather, if I was *too* careful. And as I drifted off to sleep that night, I actually wondered if I would ever be that close to her again. I knew there was a good chance our moment had already passed. I also knew that if I lost her, it would be because I didn't have what it took to hold on to her, and that loss would be something I would have to live with for the rest of my life.

Desiderium.

The unrequited.

Even now, years later, when I think about that night, my jaw tenses and my dick gets hard, and there's an emptiness, a craving, an *ardent longing* in my chest and in my gut that seems to define the word "desiderium" so completely, I almost feel as though I conceived of the concept myself.

TEN.

OCTOBER WAS GONE when I woke up, and I wandered over to her house and found her in the middle of preparing breakfast. Eggs, potatoes, toast, fresh berries. She was wearing the bottoms to the pajamas she'd had on the night before, along with the T-shirt I'd left on the floor, which explained why I couldn't find it in the mess of covers before I'd pulled on my jeans and went looking for her.

I tried to help, but she wouldn't let me. Cooking was another kind of art project to her, she explained. She preferred to make the food and, more importantly, to plate it herself. She had a fancy Italian coffee machine, though, and when I told her I had been a barista in college, she put me in charge of the cappuccinos.

Over breakfast we talked about spending the day together. It was warm and sunny, and I suggested we drive up to Point Reyes, hike around all afternoon, and then have dinner at Nick's Cove and watch the sun set on the water.

As far as I could tell, I hadn't disappointed her yet. And although my unquiet mind and heavy heart were pushing for me to question everything and assume the worst, I didn't cave. I felt strong that morning. Wide open and available. The man I wanted to be.

And I had an intense desire to *talk* to this woman. On our drive to Point Reyes, I planned on telling her everything I hadn't told her yet—about Bob and Ingrid and Sam, about growing up in Mill Valley. I would tell her how I'd never gotten over my brother's death and how I hadn't talked for two years, and then I would tell her about my best friend, Cal, and how much he'd meant to me. I'd tell her how I'd let him down, and how I'd let myself down too.

But the part that surprised me the most? I wanted, more than anything, to play guitar for her.

We were standing at the sink doing the dishes, and I guess I'd zoned out because October nudged me and said, "What cha thinkin', Lincoln?"

It was all I could do to piece words together. "You. Last night. That madrone tree outside the window." Diego stuck his whole head into the sink and tried to lick remnants of scrambled egg from the plates. "This dog. Coffee. You in my T-shirt." I was used to vacillating between numbness and regret and was shocked at the encouraging emotions I was experiencing. "It feels nice. Good. I don't know."

The door opened behind us and Rae walked in with a handful of mail, her laptop, and the Ziploc bag of nuts and raisins she was always carrying around. I'd forgotten it was a workday and was startled to see her, but not as startled as she was to see me. There I was, shirtless at 9 o'clock in the morning, standing beside my boss, who was wearing what looked like tangled sheets. Our arms were touching at the sink, and there was a fluency to our body language that we hadn't had time to adjust.

I stepped to my right to create some distance, but it was too late.

"Morning," October said to Rae, nonchalant and unapologetic.

Rae didn't say a word, but she gave me a wicked side-eye when October went back to the dishes. Then she set the mail on the counter and started sorting through it.

"Joe makes an award-winning cappuccino," October said. "Joe, make Rae a cappuccino."

"I don't want a cappuccino," Rae said.

She walked around me and grabbed a bottle of sparkling water from the fridge. Then she sat down at the kitchen table, opened her computer, set her snacks beside it, and began running through the day's schedule with October, all the while picking raisins out of the bag and plopping them into her mouth. Evidently, October had a daylong meeting at Ribble she'd forgotten about, and then she had to make an appearance at a cocktail party at the gallery that represented her later that night.

"I can't go to a cocktail party tonight," October sighed. "There's going to be too many people there. And I have plans."

"You have to. Your name was on the invitation," Rae told her. "Besides, you promised Thomas. Go get a shower, yeah? We need to leave in forty-five minutes."

October looked at me and made a sad face. Then she swallowed the rest of her cappuccino and headed down the hallway. A second later she said, "Joe, come here for a sec."

I walked around the corner, out of Rae's sight. October stepped in close and whispered, "I'm sorry we can't spend the day together. Rain check for tomorrow?"

"Deal," I said. "Rae seems pissed."

"She can be overprotective. Don't worry, I'll talk to her."

We kissed, and October slipped her hand down into the front of my jeans. I pulled her hand away and backed up, because the last thing Rae needed to see when I returned to the kitchen was a hard-on in my pants.

When I rounded the corner, Rae was still at the kitchen table on her computer. She waited until she heard October's bedroom door close, then looked at me and said, "What do you think you're doing?"

"Sorry?"

"She has a boyfriend. You know that, yeah?"

"I think you know it's more complicated than that."

"And what exactly do you foresee happening here? You think she's going to leave *him* for *you*?"

"I don't feel comfortable talking to you about this."

"I knew you had an agenda the minute you showed up."

I laughed at that. "I don't have an agenda."

"What happened to all that drivel about not knowing who she was and keeping to yourself? It doesn't look like you've been keeping to yourself."

I didn't want to argue with her, and under the circumstances I didn't really know how to defend myself. Though I did get a small kick out of the fact that Rae thought I was capable of premeditated seduction, because nothing was more outside the realm of my skill set than that.

I walked toward the door and Rae said, "Normally, a person would get fired for sleeping with their boss."

"Is that a threat?"

"No. It's a statement about how unprofessional your behavior is."

"Well, October is my boss. And if she wants to fire me, I suppose she will. What's it to you?"

"Part of my job is to look out for her. Shield her from the wrong kinds of people. You suddenly look like the wrong kind of person."

"You don't even know me."

"She's just lonely. This will end when Christopher gets home, yeah? She'll forget all about you."

"Have a nice day, Rae."

I went back to the studio, straightened up a bit, and then spent the rest of the afternoon—wait for it—playing my guitar until one of my fingers started to bleed. I hadn't taken the guitar out of its case in a long time; it took me a while to clean it up and get it in tune, but once I did it sounded as warm and as beautiful as ever. And besides lacking the necessary calluses on my fingertips, I wasn't nearly as rusty as I thought I'd be. It's astounding how the body remembers what to do if it's spent thousands of hours doing it, even if it hasn't done it in years.

I tried not to think too hard about what Rae had said, but I figured she was right. I probably was nothing more than a distraction. Furthermore, October *was* my boss, and my behavior *was* unprofessional. Throughout the day I found myself wondering why Rae could see what a shit I was but October couldn't.

What did that say about either of them, I wondered?

October didn't get home until late that night, and it was all I could do not to call and ask her if I could come over. It should be noted that throughout my entire adult life, I had only entered into relationships with women I could live without. That was my modus operandi: Stay safe. Don't care too much. So I was anxious about the way I was feeling. I had a hard time falling asleep, and by the time I woke up the next morning, it was already after nine.

I showered and dressed in a hurry. On my way out the door, I grabbed my phone and noticed a couple of texts from October, but I was seconds away from her house and didn't bother to read them.

The front door was unlocked, and I strolled into the kitchen. October was at the sink filling Diego's water bowl, and she looked startled when she saw me.

"Joe," she said quietly, looking over her shoulder. "You didn't get my texts?"

I shook my head. "I slept in. Came straight over."

I heard a voice coming from the back of the house. A man's voice. Talking in an animated tone that led me to believe he was speaking to the dog.

October leaned in and whispered, "Chris came home this morning. He wasn't supposed to be back until the end of the month. He just showed up. To surprise me."

"Ah." I hadn't had coffee yet and couldn't process this information in a swift or proficient way. I didn't know if I was supposed to run from the house or act like nothing out of the ordinary was happening. "What should I do?"

"I don't know." October bit at her thumbnail. "He wants to meet you."

"Now?" I rubbed my eyes and tried to focus. "What did you tell him?"

"Nothing. I mean, I told him you were my assistant and that you were great. That's all. He caught me off guard."

The confidence I'd had the day before was waning fast. Now that her boyfriend was real, now that he was here, I didn't think for one second that I would be able to compete with him, and I certainly didn't want to meet him without some mental preparation.

October met my eyes and touched my arm, and who knows what she felt there, because she said, "I know. I'm sorry. We'll sort this out."

Diego came bumbling into the kitchen, and I could hear Chris a few steps behind. October went to the table and sat down with a mug of coffee in her hands. I backed up as far away from her as I could get, all the way to the sink.

From the vantage point of the hallway, Chris saw me before I saw him. He was saying something to October about how good it felt to shower in a familiar bathroom, but he stopped abruptly, midsentence, presumably when he spotted me. That's when I glanced his way, and he and I made eye contact.

"Jesus Christ," he said.

I was about to say the same thing.

"*Harp?*"

If I hadn't been leaning on the counter, I would have fallen over.

"*Cal?*"

October was looking back and forth between us, bewildered.

"*Cal?*" I said again.

"*Harp?*" he repeated.

The shock wore off for him faster than it did for me. He threw his arms around my neck and pulled me into his chest like I was his long-lost brother. And, in a way, I was.

"Is it you?" He was shaking me and grinning, and his breath smelled strong and medicinal, like he'd just used Listerine. He held me by the shoulders and looked at my face. "How is this possible?"

"Hold it." October looked at me, mortified. "*You're Harp?*" Then she looked at Cal. "*Joe is your best friend, Harp? From high school?*"

Cal nodded vigorously. "I can't believe this. I can't fucking believe this."

He hugged me again, and for one second I forgot everything except that Cal Callahan was standing in front of me. I hadn't seen him in fourteen years, and even though I thought of him at least once a day, I couldn't have quantified how much I'd missed him until that moment.

And then everything inside of me started to tear apart.

"Shit. *Cal.*"

He threw his head back and howled with laughter. "No one's called me Cal since high school! Come to think of it, you're the only person who *ever* called me Cal." He looked at October and said, "I'd declared, the summer before our freshman year, that I was dropping my first name, and I asked everyone to call me Cal. I wrote it on all my papers and tests, but nobody bought it. Not my teachers, not my mom, not Harp's mom. Only Harp."

"And Bob," I reminded him. "Bob called you Cal too."

"But with contempt!" Cal laughed.

"Who's Bob?" October asked.

"My dad."

"How *is* old Bob Harper?" Cal said. "Still as pleasant as always?"

I wasn't ready to start catching up. There was already too much to process. I shook my head and said, "I need to sit down."

Cal ran his hand through his hair, pushing it off his face. "Fucking Harp."

October looked at me and said, "You told me you were from Spokane." She didn't seem angry, just confused.

Cal laughed again. Then he went to the window, pointed and said, "He's from that ridge right over there! Bob's from Spokane!"

Cal went to the fridge and pulled out a bottle of champagne. "This calls for a celebration."

"Christopher, it's ten o'clock," October said.

"And I'm with my two favorite people in the entire world!" He looked at me. "She was just telling me about her new assistant, how smart and creative and amazing he was. What are the odds it turns out to be *you*? What are the fucking odds?"

I didn't know the fucking odds, but I was going to calculate them and perhaps play the lottery since I was so lucky.

Cal popped the cork over the sink and pulled out some juice glasses from the cupboard. I could feel October looking at me from the table, needing something, but I didn't know what. I couldn't face her. Nor could I take my eyes off of Cal. He was even taller now, over six and a half feet. His hair was shorter and more stylish than it used to be, and he'd grown into his face in a good way. Birdlike features on a kid look weird, a little sinister even, but on a grown man with some depth and character, the effect is striking. Cal had transformed from an owl into a hawk.

He handed out the champagne, we clanked glasses, and I drank mine in one gulp. October didn't touch hers. Cal took two sips and forgot about his.

"Seriously. How long has it been?" he asked, refilling my glass.

"Fourteen years."

"Tell him," he said to October. "Tell him how much I talk about him. I can't tell a story from my childhood that doesn't involve you."

October nodded. "He talks about you all the time." All the sparks were gone from her voice. She looked beside herself. "Blood Brothers."

"Blood Brothers!" Cal shouted. "See! She knows!"

I wasn't ready to talk about Blood Brothers either. I drank my second glass of champagne, even though I don't like champagne, and it provided me with the dizzying kind of kick in the ass I needed to ask a question I was suddenly obsessed with knowing the answer to.

"How the fuck did you two meet?" I asked with too much gravity, glancing back and forth between Cal and October. "How long have you been together?"

"You want to tell it?" Cal asked October.

She shook her head and stared at the table. Now it was she who couldn't look at me. The question had clearly unnerved her, and I felt bad about that. But I desperately needed some context to their relationship.

"She bought this property from me," Cal said. "I'd purchased it for my mom, and after she died and I put it on the market, I was—"

I cut Cal off. "Wait. *What?*"

Terry had died? Another shock. I felt awful that I hadn't known, that I hadn't kept in touch with her, that I hadn't been there for Cal when he lost his mother. I was the worst kind of human: a terrible friend.

"Good God, Cal. I'm so sorry."

"Cancer," he said. "She was sick for a long time. She did get to see me win a Grammy though. That meant a lot to her." Cal picked up his glass of champagne but didn't drink out of it, he just rolled it around in his palm. "I bought her this place right before she got sick. She didn't have time to enjoy it for very long, and before she died she made me promise I would sell it to someone who would love it as much as she did." Cal leaned over and kissed the top of October's head. "Enter this incredible woman."

October squirmed in her seat. I'd never seen her so ill at ease.

"She showed up and gawked at the trees," Cal said. "No kidding; the first thing she did when she got out of the car was wander through the backyard, looking up and touching and smelling all the trunks. I asked her to have dinner with me before she went into the house. She just had this vibe, you know? Turned me down though. Wouldn't even give me her phone number. I had to bribe her real estate agent for it."

"Why not?" I asked her. I couldn't imagine any girl turning Cal down.

"I'll tell you why," Cal responded. "Because I made the mistake of saying, 'Don't you know who I am?' and after that she thought I was a dick."

Cal cracked up at the memory. October gave him a half-hearted smile then looked my way. "I knew who he was. And I didn't think it made sense for me to date a man whose job requires him to stand in front of thousands of screaming people every night." She stared into her coffee. "Especially one who lived in New York, had a somewhat infamous reputation as a womanizer, and was in the middle of a divorce."

"Divorce?" I couldn't believe how much of Cal's life I'd missed. "You were married?"

"Not for very long."

"Please don't tell me you have kids."

"No kids," he said. "Anyway, I dropped the price of the property so that she was basically stealing it from me, under the condition that she let me take her on a date. I really wanted to hit it out of the park, so I whisked her off to Mexico City because she told me she loved Frida Kahlo, and there's a Frida museum down there. I rented out the whole place so there were no crowds to bother her, and it was all epically romantic until she got food poisoning from some street tacos we had for lunch. The rest of the trip was me taking care of her for two days while she puked into a wastebasket beside the bed because she was too sick to make it to the bathroom. That's how I got her to fall in love with me. By holding her hair back while she barfed."

"Chris. Stop."

"Come on. You love this story."

"So, you moved back here then?" I asked him. "From New York?"

"Technically, he still lives in New York," October said with a tone.

"Not true." He ruffled her hair. "I still have my place in Brooklyn, but when I'm not on the road I'm mostly here."

October stood up suddenly and said, "I need to go lie down."

Cal wrapped her up in his arms. He was so much bigger than she was, and he engulfed her. "What's wrong?"

"Nothing. I have a headache."

Cal kissed the top of her head. "OK. Go lie down. Harp and I are going to catch up."

"Chris," she said nervously. "I'm sure Joe has stuff to do. And you must be exhausted." She turned to me. "He took the red-eye in from Chicago." Then she looked back to Cal. "Don't you want to rest or something?"

"*Rest?*" he shouted. "I've just been reunited with my long-lost best friend. How can I rest at a time like this?" He narrowed his eyes at me. "You don't have any plans today, do you? Tell me you don't have any plans."

I looked to October for an answer, but her face was blank.

"No plans," I said.

"Fucking Harp," he said. "Fantastic. Follow me."

ELEVEN.

FOURTEEN YEARS HAD PASSED since Cal and I had seen each other. In a way it seemed like a lifetime, and yet after five minutes together it was as if no time had passed at all. We picked up right where we'd left off.

Blood brothers.

After October wandered off to nap, I followed Cal to the garage. It turned out the garage was a small recording studio, which explained why all the windows were covered up and it had been padlocked since I'd moved in.

Cal said the equipment was state of the art, but I know very little about recording; when I looked at it, all I saw were three large computer screens and a console with lots of knobs and buttons. However, the studio feature Cal was most excited to show me was the wall of guitars just outside the live room.

"Check it out," he said, presenting the wall to me like a game show host revealing the big prize.

There were over a dozen of them, each one more beautiful than the next. The real-life version of our childhood bulletin board. Our Wall of Dreams. And the dream belonged exclusively to Cal.

One particular guitar ripped my heart out. The 1953 butterscotch Fender Telecaster hanging in the center, just like it had on the corkboard in my bedroom. Cal saw me eyeing it and started grinning.

I looked at him, wide-eyed and in disbelief. "Don't even tell me that's a *Micawber*..."

He nodded like crazy. "Go ahead. Play it."

I couldn't even reach for it. The guitar rendered me starstruck.

Cal took it down and handed it to me. "There is no one in the entire world I would rather hear play this than you."

I ran my fingers up and down the neck and held it in my arms for a while, feeling its weight, admiring it, absorbing its energy before I felt ready to pluck a note or strum a chord.

Cal laughed. "That's *exactly* what I did the first time I touched it."

"I can't believe you have this."

Allegedly, Keith Richards had named the guitar Micawber after a Dickens character, and back when Cal and I were first discovering different makes and models, we thought the Tele sounded too country for us—until we listened to *Exile on Main Street* a couple dozen times and Keith set us straight.

Cal sat on the chair near the console and I sat on the couch across from him. He was eager to relay the story of how he'd come to acquire this instrument. "There's a shop I go to on Broome Street in SoHo. They've got all these old, incredible guitars. I mean the place is a gold mine. One day about two years ago, I walk in, and that's the first thing I see. No kidding, I literally begin to shake and sweat at the sight of it. My buddy who owns the place, he hands it to me, and for a while I don't even play it, I just hold it like you just did, wondering who else had touched it and how it had ended up in my arms. I could tell it had been around the block, you know? I mean look at it. It has a history. A life. A *soul*. Finally, I plug it in and, well, you'll see. I dabble in guitar. I'm not a player like you. But when I play Micawber it's like I'm a fucking prodigy."

I still couldn't believe I was holding it. "How much did this cost?"

He chuckled. "Well, that was the thing. I asked my buddy the price as I'm cradling it in my arms, and after he told me I remember thinking, *This fucking thing costs more than my mom made in a decade*, and I decide right then on principle that I can't buy it. I just wanted to hold it a little while longer." Cal leaned in, animated. "October walks in a minute later. She'd been in a clothing store across the street, and she comes over and puts her arm on my back for a while—you know, does her thing—and she says, 'Wow. I guess you have to buy that guitar.' I asked her why and she said, 'I can feel how much it means to you.' She asked me what was so special about it, and you know what I told her? I swear to God, Harp, I told her it reminded me of you."

I looked down and focused on the neck of the guitar, trying to keep his words from getting too far down inside me. This is one of my biggest character flaws. I often feel things much deeper than I let on.

"You know what?" Cal said. "October asked me that day, as she and I were leaving the store, why I didn't look you up. She said I talked about you so much I should just find you and reach out, but I never did. I don't know why. You'd stopped returning my calls so long ago, I guess I didn't think you wanted to be found. But she ended up bringing us back together anyhow. Crazy, huh?"

I couldn't even begin to chronicle the absurdity.

Cal nudged me to play the guitar. He was insistent, like the moment was getting too heavy and we needed to shake it off with some sound.

"Go on. Show me what you've got."

I confessed that I had only recently started playing again after a long hiatus. I pulled off my shoes and socks, and Cal laughed at that in a sentimental way that made me feel happy and sad at the same time. Then I plugged in the guitar and dove into "Tumbling Dice," and it didn't matter that my fingers were sore and my timing was off. Cal was right. The guitar was magic. It practically played itself. And with the exception of the night I'd just spent with October, sitting across from Cal and playing that guitar was the single most satisfying experience of my adult life.

Cal and I spent the rest of the day in the studio. He showed me how the Pro Tools rig worked; we played with all the different guitars and jammed to all the old songs we used to play back in high school. In between songs we were memory banks of stories, the two most common phrases we repeated that afternoon being: "Remember that one time . . ." and "How about when . . ."

When it started to get dark, we realized we hadn't eaten all day and decided to go down to town and grab some food. Cal ran back to the house, hoping to talk October into joining us, but he returned alone a few minutes later and said she didn't want to come.

Cal didn't know how to drive. He'd never gotten his license when we were kids for two reasons: One, he couldn't afford a car and figured there was no point in having a license if you couldn't have a car. Two, he said New Yorkers didn't need to drive, and in his heart he was already a New Yorker.

We hopped in my truck, and as I shifted into reverse, Cal said, "You obviously spend a lot of time with October. Has she seemed off lately?"

I shrugged, instantly uncomfortable. "Off, how?"

"I don't know. Quieter than usual, I guess."

"I'm not sure I know her well enough to answer that," I said, hoping it sounded believable.

He nodded. "Yeah. Don't take it personally. She can be a hard nut to crack, which is pretty ironic when you think about it."

"What do you mean?"

"Oh, you know; she's so good at honing in on other people's feelings, but not as great at talking about her own."

I remember thinking that Cal's description of October didn't correspond with my perception of her at all. She didn't seem like a hard nut to crack to me. On the contrary, she seemed split wide open.

"Between you and me," Cal went on, "Rae called me yesterday and told me she was worried about October. She was the one who suggested I come back. I canceled a bunch of radio promos to get home for a few days, which did *not* make my label happy. I expected October would be glad to see me, glad I'd made the effort, but when I walked in this morning she seemed more spooked than excited."

Fucking Rae, I thought. What a yeah-saying, feet-shuffling, raisin-and-almond-eating buttinsky she was.

"Did she say anything else?" I asked nervously. "Rae, I mean."

Cal shook his head. "October gets like this when she's overworked. Super-introverted. Doesn't like to be around people. But I'm usually an exception to that."

"She has been working like crazy the last couple of weeks."

"I'm sure that's it," he said.

Cal and I went to a local brewpub for burgers and beers. At first we were seated near the window, but Mill Valley is a small town. Cal kept getting tapped on the shoulder by people who knew him and wanted to say hi or knew who he was and wanted to meet him. Especially women. He still clearly commanded—and enjoyed—the attention of women.

I found it amusing and fascinating that so many people recognized my old friend. Of course I was aware of how successful he had become, theoretically anyway, but I'd never considered how that success might play itself out in his daily life. I'd never even imagined Cal in Mill Valley as an adult. I'd always imagined him wandering the streets of New York, cool, carefree, and invulnerable, a force field around him like a rock star superhero.

It was touching for me to see how well he handled the attention. Despite all he'd accomplished, he was the same person I'd known in high school—funny, talkative, focused, and flirty. Success hadn't seemed to change him in any overt way. If anything, it had loosened him up a bit. He finished his first beer before I finished mine and asked for another round before we ordered our food. The teenage Cal would have stopped at one and lectured me about discipline. The adult Cal was a lot more relaxed.

After a pushy man with a sweater tied around his neck came over and insisted Cal take a photo with his son, Cal chatted up the hostess, who agreed to move us to a reserved table in the back of the restaurant where Cal could sit facing away from the room; we weren't bothered again.

"Wow," I said. "You're really famous."

He ignored the remark. Then our food came and we both ate like we hadn't eaten in a week. Minutes passed, and there was quiet between us for the first time all day. But it wasn't quiet in my head. I was thinking about all the things I had imagined I would say to Cal if I ever saw him again. This was something I'd imagined a thousand times in a thousand different ways. Now here he was, sitting across from me. I had to start somewhere.

"Fuck, Cal. I'm sorry."

He looked up, burger in hand, mouth full. "Harp, no. It's fine."

"It's not." I was on beer number three and stirred by liquid courage. "Just hear me out, OK?"

He wiped his hands on his napkin and gave me his full attention.

"Here's what I want to say. You did it. You did everything you said you were going to do and more. Seriously. *Everything*. I'm proud of you. And I'm sorry I let you down. I'm sorry for dropping out of your life. I'm sorry for not being there for you. I'm sorry for so many things."

He drained his beer and peered at me through a wispy chunk of hair that had fallen across his eye. But he didn't shake me off or contradict anything I said. He just listened.

"This is hard," I admitted. A lot of emotions were hitting me at once. I thought of all the years of Cal's life that I'd missed. I thought of Terry dying, and I thought about the night I'd spent with October. Sitting there with Cal, realizing what I'd done, I swore to myself that nothing else would happen between October and me. I didn't care what kind of free-love shit they had going on or how I felt about her, I could see right away that he loved her, and I wasn't going to get in the middle of that.

"The thing is," I said, "I'm just so fucking sorry."

"You don't need to keep saying that."

"I do. You don't even know." I shook my head and felt myself getting shaky. "You got *married*, Cal. You fucking got married and I wasn't there. You got *divorced* and I wasn't there. Terry *died* and I wasn't there. You won a fucking *Grammy* and I wasn't there."

"None of that matters now."

"I don't understand why you're not pissed at me."

"We were kids, Harp."

"But I *bailed* on you. I made you promises, and I didn't keep *any* of them."

There was a small votive candle in the middle of our table. Cal reached out and put his finger on top of the flame, and at first I flinched, thinking he was going to get burned, but then I realized the flame was fake, plastic, battery-powered.

He said, "I figured you had your reasons for not coming with me. And I knew you well enough to guess at what those reasons were. You wrestle with your demons in a different way than I wrestle with mine. You always have." He shook his head slowly, contemplatively, rubbing his chin. "I was never mad at you, Harp. I want you to know that. I was just super fucking bummed, for a *really* long time, that you weren't along for the ride." He leaned across the table, his eyebrow arching sharply, devilishly. "It's been a fun fucking ride, bro."

Despite how much we'd already had to drink, when the server came over and asked us if we wanted one more round, we both nodded.

"Catch me up," Cal said. "I want to know what you've been doing all these years. Figured you'd be running the family business by now."

"Yeah, well, that didn't pan out."

Cal wanted details, and I explained to him about how when I first started at Harper & Sons, I spent years in the actual construction part of the job. "It was hard but really satisfying work. Building things is like moving meditation. You can forget who you are and what you feel when you're using tools and making things. And when you're finished, there's something to show for it. A tangible object that represents your time on the planet."

"Kind of like making music," Cal smirked.

"Kind of," I said sadly. "Maybe that's why it suited me. But Bob refused to let me stay in that role. If I was going to take over the company someday, he insisted I start climbing the ladder. And once I moved into the office, every aspect of my job depressed me. Inputting data for time cards and cost codes, filing invoices, preparing liens, validating insurances for subcontractors, the hours I spent commuting in and out of the city every day, my gray cubicle. And let's not forget Bob's constant, condescending tone regarding my lack of leadership skills. I couldn't please him, no matter how hard I tried, and I swear, each day shaved off a little piece of my soul."

"So, what? You quit? Good for you."

"Oh, it's better than that." I took a long pull of my beer and smiled sarcastically. "I got fired."

Cal's brows rose.

"You heard me. Bob fucking fired me."

I stuffed a couple fries in my mouth, shrugged, and then told Cal the whole story, beginning with the argument that had resulted in my termination. "I'd been cross-checking a set of invoices and discovered that Bob had purchased and charged one client for building materials— considerably more than the project had called for—and then used those extra materials on another project, while overcharging the second client too."

"That dirty dog."

"I confronted Bob about it and he shrugged it off, said it was no big deal, that everyone did it. But I refused to send the invoices like that. It was the first time I'd ever really stood up to him, and it didn't go over well."

"What happened?"

"He said, and I quote, 'Christ, Joe. You're as much of a pussy now as you've always been.' I told him being a pussy was better than being a crook, and he took a wild swing at me."

"*He hit you?*"

I shook my head. "I ducked, and he missed. And then I laughed because I knew that would piss him off even more. After that, he told me to clean out my desk, get the fuck out of his office, and never come back."

Cal was peering at me, rapt. "Jesus."

"I guess he felt bad after that. A couple days later he sent me an e-mail apologizing and asking me to come back, but I never responded to it." I shrugged, stared down into my glass. "He sold the company a few months later, retired to Vail, and no doubt wrote me off as another dead son. We haven't spoken since."

"Damn, Harp. I'm sorry to hear that. Really. What about Ingrid? How's she doing?"

"Happily remarried and living in Texas. She's going to flip when she hears we've reconnected."

We finished eating, ordered more beer, and Cal fixed me with his eyes. "Do you ever think about it?" he said. "Playing music, I mean? Do you ever wish you'd come to Brooklyn?"

I bit the inside of my cheek and ran my thumb along the metal edge of the table, pressing it into the pointy, ninety-degree angle of the corner until it hurt.

"Every day," I mumbled.

Cal looked crushed when I told him that, and right away I wished I'd lied.

"What about now?" he said, his brow furrowed, concerned. "You're happy, right?"

"Happy?" It was like I didn't even understand the question. Then a vision of October making breakfast in my T-shirt flashed before my eyes and I smiled, but the magnitude of that insight racked me with guilt and dread.

"Marriage? Kids?" Cal asked.

"Not even close."

"You seeing anybody?"

I shook my head. "Broke up with someone a couple months ago. Haven't really had time since I got this job."

Cal and I closed the pub down that night, and even though Casa Diez was less than two miles away, I didn't think I could drive up the dark, winding road to get there as shit-faced as I was. I suggested we walk home, but Cal didn't think he'd make it. He called October and asked her if she would come and get us.

We sat on the curb laughing at everything funny and not funny, the way only intolerably drunk people do, finding it uproarious that we'd never ended up shit-faced and stranded in high school but were doing it as adults.

October arrived to find us on the sidewalk, FaceTiming with Ingrid. Cal had grabbed my phone and called her, and despite the fact that he'd woken her up, she started to laugh *and* cry as soon as she recognized him.

October ordered us into the car.

"I'm talking to Harp's mom!" Cal shouted.

October seemed irritated, and I took my phone from Cal and told Ingrid we had to go.

"You boys be careful," Ingrid said, just like she used to when we were teenagers. "And have fun."

Cal got in the front seat and I hopped in the back. I could see October's mouth, straight and livid in the rearview mirror.

"Baby, you saved us," Cal slurred. He leaned in and kissed her neck as she drove, and I closed my eyes to avoid seeing Cal's sloshy displays of affection, until I heard October say, "Stop it, Chris. You smell like a frat house."

Cal turned around and whispered, "I think we're in trouble." Then he leaned toward October. "Don't be mad. I love you *so* much."

October met my eyes in the rearview mirror. "How much did he have to drink?"

"Maybe four beers," I said. It had actually been six or seven, but I decided to round down for Cal's benefit.

"*Four?* Jesus, Joe. He doesn't normally drink that much, you know."

I wanted to tell her I knew that about him long before she did, but instead I slumped down into my seat and stopped meeting her eyes in the mirror.

Cal was still chuckling under his breath, mumbling about being in trouble. Then he started going on about how beautiful and amazing his girlfriend was, pressing me to agree with him. "Isn't she beautiful, Harp? Isn't she amazing? Even when she's pissed."

I didn't know if it was all the beer, Cal's questions, or October's serpentine driveway, but I felt like I was going to throw up.

Back at the house, October asked me to help her get Cal inside. As we walked him to the bedroom, Diego followed behind us while Cal continued droning on. "I'm so happy to see you, Harp," and "You're still my best friend, Harp," and "I missed you, Harp."

October got Cal to lie down, I took off his shoes, and by then he was out cold.

I stepped out of the room and the dog shadowed me. October turned off the lights, followed us into the hallway, and shut the bedroom door behind her.

In the kitchen she sat down at the table, rubbed her temples with the meaty parts of her little palms, and let out a long, mystified sigh. Diego dropped to the floor beside her, clattering like a bag of bones.

"So, you're the illustrious Harp," October said.

I didn't know why I was still standing there. I didn't want to be in that kitchen with her, but I didn't want to be alone either. I felt a quiet rage building up inside of my chest, and the longer I stood there, the angrier I got, though I couldn't pinpoint exactly what I was angry about. Too many possibilities.

"Joe . . ." Her eyes welled up with tears. "I didn't know. Obviously." She paused. "He cares about you so much. We can't—"

I pounded on the counter to stop her from talking. She and Diego both jumped.

"I know we can't, OK?" The volume and tone of my voice surprised me. "You don't need to say it, because I know."

We looked at each other, and my regret was as dense and as dark as the forest behind the house. Then something dawned on me, something that flipped my anger over to the other side. The other side of anger, I have discovered over the course of my life, is a deep, dark sadness.

"That was his sweatshirt, wasn't it?"

October looked at me, puzzled.

"The day we met, you were wearing this old, ratty sweatshirt, and I remember thinking, *That looks like the sweatshirt Cal used to wear.* It was his, wasn't it?"

"I don't even know who you're talking about when you call him Cal."

"Well, that's what I call him, so get used to it."

"Hey." She raised her eyes but lowered her voice. "Don't speak to me like that. This is hard for me too."

I shook my head and turned to leave, but when I got to the door I stopped, spun back around. "Why the fuck didn't you tell me who your boyfriend was?"

Her brow rose sharply. "Why the fuck didn't you tell me you grew up in Mill Valley?" I had no good answer to that question, but it didn't matter, because she didn't wait for one. "Besides," she went on, "I figured you knew. Everybody knows. All you have to do is search Chris's name on the internet and you'd find out in two seconds."

"I haven't been able to search his name on the internet in ten years."

I saw recognition on her face then. And pity. Cal had told her too much. All the things I'd tried to hide, she already knew. I could see them coming to her in flashes like a slide show blinking inside her mind.

She tilted her head to the side, and in the warmest voice she whispered, "Wait . . . you play guitar. . . ." There was a pause. Then, "And your brother. Something happened to your brother. . . ."

She stood up and started to come toward me, but I backed away and walked out the door without saying goodbye.

Back in my apartment, I opened my laptop and, against my better judgment, typed "Chris Callahan" into my web browser and pressed "Return."

October was right. One of the first images that came up was a picture of the two of them walking hand and hand down some charming street in Brooklyn. It must have been winter, because they had on scarves and hats and heavy coats. The caption read: *Musician Chris Callahan and his girlfriend-of-the-moment, performance artist October Danko, out and about in Williamsburg.*

In another shot they were walking through SFO. October was holding a book and looking up at Cal—he towered over her—and she was smiley and bright. She loved him; I could see it. Or at least she *had* loved him. Of course she had. Surely she still did. Why wouldn't she?

I spent hours scrolling through photos, watching videos, and reading interviews and articles that had been written about Cal. I found pictures of him rubbing elbows with just about every musical hero he and I ever had, and he didn't look out of place in any of them.

I also discovered that not long after they started dating, he and October had collaborated on an exhibit for a gallery in Brooklyn. Something about painting to music. All the songs were original; Cal was writing them on the spot, stream of consciousness, while October interpreted them on canvas. The paintings were then auctioned off, along with a vinyl pressing of the music Cal had created, and some of them sold for more than I'd made in the last three years combined.

I read about Cal's ex-wife too, a fashion designer, Anna Holland. According to a few gossip blogs, Cal and Anna had married impulsively in Las Vegas after knowing each other for only a few weeks. The marriage ended on account of Cal having an affair with the daughter of an old British rock star. From my research, it was clear that Cal had a weakness for beautiful women, and I had to admit it made me feel a little better knowing that even Cal could fall prey to human foible.

But getting lost in the internet life of Chris Callahan only sunk me deeper. Drunk, exhausted, and woozy, I got in the shower and turned it on as hot as I could stand it, hoping it would sober me up and burn away the weight of the day.

As the water ran down my face, I thought about how funny Cal had been sitting on the curb talking to Ingrid, and it made me laugh all over again. But then a switch flipped and I started to cry. Hard tears. I hadn't even cried like that when Sam died, and I guess I'd built up quite a reserve, because I couldn't stop; after a while I couldn't tell if it was the scalding water or the tears that were burning my skin.

When I finally got into bed, I had a dream that Cal was a centaur. His top half looked like him only younger, the age he was when I'd last seen him; the bottom half was a shiny, buckskin-colored horse. In the dream I was chasing Cal through Muir Woods. He was dodging trees, weaving in and out of the brush; as he galloped up the Dipsea Trail, I cut him off and we came face to face at the top of a hill. I had a hat on like Robin Hood and a bow and arrow in my hands; I yelled for Cal to stop, to freeze, but he kept running, and without blinking I pulled back the bow and let the arrow fly.

I shot him clean through the chest, but then, in a weird twist, I woke up clutching my own heart, trying to catch my breath.

TWELVE.

IT WAS ALMOST NOON and I was still in bed when I heard footsteps on the stairs up to my apartment. I had a headache the size of El Capitan, my eyes burned like someone had poured gasoline in them, and the only reason I got up and went to the door was because Cal wouldn't stop pounding on it.

"I know you're in there, Harpo! Get your ass up!"

I opened the door and he smiled and said, "We're neighbors! How awesome is this?"

It was the best and worst thing imaginable.

"You look as bad as I felt this morning, my friend." He handed me a mug, and for one second I anticipated the rich, soothing salvation of coffee. But the mug was cold and contained a thick green sludge. "Avocado and spinach smoothie. Really good for a hangover."

It smelled like the compost bin in the backyard. I carried it to the kitchen, set it in the sink, and went about making coffee while Cal poked around my room. He had come over to tell me he was having a dinner party that evening and insisted I come.

"Does October know you're inviting me?" As soon as the words fell from my mouth, I worried the question might seem suspicious. I added, "I mean, I'm just an employee."

He was inspecting a book on my nightstand called *The Forest Unseen*. "Fuck off," he said, skimming the back cover. "You're family, you nerd."

I told Cal I didn't think I would feel comfortable around a bunch of people I didn't know, but he said it was going to be a small group and wouldn't take no for an answer.

"I'm only in town for a week and a half, then back on tour for a couple more months. I want us to hang out as much as possible. Plus, it's Sunday. What else do you have to do?"

After Cal left, I drank some coffee and played guitar for a couple hours. It felt good to make sounds that communicated all the feelings I had inside me, feelings I didn't know how to express any other way. That was the reason I'd picked up the guitar in the first place. Because there were chords and notes that, when I played them, made me feel as though I was expressing emotions for which I had no other language.

When my fingers got too tired to keep moving, I walked into town to get my truck. I stopped at Equator for more coffee, sat and read a while, and then went into a clothing store down the street and bought a new shirt to wear to dinner. It was black with thin white stripes, and I thought it would make me feel better around Cal and his friends. Cal's clothes were a lot nicer than they used to be. He still wore jeans and T-shirts, but they were the expensive kind now.

Before I headed home, I ducked into Mill Valley Market and picked up a bottle of tequila that I spent way too much on, but I didn't think it was right to show up to a dinner party empty-handed and figured I was going to need it to get through the night.

By the time I got back to the house, a long dining table had been set up in the yard. I was sure October had been the one to decorate it, because it looked like the dinner table of a gypsy princess. Gardenias floated in long rectangular boxes all the way down the middle of the table, and the scent they gave off mingled with the scent of redwood, eucalyptus, and jasmine so that the air smelled like some sort of sexy heaven. Candles and leaves and more flowers were strewn around colorful, mismatched plates and glasses, and strands of lights illuminated the trees. The yard could have doubled as the set of a hip *A Midsummer Night's Dream*.

More candles lined the path to the front door, and I worried about Diego knocking them over and catching the place on fire, but I looked closer and saw they were the same candles the brewpub had on the table the night before. Of course, battery-powered candles made perfect sense in the middle of a forest, but they made my heart clench up like a fist. I felt as if they somehow represented me. The safe kind of fire. Or, rather, no real fire at all. October was all sparkles and warmth. Cal was combustion. I was that fake flame. And trust me when I say it hurts to be a spirit inside a body that yearns to burn far hotter and brighter than it actually does.

I went back to my apartment, took a shower, shaved, and then headed across the yard. I could see October through the kitchen window. She was ripping up lettuce with her hands, tossing it into a big wooden salad bowl.

I hesitated to approach, nervous to talk to her after how I'd left the previous night. But she looked up and, with a weary expression, gestured for me to come in.

"Hey," I said.

"Hey yourself."

I set the tequila on the counter and she thanked me, but she didn't say anything else. She was slicing a tomato with a knife that had a white blade.

"I was a shithead last night, wasn't I?"

She put the knife down and sighed. "Can we not talk about last night? I just want to get through this dinner in one piece."

She was obviously still sad or mad, and completely on edge. But despite all of that she looked so stunning it was hard for me to be in the same room with her. She was wearing a long, pale-colored dress that had wooden beads embroidered around the neckline. Her feet were bare, and the dress dragged on the floor behind her, making it seem as though she were floating around the kitchen when she walked. She had on shimmery earrings that hung down to her shoulders, and stacks of bracelets on her wrists jingled like tambourines as she sliced.

"You look pretty," I mumbled, hoping to allay her a bit.

She turned toward me, her eyes fierce, and said, "Pretty is the lazy way to describe a woman."

I laughed hard. I couldn't help it. Every woman I've ever dated has all but begged me to tell her how pretty she was, and here was this one chastising me for it.

October laughed then too, and the mood softened.

"I'm glad you came, Joe."

She chopped up a handful of mint, turned to the stove, lifted a hefty, cone-shaped lid off of a big clay pot, and stirred whatever was inside. It smelled like garlic, cinnamon, and rich, stewed meat.

"Moroccan lamb curry," she said when she saw me eyeing it. She scooped up a small bite with a wooden spoon, sprinkled a pinch of the mint on top, and held it out to me with her tiny palm cupped under the spoon. "Here. Be my taste tester."

She didn't hold the spoon out very far, and I had to get way too close to her to reach it—so close we were almost-but-not-quite touching—the kind of closeness where you might as well be touching because your energies or whatever you call them are overlapping like some spiritual Venn diagram. I could feel her body as if she were pressing it against mine, even though I was still a few inches away.

I tasted the curry and took two steps back.

"It's good," I said.

She offered me a sad smile. "I like your shirt."

As soon as she said it, I realized it wasn't Cal's friends for whom I'd made an effort. It was for October. I wanted her to notice me above the others at the party. But then I felt guilty for thinking that and wanting that; to distract myself from those feelings, I asked after Cal's whereabouts, only for the first time in my life I called him Chris so as not to annoy her.

"He took Diego for a walk. He'll be right back. There's beer in the fridge. Oh, and an antipasto plate up there if you're hungry." She pointed to the top of the refrigerator. "Do me a favor and grab it down."

Cal must have put it up there because I could barely reach it, and if I could barely reach it, October definitely couldn't.

"Why is it on top of the fridge?"

"Diego has a weakness for prosciutto."

It was a long, heavy wooden board filled with vegetables, cheeses, and meats, plus olives, nuts, and crackers. I lifted it carefully and set it on the counter. Like the table outside, the board looked like a work of art. October had arranged flowers, berries, and branches with imagination and precision all around the food, and even though I was hungry, I decided it was too beautiful to mess with before the guests got a chance to see it.

I grabbed a beer while October drifted over to her laptop. She pushed a few buttons, and seconds later music started playing softly inside and outside the house. Subtle singer-songwriter stuff that amplified my melancholy. I looked out the window and nursed my beer while a mopey guy playing what sounded like a prewar Martin whisper-sang, *It's not that we're scared, it's just that it's delicate,* and I wanted to say: Speak for yourself, buddy; I'm fucking terrified.

I could see October was listening to the song too, and I felt relieved when I spotted Cal and Diego walking up the driveway, because I didn't want to be alone with her and all my leaden, Martin-tinged emotions.

I walked out to greet Cal just as a big Mercedes SUV pulled up. A tall, light-skinned African-American guy got out and then helped his wife out of the passenger side. Cal embraced them and introduced me as his oldest and best friend. They shook my hand and told me their names, but I'm terrible with new people and names, and a second later I couldn't recall what they'd said.

We went inside; more cars pulled up, and before I knew it the house was filled with people talking and drinking and messing up October's beautiful antipasto board without ever telling her how incredible it looked. They took her talent for granted. Or, as she might say, they missed the point. Even Cal seemed to miss it. But October didn't care. She didn't do it for them. She didn't make interesting and beautiful things so that people would notice and tell her how interesting and beautiful they were. She did it because it moved her to do so. She did it for the doing itself. That's what art is to her. Doing. Living. The expression of oneself in action and in creation. You know that old question about if a tree falls in a forest but nobody hears it, does it make any noise? October was the art equivalent of that. If you make something and nobody ever appreciates it, is it still art? I would argue it most certainly is. October would surely argue the same.

The only good part of all the socializing and mingling was that I couldn't hear the mopey guy singing anymore.

Cal went out of his way to make me feel comfortable. He introduced me to his manager, Nancy, and her husband, John, and I talked to them for a while. They both had soft handshakes and shiny silver threads of coarse hair at their temples, and had come with one of Nancy's other clients, Loring Blackman, another famous musician who writes songs for other artists now. I got a kick out of meeting him because I'd listened to his music a lot in college. Loring and his wife, a jewelry designer, told me they lived in a brownstone three doors down from Cal in Brooklyn and were in town visiting one of Loring's sons, who went to UC Berkeley. Cal told them I'd graduated from there and they asked me a lot of questions, the kind it didn't bother me to answer. They were sweet and attentive with each other, and something about the way they interacted made me imagine for an instant that October and I could have ended up like that, had it not been for Cal. Deep down I didn't believe it—I didn't think I was brave enough to go the distance with a woman like October. Nevertheless, it made me feel better to have someone to blame other than myself.

The last to arrive was a photographer named Guy. He had a big, egg-shaped head, a long beard, and a loud, fuzzy voice like he was speaking through a distortion pedal. The first thing he told me was that he'd shot Cal's last two album campaigns "but not his first one, because he couldn't afford me then." Guy was wearing a fur vest, and I disliked him within thirty seconds of our meeting. He was twitchy, reminiscent of an old neighbor in Berkeley who did a lot of bad drugs. The other thing I disliked about Guy was that he was very touchy-feely with October, resting his hand on her back as he spoke to her. And I could tell by the way she flinched and walked away that she disliked him too. She's sensitive to touch, especially to someone who's full of negative energy.

Guy had arrived with two models in tow. They had similar names that I can't recall now, Carla and Claire, or something like that. They seemed nice enough, but they spoke with extreme Southern California accents—you know that monotone way of talking as if nothing matters—that made me want to bang my head against a wall.

Eventually I got tired of talking to strangers and went back into the kitchen to see if October needed any help, but she waved me off, and I could tell by her demeanor that the last thing she wanted to be doing was entertaining a houseful of people. Cal strolled in a second later and put his arms around her. She whispered something to him that I couldn't hear, and he rolled his eyes and said, "I *dare* you to have a good time tonight," before grabbing a couple crackers and walking back into the living room.

Diego was sprawled underneath the table, either hiding from the partygoers like I was or waiting for someone to drop food. He looked up at me, and I fed him a slice of prosciutto. After that he followed me to the couch, where he sat at my feet and kept me company until October told everyone to go outside and sit down for dinner.

I ended up with the tall African-American man on my left and Loring's wife, Bea, on my right. Model Claire sat directly across from me, Carla next to her.

"Are you a musician too?" Claire asked, and I knew that listening to her talk for too long would've turned me into a serial killer.

I told her I was not a musician, but Cal, who was at the head of the table, waved his napkin in the air like he was trying to shoo away a swarm of mosquitoes and said, "Don't listen to him! He's the single greatest guitar player you've never heard of!"

That egged Claire on, and she began asking me more questions—the kind I hated, like where I was from and what kind of music I played. In an effort to get her to leave me alone, I turned and asked the man on my left the same dumb questions, which turned out to be the most amusing part of the whole night. I had assumed he was someone with whom Cal worked, maybe a band member or a roadie, and when I asked him what he did, the entire table went silent.

"I play basketball," he answered softly.

"Professionally?" I asked. He did seem tall, but not as tall as Cal, and certainly not as tall as I imagine basketball players to be.

Once the guests realized I was serious, laughter erupted. Then Guy explained, at volume ten and with an offensive amount of disbelief regarding my knowledge of sports, that the gentleman on my left played for the Golden State Warriors and was arguably the greatest point guard in the NBA.

I didn't know what a point guard was, but I congratulated the man. Claire then announced that she wasn't into sports either, as if that inextricably linked the two of us, and Cal immediately came to my defense like he used to when we were kids.

"Harp and I were too busy practicing our crafts to care about sports."

That made me think about the way Bob used to bark, "What are you, his lawyer?" whenever Cal stuck up for me or made my case. I reminded Cal of that, and he told a story about the time Bob took us to a 49ers game during a short-lived phase when he was trying to spend more quality time with me. Why he had chosen football as the venue to express that, I'll never know. But it was a Sunday, and Cal and I had plans to go to Tower Records that day, so naturally we'd protested wholeheartedly—and by "we" I mean Cal—but Bob told us we didn't have a choice.

"We brought *Spin, Guitar World,* and the *NME,*" Cal said. "And we read magazines the whole time."

"Man, was Bob pissed," I laughed. "He didn't let you come over for a while after that, remember?"

October had barely said a word throughout dinner, but she smiled as we told the story, and I didn't know if it was a happy smile or a sad smile, or if it was directed at me or at Cal.

After we finished eating, October gathered a handful of dishes and took them into the kitchen; Cal followed her with the rest. I watched them through the window. Cal stood close to October as he separated the dishes from the silverware and stacked the plates in the sink. Then he said something to her that made her swat him in the arm and laugh, and they kissed.

When they came back outside, October was carrying a white cake that she'd decorated with rosemary and manzanita berries. Cal had a bunch of small plates in one hand and the bottle of tequila I'd brought over in the other.

"How about a song before dessert?" Guy shouted.

The basketball player chimed in, the models started droning on about it too, and soon everyone was pestering Cal to play something.

"Fine, fine," Cal said. "Hold your horses."

He ran off to the studio and came back with a Gibson SJ-200E and an old, beautifully weathered Takamine with a worn-down pickguard and scratches all over the finish. He presented the Takamine to me and said, "I'm not playing unless you play with me."

I didn't protest. As insecure as I was about most of my abilities, making music with Cal was not one of them. I pulled off my shoes and socks, took the guitar in one hand, poured myself a shot of tequila with the other, and tossed it back quickly.

Cal and I moved our chairs out from the table and formed a semicircle a few feet away. Then, like I used to do in high school, I asked Cal what we were going to play—it was always up to him, he was the ringleader, the mastermind behind our performances—and he said, "The Tam High set list, obviously."

He didn't have to remind me what songs were on that list. I remembered.

We tuned our instruments and did some funny vocal warm-ups that Mr. Collins, our freshman year music teacher, had taught us. Even when we were kids, I laughed through them, but Cal took them seriously, claiming he still used them before every show.

I'm not a great singer, but I can hold a decent tune. And I'd learned to sing by harmonizing with Cal, so I knew he and I sounded good together.

As soon as Cal gave me the nod, I counted to four and we hit our D strings in unison.

Our first tune was a slower, bluer version of "Peaceful Easy Feeling" that silenced everyone at the table, even Guy.

During the song I kept glancing over at October, to see if she was paying attention, and every time I did her eyes were on me.

We followed the Eagles with Oasis, then Petty, and then Cal told me to show off, and I lost myself noodling around on my own. When I finally stopped playing and looked up, everyone at the table was staring at me as if they'd just noticed I was an octopus. They seemed stupefied. Then they started clapping like crazy, and I put the guitar down to make it end. The rush of playing and the reaction of the guests felt like a great dam breaking inside of me. A tiny glimpse into a world I'd missed. No, not missed, but had forsaken.

My heart was pounding, my breath shallow, and I knew I needed to get away from the table. I slipped my shoes back on, excused myself, and snuck off to the trail behind the house. I walked slowly in the dark, my steps heavy as I inhaled and exhaled deeply, audibly, trying to calm myself, trying to crack the silence around me, hoping to stave off what felt like an imminent collapse. And I was just starting to settle down when I heard the drone of Claire's voice call my name and ask me to wait.

"What are you doing?" she said, plodding behind me.

I stopped to help her up the hill despite wanting to pretend I didn't see or hear her. "Taking a walk."

"It's dark out here," she said, grabbing onto my arm. A small purse on a gold chain dangled diagonally across her body. She pulled her phone out of it and turned on the flashlight, lighting up a stretch of trail I didn't want or need illuminated.

We walked for a bit, but Claire wasn't wearing footwear for hiking, and by the time we made it to Beanstalk she asked if we could sit down.

I sat against the trunk of the tree and she sat beside me, fidgeting and scanning the area above her head and along the ground with her flashlight, plainly uncomfortable about being outside. "Are there spiders on this tree, do you think?"

I told her there were most likely hundreds of species of bugs we couldn't see crawling around that very moment on the tree, including spiders.

It was the truth, and I'd hoped it would send her running back to the house, but she laughed like she thought I was teasing.

"Want to smoke some pot with me?" she asked, pulling a joint and a lighter out of her purse.

"Yup," I said. Anything to avoid the tsunami of emotions surging inside me.

She lit the joint, and we passed it back and forth without talking. Then Claire said, "You were really good back there," although she was texting someone on her phone at the time, not even looking at me. "Do you play in Chris's band?"

"No."

She started scrolling through Instagram. After a while she put the phone down and said, "You don't talk much, do you?" Her voice was deeper and less annoying when she was high. Or maybe it just seemed that way because I was. "Gloomy. Like a lost dog."

I took one last hit of the joint and held it in until I was dazed. As I exhaled, I coughed a little and said, "Is the stench of my misery and self-loathing that strong?"

She turned her head and looked at me. It was dark, so I couldn't fully make out her expression, but it might have contained a modicum of fear.

"Sorry," I said. "It's been a weird weekend."

I spit on the remnants of the joint to make sure it was burned out and buried what was left of it in the dirt. When I stood up I felt lightheaded, but strangely heavy too, as if my head were a helium balloon and my body the string attached; only the string was tied to a brick.

I walked to a small redwood a few feet away and rested my forehead against its trunk.

Claire giggled and said, "What are you doing?"

"I love this tree," I told her. I stepped back and looked around at the other trees nearby, at Beanstalk and at all the different-size redwoods, oaks, and madrones, all smaller than Beanstalk but just as beautiful. "I love *all* these trees."

The whole forest was starting to come into focus as my eyes adjusted to the dark. I could pick out sword ferns and Indian paintbrush, and even some wild irises farther up the trail. But then Claire swiped her stupid flashlight back on and everything beyond a two-foot radius went black again.

I ran my hand down the redwood's bark. It was hard and soft, damp and dry, depending on where you pressed. And underneath that, an ancient history. A whole world inside itself. "Do you know that redwoods don't go from youth to adolescence until they're about eight hundred years old?"

Claire stared up at me, nonplussed. She was a beautiful girl. Big eyes and blond hair that, in the glow of her flashlight, shone like a halo around her face.

"This tree is still a baby," I told her. "It seems so big, right? It's a toddler."

Claire let me ramble on about trees for a while, and I explained all the different parts to her, from the cambium layer to the sapwood and the heartwood, all the way down to the pith. And to her credit, she listened, even though I could tell she was bored.

At some point during my homily, I had an epiphany about why I was so drawn to redwoods. Because, metaphorically speaking, I decided, I was one. Breathless with weed-induced insight, I said, more to myself than to

Claire, "Redwoods can live at the bottom of the forest, often times in the shade of their older and stronger brothers. In the kind of darkness where most species would die. But they don't die. They grow slowly. And they endure." I paused, and then added, "Let that be a lesson to *me*."

Claire said, "You're an odd duck." She ran her hands through her hair, pulling and smoothing it down around her face with her fingers. "Super cute, but odd. Do you want to make out?"

I clammed up and made some grumbling noise meant to indicate that making out wasn't likely.

"A girl?" Claire asked with borderline indifference. "Is that your problem?"

"One of them."

She stood up and wiped dirt from her jeans. She'd had enough of me. She put on some lip gloss and said, "I'm cold. Can we go back?"

By the time we returned, all the other guests had gone. I told Claire I would drive her home, even though I didn't want to, and as we walked in front of the main house, I could see October and Cal through the front window. They were cleaning up and talking. I didn't think they spotted me or Claire passing by, but they couldn't have missed my truck pulling out.

Claire lived in San Francisco, near the marina. At that hour the round-trip from Mill Valley to her apartment and back took forty-five minutes.

When I pulled back up the driveway, all the lights in the kitchen were off, but I noticed a glow from October's studio. I parked and walked over, thinking she'd left a light on by accident, but when I went in to shut it off I heard music playing quietly in the back.

I followed the sound and found October sitting in front of an easel, tiny paintbrush in hand, working on a small canvas. Her face was maybe an inch away from the painting, like she was perfecting some minute detail. She was still wearing her dress, though she had a smock over it. Watercolor paints and a small Mason jar of water sat on another stool beside her.

She turned her head when she heard my footsteps, sighed, and said, "Go away."

I kept heading toward her. And I think I expected to see an image more representative of her apparent mood on the canvas in front of her, but it was Diego. She was painting her dog.

I asked her what she was doing, and without taking her eyes off the canvas, she said, "I'm pretty sure the answer to that question is obvious."

"I mean, why are you up at this hour?"

"I could ask you the same thing."

I grabbed a stool, pulled it up beside the easel, and sat down and watched her paint for a while. Eventually she huffed and said, "Do you mind? I really want to be alone."

I shifted uncomfortably. I wanted to tell her things, but I didn't know how. Story of my life, I know. My words were locked somewhere inside of me, and I had long ago lost the key.

Finally I said, "Nothing happened with that girl. I went for a walk and she followed me. I was—I don't know—I just needed to get some air, and I lost track of time. But I didn't—"

"Stop!" She slammed her paintbrush down on the stool beside her and the jar of water fell and spilled all over the floor. "Jesus Christ, Joe. Just leave me alone. Please."

"I'm trying to explain something to you."

"Well, you don't have to. It makes no difference to me if you fucked that girl or not." She put her elbows on her knees, her head fell into her hands, and she said, "What a mess."

I didn't know if she meant the spilled water or our lives, but I went to the sink, grabbed a bunch of paper towels, then walked back over and cleaned up the floor. After I threw the paper towels into the trash bin, I sat back down and said, "Can I ask you one thing before I go?"

She didn't say I could, but she set the paintbrush down and turned toward me. Her eyebrows came alive and she blinked like crazy.

"If it doesn't matter to you, then why are you so mad at me?"

She reached toward my chest, and I thought she was moving to touch me, to take my hand, to use her *gift*, but she just brushed dirt off my shirt.

She shook her head and said, "I don't think you want me to answer that question."

"Why not?"

"Because every question answered is another can of worms opened, and I'm trying to put the worms *back* in the can."

"Please?"

She scratched at a splatter of dried paint on her smock and sighed. "First of all, I'm not mad. It's just that I watched you walk away from the table tonight, and I knew where you were going, and why, and I wanted to go with you. And that feels like a problem. Here's something else that feels like a problem: When I'm with you, just sitting here working, or talking, or not working, or not talking, I don't want to be anywhere else." She rubbed her eyes and looked up at the skylights, then back at me. "I could see what you were feeling after you played those songs, and all I wanted to do—" She caught herself, shook her head. "Forget it. I can't say it. It's not right."

I was glad she didn't say whatever she held back, because I had a feeling that if she had it would have haunted me for a long time.

She was spot-on about the worms though.

I looked down at her watercolor palette. The little black circle of paint she'd been diluting to color in some of the dog's gray fur was wet and tacky, and I pressed my thumb into it. But then I lifted my thumb and it was covered in wet black paint; I didn't know what to do with that, so I pressed my thumb into my jeans, on my thigh, right above my knee. I held it down for a few seconds so the denim would absorb the water and the pigment, and when I lifted it back up I saw a black thumbprint there.

"Should I quit?" I said, voicing a question I'd been pondering all day. "Do you want me to leave?"

She shook her head. "That would shatter me right now."

"What if I want to quit?"

"You don't."

She was right. I didn't. "That doesn't mean I think staying is a good idea. It's certainly not going to make this any easier."

She shrugged and said, "I don't need it to be easy. Besides, we're adults. Surely we're capable of boundaries."

I nodded, but I wasn't so sure. And I had a notion that I would be better at boundaries than she was. Cal might have been a boyfriend to her, but he was a brother to me. Intuition told me brother held more weight than boyfriend.

October looked down at my thumbprint. Then she pressed her thumb into the black paint like I'd done and pressed it onto my jeans, right on top of where I'd put mine, and our prints merged into one.

"Look." She smiled for the first time since I'd arrived. "We made art."

I smiled too, but the loneliness and longing I felt for her throbbed and stung like everything else. A moment later October lifted my hand and pressed the tip of her black thumb into the tip of my black thumb and twisted them together, much like Cal and I had done as kids, only we'd used blood instead of paint.

"Friends," she said.

"Do you really think we can be friends?"

"I think we already are."

I dropped my head backward and gazed up at the ceiling. The skylights were filthy again. I couldn't see anything but sticks and dirt and fallen leaves, and that made me sad too. All that dead stuff.

I stood to go, and October said, "Everything will be all right, Joe."

"How do you define *all right*?"

"You and I are going to be friends, and you and Chris are going to be friends, and we're going to work together and make art, and put this thing to bed." She pointed back and forth between the two of us. "Whatever *this* is. We'll get over it. We have to."

I thought about the song she'd played for me the night we first talked in my apartment. The title of that song, I'd since learned, was "Sorrow," and I'd listened to it a couple dozen times by then.

I don't wanna get over you . . .

I went back to my apartment, but I didn't go to sleep. I watched and waited for October to leave the studio. After she did, I went over to get some varnish and applied three coats of it to the spot on my jeans where we'd left our thumbprints. I'd only ever used that varnish to protect acrylic paint on canvas and wasn't sure it was going to work on watercolor and denim, but I applied it anyway.

I still have those jeans.

I'm wearing them right now, as a matter of fact.

The little oval of our thumbprints is still there.

It's faint, the palest shade of gray now, but it's still there.

THIRTEEN.

THERE WAS A NOTE on top of a stack of papers waiting for me in the studio when I got to work the next morning. I saw my name, written in the same architectural script as the note October had left on my door, and for one reckless instant I both hoped and feared it was going to say *Run away with me*, or *I still can't stop thinking about you*, or *I don't wanna get over you*, or something that would erase the boundaries I had sworn to uphold the night before.

In fact, the note contained information and instructions for an upcoming exhibition October had committed to participating in with a handful of other artists. The show would be for charity, held in a few weeks at the Thomas Frasier Gallery in San Francisco. According to the printout, the gallery welcomed painting, sculpture, photography, or installation. The theme was FREEDOM, and all the profits would go to an organization that supported women's reproductive rights.

October wanted me to build her a birdcage large enough to fit into. She'd drawn a rough sketch of what she was picturing and left me a dozen other images for reference and inspiration. *But*, she wrote, *just suggestions. Be your amazing and creative self. I trust you.*

The note ended with her explaining that she was going to work on the next selfie on her own and would send it to me to catalog once she'd finished. Then she wrote:

Chris thought he and I should spend some time together before he goes back on the road. We'll be away for a few days. Rae will be staying at the house with Diego. Text if you have any questions. Thank you.
Oct.

I sent her a text right away: GOT YOUR NOTE. BIRDCAGE WILL BE COOL. I WOULD'VE WATCHED DIEGO.

I was hoping to get a response, to be able to keep a dialogue going with her while she was gone, but all she sent back was the smiley-face-with-heart-eyes emoji, and I didn't know what to make of that.

I spent all day researching birdcages, trying to design something as visually interesting as what October had drawn, yet functional and easy to build in the limited time I had. I also came up with an idea I thought would elevate the installation to the next level, but I needed to explore its feasibility before I talked to October about it.

I could have done most of my research on my computer at the studio, but to avoid any confrontations with Rae, I went to the Mill Valley Library to work. I was glad to be busy. The idea of October and I being friends sounded hypothetically conceivable, but I realized it was agreed to under the guise of getting to spend my days near her, being productive and creative with her. The work connected us, and in theory that enabled me to accept all the other things we couldn't do together. But thinking about her and Cal off on a trip, wondering where they were and what they were doing, tangled me up in knots.

After much debate and a call to Shane, an old site supervisor from my Harper & Sons days, I decided to build the cage out of bamboo, first and foremost because it's a renewable resource, but also because it's strong, light, and flexible enough to bend without snapping, which would be necessary if I ended up being able to pull off my idea.

Tuesday morning I went to San Rafael to get the materials I needed to build the cage and then went back to the studio to start prepping the wood. I was unloading everything from my truck when Rae left to take Diego for a walk; I was still out there when she returned. She didn't acknowledge me, and I didn't acknowledge her, not even when Diego ran over to investigate what I was doing. I assumed this meant Rae and I had a mutual understanding that we would steer clear of each other while October was out of town, and that suited me fine. But later in the afternoon, as I was measuring for the double grid that would be the floor of the cage, Rae came back outside.

She walked to the opposite side of the table and used a hand to shield her eyes from the sun. Instead of her usual almonds and raisins, she had a bag of dried apricots, and as she held one between her thumb and index finger, the sun shone through it the way a flashlight illuminates the veins of a hand.

I took my time with the piece of wood I was working on and then put down my pencil and waited for her to say whatever it was she wanted to say. Sweat dripped into my eyes, and I wiped my brow.

"I told you everything would go back to normal once Chris got home, yeah?"

I think she was waiting for me to put my hurt feelings on display for her, but she would wait a long time for that. I could feign indifference better than anyone. I gave her nothing.

"They're in Big Sur, in case you're wondering." She ate the apricot she'd been holding. "A little romantic getaway at the Post Ranch Inn."

I watched foamy saliva collect and pool in the corners of her mouth when she talked and chewed at the same time. And as I stood there listening to her, I wondered if she was deliberately trying to hurt me or simply trying to prove her point.

"I happen to know you're the one who asked Cal to fly home," I said. "He told me."

She looked confused, and I corrected myself. "Chris, I mean."

"Right. October mentioned you and Chris are what, childhood friends or something? What a coincidence, yeah?"

She was doing it again. Insinuating that I had some ulterior motive to come in and steal October from Cal. She had no clue.

"Some friend you are," she said.

I hesitated to respond. In my opinion, this was none of Rae's business. But I didn't want her meddling any further. More specifically, I didn't want her telling Cal anything that would hurt him.

I took a deep breath, tried to center myself and said, "Listen, this job is important to me, and I'm not here to mess up anyone's life. What happened between me and October was a mistake. I get it. She gets it. It's over."

"Very happy to hear that," Rae said.

She made like she was going to walk away, but then she stopped, looked at me, and when she spoke again it was as if she'd taken off a mask.

"You know, I went to art school for a while," she told me. "I thought I wanted to be an artist, but I quickly realized that I didn't like making art as much as I liked being around it. I dropped out. After that I couldn't get a job in the art world to save my life. When I met October, I was working as a receptionist at a company that makes pasta sauce. I thought her work was special. I told her that if she ever had a place for me, to call. About a year later, she did." Rae paused, seemed to waffle a little, as if perhaps she was revealing too much. "I appreciated that. I owe her a lot. All I'm doing here is looking out for her."

"Maybe you underestimate her. Maybe she can look out for herself."

"Maybe you don't know her as well as you think you do, yeah? Maybe I've seen her get hurt. And maybe I know that when she gets hurt, she doesn't get over it for a long time. Chris has his issues, I know. But he can't hurt her. Do you understand what I'm saying?"

I nodded.

"Good," she said. "I'm glad we had this talk."

I nodded again, and she went shuffling back into the house.

The following night, October sent me a file to catalog for the *365 Selfies* site. The subject line of the e-mail read: "Reverse Suicide Selfie." It was a video of her walking out of the ocean, and it began with a shot of the waves. October was completely submerged under the water, so much so that I didn't expect to see her. A second later she was there, heading toward the camera. I'm not even sure how she managed it, because she was wearing a long dress, similar in shape to the one she'd had on the night of the dinner party, but the one in the video was belted, and the belt had big leather pockets with fringe hanging down on each side.

The pockets were filled with rocks, and as October emerged from the water, she lifted the rocks from her pockets. One at a time she dropped the rocks into the sea and then, once she reached the beach, onto the sand.

The water in Big Sur is frigid, even in summer. October was trembling, and her skin was translucent. And it wasn't just her skin. Her dress was light, gauzy, drenched, and it became diaphanous as it clung to her body. She wasn't wearing anything underneath, and I could see her nipples, the outline of her waist, the curve of her hips, everything. The night we'd slept together, I'd only gotten glimpses of her body. She'd been either lying down, on top of me, or under the sheets, and it was fairly dark once I'd turned off the lights.

I didn't know if she meant for the clip to be so erotic, but it was impossible for me to see it any other way.

After I uploaded and cataloged the video, I tried to read a book on edible plants of Marin County, but every time I got to the end of a page, I realized I hadn't absorbed a word; I put the book down. I kept thinking about the night October and I had spent together, remembering how soft she was; the way she whispered into my ear, telling me what she was going to do and how she was going to do it; and how she tasted like tangerines and mint and fit so perfectly in my arms.

I went back to my computer, watched the video again, and wondered if Cal had been manning the camera. Then I started to imagine what might have happened after he turned it off. No way he didn't have the same reaction I had to seeing October like that. No way he hadn't wanted her.

I tried to stop thinking about it, but that backfired, and things took a darker turn. When I closed my eyes, all I could see was Cal fucking October on the beach in that dress. In my fantasy, Cal was rough and violent, ripping the dress apart, forcing himself on her as she screamed and fought.

October once told me that no one should be ashamed of their fantasies, but jacking off thinking about my best friend hate-fucking the woman I was pretty sure I was in love with did not make me feel like I was dealing with the situation in a healthy or constructive way.

October and Cal didn't come home until Thursday night. I was standing in my kitchen eating takeout from Sol Food when I saw her SUV pull up the driveway. Rae came outside with Diego, and the dog went crazy when he saw October, running and bouncing around in big, clumsy circles, almost knocking her over.

I stood in the window and tried to will either October or Cal to look in my direction, to wave and invite me down, but neither did.

October, Rae, and Cal stood in the front yard talking for a few minutes. After Rae got in her car and drove away, Cal put his arm around October; they walked into the house with Diego loafing behind.

I went to the studio early the next morning to do more work on the birdcage before October saw it. She came in around nine o'clock carrying two cappuccinos.

"Hey," I said.

"Hey." She handed me one of the mugs. "Disclaimer. I don't make them as well as you do."

I tried to assess her reaction to being back, tried to measure how things were between us, but I didn't have her gift, and from my point of view she seemed unfazed and unattached, not all torn up inside like I was. Reluctantly, I asked how her trip to Big Sur had been. Her answer was ambiguous and deflective.

"Fine," she said. "Tell me about your week."

"How about I show you?" I was nervous, desperate for her to like the cage, and I walked her to the back of the studio so she could see the progress I'd made.

Before she was even close enough to see any of the particular details, she stopped in her tracks and said, "*Woah . . .*" As she continued to approach, she looked at me, then at the cage, then back at me. She walked all the way around it, ran her hand up and down the small section of bars I'd already installed, and then took a few steps back to take it all in.

"Joe . . ."

"It's not done yet. Obviously."

She was shaking her head. "I don't know what to say. . . . It's already beyond what I could have imagined . . . and it's so . . . I don't know . . . *pretty.*"

Teasing, I said, "Pretty is the lazy way to describe a birdcage."

She elbowed me in the ribs. "I mean it. I'm speechless."

"Check this out," I said, galvanized by her reaction. "I'm in the process of making the door." I pointed. "It'll latch from the outside. Right here." I showed her the drawing I'd made as well, so she could see what I was talking about. "This is where the clasp will go. I'm thinking of putting a small box around it, if I have time, so you can't reach through and open it. Apparently that's a thing. Some birds can open doors." I took a drink of my cappuccino. She was right. It was terrible. The espresso tasted like burnt popcorn and there was too much milk, but I drank it anyway. "And, well, there's this other crazy idea I've been working on, but I can scrap it if you think it's *no bueno*. It sort of depends on the statement you're trying to make about freedom. I mean, is this an *I Know Why the Caged Bird Sings* sort of thing? Or a literal absence of freedom? Or a commentary about freedom of choice regarding women's rights? Given the charity we're supporting, that's what I would imagine, but you tell me."

She didn't answer my questions. She just squinted and said, "Tell me your idea."

"OK. Like I said, if you hate it, it's not too late to dial it back. But here's what I was thinking: What if I put a mechanism on the cage so that as the night rolls on—we have what, two hours? So, imagine as those two hours tick by, the cage is *literally* closing in on you. It'll happen slowly and be barely perceptible, but perceptible *enough*, like if it wasn't for the base sticking further and further out from the bottom of the bars, people might not even notice it until the cage is pressing up against you. But they'll *sense* it. It will make them uncomfortable. And by the end of the night, you won't be able to move. You know, as a sort of interpretation of how women seem to have all this freedom but are still caged in a lot of ways, and it's stifling, and some people are still trying to take it away."

Her expression had been expanding as I spoke. Her eyes were huge and sparkly, and she was pointing at me, pressing her finger into my chest. "Joseph Harper, do *not* get me excited about this unless you're confident you can build it in a couple of weeks."

"If this is *all* I'm doing, then yes, I'm confident I can."

She pursed her lips as though she were holding a secret between them.

"What?" I said.

"Nothing." She was smiling now, big and bright. "I just love this idea so much."

"You do?"

She nodded. "It's perfect." Then she tilted her head to the side and stared at me, and I saw a glimmer of something return. A pillowy softness in her eyes that I recognized as the kind of affection a person can't hide even if they try.

"What?" I said again.

She caught herself, regained her composure. "Nothing. You're a genius. I'm excited about this, that's all."

I escorted her into the cage. The space was tight for two people and we had to stand close. "I'm going to hang a bar in the center, right here, with a perch. It will look nice, don't worry." I pointed to the spot on the drawing too, so she could reference where we were. "It may or may not be weight-bearing, I'm not sure yet. For you, it will probably be fine. But you definitely won't want Diego sitting on it."

She laughed and said, "Duly noted."

"Oh. Wait. I have to show you my favorite part." I put the sketches down and walked to the corner of the room, where I'd left a long cardboard box. "I found this wallpaper to put on the bottom." I opened the box and unrolled the paper for her to see. It was made to look like old editions of the *New York Times*. "Get it? Every birdcage I've ever seen has newspaper on the bottom. *And* these aren't random newspapers. I got to pick the year when I ordered it. These are headlines from 1973, the year of the Supreme Court's decision on *Roe v. Wade*."

"Incredible. Honestly, you're blowing me away."

We drank our awful, now cold cappuccinos and talked more about how I was going to make the mechanics work, as well as how the night would unfold. October told me we were having a meeting with the audiovisual engineer from the gallery the following day, and she couldn't wait for me to explain this to him.

We worked separately for the rest of the day. I concentrated on the birdcage, and October concentrated on a selfie. She spent over an hour photographing her eyes in extreme close-up with a forensic camera. Then she edited the photos into a video montage, put a bunch of weird filters on them, and intercut the video with images of masochistic, hard-core pornography. The porn flashed by in quick, short bursts so that if you blinked you missed it and if you didn't blink you weren't quite sure you'd seen it at all. It made me uncomfortable when she showed it to me, mainly because it reminded me of the fantasy I'd had of her and Cal on the beach, and even though I knew it was impossible for October to have gleaned those thoughts from me, or sensed my shame all the way from Big Sur, I couldn't exactly put it past her.

At some point later in the day, it must have been around four o'clock, Cal burst into the studio like he'd been shot out of a cannon and declared the workday over. "Enough of your toiling," he said. "I'm only here for two more days. I want to hang out."

October and I were at opposite ends of the room. We both stopped what we were doing and looked at him.

"Which one of us are you talking to?" she asked.

"Both of you. Come on. Let's do something."

October didn't make a move, so Cal sauntered over to her, lifted her up, and flung her over his shoulder.

"All right," she laughed. "Put me down."

He slid her back to the ground. Then he rested his hands on her shoulders, looked at me and said, "Drop the tools, Harp. I'm not above picking you up either."

I walked over, wiping my hands on my jeans. "I could use a break."

"Excellent. How about we go for a drive?"

"For a drive," October repeated, rolling her eyes. "As you know, what Chris means when he says 'Let's go for a drive' is 'Drive me somewhere.'"

I offered to do the driving, but October predicted we were going to end up at a bar and said, "You guys have fun. I'll be the chauffeur."

A second later Cal said, "I got it!" He looked at me when he said, "the Pelican Inn."

The Pelican Inn is an authentic British pub off of Highway 1, on the way to Muir Beach. Cal and I used to hike there from my house when we were kids. We'd talk Ingrid into giving us some money, and when we got to the Pelican Inn we'd eat fish-and-chips and drink a couple of sodas before heading home. It used to make us feel like adults to sit in the bar, order food, and pay the check by ourselves. And we would feign British accents whenever we were there. Actually, it was more specific than that. We would feign the exact Manchester accents we had perfected by watching Noel and Liam Gallagher in interviews. We would introduce ourselves as Noel and Liam too. Cal was always Noel because he was the leader of our band, and because he is a month older than I am—Noel is the elder Gallagher brother.

More than once when we were kids, we'd talked about how we were going to go back someday, after we were grown up, and actually order beer. So when Cal suggested we go to the Pelican Inn, my first thought was: *This is one shared dream he and I will realize together.* And there was a sense of contentment in that. A softening in my heart. But right away the softness gave way to an impending melancholy, a pressing in of regret, of all that had been lost.

Cal hopped into October's SUV with the gusto of a windstorm, and I couldn't help but follow. This is why Cal had always been a good ally for me. His enthusiasm is contagious. It's hard for me to get excited about most things, but Cal has the ability to flip a switch and turn on my fun side.

October drove through downtown Mill Valley and headed up Marion Avenue toward our intended destination, but when she got to Edgewood, instead of continuing straight, Cal said, "Make a right."

October turned, and as soon as she did I knew where Cal was taking us. October did not and said, "This isn't the way to the Pelican Inn."

"Detour down Memory Lane," Cal told her. A minute later he said, "Up there, on the right. Pull over." He pointed down a long, sloping driveway and said, "There it is. Bob Harper's masterpiece."

Masterpiece was a facetious term. The house was three stories of cutting corners made to look fancy. Bob's clients typically wanted the biggest, showiest houses on the block, not the most well-built ones, and Bob had constructed our family's house in a similar manner. The house was still standing though, and it didn't look much different than it looked back when Cal and I were teenagers, so maybe it was a masterpiece and I was an ungrateful shit.

October parked on the side of the road just north of the property and looked over her shoulder at me. "I'm assuming this is where you grew up."

I nodded.

"I grew up here too," Cal said. "In high school, I spent more days and nights in this house than in my own. As a matter of fact, the first time I ever touched a boob was right there in that garage."

"Shit," I mumbled. "Kathleen Kelly."

Cal threw his head back and laughed. "I can't believe you remember her name!"

"Of course I do. She traumatized me."

Cal's laugh came from deep in his gut. "Tell October the story! You tell it way funnier than I do!"

Most people would describe me as dry and somber, but for some reason Cal found me uproarious. I looked at October and said, "Kathleen Kelly wasn't some girl from our school. She was one of Ingrid's friends."

"Ingrid is Harp's mom," Cal clarified.

"Yeah. So, my mom is having this party one night. Cal and I were what—sophomores at the time?"

"Not even. It was the spring of our freshman year."

"Right. And Kathleen comes out to the garage where we were practicing; she's drunk out of her mind, and wearing this low-cut blouse."

"Like, to here," Cal said, pointing to his bellybutton.

"Pretty much," I agree. "And she asks us straight up if we've ever seen a topless woman before."

At this point Cal is laughing so hard he can barely get the words out. "Tell October what you asked Kathleen!"

I shrugged. "What? All I said was 'In person?' because I didn't know if she meant in real life or on TV. We'd obviously seen naked women on TV. It seemed like a legitimate question."

October was chuckling now too, looking back and forth between Cal and me.

"Anyway," I went on, "Kathleen unbuttons her shirt and unhooks her bra right in front of us. The door to the house wasn't even closed. And then she says, 'Who wants to touch them?'"

"And they're huge and fake and, like, *rippled*," Cal explains. "Imagine unripe cantaloupes."

October made her paper-belly face. "*No . . .*"

"Both of us are standing there, frozen and terrified, our jaws on the floor, and Kathleen is saying, 'C'mon, c'mon, doesn't anybody want to touch them?' and finally Cal raises his hands. *Plural*. He raised *both* his hands." This is where I started to crack up. "Your face," I said to Cal. "I remember how concerned you were. Like you felt bad I wasn't volunteering and had to do Kathleen a favor."

"That's exactly how I felt!"

I tapped October on the shoulder so that she would look at me, and then I raised my hands and stretched out my fingers like Cal had done, to show her. "No kidding, his hands are like this, and he says, 'Fine, fine, I'll do it,' and he walks up to her and grabs them like they're two clown horns. And he squeezes."

October covered her face and giggled.

Cal said, "I learned a very important lesson that day. Don't squeeze."

After our laughter died down, Cal hopped out of the car and said, "Come on. Let's look around."

October and I followed Cal as far as the driveway, but he kept going.

"Chris . . . ," October said.

"Nobody's home," he told her. And while there were no lights on and no cars around, there was no way he could know that for sure. "I just want to peek in the windows. For old time's sake."

He was all the way to the front door when October took a step closer to me, put her palm on my back, and said, "Just checking to make sure you're OK. Being here, I mean."

"I'm fine." I nodded and stepped away from her. "Thanks, though."

It was true when I said it. Seeing the house wasn't a trigger for me. I had hiked past it a few times since I'd moved back and didn't feel much of anything when I did.

It wasn't until I looked up and saw Cal standing near the front door, calling my name the way only Cal ever did, that my mood took a nosedive.

The last time I'd seen Cal in that doorway was the day before he left for Brooklyn. He'd come over to make one last appeal, and he'd used the same argument I'd tried on Bob. "Give it a year. If we don't make any progress you can come back and go to Berkeley. What do you have to lose?"

I had assured him I would give that serious thought and, to make us both feel better, told him I'd probably be in Brooklyn by Christmas.

I could see the internal debate on his face then, and the concern. "Harp," he'd said, "promise me one thing. Promise me that no matter what happens, we'll always be best friends."

"I promise."

The Pelican Inn opened in the late 1970s and is meant to look like a cozy medieval pub. The walls are brick and white plaster; the floors thick, wide planks of five-hundred-year-old redwood; and in the back corner of the restaurant there's a walk-in fireplace with a big cauldron in the middle of it.

It was Friday, and the place was packed when we arrived. Right away I could see that all the people waiting in the entryway made October uncomfortable. She didn't take her eyes off the floor, and she kept snapping the elastic hair band she wore around her wrist. I wondered to myself if we should go somewhere less busy, but Cal didn't seem fazed by October's behavior, and I didn't think it was my place to step in and say anything if he didn't.

There wasn't a table for three available, but Cal sweet-talked the hostess, and she said that if we didn't mind squeezing in at a table meant for two, she could seat us right away.

"Bloody brilliant," Cal said in his Noel Gallagher brogue.

"Sounds fantastic," I said as Liam.

October looked at us like we were two strangers she'd picked up on the side of the road.

The waitress led us to the back corner of the dining room, to a small table right beside the fireplace. The table had a chair on one side and a bench on the other. The bench was actually a section of an old church pew. It faced the room, and right away Cal took the single chair so he could sit with his back to the other diners.

I slid onto the bench first, all the way to the wall, but the space was so tight that when October slid in beside me, our legs and arms pressed against each other's. I remember trying to hold my breath, trying to shut my body down so that she wouldn't pick up on my reaction to being that close to her. But my leg palpitated like it had its own heartbeat, and I realized with resigned mortification that there was no way for me to hide my feelings from her.

Luckily, glancing across the table at Cal distracted me. He looked elated and proud, and it made me homesick to be there with him, though not for my literal home. I was homesick for the feeling I used to have when I was with Cal and could see the world through his eyes. There's a certain sort of hope that kids have, even in the direst of circumstances, because they don't yet understand the constraints of time and the complexities of adult life. When I was young, I used to imagine time as a wide-open space, like a big field that Cal and I ran around in. Now that I'm older, I see that time is really more like a funnel, getting narrower and narrower as we move forward into it, limiting our space, our options, until one day there will be nothing but a tiny hole that we'll drip through into nothingness.

I stared at the candle in the center of the table. Finally, a real one, in a real, old-fashioned pewter candleholder, with a real flame; I took comfort in that.

Cal and I both ordered Guinness, and October asked for a lemonade. After the waitress came back with our drinks, we ordered fish-and-chips and shepherd's pie. Then Cal lifted his glass, looked at me and, still committed to his accent, said, "Here's to brothers." He leaned across the table, grabbed me, and kissed me on the forehead. Then he kissed October on the lips, adding, "And to the woman who brought my brother back home."

Cal was smiling, the moment was poignant, and I remember thinking that if October and Cal were both in a sinking ship and I could save only one of them, I didn't know which I would pick.

After we ate, the waitress offered us another round of Guinness, but Cal shook his head and asked for the check, which he paid right away. When I tried to leave the tip, he said, "Fuck off, you bloody cunt." This was something we'd heard Noel and Liam say, and it made us laugh every time.

A second later, Cal got October's attention and went back to talking like himself. "Baby," he said, "would you be bummed if you had to drive home without us?"

She started fishing through her purse for the car keys and didn't immediately respond.

Cal looked at me and said, "I was thinking . . ." And before he said it I finished his sentence with: ". . . that we'd hike back."

Cal nodded, and October said, "You guys are cute. But it's going to get dark soon."

"Not that soon," Cal said. "And it wouldn't be the first time we hiked in the dark."

"We were never very good at knowing what time the sun was going to set."

"Besides," Cal added, "I could blindfold Harp and he could still get us home from here." Cal looked at October. "Can we?"

She rolled her eyes and playfully smacked him in the arm. "I'm not your mom. Do whatever you want. Just don't call me to come and pick you up if you get lost."

We walked October to the car, and I promised her we would most definitely not get lost.

Cal gave her a long, deep kiss and said, "You're dope."

We had to walk down the street a ways to catch the beginning of the trailhead. It wasn't even seven o'clock yet, and that meant we had plenty of decent light left. As long as we kept up a good pace, we'd have a mile or so in the dark, but we'd be on the fire road to October's house by then and, like Cal said, I could hike that trail in a blindfold and still make it home.

Instead of reminiscing, which is what we'd been doing most of the evening, Cal and I talked about some of the things we had coming up. I was excited about the birdcage and described it to him in great detail. He, in turn, told me how much he was looking forward to his upcoming show at the Greek Theater in Berkeley. It was a couple months away, already sold out, and would be the last performance of the tour.

"I really want you to be there," he said. "You'll come, right?"

"Of course," I assured him. "Wouldn't miss it."

By the time we hit the Gravity Car Fire Road, I could tell Cal had something on his mind. He'd gone quiet and his eyes were pointed at the sky. Anytime Cal was feeling contemplative, he stared at the sky.

Further down the trail, he climbed a small embankment and watched the lights of San Francisco twinkling in the distance. A moment later, his eyes glazed out on the view, he said, "Harp, can I talk to you about something?"

"Sure."

He picked up a long, narrow stick and poked at things in the dirt. "It's about October."

My jaw tightened. For a moment I said nothing. Then, "What about her?"

A beep came from Cal's pocket. He took out his phone, responded quickly to a text, and put it back. Then he skidded down the little rise he'd climbed and resumed the hike. He was looking straight ahead when he said, "Something's been bothering me all week, and I need to get it off my chest."

His words and tone gave me pause, and I gulped.

"Something's not right with her."

"What do you mean?"

He broke the stick into two pieces and then started to break those pieces into even smaller pieces, tossing the fragmented twigs off the side of the trail as we walked. "I realize it's not cool for me to put you in this position, being that she's your boss. And if you and I didn't have the history we have I wouldn't even bring it up."

"It's OK," I told him.

He ran his hand through his hair and said, "I think she's seeing someone."

My mouth went dry, and I had to swallow too many times to get any words out. "What makes you think that?"

"You can't tell her we had this conversation."

I made some gesture to indicate I wouldn't.

He rolled the last piece of stick back and forth between his fingers and said, "She won't fuck me."

This caught me off guard for a couple of reasons, the main one being that I'd assumed they'd been fucking all week while I was alone in my room thinking about all the fucking they were doing.

Cal looked to his left, into the woods, and said, "Not once since I got back. Not even in Big Sur. And if your girlfriend won't fuck you in Big Sur, you've got a problem." He shook his head. "Every time I try, she makes an excuse. Fine, she jacked me off after I bugged her long enough, but that's it. And trust me when I say October is a passionate woman. She usually jumps my bones the minute I get home. But for the last week and a half, nothing."

I felt a rush of panic coming on and picked up the pace to get us home before I started acting guilty. "Have you *asked* her about this?"

"Sort of."

"Sort of?"

"I brought it up a few times while we were gone, but she didn't want to talk about it. Then I pressed her on it again this morning; she told me she's going through some emotional stuff, and sex is too intense for her when she's emotionally overwhelmed. She asked me to give her space. I said sure, and then I asked her if she could elaborate on what kind of emotional stuff; she told me that agreeing to give her space means agreeing to stop asking her questions." Cal shook his head. "The last time I used that line, that I needed space, I'd married a woman I hardly knew and was screwing my ex-girlfriend behind her back."

Apprehensively, I said, "Have you asked October specifically if there's someone else?"

"See, this is where it gets complicated. I can't ask her that. I'm not allowed."

"I don't understand."

It was getting cold out, and I zipped up my jacket. Cal didn't have a jacket. He dropped the last remaining twig, put his hands deep in his pockets, and hunched up his shoulders.

"We have this arrangement," he said. "Since we spend so much time apart. We're supposed to be allowed to see other people, as long as it's a no-strings-attached sort of thing. You know, casual. Believe it or not, it was her idea. I went along with it because in theory it sounds awesome, right? And because I was in love with her and wanted her to think I was open-minded and all that shit. But I'm not, really. Anyway, *not* asking each other about our extracurricular activities is one of the rules. It's the biggest rule. Don't ask, don't tell. Our relationship is like the fucking army."

Thank God for that, I thought.

It was almost fully dark, and Cal said, "You know where we are, yes?"

I could see Beanstalk up ahead and nodded. "Less than a quarter mile from the house."

Cal was looking at me like he was waiting for me to give him advice, but I was at a loss and ended up asking him a question that was more pertinent to me than to him. "So, you see other women then?"

He shrugged. "Sure. Though I usually feel guilty as fuck when it happens, even though I'm allowed to do it." He rubbed his hands together to warm them and blew into his palms. "And not that this makes it any better, but it never means anything, you know? I follow the rules. What's going on with October is different. She doesn't just connect with random people. She's not like that. I can count her friends on one hand. She's pulling away from me, and I'm freaking out. I don't want to lose her." He came to a halt in the middle of the trail and said, "I'm sorry, but I have to ask . . ."

I braced for it. Because I knew that if Cal asked me straight up if something was going on between October and me, I wouldn't have been able to lie to him.

He said, "Have you seen anyone around? Anyone coming or going that may be worth mentioning? Is she ever gone all night?"

Cal misinterpreted the look on my face and said, "Fine, fine, I know. It's not fair of me to be asking you this. But the only other person I could ask is Rae, and I have no confidence in her. She'd tell October I was prying."

"I haven't seen anybody," I said.

That wasn't a lie.

"Thanks, man." Cal stepped closer and put his arm around my shoulder the way you do when you trust someone. "You'll keep an eye on things while I'm gone, right? Let me know if that changes?"

I told him I would.

But that wasn't even the shittiest part. The shittiest part was that when I got back to my apartment, I didn't sit around thinking about what Cal was going through. I thought about what it meant that October wouldn't have sex with him. And while I came up with numerous possible conclusions, the only logical one seemed to be the same one Cal had come to.

She was thinking of somebody else.

FOURTEEN.

GUITARS ARE LIKE PEOPLE. Each one is an individual. Especially vintage guitars. And almost all of the guitars on Cal's Wall of Dreams were older than I was.

The morning Cal left to go back on tour, he gave me a key to his studio and told me I was welcome to hang out and play the guitars whenever I wanted. In the days following his departure, I spent virtually all my free time doing just that.

The guitars saved me. Being around October all day was tougher than I thought it was going to be. I felt like I'd spent my life perfecting the art of pretending—pretending to care, pretending not to care, pretending I didn't feel things, pretending I did—but I couldn't seem to figure out how to pretend I didn't want to be with that woman.

I had a little over a week to finish the birdcage, and that kept me busy in my corner of the studio without having to interact with October too much. Plus, Rae was around a lot then. She usually worked out of the house, doing whatever it was she did—taking care of October's personal business and eating trail mix—but following Cal's departure, Rae seemed to find myriad reasons to stop by the studio throughout the day. I figured she was there to make sure I was keeping my distance, and I was.

127

In the meantime, October had begun working on the series of vintage ship paintings that had been lying dormant against the wall since my first day on the job. The series was part of a nautical-themed exhibit she would be debuting at a Thomas Frasier popup gallery in Chicago the following summer. When she wasn't working on selfies and Ribble scribbles, she focused on those.

But sharing the space with her was hard. Sometimes I would glance up and watch her from across the room, the way she puckered her lips and shifted them to the side when she stepped back to survey a canvas; the way she tilted her head, squinted and bit at her left thumbnail when she was focusing on the details of a piece; the way she had to lift her head up to see when her hair fell across her eye.

She was extra quiet that week. Kept to herself and seemed pretty down. And the minute she left at the end of the day, I felt lonely. If it hadn't been for Cal's guitars, I'm not sure what I would have done.

Actually, I do know.

I would have left.

And in hindsight, maybe running off sooner rather than later would have made it easier for all of us. Maybe if I'd left that week, I wouldn't have ended up working as a guitar instructor in a sleepy mountain town in northwestern Montana, living in Sid's guest cabin without Wi-Fi, wishing I'd done everything differently.

In any case, I can't say that playing Cal's guitars made my loneliness go away. But I could make those guitars feel what I was feeling, and that made me less lonely. I could transfer my longing to whatever instrument was in my hands, and I could turn it into beautiful sounds. It didn't heal me, but it comforted me, and I needed comfort more than I needed anything. Each guitar was a companion, a friend with whom I could commiserate. I wasn't alone when I was with those guitars.

There was one instrument I got particularly attached to. Like the mythical Micawber, it was also a Telecaster, but this one was a 1961 Sunburst. In 1961 it was a cheap and unremarkable guitar. Cal bought it in 2014, and by then it was neither of those things. In fact, it had purportedly lived an incredible life as *the* guitar a couple of Nashville session players had traded around to record with Roy Orbison. Rumor had it that Roy had dubbed the guitar "Sammy" in honor of Sun Records founder Sam Phillips. Obviously that name bore a different, but no less powerful, significance to me.

I hold a mystical belief that people leave behind their essence or energy on anything they touch, anything they care for. That's why vintage guitars are so special. History gives a guitar a character you can feel when you play it. Like a living thing, a guitar has a spirit, and the spirit of the 1961 Fender was deep and kind and, above all, wise. I know it sounds crazy, but this Tele was the wisest guitar I've ever played. When I had a question, it had an answer. When I didn't know what to say, it said it for me. When I wanted to pick up and run, it talked me into staying.

Sammy also had the best neck of any instrument I'd ever held. Before holding that guitar, the best neck I'd ever touched was on a 1952 Les Paul that belonged to Elvis Costello. Right before our senior year, Cal and I had summer jobs at The Sweetwater, a small music venue in Mill Valley where Elvis would occasionally show up to play. We happened to be working one of those nights, and Cal being Cal, he sauntered up to Elvis's guitar tech and told him I was the best guitar player under thirty in the whole Bay Area. The tech took one look at me and laughed, but he let me tune some of the guitars, including Elvis's '61 Tele and his '63 Jazzmaster. Once I'd sufficiently impressed him, he handed me the Les Paul. It was a hard, feisty guitar. It fought me, taunted me, made me work for the magic. The damn G string wouldn't stay in tune, so I was on edge the whole time it was in my hands, but on edge in a way that made me feel alive.

When I held Sammy, the neck felt as if it had been broken in by my hands. And I wasn't alone in my feelings for that guitar. When Cal texted me on Wednesday to see how things were back home, I told him I'd fallen in love with Sammy, and he wrote: "I'VE YET TO HAVE SOMEONE PLAY THAT GUITAR WHO ISN'T IN LOVE WITH IT. NO KIDDING. I BOUGHT IT FROM MY BUDDY DON, AND HE STILL CALLS ME EVERY COUPLE MONTHS TO ASK ME HOW IT'S DOING."

The funny thing is the 1961 Tele isn't even a rare guitar. They're expensive as hell, but easy to find. Hell, Cal has another one in custom black on his wall. But I played the black one too, and it didn't deliver like Sammy delivered.

On Thursday night I decided I needed a break from Casa Diez. I went over to Berkeley for the first time since I'd moved back to Mill Valley and met up with one of my old coworkers for a drink—and to get October her mushrooms, which I hadn't forgotten about.

My buddy, Len—the shroom purveyor, and hands-down the best electrician I'd ever worked with—wanted to hear about my new job. At first I was reticent with my answers, conscious of October's privacy, and careful not to give too much away. But after a beer and a shot of tequila, I guess I dropped my guard a bit, because when Len pressed me on what October was like, I stumbled over my words, and Len's face cracked.

"You're sleeping with her!" he said, loud enough for half the bar to hear.

"What? No." I tried to sound sincere. "Definitely not."

"Ah. Then you *want* to sleep with her?"

I shook my head. My face felt hot. "It's not like that."

Part of me wanted to confess to Len, get it off my chest. But the truth of the matter seemed impossible to convey. So I changed the subject to another uncomfortable topic. "Have you heard from Bob lately?"

Len had spent seven years under Bob's tutelage, and they'd gotten on well.

"Nah," Len said. "Not since he left. How's he doing?"

"Dunno." I shrugged. "I haven't heard from him either."

When I got back to my place, there was a Mason jar filled with cookies in front of my door, with a note on it that said:

Homemade Oreos.
(No hydrogenated oil!)

October wasn't kidding. The cookies looked just like Oreos, only they were twice the size of the store-bought kind. I took them to the kitchen and ate one the same way I used to eat real Oreos when I was a kid—by twisting off the top, eating that first, and then eating the bottom half like an open-faced sandwich. The cookies tasted like real Oreos too, if real Oreos could ever be soft and fresh. I ate a second one and thought about how October told me she baked when she was anxious; I wondered what was on her mind.

After much internal debate, I sent her a text that said: Thanks for the cookies. She sent me back a smiley face. I hated when she responded with emojis because I didn't know how to interpret them. In a moment of weakness, I typed Feel like hanging out? But I knew that was a bad idea and deleted it before I pressed "Send."

There seemed to be a gaping hole in the night, down which I was in danger of falling. And here's how absurd I got: I tried to send October a message telepathically. Much like my psychic relationship with Sam, I didn't necessarily believe October could receive my communiqué, but I felt powerless in life almost all of the time, and attempting extrasensory contact was my way of pretending I was capable of controlling my destiny.

The bottom line was: I wanted to see her. So I closed my eyes and imagined that she was sitting on her couch and that my spirit was beside her, whispering in her ear, telling her that *she* wanted to see *me*.

I felt stupid after that. And because I didn't want to be tempted to communicate with her like a normal person, I left my phone in the kitchen, took off my shoes and socks, and went downstairs to play.

I was in the mood for an acoustic and selected Cal's Gibson SJ-200E, the guitar he'd used the night we played together at the dinner party. The Gibson had volume knobs and a pickup like an electric, so it was really more like an acoustic on steroids. According to Cal, the knobs and pickup were put there by the original owner, and Cal was told upon purchase that only two people ever did that to their acoustic guitars back when these knobs and pickups would have been installed: John Lennon and Elvis Presley.

"It's probably a bullshit story," Cal said, "but I choose to believe one of them owned this guitar."

My choice was more specific. I chose to believe it had belonged to John Lennon, and I played "Across the Universe" in his honor as my warm-up.

And then something extraordinary happened. I'd barely played the last note of that song when I heard a quiet tap on the door; a second later, October walked in with Diego at her side. She had two beer bottles in her hand and a woolly lavender blanket wrapped around her shoulders.

My heart stopped and then raced.

"Hey," I said.

"Hey." She handed me a beer. "I saw the light on. Thought I'd come over and listen to you play for a while."

She curled up on the couch, across from the chair where I was, and drew her knees into her chest. Diego settled on the cool concrete floor by the door and could have been mistaken for a shag rug.

I opened the beer and took a couple of long drinks. October sipped at hers. I was staring at her, and she was looking around the room at everything but me. We didn't speak, and it was uncomfortable, but uncomfortable in a way that borders on exciting, like when two people feel too much when they're alone together, and for one reason or another can't show it or tell it.

Then I realized I could tell her a lot; I just had to start strumming.

"Any requests?"

"Sad songs," she said. "Only sad songs."

I took another drink of my beer and then played "Slip Slidin' Away" because that song is about missed chances, regret, and fear, and because the closer I got to October, the more I felt like I was sliding in the opposite direction. Moreover, whether I'm listening to that song or playing it, I find myself wondering how any of us make it through the peaks and valleys of our lives with any grace and hope at all.

In the middle of the song, October set her beer on the floor, stretched out on the couch, stuffed a pillow under her head, and lay down. Then she closed her eyes and hummed along to the music.

I played a couple of Leonard Cohen songs, one of which I could've written about October if I were as cool and poetic as Leonard. And then I noodled around, making stuff up as I went along, and she fell asleep.

She was on her side, hands together in front of her chest as if she were holding a baby bird in her palms. I watched her as I strummed soft chords and plucked at sweet lullaby notes with my fingers, and when I finally got tired and put the guitar away, I thought she'd wake up, but she didn't. Then I remembered she'd once slept through a Bruce Springsteen concert.

She looked comfortable, and I saw no reason to rouse her. I pulled up the blanket to cover her shoulders, shut off all the lights except for the small one near the door, stepped carefully around Diego, and walked out.

When I got back upstairs, I felt electric. Knowing October and I would be sleeping under the same roof filled me with an odd combination of peace and desire that wrestled with my body and calmed me down all at once.

This is the good kind of loneliness, I thought. The kind that's really a longing for something your imagination can hold onto until morning.

My sheets were glacial when I got in bed, and I swore I could feel October's closeness in the shivers on my skin. Then I thought of Cal and wondered how I was going to hold this all together.

Right before I fell asleep, I realized I'd forgotten to tell October about the mushrooms.

FIFTEEN.

I WAS SITTING at the table in October's studio, eating a bowl of muesli and paging through a book on redwoods, one Ingrid had recently sent me, when October and Diego got there the next morning.

October seemed lighter in spirit than she had all week. Her movements were smooth and floaty, like she was on roller skates, and she glided over to where I was, sat down across from me with one of her legs tucked underneath her, leaned halfway across the table and said, "Whatcha readin'?"

I had a mouthful of cereal and showed her the cover. She spun the book around and opened it to the inside flap, where Ingrid had written:

> *Dear Joey—*
> *Thought of you when I saw this in the bookstore.*
> *Love you,*
> *Mom*

"Ha-ha," October giggled. "*Joey.*"

"Just so you know, Ingrid is the only person on the planet who is allowed to call me that."

She began paging through the book. I watched her eyes moving right to left, widening as they skimmed the words and looked at the pictures. Every so often she would shake her head and mumble, "Holy cow."

As soon as I finished my breakfast, I said, "I forgot to tell you last night. I got your mushrooms."

At first she didn't seem to know what I was talking about. Then she did. She leaned in and began to ramble nervously. "You have them? Wow. OK. You can't just give them to me, though. You know that, right? I can't do them alone. That doesn't seem safe. Are mushrooms safe? Maybe we should film it. No. Probably not a good idea. No filming. Private is better, right?"

"Private is definitely better." I saw Rae pull in and said, "Can we discuss this later? I don't need Rae accusing me of being a drug pusher."

October laughed and made a zipping motion across her mouth, and I quickly took my bowl to the sink in the back. All week long I'd been making sure I was nowhere near October when Rae arrived in the morning.

Rae came straight into the studio, presented October with a handful of bills, and asked her to sign some checks.

October set my book on the table with the page she was reading splayed face down. She scribbled her signature on the checks and then picked up the book again. Looking at Rae, she said, "The tallest tree *in the entire world* lives in a park in Northern California."

Rae feigned interest, but I could tell she didn't really comprehend what October was trying to tell her. I walked over to join the conversation and noticed Rae didn't have any nuts and raisins with her. This meant she wasn't staying long.

"Hyperion," I said. Rae and October both looked at me. "That's the name of the tree. It's about 380 feet tall."

"*Three hundred and eighty feet?*" October exclaimed. "That's as tall as the Empire State Building!" She seemed to find this awe-inspiring. Rae acted like it was ordinary, but probably only because I said it.

"I camped in that park after Hyperion was discovered," I told them. "It's phenomenal."

I turned to a photo of Hyperion and pointed it out to Rae. In the photo, a man was standing beside the tree. He was listed as being six feet eight inches tall, and that really showed the scale, because he looked like a tiny toy soldier that had been placed beside an upright bass.

Rae's eyes finally widened, and she said, "Wow. That is big, yeah?"

I flipped back a few pages and pointed to Giant Tree. "This one's my favorite. He's not the biggest or the prettiest, but in person he really moves me."

"He *moves* you?" Rae said, with a slightly comic tone.

"Where does he live?" October asked.

"Avenue of the Giants. In Humboldt. I once drove all the way there, had lunch with him, and drove home."

Rae said, "Did you sing 'Kumbaya' to him too?"

I chuckled. "That's actually funny, Rae."

"You know, I can be funny, Joe."

October said, "Let me see."

I pointed. "Look at the way the sunlight reaches down through his crown. Incredible, right?"

October said, "I can't believe I've lived here for as long as I have and didn't know about these trees. I thought the trees in Muir Woods were giants."

I could tell Rae was paying close attention to the way October and I were bonding over the trees. Or maybe she was just surprised by my passion and enthusiasm, which was rarely on display in front of her, or anyone for that matter.

I handed the book back to October and said, "I could talk about trees all day, but I have a birdcage to finish."

I went back to my corner—I was about two full workdays away from being done. Meanwhile, Rae went into the office and printed something on the computer and then left to run errands.

October was still at the table, still engrossed in the book. Usually she had music playing during the day, but that morning I worked in silence while she read about the redwoods.

Around lunchtime she came back to see me with the book still in her hands.

I wiped my face on the bottom of my T-shirt and gave her my attention.

"Do you have plans tomorrow?" she said.

"No."

She stepped closer and pointed to the cover of the book. "Will you take me here? To see the trees?"

"Tomorrow?" I laughed. "We can't go all the way up there tomorrow."

"You just said you didn't have anything to do."

I cracked my knuckles and stared at her, which caused her to point more vigorously at the cover.

"This is where I want to do the mushrooms."

My body tensed and shook as though it were feeling the approaching future and all it held. October's phrase "can of worms" popped into my head, and I mumbled something that was unintelligible, even to my own ears.

"Come on," she purred. "Doesn't this seem like the *perfect* place to do mushrooms?"

Fucking hell, I wasn't going to lie to her.

"Well, yeah," I said. "As a matter of fact, it does."

Initially, October wanted to see Hyperion, but he's pretty far north, almost to the Oregon border, in a fairly remote area of Redwood National Park. It would have taken us a good five hours to drive there, and another couple to hike to the tree. Avenue of the Giants was only three hours away, in Humboldt County, and the state park there was filled with tons of notable redwoods worth visiting, including my favorite, Giant Tree, as well as the Flatiron Tree, and the Albino Redwood—a tree not many people knew how to find, but I did.

I suggested we leave early so we had the whole day to explore. I also wanted to make sure October was coming down off her trip before we drove home.

As we were making our plans, October pulled out her phone and said, "Before I get too excited, let me text Rae to see if she can spend the night with Diego."

She began typing, and I let her words sink in.

"Wha . . . huh?" I stuttered, my brow furrowing against my will. "You want to spend the night there? *Together?*"

She paused, biting at her thumbnail while she pondered my question, as if the trouble with the idea had only just occurred to her. "Well, I thought . . . I mean . . . We certainly can't drive home on drugs, right?"

"I'm not planning on *doing* the drugs. I'm planning on supervising."

"Joe, no. You can't let me do them alone."

My stomach felt like it had been tossed off the top of a tall building.

"Come on," she said. "It's a long way to go for just a few hours. If we find somewhere to crash for the night, we can spend a lot more time with the trees."

I didn't want to be responsible for making a decision like this. On the one hand it seemed like a horrible idea for us to go away together overnight;

on the other hand there was nothing I wanted more than to spend the night in the middle of an ancient redwood forest with her.

She touched my arm and said, "It'll be fine. We're friends, remember? Friends do this kind of stuff. Don't worry."

I wasn't worried. I was terrified. And weak.

"We can get separate rooms if that makes you feel better. However, if I'm still tripping when I go to sleep, I'm going to need you to sit by my bed and make sure I don't die."

I laughed. "You're not going to die."

She laughed too. But then she got serious. "Really though, if you don't feel comfortable with this, I understand. I can ask Rae to go with me."

I scoffed. "You *cannot* do mushrooms with *Rae*."

Her megawatt smile returned. "OK. What I'm hearing you say is that it's cool and you'll take me?" She raised her phone. "Blink once for *no* and twice for *text Rae about the dog*."

My conscience wrestled with all the other parts of me and lost, because as much as I believed *no* was the correct answer, I blinked twice, and the words that came out of my mouth were "It's cool. Text away."

"Thank you! I promise it will be fun!"

Fun was not what concerned me.

She pushed "Send," and we waited for a response. Less than two minutes later, Rae wrote back and told October she would be at Casa Diez by seven.

The next morning I walked down to Equator before Rae got to the house—I didn't want her to see me leave with October.

October picked me up at the cafe a little after seven, asked if I minded driving, and then climbed over the middle console to the passenger's side of the car.

As we headed north on US 101, she propped her feet up on the dashboard and reclined her seat as if she were relaxing on a beach lounger. She had my redwoods book in her lap and was reading facts aloud—facts I already knew—but I let her go on because her reverence for the trees made me feel closer to her.

"Redwoods have been around for 240 million years!" she gasped. "That's before humans."

"Yup. Before birds and spiders, even."

"They can live to be two thousand years old? Jesus. It doesn't seem fair that a tree gets to live for centuries and all we get is a handful of measly decades."

"You'd really want to live for a thousand years?"

"You wouldn't?"

"I've barely made it this far." It was warm in the car, and I asked October to hold the wheel while I took off my fleece jacket. "Anyway, trees are so much smarter, stronger, and more reliable than humans. If we could actually live that long, imagine how much more fucked up the Earth would be." I tossed my jacket into the back seat. "Who am I kidding? We would have destroyed the Earth by now. We'd be long gone."

"That's very pessimistic, *Joey*." A minute later she said, "Wait. The coast redwood is actually a cypress tree, not a sequoia?"

"Coast redwoods and sequoias are both part of the cypress family."

"And the coast redwood is the tallest?"

"Yup."

"And that's what Hyperion is? A coast redwood?"

"Correct. All the trees we're going to see today, those are coast redwoods too. The giant sequoias grow in the Sierra Nevada."

"*Sequoia sempervirens.*"

"Always alive. Forever green."

"Redwoods are nature's art installations," she decided firmly.

A quote came back to me, one I'd memorized when I was doing research with Sid for my college thesis. "Aristotle once said: 'There is more both of beauty and of *raison d'être* in the works of nature than in those of art.'"

She nodded with so much enthusiasm she had to sit up to do it. "That's why I love these trees. They're universal symbols of strength, perseverance, and survival. They're living poems to time."

I'll admit it: I wanted to fuck her when she said that. And as I drove on, an image popped into my head. I saw myself as the pith inside one of those colossal trees, living in darkness, buried deep inside the trunk, hidden under centuries of growth, a heartbeat muffled and faint. And then I imagined October coming along and scraping off long pieces of bark, peeling away layer after ancient layer, trying to reach me. And still it would take years to get deep enough to set me free.

She said, "Redwood trees are poetic, don't you think?"

Her voice brought me back into the car, back into my body.

"Yup," I told her. "Always have."

We made it to the little town of Willits, known as the gateway to the redwoods, in two hours and stopped at a coffee shop on Main Street for breakfast. There were few patrons inside—couple of burly loggers and some old hippies. We drank strong coffee and ate runny egg sandwiches, and after we finished, October got out her sketchbook and asked if she could do a portrait of me.

The plan, she said, was to do one now and then another later, after the mushrooms kicked in.

"No talking, no moving," she directed.

I sat still and stayed quiet while she focused on my face. The entire time she was drawing, I had a strong, somatic, dare I say *synesthetic* response to her attention. What I mean is I felt as if she were touching me with her pencil. Her hand made broad, sweeping strokes and small, intricate marks on the paper, each one like a gentle caress on my face. And as she tilted her head and squinted at my features, I had the sense she was examining my interior as much as my exterior.

"You have a beautiful mouth," she told me matter-of-factly. "And your eyes are almost symmetrical."

She used her hand for a bit, shading and smudging until her fingers were gray from the graphite.

"This is fun," she mumbled, as if she were talking to herself. "There's so much going on behind your eyes, and that makes for a very nuanced portrait. On the surface you're all still water. But man, that water runs deep."

"Swampy," I mumbled.

"No talking." She shook her head. "Besides, you're wrong. I can see people's spirits when I draw them, and yours isn't swampy. It's a little marine flare blinking at the bottom of a deep, dark ocean."

She put her pencil down, examined her work, made a couple of additional adjustments, and then flipped the pad around for me to see.

"Well?"

She'd drawn me with a cup of coffee in my hands, looking a little off to the right, the cafe's one big window behind me and to the left.

I studied the portrait for a while before I said anything. It looked exactly like me, and yet it looked like a stranger. She'd drawn a fiery light in my eyes that I didn't think was really there.

"That's how I see you," she said.

Then I understood. She'd drawn the potential Joe Harper, not the actual one. Because that's what a spirit is, right? Our best, brightest, purest self?

"I like it," I told her. What I meant was I liked who I was in her eyes.

My coffee had gone cold, I went to get a refill, and when I returned to the table a young man who said his name was Finster had taken the seat beside October. Finster had no food or beverages in front of him and claimed he had been a lobster in a previous life.

"I had a beautiful lobster wife and a lobster daughter," he explained.

Finster had broad shoulders like a swimmer, a square forehead, a square jaw, and wild, crystal-meth eyes.

"We lived peacefully in the ocean for years," he said. "Then one day my family got scooped up in a net and ended up in a tank in a seafood restaurant near the wharf."

I tried not to laugh. October listened politely, her chin in her palm, elbow on the table.

"I watched my family get picked from the tank and cooked alive."

"I'm sorry . . ." October said.

"I prayed for death," Finster told her. "I wanted to end up on a plate too. I wanted to get chewed up and turned to shit like them. Instead I got rescued by a militant vegan who drove me back to the ocean and set me free."

That time I laughed out loud; October shot me a look.

"A few days later I got snagged by a fisherman's hook." Finster curved his index finger into the shape of a "J" and hung it from his mouth to demonstrate. "*Mort*."

With obvious trepidation, October touched the man's hand, and I saw her flinch when her fingers made contact, like whatever she felt was not good.

"We should go," I mumbled.

October said she needed to wash her hands and wandered off to the bathroom. While I waited, Finster stared at me with deranged scrutiny, and I imagined he could see in me what I saw in him—blackness.

"You miss her," Finster said.

"Who?"

"Your girlfriend."

"She's not my girlfriend."

"Don't worry, she's coming back."

"I know she's coming back. She just went to the bathroom."

October's sketchbook was still open on the table. Finster looked at the drawing and said, "It's you. Without the rage."

"Excuse me?"

"Where's your rage come from? Daddy? Mommy?" He sniffed the air like a dog. "I can smell it."

I shut the sketchbook, stood up, and began to bus our table. Before I took the dishes away, Finster grabbed what was left of October's egg sandwich and shoved it into his mouth.

As we were leaving, Finster pulled on October's sleeve and said, "Your sweatshirt is nice."

She was wearing her oversized gray hoodie. There was nothing especially nice about it, and October took it off and gave it to the guy.

"What are you doing?" I said. "What if it gets cold later?"

"I have a sweater in the car."

"He's not a lobster," Finster said to October, pointing at me as we were walking out the door. "You can't catch him."

The redwoods along the highway start to get noticeably bigger after Willits, and October kept leaning her head out the window, trying to see their crowns. "Look at that one," she would say, and I'd remind her that these were still the small trees.

As we approached Avenue of the Giants, she asked to see the mushrooms. I reached behind my seat, grabbed them from my backpack, and handed them to her.

"Wait," she said. "I was literally expecting a bag of dirty mushrooms. These look like candy bars."

"My buddy Len isn't kidding around. This is *his* art. He melts down high-quality chocolate, chops up the mushrooms, mixes it all together, and makes those by hand."

Each bar was a two-inch square, individually wrapped in metallic foil, with pretty paper labels on top. The labels had images of Hindu goddesses printed on the front and a Hunter S. Thomson quote on the underside that read: "Buy the ticket, take the ride."

"The one in the pink wrapper is dark chocolate with dried cherries. The gold wrapper is milk chocolate with honey. And Len wanted me to mention that he uses all organic ingredients."

October looked sideways at me, playful and flirty. "There's two. One for you and one for me."

"We'll see."

"We'll see," she repeated, mocking my deep, humorless tone.

She smelled the bars and said, "I call the milk chocolate."

The "Welcome" sign near the entrance to Humboldt Redwoods State Park has a John Steinbeck quote on it, something about how the trees are ambassadors of another time, but October said it felt more like a prehistoric place where time stood still.

"If a triceratops walked past me right now, it wouldn't seem weird," she said.

The air smelled of dirt, bark, and moss, and inside that miasma I could taste the ocean. It was in the wind that blew over the hill from the Pacific and kept the earth soft and damp under our feet.

We had decided we would hike around for a couple of hours, visit the specific trees we'd been talking about, and then find a motel where one or both of us would eat the chocolates. If all went well after they started to kick in, we'd go back out into the woods, let the magic unfold for a while, and at some point October would draw me again.

We started down the trail, and as soon as October saw the wooden platform that led to Giant Tree, she ran toward it. When she got to the tree, she stretched her arms out and said, "Nice to meet you, sir. I've heard so much about you from my friend over there." Then she looked back at me and said, "Joe, he's magnificent."

"You look like a child next to that behemoth."

We walked deeper into the forest, October and I both petting random, unnamed redwoods as we went along.

"Wow, look at this one," she would say. Then we'd walk a few more feet. "And this one."

Near Drive-Thru Tree, I asked her to turn around so I could take her picture. She stepped back into the naturally carved out tunnel that ran through the middle of the tree's trunk, raised her arms into the air, and smiled.

That was one of only two photos I took of October back then. I must have looked at it a thousand times after I left California, and every time I did, I saw so much more than her face and body in it. I saw her spirit, the way she had seen mine. As if she were lit from within. Other times I looked at that photo and saw the future. I saw how careless I was with her. How stupid.

She said we needed a pic of the two of us together and motioned for me to stand next to her. Then she gave her phone to an older man hiking nearby, and he snapped a shot of us side by side, October's arm thrown around my shoulder, my hands deep in my pockets.

We lost track of time in the forest, and the last tree we visited was the albino redwood. On our drive up that morning, I had predicted that Albino Tree would be October's favorite.

"You were right," she said as we stood beside it.

"Naturally. It's the weird one."

"You're calling me weird?"

"I'm calling the tree weird. Then again, you once had me film you standing on your head reciting the Declaration of Independence."

"Touché," she laughed.

Albino Tree was tiny compared to the others—only about sixty feet tall—but it was exquisite, with white, frosty leaves due to its inability to make chlorophyll. Sometimes called the forest ghost, Albino Tree appears to glow when the light hits it just right.

October said Albino was her spirit tree and contemplated filming it to use in a selfie. "Cool or dumb? I can't decide."

"Cool," I assured her.

She nodded and proceeded to record a long, static shot of the tree, though why she trusted my estimation of cool is one of my life's great mysteries.

By the time we got back to the car it was after four, and we still needed to find a place to stay and get some food before we were ready for the mushrooms. I drove us back toward the highway while October used her phone to look for nearby motels. She found a place in Miranda, right on Avenue of the Giants, promising quaint cottages in the middle of a forest. She called the number on the website and booked us a two-bedroom bungalow with a fireplace and a kitchen and told them we'd be there soon.

After she hung up, she said, "Judging from the price of a two-bedroom cottage, I suggest we don't get our hopes up for luxury."

I shrugged. I'd sleep in a muddy trench if it was surrounded by redwoods.

We stopped at a dodgy convenience store down the street from the motel and picked up some snacks. It was slim pickings in there, and we made do with what seemed edible, which was limited to a bag of tortilla chips, a small lemon pie in a box, and two bottles of water. October suggested we get beer too, but I told her we weren't going to want to mix alcohol with the mushrooms.

As we were turning into the motel, October looked over at me and said, "Time for you to decide if you're going to buy the ticket and take the ride."

I didn't say anything as I pulled into a parking space next to the small office, where a "Vacancy" sign blinked in the window. I could see all the little cottages behind the main building, and a grove of redwoods behind that. October was right. It wasn't luxurious. It was old and shabby and mundane. But there was something nostalgic about it. Something woefully charming.

She was waiting for my answer, and I thought of what Cal used to say when I tried to convince him to get high with me.

"Fine, fine," I said, my bones tingling with both excitement and doom. "I'll do it."

SIXTEEN.

THE OLD LADY who checked us in called the place a resort and told us it had been built in 1929 for city folks looking for a quiet retreat in the forest. She had a spiky gray buzz cut and saggy triceps that hung like raw crescent rolls as she walked us around the grounds. First she showed us the pool, littered with leaves and sticks that had rained down from the trees, and then she pointed out a gate at the back of the property. The gate, she said, led to a trail that meandered through a small redwood grove. She gave us our key, which dangled from a keychain shaped like Giant Tree, and told us our cottage was the only one that still had the original wainscoting.

Our cottage reminded me of the apartment where Cal and Terry had lived in Marin City, with its pine-green carpet and Walmart furniture. There was a double bed pushed up against the far wall in the living room, a smaller bedroom on the other side of the house, and a shared bathroom in between. Two pleather recliners sat across from the living room bed; a hexagonal dining table of wood veneer sat to the left of those. There were dark water stains on the ceiling tiles. The fluorescent lights were way too bright, even before we ate the mushrooms. The venetian blinds were covered in webs and dust. And they'd lied about the fireplace. There was no fireplace.

"I told you it wasn't going to be fancy," October laughed.

I went and got our stuff from the car and set it all on the table. We didn't have much. I'd brought a backpack with my toothbrush and a change of clothes. October had a small duffle bag, her sketchbook and pencil case. And we had the food and water from the market.

The cottage had a damp, musty odor, and the first thing October did was light an incense stick that instantly transformed the smell of the room from "dingy motor inn" to "woodsy bohemian den."

We hadn't eaten since breakfast and contemplated snacking before we ate the mushrooms, but from what I recalled they were more potent on empty stomachs.

October sat on the bed in the living room, smiled apprehensively and said, "OK. Let's do this."

I got the chocolates from my backpack and sat down across from her. I handed her the milk chocolate square and kept the dark one for myself. It was hard to get the foil off because some of the chocolate had gotten a little gooey in the afternoon heat of the car, but we managed to scrape it all out.

I snapped my piece in two, put both halves in my mouth and ate them at the same time. October held hers in her hand and made a face.

"Oh, no. You can't paper-belly the mushrooms."

She laughed and said, "I'm scared."

I loved October's vulnerable side. It made me feel useful. "Don't worry. I won't let anything happen to you."

Her expression softened as soon as I said that. She took one bite, chewed and swallowed, and then wriggled her nose and ate the rest.

"Ticket bought," she said.

"Now, we wait for the ride."

"Let's wait in the forest."

We made our way to the trail behind the resort. The hike down into the grove only took a few minutes and wasn't as picturesque as we'd hoped. There were old tires and the blackened chassis of a car from the 1930s at the bottom of the hill, and huge stumps of old-growth trees that had been cut down among the new ones.

"These are babies," I said, touching random redwoods. "Less than a hundred years old, I bet."

It had been only about twenty minutes since we'd eaten the mushrooms, and I didn't feel anything yet, but October's were starting to kick in; I could tell because her pupils were beginning to take over her irises. Black and shiny, they looked like little vinyl records spinning in her eyeballs. And there were sharp, weather-bleached branches all over the ground that she thought were animal bones.

We walked a little farther and came upon a creek. That's when I noticed something starting to happen in me because I knew it was water I was looking at, but it didn't *look* like water. It looked like Jell-O. I touched it and swore it felt rubbery and gelatinous like Jell-O too.

Regrettably, I couldn't think of Jell-O without thinking of the day Sam died, and I tried to push "Eject" on that memory before I got sucked down into it. The last thing I wanted to do on this trip was to take a wrong turn. Or worse, to bring October down with me.

I tried to walk away from her because I didn't want her to feel my darkening thoughts, but she was following too close behind, holding onto my arm, imploring me not to leave her alone and whispering that everything looked weird.

I turned around, leaned against a downed tree, and asked October to stay where she was. She stood in place like I'd requested, but in this case she didn't have to touch me to know something was wrong.

"What?" she said, her face changing from amazed to concerned in an instant.

I'd never spoken to her about Sam, but I was on the ride now, and the walls of impassivity I usually hid behind were crumbling.

"The Jell-O," I said, rubbing my face.

"Jell-O?"

"It was my fault."

She tilted her head to the side, and after a good twenty seconds of squinting at my face, she said, "What was your fault?"

"My brother." I started rambling, beginning with how Ingrid and I had been at Tam High to watch Sam's swim meet. "He swam freestyle and butterfly and was good enough that his coach thought he'd be able to get a scholarship if he wanted one."

October's eyebrows rose as if they'd been animated, and the air around her face started to look pink and hazy, like there was a summery filter over it.

"Sam had this prerace ritual of eating raw strawberry Jell-O. He would rip open the packet, lick his finger, dip it in the powder and then lick it off, over and over, until his tongue and teeth were red and he was, as Ingrid used to say, bouncing off the walls."

October reached out for my hand, but I shook my head, pressed my palms hard into my temples.

"Joe—"

"No, just let me talk. Before we left the house that day, Ingrid handed me a packet of Jell-O and asked me to bring it to the meet. I was on the couch playing *Mario Kart* and set the Jell-O to the side. And then I forgot about it."

I moved my palms to my eye sockets, pressed harder, and saw thick swirls of dark green and purple, like paint being splattered on a black canvas. When I lowered my hands, I was sure October had taken a step forward. She seemed too close.

"About thirty minutes before Sam's first event, he rushed over and asked for his Jell-O, but I didn't have it. And he was so pissed at me. He huffed and cursed and stomped his feet. And you know what Ingrid said to him? She said, 'Calm down, sweetheart. It's not the end of the world.' But it was. For him, it was."

October's face was melting into so much waxy softness I had to look above her head to get away from it, and the same dark swirls that had been behind my eyes were now in the sky.

"Joe, what happened?"

"Ingrid gave Sam ten dollars and told him to run to the Safeway across the street to get his Jell-O. Naturally, I begged her to let me go too, because I was twelve and Sam was sixteen, and I wanted to do everything my big brother did. Ingrid told Sam to take me with him, and to get me a snack. I remember I had to stop to tie my shoe and Sam huffed and said, 'Come *on*, Joey. You're such a frickin' turtle.'"

October was still wide-eyed. Her body was twirling side to side as her hands went to her hair, and she began twisting her locks in circles around her fingers.

"I followed after Sam fast as I could, yelling about how I wanted him to get me a Dr Pepper and some Doritos, but he was sprinting by then, not paying any attention. And he was a considerable distance ahead of me when he darted into the street without looking to his left or right." I could feel the tears starting to roll down my face, and they felt automatic, as if someone had flipped a switch and turned on my sorrow. "The driver of the Porsche didn't see Sam until it was too late, but I saw the whole thing unfold from the top of the steps, and watching it was like watching a premonition come to life. What I mean is my point of view was wide enough that I knew the car was going to hit Sam before it did. I even shouted for Sam to look out, but by then the outcome was unchangeable. Sometimes the future gets locked into place and there's nothing we can do about it except feel a powerless sense of regret, you know?"

I glanced down at the ground and swore I could see my tears hitting the dirt like raindrops. When I looked back up at October, I saw tears streaming down her face too, and they seemed to be falling in sync with mine, as if she were a mirror of me.

"Joe—"

"No. *Listen*. I remember the sound of the Porsche's tires screeching and then a loud, dull thud, like a fist hitting a pillow. A second later I watched my brother land on the grassy median that runs through the middle of Miller Avenue." I inhaled, but I couldn't get a deep enough breath. "Almost immediately I remember thinking, *This is all my fault*."

October shook her head. Her face was all twisted up.

"I ran to Sam and pulled on his arm, tried to get him to stand, until someone dragged me away. And I must have passed out then, because the next thing I knew I was lying on the sidewalk with a puffy down jacket under my head, listening to a paramedic tell Ingrid that Sam most likely died instantly. *He didn't suffer*. That's what the guy said. I sat up and saw my mom with her hands over her mouth, making a sound like someone was tearing her limbs off her body. It's a sound I still have nightmares about." I wiped my eyes with the sleeves of my fleece. "A bunch of fucking parents and kids from the swim meet had congregated around by then, and they were all gawking and crying and not minding their business like I thought they should. And you know what? If I had to pinpoint it, I would say that was the exact moment I started to disappear. Everyone was busy trying to help my mom, and as soon as I stood up I walked to Sam's body—he was on a stretcher by then, covered in a plastic sheet next to the ambulance—and I pulled the sheet down to see his face, and despite what the paramedic had said, I was sure Sam had only been knocked unconscious because I didn't see any blood on him, and that made me believe he was going to wake up and make it to Safeway for his Jell-O. It was explained to me later that Sam had been all broken on the inside, but on the outside he looked like a normal, still-living person who might just be taking a nap. After his death I imagined Sam and I had that in common: being all broken on the inside, while appearing to be normal, still-living people."

At this point, my stream of tears had become a violent sobbing. I'd never cried that hard for Sam, and I welcomed the release, imagining years of grief being set free. I could feel the salty sadness melting down my face, and when I was done talking I was lighter, calmer, at peace.

Sam's death lived deep in my body, and I'd never felt peace with regard to losing him. But I felt it then. And it felt real.

October's big, wild pupils were trained on my face, her expression solemn, sympathetic, hyperalert. I was still leaning against the horizontal tree, still keeping her at a distance, but when I got quiet she moved toward me, and I let her fold herself into my arms, let her rest her head in the curve of my neck, buried my face in her hair.

"It's OK," she said. "You're OK."

She placed her palm on my chest and began petting me as if I were made of fur. She leaned on me, and even though she was so small, she felt heavy. We stood like that a long time. Or maybe only a few seconds. Time was a blur. And at first being that close to her was fine. She was my friend and she was comforting me, and that felt safe, appropriate. But then it shifted. Only a fraction, but sometimes a fraction is all it takes to slip the whole world sideways.

Suddenly I was awakened to the heat coming from between her legs, pressing into my thigh. I felt her lips resting against my neck, her eyelashes fluttering across my skin like a paintbrush every time she blinked.

All my senses were alive, and I didn't want to think anymore; I only wanted to feel. I reached up and put my hands in October's hair, and it was fur too. I lifted her face, pressed my forehead into hers, closed my eyes, and in that darkness I saw us connected by thin, fuzzy strings of light that kept wrapping around us in big, electric circles, binding us together. I wasn't completely on psychedelic autopilot though, because I remember struggling *not* to kiss her. And I remember thinking *I don't have to kiss her*, because I was positive it would be just as satisfying to stand there and *inhale* her. My eyes were still closed, and I took long, deep breaths through my nose. And then I thought, *How do I get inside of her? I need to be inside of her.* But I didn't mean fucking. I wanted all of me inside all of her, and I had a notion there might be a zipper somewhere on her body, and if I found it I could climb in and live there for the rest of the night.

When I opened my eyes, I saw thousands of little gnats flying around us. Real ones, not hallucinations. I wanted to shoo them away, but my hands wouldn't move from October's hair.

She rubbed harder against my leg and then caught herself and tried to pull away, but I didn't let her go.

"Joe—"

Gently, I tilted her head up so that I could see her eyes. I didn't think I would be able to hear her talking if I wasn't looking into her eyes.

Her glassy pupils met mine and she said, "Let's go back to the cottage."

I took her hand and we floated up the hill.

Inside, I was paranoid that the gnats from outside were all over us and said, "We need to take a shower."

She nodded, and we dropped our jackets and shirts on the floor by the table, and our jeans and underwear on the bathroom tile. I turned on the shower and we waited by the tub until the water got warm. Once we got in, our hands had minds of their own.

The water didn't feel strange like I thought it would, but October's wet skin did. She was slippery and unctuous like mercury. Her breasts felt bigger in my palms. Her hands on my dick felt like a warm mouth. The stream from the showerhead above us was a waterfall; the soap on our bodies smelled like the wild fennel that grew all over the trails on Mount Tam, and I was sure I had never wanted to fuck a woman more than I wanted to fuck October then.

"We can't," she kept saying.

"I know."

But when we stepped out of the shower, we didn't towel off, we went straight to the living room. October tore the comforter to the floor because she said it was covered in germs, and then she fell across the bed. I pulled her to the edge, got on my knees, and went down on her. And that wasn't something I ever did without being pressured or prompted. It wasn't something I'd ever been comfortable doing. I didn't think I was good at it, and it made me feel feeble and awkward. But in that room I was free, and I still wanted to open October up and crawl inside of her, and I think I figured that was my way in. I swore she tasted like cake batter, and part of me thought it would be a beautiful dream to stay down there all night. But right before she came, she pulled me up so that I was on top of her, took my face in her hands, and said, "Joe, gravity makes perfect sense to me now. I can feel the pull of the Earth on my body. I can feel the weight of my spirit *inside* my body. And it weighs *so much more* than my *physical* body. I understand now. Gravity is Earth's way of keeping our spirits on the ground."

I kissed her then for first time all night, certain there was nothing else happening in the entire world but that kiss. I even said those words to her, to which she replied, "Kissing is art. So is fucking. You need to fuck me."

She opened her legs and pulled me in, and it *did* feel like art. It felt like magic too. And religion. And eternity. And even though I was inside her, I could feel her inside me too.

After we made love, October turned on the room's old clock radio to a station that played mellow classic rock, and the crackly static of terrestrial broadcasting made the music sound even more mawkish than it already was.

We lay in bed, talking, listening, and laughing at everything.

We laughed at the things we saw in the paintings on the wall above the recliners. One was a painting of a mountain range, but I saw a menacing Jesus and October saw a goat man.

"What's a goat man?"

"A man who is half human and half goat, *obviously*."

We laughed.

The other painting was of a wave about to crash onto a beach, and we both swore we saw the wave moving in slow motion, both thought that once it broke onto the shore the recliner was going to get all wet.

Hilarious.

We laughed about the man at the cafe in Willits who used to be a lobster, and how his story all of a sudden seemed plausible.

We got hungry and ate the miniature lemon pie with our hands. I couldn't stop laughing about how good it tasted, and October laughed at me laughing.

We even had a conversation about Cal and the predicament we found ourselves in. On our foggy, drug-induced ride, we both professed our unending love for Cal and came to the conclusion that if he loved us back he would *want* us to be together.

"We need to tell him," October said. "Tomorrow."

I nodded and agreed because at the time it made sense—but so did the idea of a man who was once a lobster.

We kept floating into outer space on the songs, and then we'd come back to Earth, laugh at something else, and float away again.

"You know what I could really go for right now?" I said after I finished the pie.

"A beer."

I nodded.

"Told you."

We laughed.

Almost two hours later we thought we were coming down from the high, only to have another wave hit us. I wanted to be inside October again; she was warm and slippery, and my body was so sensitive I almost had to pull out. But then I lost myself in a vision of us being ancient Egyptians, fucking deep in a pyramid, surrounded by torches, and after I came I was so tired I wasn't sure if we'd just had sex or if I'd hallucinated it.

Minutes later, as I teetered on the edge of sleep, October gasped and said, "Joe!"

I half opened my eyes, but they wouldn't stay that way; words wouldn't come, and I groaned so she knew I was listening.

"I forgot to draw you!"

The radio was playing an old Elton John song, but the last sound I remember hearing before I drifted off into dreamland was the sound of us laughing again.

When I woke up, October was still asleep and I was hungry. I took a quick shower and went to the lobby for the free continental breakfast. The same lady who checked us in the night before was there, wearing a blue short-sleeved shirt with little American flags all over it. She barked "good morning" through a raspy smoker's cough and handed me a tray.

I wasn't sure what October would want to eat, and I piled the tray with random options—two little boxes of cereal, milk, a banana, a cherry Danish, a bagel, two packets of peanut butter, a handful of bacon that I scarfed down on the way back to the room, and two cups of coffee with half-and-half.

My head was all messed up, and I didn't know how I was supposed to act. At first I felt light and alive, still coasting on the euphoria of the night we'd had. But then I made the mistake of looking at my phone while

I waited for the bagel to toast. I had a text from Cal that said: HOW ARE THINGS? HOW'S MY GIRL?

Kill me now, I thought. I was reprehensible, and I wished for bolt of lightning to strike me dead so that I didn't have to face the consequences of what I'd done.

October was in the shower when I got back. I sat on one of the recliners, drank my coffee, ate a banana, and considered walking out to the highway and hitchhiking as far away from there as I could get.

When October came out of the bathroom, her hair was wet, and she was wearing her jeans and a lacy bra that was almost the same color as her skin.

"Hey," I muttered, nodding toward the tray of food.

"Ah. Thank you. I'm starving."

She grabbed a sweater from her bag and slipped it on. Then she smeared peanut butter on half of the bagel and came over to the recliner where I was, even though there was an identical one right next to it. She sat down and nestled in beside me while she ate.

I felt myself freeze up. Went dead inside. I didn't want to be that close to her, and I almost asked her to move to the other chair, but she noticed the other cup of coffee on the tray and got up to get it.

I got up too and relocated to the table, where I poured myself a bowl of cereal and pretended I was reading something on my phone while I ate.

I'm certain it was obvious to October, notwithstanding her *gift*, that I wasn't right that morning. But she seemed uncomfortable too, and when she spoke again, her voice was timid.

"I can't believe I forgot to draw you."

She drank her coffee and finished the bagel, and then she said, "We should head out. I told Rae I'd be home by noon."

I packed up my stuff while she packed up hers, and we walked out, stopping in the lobby to give our room key to the old lady in the American flag shirt.

October wanted to drive, and as she turned onto the highway I leaned my head on the cold, dewy window, closed my eyes, and tried to isolate what I was feeling. The trouble was, I wasn't feeling anything at all. I was numb. But it was the kind of numbness that felt like pain.

Feeling nothing can sometimes hurt like hell.

When we got to Ukiah, October pulled into a gas station and asked me to fill up the tank while she went to the bathroom. It was the first time either of us had spoken since we'd started the drive.

We drove in silence for a little longer, but near Novato, October said, "Are you going to pretend to be asleep the whole way home, or can we talk?"

Here we go, I thought. But I didn't say anything. Once again, I was Mutant Joe.

October tried to touch my hand, but I pulled it away and started playing *Tetris* on my phone.

"Joe, please tell me what's going on in your head."

"Don't you know?" I snapped. "Aren't you a mind reader?"

That agitated her, and she said, "There's no reason to act like an asshole."

"Fine." I tossed my phone onto the dash and rubbed my face. "You want to know what I'm thinking? I'm thinking about the text I got from your boyfriend this morning. He wants to know how you are. What should I tell him? She's a little groggy today, but she seemed great last night when I was eating her out on a cheap motel bed?"

She looked at me and said, "Maybe you should tell him that."

"Jesus Christ, October."

"So, this is about Chris? You're acting like this because of Chris?"

"Don't you feel even a little bit guilty?"

"You know I do. But I thought we decided something last night."

"What did we decide?"

"That we're going to tell him. Today."

"Are you fucking kidding me? We were on drugs last night. We can't tell him."

"We have to. It's the right thing."

"Oh, *now* you want to do the right thing?"

She glared at me, looked back at the road, then at me again. "Come on, Joe. Life is messy sometimes. And I know that what happened last night probably shouldn't have, but it did, and it was incredible, and I'm not sorry about that. Besides, technically we didn't do anything wrong."

"I bet Cal would disagree."

"Well, no one will ever be able to convince me it's wrong to listen to your heart. If Chris were in this situation, I'd want him to do the same thing."

"I wasn't listening to my heart last night, I was listening to my cock."

I'd hoped that would set her back, but she shook her head and said, "No, you weren't."

She tried to touch my hand again, but I wouldn't let her.

"Joe—"

"No. Pay attention to what I'm about to say. This can't happen. And if you know what's good for you, you'll fire me, kick me out, and forget we ever met."

"I have no intention of firing you. You're too good at your job. If you want out, you're going to have to quit." She reached for my phone because hers was in her bag in the back seat.

"What are you doing?"

"Calling Chris."

I grabbed the phone before she did. "Are you still high? You're not calling him! Do you hear me? You're not going to take him away from me!"

She turned her head and looked at me fully, for as long as she could before it became dangerous and she had to look back at the road, and I almost thought she was going to pull over so she could stare at me some more.

The truth of the matter had dawned on her though. "I get it," she said. "For you, this is a choice. It's me or him."

"Yup," I said sharply.

"And you choose him."

I nodded. "I choose him."

I saw that hurt her. Finally. And my numbness had obviously turned to malice, because I distinctly remember feeling victory over that. I had wanted to hurt her. I wanted her to hate me.

For the rest of the way, we drove in silence. And when we pulled in to Mill Valley, I said, "Drop me off at Equator."

She parked across the street from the coffee shop and said, "Don't leave. Please. We need to talk."

I grabbed my backpack from the back seat. Before I got out of the car, I said, "Don't tell him. There's nothing else to talk about."

She glared at me. "You don't get to tell me what to do, Joe. You don't get to be the only one who has a say in what's happening between us."

"There is no *us*!" I shouted. "That's why there's no point in telling him. This is nothing. And if you hurt him for nothing, then you're just cruel."

I got out of the car, walked across the street and into Equator; only then did I look back to see if she'd driven away.

She had.

I didn't order any coffee—too many people in line. I sat at one of the small tables against the wall of windows and waited for the queue to die down. It was a warm, sunny Sunday, and the place was packed. To my left, a mom was cutting up a waffle for her young daughter. To my right, a couple in yoga clothes were discussing their food allergies with the gravity of a United Nations Security Council meeting. A group of guys in cycling gear were loitering out on the sidewalk with little cups of espresso. Everyone talking and snacking and living the lives they wanted to be living, and I was alone.

I took out my phone and sent Cal a text that said: ALL IS WELL HERE. WE MISS YOU, BROTHER.

I saw Rae's car turn the corner and head out of town.

I looked down at my jeans, pressed my thumb onto the black fingerprint above my knee, and imagined October could feel it on her leg.

Pathetic.

SEVENTEEN.

THERE'S A TYPE of spider native to southern Africa. It's called the wheel spider, and it cartwheels away from threatening situations when it senses it's in danger. In fact, it's so adept at getting away from perilous circumstances that it can do almost fifty cartwheels a minute to escape.

I was the human equivalent of the wheel spider, constantly tumbling away from anything that had the potential to hurt me. Because I can talk until I'm blue in the face about how I hadn't wanted to hurt Cal, and that was true, I would have rather cut off my strumming hand than betrayed him again. But I had a hunch that even if October's boyfriend had been a stranger to me, even if she hadn't had a boyfriend at all, I would have made up a dozen other reasons to spin away from her.

Later that afternoon, when I got back to Casa Diez, October was in the yard with Diego, playing the wolfhound version of fetch. Wolfhounds aren't known for their retrieving skills; every now and then Diego would go get the ball if you threw it, but he wouldn't bring it back. He would just hold it in his mouth and circle you in big, gawky gallops, trying to coax you into chasing him for it.

Diego dropped the ball and ran to my side when he saw me, his tail wag like a whip against my leg. October stood still, arms crossed in front of her chest, watching me.

The walk home had made me more lucid. I felt as if I'd been pulled up the driveway by big, heavy thoughts. I went to October wanting to lay them at her feet, but all I could say was "Sorry."

She didn't say anything. She just picked up the ball and threw it toward the garage. Diego followed the ball with his eyes but didn't go after it.

October crossed her arms again, this time higher and more rigidly, as if she were protecting her heart. She stood straight and dignified like the redwoods that surrounded her, like they were all a gang and she was their tiny leader.

"Listen," I sighed. "These last couple of months . . . Moving here . . . Meeting you . . . Reconnecting with Cal . . . It's a lot. And I know that's not an excuse for being an asshole, but that's just who I am."

She shook her head. "That's not all you are."

Diego took a step closer and leaned so heavily into me I had to steady myself to keep my balance.

I said, "I don't want people to get hurt, OK?"

"Oh. *OK*. Well, either you think I have no feelings or you mean you don't want Chris to get hurt."

I shrugged. The truth is, I wasn't thinking about Cal or October. I was thinking about myself. I was thinking, *One day she'll see me for who I really am and she'll crush me*. I was thinking, I *don't want to get hurt*.

She studied me, and her face relaxed and paled, as if it were emptying itself of blood. Then she nodded and said, "I understand." And I believed her, because her eyes were bristling with a sad tenderness I didn't think I deserved.

I turned and started toward my apartment. A moment later she said, "You're going to die someday, you know."

I stopped at the steps and turned back around. Diego's ball was at my feet.

"I know that," I said, gruffer than I'd meant to.

"I'm not sure you do," she said. "Because you live like someone who doesn't understand how quickly all of this is going to be over. You live like someone who doesn't understand how fast the sand moves through the hourglass. You live like someone who doesn't understand how much all these decisions matter. How much your dreams and desires matter. How much your happiness matters. Or maybe you don't care. But I think you do. I think you care so much."

I glanced off into the trees, looking for a retort, for a spark of wisdom I knew lived out there. I thought about the thesis I'd written on Aristotle's notion of happiness, and how Sid used to tell me that it was useless to study philosophy and ethics if you couldn't actually put what you'd learned into practice.

"Before you know it, the majority of your life is going to be behind you," October continued. "Hell, it may already be behind you. And in the end, nothing is going to seem as scary or as painful as the realization that you walked away from everything you ever wanted."

I felt that heavy pull again, a tension in my skin, in my body, in the weight of my feet on the gravel below me. It was like what October had said the night before about gravity being Earth's way of keeping her spirit grounded. Only my spirit felt chained.

"You think you know what I want?" I said.

"I don't know it. I feel it."

I picked up the ball and threw it hard across the yard. Diego didn't flinch.

Without another word, October turned and went into her house. The dog waited, watching for my next move, but he soon turned and went into the house too.

I made it halfway up the steps to my apartment, changed my mind, and went back down to Cal's studio.

I tore off my shoes and threw them against the door. Then I grabbed the '59 Les Paul Standard and spent the rest of the day using it to channel my rage.

EIGHTEEN.

OCTOBER AND I had a demanding week in preparation for the exhibit on Friday. We had no time to talk about anything except work, and that was a relief. But the vibe between us was strained. October was distant, and I was too sheepish to address the situation directly. On Monday morning I offered to make her a cappuccino and she looked at me as if we were strangers, as if it were a preposterous idea that I might fix her a cup of coffee. I kept meeting her eyes, searching for that familiar softness, but what I saw looked like disdain.

I was at the studio until after midnight on Monday, putting the final touches on the birdcage. On Tuesday we did two abbreviated run-throughs, contracting the bars with October inside to be certain the machinery worked smoothly, and to make sure I knew exactly when to stop it so that it didn't crush her.

I'd ended up making the mechanism work by floating the cage over the base and attaching the cage to the base by pegs that sat in tracks. The tracks were embedded into the base of the cage, under the grid so you could barely see them. The tops of the cage bars were connected to a single hinged point, gears and pulleys inside the base drew the pegs toward each

161

other along the tracks, and the hinged point allowed the curved bamboo to straighten toward the ceiling as the bars got closer.

It sounds complicated, but it all worked on a simple system that could be controlled via an app on my phone that was normally used to turn lights on and off in houses.

It took me a couple of tries to get the timing dialed in, but once I did, I felt certain it was ready; I disassembled it for transport the following day.

I spent Wednesday packing everything up with the help of two husky handlers the gallery had sent over. October had her final dress fitting, met with a hair and makeup artist, and ran through the audiovisual portion of the performance on-site.

On Thursday, October, Rae, and I went to the gallery to supervise the installation.

The Thomas Frasier Gallery is a large, pristine, L-shaped building in the SoMa neighborhood of San Francisco. It has high ceilings and walls the color of brand-new teeth, with two gallery spaces inside. The main one was a long, narrow room with a small reception area—the bigger of the two, this was where the paintings and photographs by the other artists were being hung, along with two sculptures set up in the middle. Beyond that room was a hallway that led to a smaller gallery where the cage was being installed.

October was the most prominent artist contributing to the exhibit, and attendance at the party, which included visiting her installation, required a sliding-scale donation starting at 250 dollars.

I worked until early evening to get the cage back together. Once it was secure, Rodney, the gallery's audiovisual engineer, showed me how to connect the equipment to my app so I could start and stop the music and video clips along with everything else. After we got that uploaded, Rae drove October and me home, and while Rae and I chatted about the details of the day, October didn't say a word.

The cocktail reception was set for 6:00 p.m., with October's exhibit commencing at 7:00 and running until 9:00, and the auction ending at 10:00.

That afternoon the gallery sent a car to get October and, by association, me. We both sat in the back seat. And even though October seemed less tense than she had all week, she was still aloof when I tried to speak to her.

"Did you sleep OK last night?" I mumbled.

"I never sleep well before performances," she said, her gaze out the window.

"Have you eaten?" She had a habit of forgetting to eat when she was preoccupied with work. "I can go get you some food when we get to the gallery."

Her phone beeped and she pulled it out of her bag. "That's not your job," she said. "And anyway, there will be food there."

"Right. OK."

I had an urge to scoot over and press against her so that she could feel my frustration, and my affection, but instead I pulled out my phone and busied myself scrolling through the trending topics on Reddit. Meanwhile, October spent the rest of the ride texting with Cal. And I knew it was Cal, because I kept taking furtive glances to my left and saw his name at the top of her screen.

In that moment, I envied Cal. And I remember chuckling a little when it occurred to me that I envied him not because he was a successful musician and I wasn't, but because he was currently commanding October's attention.

We were met at the door by the gallery manager, a tall woman in a white pinstriped suit named Helen Driver. She took us up to the green room—a nice studio apartment a floor above the gallery that they'd set up for October to relax in and prepare. Rae was waiting there, as was October's hair and makeup artist, Shelly. A platter of fancy cheese and crackers had been laid out, along with what I called vegetables but what Rae kept calling "crudités" like she was the Queen of England.

Rae was carrying a clipboard and, on top of that, her usual squirrel food. As I watched her shuffling around, I could see she was in her glory—giving orders, eating dried fruit and nuts, and acting like hers was the world's most stressful job.

More reassuring to me was the bar cart near the couch. No tequila that I could see, but I spotted some top-shelf whiskey and planned on dipping into it prior to the reception.

I had originally planned on avoiding the reception altogether. In my mind the night was going to go like this: I would hang out upstairs until it was time to put October in the cage. Then I would go down and man the cage and not have to talk to anyone. And then I would go home. But Rae informed me that October was going to need some alone time before the performance, and that meant I would have to make myself scarce right around the time the reception was set to begin.

I let out a discernable grumble and October said, "You need to mingle anyway."

"Me? Why do I have to mingle?"

"Joe . . ." She was sitting in a tall chair with her eyes closed and her head tilted up at Shelly, who was applying dark, sparkly shadow on her lids. I wasn't used to seeing her with makeup on and thought she looked like she was wearing a theatrical mask of her own face.

"You built this thing," she said. "You need to talk about it. Toot your horn."

I mumbled something about not having a horn to toot, and she said, "Well, then toot your kazoo. You have to. It's for charity."

I sat on the couch with my arms crossed in front of my chest, and Rae said, "I think he's pouting now."

Moments later, Helen Driver summoned Rae downstairs to finalize the guest list, and she walked out just as Mr. P and his husband, Thomas, walked in. They were well-dressed men, late fifties, and though I'd seen them coming and going around Casa Diez, I'd never officially met them.

They greeted October with air kisses and loud affection. Mr. P was the more handsome of the two. Tan and fit, he looked like an aging surfer, not a Silicon Valley mogul. Thomas was tall and elegant, with smooth, shiny, almost pink skin unnatural to someone his age. He wore round, gold-rimmed glasses, and his teeth were glow-in-the-dark white like the walls of the gallery.

Thomas was carrying a small black vase filled with yellow lupine wildflowers. He held it up in front of October and said, "From Christopher."

He set the vase on the table and handed October the card that went along with it, but she didn't read it because Shelly told her to close her eyes.

Seeing the flowers from Cal reinforced my belief that I wasn't good enough for October. If I were half the man she seemed to think I was, I would have been considerate enough to send her a vase of native wildflowers and a card too.

Neither Mr. P nor Thomas noticed me slumped over on the couch until October pointed her thumb in my direction and said, "Guys, this is Joe." She paused, and then added, "My assistant." I stood up just as she said, "Joe, meet Phil Pearlman and Thomas Frasier." Only then did I realize that Mr. P's husband was Thomas Frasier, the gallery owner.

When October said my name, their eyes widened, and when they shook my hand, it was with a suspicious amount of interest.

"Well, *hello* . . ." Mr. P said.

"We've heard *so* much about you," Thomas added.

These were two of October's closest friends. I knew by the tones of their voices that she'd told them what had happened between us, and I didn't know whether to be flattered or humiliated.

"Joe doesn't want to go to the cocktail party," October said. "Will you guys take him downstairs and keep him company?"

"Of course," Thomas promised, slipping his arm through mine. "You're a cutie, aren't you?"

I blushed, and Thomas said, "Look, he's blushing."

"Mr. Pearlman," I said, trying to deflect the attention. "Have you seen the birdcage?"

"Oh, sweetie, call me Phil. And no. I'm waiting for the big reveal."

"*I* saw it!" Thomas exclaimed. "It's ex*cep*tional."

Rae came back with the clipboard still in her hands and her snacks still on top.

"Good god with your trail mix," Phil said to her. "There's smoked Gouda, *jamón*, and Marcona almonds over there, and you're eating bird shit."

Rae was all business. "Ten minutes, and you guys have to clear the room."

Thomas leaned down toward my ear and mumbled "bossy bitch" under his breath, and I couldn't help but laugh.

In preparation for our exodus down to the party, I went to the bar cart and poured myself a double shot of whiskey. Phil saw what I was doing and said, "Make it two, Joey."

I handed him the drink and fixed another one for myself.

Phil raised his glass and said, "To brilliant women. And the men who put them in cages."

I mumbled, "To art."

Shelly was in the middle of applying mascara to October's eyelashes, but October managed to look over at me when I said that.

The whiskey never kicked in. No doubt I appeared aloof and composed to everyone around me. That's my superhero skill in life. But inside I was a basket case. I wanted the exhibit to be a success. I wanted to fit in. I wanted

October's friends and colleagues to like me. And I wanted the mechanics of the cage to function without issue. All of that, combined with a roomful of strangers I assumed knew more about art than I did, triggered fear, anxiety, and feelings of inadequacy rooted so deep in me I wished I could summon the numb, checked-out Joe Harper to represent me for the night.

Downstairs, people were starting to arrive. Many were from the tech world, Phil told me: young, obscenely paid, and dressed like kindergarteners. Lots of colorful hoodies, sneakers, and slouchy jeans. I had on black pants and the black striped shirt I'd bought for Cal's dinner party and felt overdressed.

"They look like they don't have pots to piss in," Phil said, "but they'll pay thousands for these pieces, just watch."

Thomas and Phil seemed to know many of the guests, and they introduced me to a handful, including the woman who ran the organization for which we were raising money. Her name was Julia, and she told me I was the spitting image of an actor from a TV show on HBO. When she walked away, Thomas claimed she had been flirting with me.

Thomas led me around the gallery, telling me about all the other pieces being auctioned off. Two in particular moved me. One was by a striking, livewire of a woman from Seattle named Jennifer, who became wide-eyed and animated when Phil told her I worked with October—I thought it said a lot about Phil that he used the word "with" as opposed to "for."

Jennifer told me she was a fan of October's work and asked me rapid-fire questions about the birdcage. She was outgoing and cool, and her piece was cool too—a large-scale square panel made of wax, paint, and gold leaf on wood, with a round, celestial form in the middle of the square. When I narrowed my eyes hard at it, I felt as if I were looking at deep space and the light of the moon, or a portal into a distant, dreamy galaxy. There seemed to be as much hidden underneath as there was on the surface, and I could relate to that.

The other piece that caught my attention was a wall hanging made of dark ropes knotted together and then hung on polished walnut rods in an intricate pattern of lines and curves that, depending on where I stood, reminded me of a guitar or a woman's body.

I overheard two young women gossiping about who October's boyfriend was. One even asked Thomas if Chris Callahan was going to be at the reception, and she asked it in a tone that made me think it was the reason she'd come. Thomas told the girl he didn't know, even though he did.

Cal had actually texted me a few days earlier to say he'd looked into making it home for the event, but he had a show in Berlin on Wednesday and one in Amsterdam on Saturday, and even if he'd chartered a plane, he said getting back to the Netherlands in time would have been impossible.

BUMMED I CAN'T BE THERE.

I'M SURE YOU TWO WILL KILL IT.

GOOD LUCK AND SEND ME A PIC OF MY GIRL.

Fifteen minutes before the installation opened, Rae shuffled over with Rodney at her side and said it was time for me to go get October.

The hallway to the stairs had been roped off, and a bearded behemoth of a man in a suit was standing guard. Big, shaggy, and gray, he looked like a hostile, human version of Diego. And even though he'd seen me come down earlier with Thomas and Phil, he stopped me from going up until Rae said, "He's OK. He's going to get Ms. Danko."

Shelly was tying October into her dress when I walked into the room. I caught a quick flash of October's bare back and left breast and darted back out, but October laughed and said, "Come in, Joe. You've seen boobs before."

I stepped into the room but stared at the carpet until she was dressed. Once she was, she walked toward me with her arms out to the sides as if she were about to take a bow.

"Well?" she said.

She looked stunning. Like a raven that had been turned into a woman. Her gown was to the floor and made of dark feathers that sounded like whispers when she walked. The feathers looked black from a distance, but when she got closer, I could see nuances to the color—reflective, iridescent hints of gold and green and blue, like a real bird. The top of the dress was sleeveless and tied around October's neck. It covered her torso but was open in the back. Her feet were bare. Her hair was big and wild. Looking at her made my chest feel like it was filling up with water.

"You're a vision," I said.

I took out my phone to snap a photo, and when I told her it was by request for Cal, she posed with her lips pursed like she was going to kiss the camera; that made me feel jealous and sad again.

"Ready?" I asked.

"One more thing." She handed me a thick, black Sharpie and asked me to write "CHOICE" on her exposed back. "All the way across. Big and clear."

I pressed my left palm against her skin, to steady my writing hand so I could print clearly, but also so I could talk to her without speaking. And maybe it worked, because once I took my hand away, she looked at me with more compassion than she had all week and said, "If it makes you feel any better, I'm nervous too."

"You are?"

She nodded, and I wondered if she'd gleaned anything else in my touch. The sadness. The frustration. The longing.

I escorted October slowly down the stairs, one hand on her arm, the other on her back, while Shelly held up the back of the dress.

At the door to the gallery, October asked Shelly, Rae, and Rodney to wait in the hallway. I stood off to the side, expecting to wait too, but she said, "You come with me."

We walked in and stood side by side in front of the cage, both of us looking up at it and then around the room. All week long, October had been keeping her distance from me, but she broke character there, hooked her arm through mine, sighed, and said, "You know, this one belongs to you even more than it belongs to me."

I shook my head. "It was your idea. All I did was build it."

"But you built it with your whole heart and soul. It's a real work of art, Joe. I hope you recognize that. And I hope you know how much I appreciate it." She didn't take my hand so much as she slipped her fingers around the tips of my fingers and tentatively grasped them. And her voice quivered when she said, "I'm happy we made this together. I'm happy you're here with me tonight. I'm happy we get to offer this creation of ours to the world. And no matter what the future holds, I'll always remember this moment with you."

I swallowed hard and felt a rush of gratitude toward her, for trusting me to create the piece, and for believing I could. There was the pride I took in the creation itself, which felt as meaningful to me as it did to her. And above all that, I had the sense that I, too, would remember the moment.

For a long time it weighed on me that I didn't articulate any of that to her when I had the chance. I didn't, for fear it would cut me open, expose my insides. But she had my fingers the whole time, and I like to think she knew.

"OK. Time to lock me up."

I helped her step inside. "I never thought to ask, but what are you going to do in there for two hours?"

"I don't know." She shrugged wistfully. "I never know. That's part of the fun."

She told me to go get the others. Shelly scurried in first, futzed with October's hair one last time, and pronounced her good to go.

I shut and locked the door. Then I opened the app on my phone, made sure the bars, lights, and audiovisual devices were all detected, and signaled to Rodney that we were ready.

Rae gave Helen a thumbs-up, and Helen removed the ropes.

The lights blinked in the main gallery to indicate the performance was about to commence, and people began entering the room.

October nodded, and I pushed "Play."

Nobody but Rodney had been allowed to see the visuals before the performance. October wanted her team to experience the installation in real time as much as possible. Films played on all three walls of the gallery, and they were provocative and disturbing—an in-your-face mishmash of statistics, social media messages, graphic photography, and video clips of everything from suffragette protests erupting in violence to botched back-alley abortions. In juxtaposition, the velvety voice of Leontyne Price, one of the first female African-American opera singers, blared from speakers hanging in the corners of the room.

I tried to focus on the gradual movement of the bars, but it was hard to take my eyes off October's mesmerizing performance. At first she was inert, resigned to being locked up. Then she seemed to notice she was trapped and began trying to escape subtly. Then not so subtly. She pulled at the bars as they steadily closed in on her. She looked frightened as the cage narrowed. She opened her mouth to scream but nothing came out, only the sound of Leontyne's tortured arias. She wrestled with her dress, and feathers blew around the cage. She pounded and collapsed onto the grate. She curled up into a ball and cried, and her eye makeup ran down her face like black wax.

At some point she accidentally cut her arm on what must have been a loose nail—my bad—and blood dripped in an abstract, Pollock-like splatter all over the *New York Times* wallpaper.

The gallery was packed, and the audience was captivated. Most guests stared and gawked. A handful of people cried along with October. A few jaded jerks laughed and rolled their eyes, but nobody was bored.

Two hours went by in a blink and without any technical difficulties, and by the end I expected October to be as exhausted as I was, but as she sat on the grate, hugging her knees into her chest, unable to move, she looked wired.

October had done with her body what I tried to do with the guitar. She used it to speak a language that all humanity, if they were listening, could understand. It was beautiful, but it touched a nerve in me. I couldn't put my finger on why right away, but something about the type of freedom she was exploring made me hyper-cognizant of the ways in which I held myself back.

There was more. I believed I knew October fairly well by then, and, yes, she was extraordinary, but she could also be vulnerable, complicated, awkward, and full of contradictions. I saw all of those qualities in her performance. I saw her humanness. What set her apart from most humans I knew was that she used those qualities to her advantage. She turned the dark and mundane into the poetic and magical.

That, I thought, *is what it means to be an artist of life.*

I didn't perceive or understand this distinction when I was a kid. Cal was the closest thing to an artist that I knew, and in my eyes he was smarter, stronger, more enlightened than I was. He was unlimited. Single-minded. Special. That's what I thought you *had* to be in order to be an artist, and that made it impossible for me to accept myself as one, because I didn't see myself as a person with any exceptional qualities. Sure, I was a good guitar player, but that was a skill, something I'd learned through thousands of hours of practice. I didn't connect it to my character or my destiny. I didn't see it as the kite that lifted my spirit out of the dirt and off the ground.

Except that it *was*.

For so long I'd assumed I was too ordinary, too mortal, too pusillanimous to be who and what I wanted to be. What I learned from watching October was that it was exactly those prosaic human qualities, expressed in authenticity, that people connected to. Art isn't about people who are better than us showing us how much better they are, it's about being reminded of the ways in which we are all the same.

I read a line in a novel once that stuck with me. It said, "People, for some stupid reason, think they can escape their sorrows." And if I learned anything from my work with October, it's that there are two ways in which one *can* escape his or her sorrows.

Art and love.

By the end of October's performance, I was fixated on the notion of *what could have been* and questioning whether cowardice was revocable.

Back when Cal was still trying to get me to join him in Brooklyn, he'd written me an e-mail that had haunted me for a long time. It said: *The thing is, Harp, everyone is always one decision away from a completely different life.*

I never responded to that e-mail. In fact, after Cal sent it to me, I didn't speak to him again until the morning he walked into October's kitchen.

Once the visuals faded, the lights went out and the music continued at a much lower volume while the crowd filed out and back into the larger gallery for more drinks. Only then did October give me the go-ahead to set her free.

She held onto my arm to steady herself, and we followed Rae and Shelly back upstairs. The green room was now full of people, and they all clapped when we entered.

October seemed uncomfortable and overwhelmed by the applause, and she went straight into the bathroom. I walked to the bar cart and poured myself another whiskey. When I turned around, Rae was there. And she was smiling.

"Great job, Joe. Well done. Really."

It was the first genuinely nice thing she'd ever said to me, and I appreciated it. I mumbled a sincere "thank you" and offered her some whiskey, but she shook her head and said, "I'm driving you guys home, yeah?"

Soon, Phil rushed into the room. "That was luminous!" He threw his arm around my back. "You two make a great team! I hope this is just the beginning of a lot more collaborations!"

Is that what October and I are doing? I wondered. *Collaborating?*

October came out of the bathroom in a black slip dress with a big, camel-colored cardigan over it. Her sleeves were pushed up above her elbows and I could see a bandage on her forearm from where she'd cut herself in the cage.

She slid into a pair of sexy snakeskin boots, looked my way, and sighed. "We have to go downstairs and mingle before the auction ends."

She'd twisted her hair up into a messy bun and wiped the dark eye makeup off her cheeks as best she could, but Shelly came over and said, "Lordy, let me touch you up before you go meet and greet."

Thomas sauntered in, brimming with excitement, and announced that the top bid on the birdcage was currently at fifty grand.

Everyone cheered again, and while Shelly was fixing October's makeup, October's phone rang and she answered it. She and Shelly had stepped into the kitchen so I couldn't make out what she was saying, but she looked sweet and animated as she spoke, and when she walked back into the room, she came straight to me and said, "Chris says congrats and thanks for the pic."

I maintained a neutral expression, but I didn't feel neutral. I felt like I was suffering the loss of something monumental.

Let her go, I thought.

My head believed that, but the little muscle in my chest was tense and tight as we shuffled down the steps to the main gallery, where the crowd still lingered, everyone waiting for a chance to meet October.

People swarmed her, and she gripped my arm, whispering, "Please don't leave my side." Then she started introducing me to everyone as the artist who built the cage. Strangers lauded my work and treated me like I was important, and while I tried with all my might to appreciate that, I remained too caught up in my own confusion to relax.

Phil pushed his way through the crowd, holding two glasses of champagne above his head. When he reached October and me, he handed each of us one. I didn't want it, but I took it and then set it down on the table behind me. Across the room, Thomas raised his glass, made a toast praising October and all the other participating artists, including me, and then he thanked the guests for their generosity.

Having so many people touching and talking at October wore her down quicker than the performance had. Before long she was snapping the elastic hair band on her wrist and staring at her shoes, and Rae went to get the car.

The three of us were quiet on the drive home. October rested her head against the window; I was behind her, so I couldn't see her face, but as we turned onto Lombard Street, I heard her sniffling in a way that made me think she might be crying. Rae glanced at me but didn't say anything, and when we were stopped at a red light, she picked up her phone and sent me a text that said:

GETS EMOTIONAL AFTER PERFORMANCES.

DON'T WORRY SHE'S FINE.

I wanted to reach up and rest my hand on October's shoulder, to comfort her and let her know I was there, but I refrained because I felt Rae and I had turned a corner that night, and I didn't want to take any steps backward with her.

Instead I wrote Cal a long text. I told him about how great the night had gone and how amazing October had been and how much one of the guests paid for the cage.

I should have left it at that, but ever since the drive into the city that afternoon, I'd been wondering where things stood between October and Cal, and I typed:

HOW'S IT GOING WITH YOU TWO ANYWAY? BETTER?

We were just getting off the bridge when his response came through.

HARD TO GET HER TO TALK.

STILL FEELS OFF.

NOT LETTING HER GO WITHOUT A FIGHT THO.

I sent him back the thumbs-up emoji and put away my phone.

As we passed the Sausalito exit that used to take me to Bob's houseboat, I thought about my father and wondered what he would have thought if he'd been at the gallery that night.

He wouldn't have understood the performance, that's for sure. But there was a part of me that wished he could have seen it anyway, wished he could have heard all the people praising my work.

It didn't escape me that this was work I only knew how to do because of him. And I like to think he would have been proud of me. But if I knew Bob Harper like I thought I did, it's more likely he would have deemed the whole thing a complete waste of wood, nails, and ingenuity.

NINETEEN.

I'D BEEN KEEPING a file of words. I'd started the list after October asked me what my favorite word was because I hadn't had an answer for her then. But after that, whenever I came across a great one, I typed it up in my phone with the intention of sharing it with her at some point.

When we pulled into Casa Diez, October thanked me for doing such a great job on the project, but she said it in the aloof, I'm-pretending-you've-never-been-inside-of-me voice she'd been using with me all week. Then she got out of the car and headed toward her house carrying the little yellow flower arrangement Cal had sent her.

Rae followed October to the door, lugging a big garment bag with October's dress. I offered to carry that for her, but she said she was fine, and I was left staring at my hands.

I waited for one of them to invite me in, but they bade me good night, and I went back to my apartment.

Just like that, the evening was over.

I felt too wired to go to bed but too drained to play guitar. I picked up the novel I was in the middle of reading and went to the couch, hoping the book might lull me to sleep.

The red taillights of Rae's car flickered across my wall, and I sat up and watched her drive off. A moment later I saw October open the front door and let Diego outside. She stood on the porch under a soft amber light with her big cardigan still on, watching the dog. The night had turned chilly, and she held the sweater tightly across her chest.

Diego peed for nineteen seconds—I counted—and headed inside. October followed him, ruffling the scruff on his neck.

I moved from the couch to the bed and lay down, the unopened book now resting on my stomach. I stared at the dank wooden planks on the ceiling. All different shades and lengths, some had big knots in them, some didn't, and the mismatched colors and sizes looked cheap and amateurish. This was a pet peeve of mine back when I built houses: when the wood was chosen and installed with no thought to art or design. I used to hand select the boards so that the ceiling looked meticulous and streamlined, which took a lot of time and drove Bob insane, but the clients appreciated it.

I replayed the night in my head, looking for an answer to the question that had been bothering me. Namely, the performance had gone better than I could have imagined, so why had it left me so unsettled?

I thought on it long and hard, and when that yielded no explanations, I changed tactics. I dug inside my body instead of inside my head. I tried to *feel* instead of *think* the answer.

And then it hit me. And it was so obvious. The whole thing—the resignation, the imprisonment, the rage, the grief—it was about me. No, not *about* me, it *was* me. Sure, October was expressing the themes of the show, and the visual portion of the piece convinced the viewers of that. But where her performance was coming from, the motivation, the depth and truth she was expressing, was calculatedly directed at me.

I was the one in the cage.

I was the one whose walls were closing in on him.

And the most jarring point of all?

I'd built it myself.

When October said the piece belonged to me even more than to her, she wasn't kidding. She had been talking to me all along, and what she had been saying was that the decisions I'd made in my life had locked me into a confining, diminishing, unbearable space from which I couldn't escape without a key.

And what was the key?

I'd written it on her back.

It was the same thing Cal had tried to tell me over a decade earlier.

Everyone is always one decision away from a completely different life.

175

One decision.

Or, in my case, about fifteen yards.

I got up off the bed and paced around the room. My heart pounded. My breath fell short. I thought I was angry. I had an urge to kick a hole through the wall. Scream in October's face about how my choices were none of her fucking business. And then I realized it wasn't anger I was feeling, it was fear.

Something shook inside me. Shook me to the edge of a place I'd never been. I looked over that edge, and it was as dark as a pool of thick, black paint, and I couldn't tell how far down it went, but I knew I had to step into it.

I felt as though the choice I had to make was between staying in a burning building or leaping out the window before the fire caught me. I would go up in flames if I didn't jump, but if I did, there was a fifty-fifty chance I'd hit the ground and shatter to pieces.

I needed a nudge.

No, I needed a fucking shove.

"Sam."

I sat back down on the bed, dropped my head into my hands, and asked my brother for help. And I swore I would listen this time, if he would just tell me what to do, if he would make it so obvious I couldn't second-guess him even if I tried.

The book I was reading had fallen to the floor and I picked it up. A decades-old novel by a Portuguese writer, I'd checked it out of the library because the blurb on the inside flap said it was about the existential nature of loneliness and chance, and that sounded right up my alley.

I told Sam the plan: I was going to close my eyes and open the book to a random page, and I was going to point to a passage on that page, and then I was going to open my eyes and read the passage, and the passage was going to tell me what to do.

I took note of the page I was on and removed the receipt from Mill Valley Market that I was using as my bookmark. I closed my eyes and turned page after page until my gut told me to stop. I ran my finger up and down the paper, lifted my finger, put it back down and decided I was ready to look.

I opened my eyes. My finger was resting on the middle of a paragraph in a chapter I'd read a couple of nights earlier.

Before I even studied the passage, I knew it was going to be significant because there was a word in it that I hadn't known when I read it the first time, and I'd lightly circled it in pencil so I could look it up. Once I did, I was so taken with the word that I added it to the list I was saving to show October.

The passage went like this:

Each morning I go out with my tea and I check on the fig tree and I think, Do what you want, my dear, but only if it means going back to the house, only if it keeps the fear of saudade close and even closer than that, do you hear me?

There was no equivalent to the word "*saudade*" in the English language, but the translation I found defined it as "a deep emotional state of nostalgic or profound longing for an absent something or someone that one loves." It went on to explain that *saudade* was sometimes described as "a nostalgia for something that never was."

I don't remember walking out the door, down the steps, or across the yard. I only remember that when I got to October's house I walked in without knocking and found her in the kitchen making a grilled cheese sandwich. She'd showered; I could tell because her hair looked like a wet rope hanging over her shoulder. And she'd changed into a pair of sweatpants and a loose, silky tank top. Her back was to me, and I could see the tops of the letters I'd written there, a little faded but still legible.

CHOICE.

The sound of the door startled her. She spun around and her hand went to her heart. "Jesus, Joe. You scared me."

Diego moseyed over from the living room floor and nuzzled up beside me, wagging his baseball-bat tail.

"I can't stop thinking about you," I blurted.

She tilted her head to the side, her face a rictus of expressions I couldn't discern.

"I've tried and I can't. It's like you turned on some faucet in me and I have no way to turn it off."

I thought for once that I might surprise her, but she didn't look surprised. She looked cautious. She shut off the burner, moved the skillet to the adjacent burner, and leaned back, her hands behind her on the counter like she was going to hop up onto it.

Fear began to rise in me, starting at my feet and filling up my body, as if I'd stepped into a pool of it.

"Say something," I mumbled.

"I'm trying to figure out what I'm supposed to do with this information. Because I'm assuming that's all it is. Information."

I took a step forward and noticed her face was pale and shiny, her eyes red from scrubbing off all the makeup.

"I know what you're thinking," I said. "I'm open and available now, but come tomorrow I'm going to turn back into the cold, asshole Joe that makes up a bunch of excuses or changes his mind, but I'm not. This is different. I can feel it. Tell me you can feel it."

She said nothing, and her silence lingered like a stranger hiding behind a door—I didn't know if it was benevolent or menacing. She turned back to the stove and used a spatula to lift the sandwich out of the skillet. She sliced the sandwich in half on the diagonal, put it on a plate, and handed it to me.

"You don't want it?"

"I'll make another one." She nodded toward the table. "Sit."

I went and sat down, and the silence resumed while Diego and I watched her make another sandwich. She was slow and careful buttering the bread and slicing two different kinds of cheese, and it took forever. When she finished, she cut her sandwich in half and put it on a plate too. Then she poured us both glasses from a half-empty bottle of Chianti.

She placed the wine bottle in the middle of the table, along with a couple of napkins, and sat across from me. The little yellow flower arrangement from Cal was on the table too, directly between us like a blooming "Yield" sign. I moved it out of the way.

I watched her and she watched me. She had a funny way of eating her sandwich. Instead of biting it like normal, she tore pieces off and put them in her mouth the way a person would eat a croissant. But sometimes she would have to pull the entire length of her arm because the cheese was all melted and gooey and wouldn't break off, and when that happened, she chuckled quietly.

After we both finished our sandwiches and were sipping our wine, I said, "The performance tonight. The cage. What was it really about?"

She smirked like she knew exactly what I was asking her and said, "The beauty of art is that it can be about whatever you want it to be about."

She poured the rest of the wine into my glass.

"Come over here," I said. "I want to show you something."

I pulled out my phone and waited while she took a sip of her wine, wiped her hands on her napkin, and moved to the chair beside me.

"Remember when you asked me what my favorite word was?"

She nodded, setting her elbow on the table, her chin in her palm, a small smile still flickering on her face.

"I've been keeping a list," I told her.

She pulled her chair closer and leaned against me so she could see over my shoulder. I could smell the clean, coconut scent of her shampoo, could feel her warm, Chianti-laced breath on my cheek.

I tapped the NOTES icon on my phone, opened the file titled "WORDS" and slid the phone over to her.

She slid the phone back and said, "Read them to me."

"*Saudade*" was at the top because it was the last one I'd entered. After I told her what it meant, she said, "That's breathtaking."

I didn't tell her it came from a passage that was part of the numinous impetus for why I was sitting in her house. That was a good story, but it was a story for another time. And that night I believed another time would someday come.

The next word was "*Koi No Yokan*." I felt shy reading its definition aloud. "It's Japanese. Loosely translated, it's the sense one can have upon first meeting a person that you're going to fall in love with each other."

"*Koi No Yokan*," she whispered, looking down at the table and, with her index finger, making an invisible drawing on my napkin. "I know that feeling."

The third word was "adamantine." "It just means "unbreakable." No biggie. But I like the way it falls off the tongue like a melody."

I scrolled to the next word. She saw it and said, "'*Cafuné*.' I know that one."

I pulled the phone toward my chest so she couldn't read the definition. "What does it mean, smarty pants?"

Another Portuguese term I'd come across in the same book, it was the word for tenderly running your hand through your lover's hair. But October didn't *say* what it meant. She reached up and acted it out, and goosebumps sprang up all over my arms.

"This last one's my favorite." I showed her the word because I didn't know how to pronounce it: *mamihlapinatapai*.

She laughed. "That's not a word, it's an alphabet."

"It's real, I swear. Indigenous to South America."

"What does it mean?"

"It's the shared look between two people who want the same thing but are reluctant to initiate it."

She looked right at me and didn't blink when she said, "I wonder if there's a word for when one person is less reluctant than the other."

I wasn't sure if she was referring to me or to herself in that instance, but the space between us was getting smaller, thicker, and as lush as the forest grass that grew in big patches behind the house.

October took my hand and held it between both of hers, the way she had the day we met. Then she nodded and said, "I can feel it."

Something relaxed inside of me then. I put my free hand on her face and moved in to kiss her, but she pulled back, got up, and stepped away. Pointing at my phone, she said, "If you really mean what you're saying, we need to call Chris right now and tell him what's going on. Otherwise you can't be here."

It would be morning in Amsterdam. I imagined calling Cal and waking him to tell him—what? That I was in love with his girlfriend? That she was in love with me? Was she? I tried to picture his face when he heard me say the words, the various possible reactions he might have, all of them catastrophic.

I'm not letting her go without a fight, he'd said.

I stood up and walked into the living room, and October followed.

I paced, rubbing my face. "Fuck."

"Not an ideal situation. I get it," October said. "But we have to tell him."

"I know. But fuck," I said again. "Can I just think this through for a minute?"

She sat on the couch while I continued to amble back and forth, trying to figure out how we could tell Cal the truth and cause him the least amount of pain. October's eyes followed me like I was a metronome she was using to keep time.

I sat down beside her and let my head fall into my hands. "He's going to hate me."

"Maybe not forever." I felt her eyes on the side of my face. "Trust me, Chris knows that what he and I are doing isn't working. He has to be able to see the inevitable end in sight. With or without you thrown into the mix."

But I doubted Cal knew that. It wasn't how his mind worked. When he wanted something, he went after it, and he got it; and if something was broken, he fixed it. Failure was not a conceivable outcome for him.

A memory came back to me then. The first time I brought Cal over to Bob's houseboat. We had only known each other for a few weeks, but we were already blood brothers. It was a Friday night, Bob had gone out, and

Cal started snooping around the house, looking for a way we could entertain ourselves in the absence of guitars. He found a couple of fishing poles in a storage closet. I have no idea why Bob had them, because I'd never known him to fish or express even a vague interest in fishing. At any rate, Cal got it in his head that fishing was simple and that it would be fun for us to catch our dinner off the side of the boat, never mind that neither of us had ever fished, nor did we know the first thing about what to do with a fish if we managed to catch one.

Cal asked me what I thought we should use as bait. I looked in the refrigerator and decided hotdogs were our best option. We both stabbed big chunks through our hooks and went out to the deck.

Cal said, "It's all in the wrist, Harp," like he knew what he was talking about, even though he'd only heard that on TV.

I flicked my rod backward with the intention of casting it out into the water, but the hotdog-heavy hook went left and caught Cal somewhere near his right eye.

With a howl, he dropped his rod, leaned over, and clutched the side of his face. A moment later he started making this *aahhh* noise that sounded like what precedes the *choo* in a sneeze. I couldn't see the damage I'd done, but a little blood dripped down his fingers, and I had a vision of Cal taking his hand away and there being nothing but an empty socket where his eyeball had been.

Over and over I asked Cal if he was all right, begging him to let me see his eye, but he just kept making that noise. When he finally straightened up, I realized it wasn't because I'd blinded him, it was because he was laughing so hard he couldn't form words.

Once he composed himself, he ran to the nearest bathroom and examined his wound in the mirror. I'd missed his eye by a hair, and the hook had carved a tiny but deep gash into the skin right below his lower lid that you can still see today if you look close enough.

"Nice job," he said. "That's *definitely* going to leave a scar."

We retold the story to each other from our individual points of view a dozen times over the next few hours, and Cal's version got gorier and gorier as the night went on. Right before we fell asleep, he asked me what had been going through my mind when I thought I'd taken out his eye, and I told him all I could think was that if I'd blinded him, he wasn't going to hang out with me anymore.

It was dark and quiet, Cal in the twin bed next to mine, a small bedside table between us, but I knew he was shaking his head because I could hear the sound of his hair pulling and swishing against the crisp pillowcase.

"Harp, we signed a contract, remember? It says we're best friends, and best friendship is bound by commitment, code, and honor. There's nothing you could do to make me not hang out with you anymore."

"*Nothing?*" I said in disbelief. "Come on, there has to be *something*."

He thought about it and said, "I guess if you stole my girlfriend. I mean, if I *had* a girlfriend, and you stole her, then I might hate you."

"Well, that's fine, because I would never do that."

"Obviously," he said.

"Obviously."

October was still waiting for me to make the call.

"Here's what I think," I said. "Now is not the right time to tell him."

"Joe—"

"No, just hear me out, OK? He's gone for what? Another month? He tells me every few days how much he's looking forward to the show at the Greek. It's a big deal for him to play it, and it's a big deal for him to share it with me. And, to be honest, it's a big deal for me to share it with him. For once, I'd like to not let him down."

October rested her head on my shoulder and sighed.

"And what difference does it make if we tell him now or when he's back?" I asked. "It's the same information, and it's not going to go over well, no matter what. If we wait, we can do it in person. And we won't ruin his big homecoming. I feel like I owe him that."

I meant every word I said to October that night. As difficult as I knew it was going to be, I had no intention of bailing on her when the time came to confess to Cal. But the situation was a lot like vowing to go to Brooklyn back when I was a kid. As an idea, it seemed utterly possible. But ideas live in very specific futures, and not all futures arrive.

"I know you're not going to like what I'm about to say," I mumbled. "But waiting until he gets home also gives you time to change your mind."

"I'm not going to change my mind," October said.

"Yeah, well, it's possible you might. And in this scenario, no harm, no foul if you do."

I was too tired to mull it any longer. I stretched out on the couch, pulled October down beside me, and for a while we were lost in our own thoughts. I ran my finger up and down her arm in a figure-eight pattern around the bandage that was still there, and she was quiet, but I could feel her ribcage moving in and out with her breath.

After a few minutes she said, "OK."

"OK?"

"We can wait until he gets home. But you need to give me your word, Joe. You need to promise me that immediately after the show, we'll sit him down and tell him. I'm going to trust you on this."

Like I said, I had absolutely no intention of bailing on her.

I lifted her hand, kissed her palm, and said, "I promise."

We fell asleep there. And hours later, as daylight was just starting to outline the trees and the sky to the east looked like it had been tie-dyed, a deep tangerine fading to apricot, I awoke in a fog and imagined a scenario in which Cal was in the house, looming over us on the couch. Only, in my imagination he was a giant, as tall as a redwood, his body stretched so that it appeared to narrow as it rose up three hundred feet high.

From above, Cal surveyed us, livid and bereft. And I tried to experience his reaction to finding his girlfriend in my arms, pictured him pulling me to the floor, beating me to a pulp, and telling me what a shit I was.

Then I thought, *no*. That's not what he would do at all. And I imagined him glaring at me with pity, laughing. Crazy madman laughter like a mental patient as he knelt down beside October and tapped her on the shoulder until she opened her eyes. Once she did, he leaned in toward her face and said, "Just so you know, Harp doesn't keep his promises."

TWENTY.

"ARISTOTLE'S NOTION OF HAPPINESS," Sid said. "Go."

We were sitting at the little round table in his office, on the second floor of Moses Hall, near the Campanile on the Berkeley campus, a pot of Folgers on a trivet between us, discussing my thesis.

"Well, first of all," I said, "Aristotle's notion of happiness isn't what most people think of when they ponder what it means to be happy. Most people confuse happiness with pleasure, but for Aristotle, happiness was the supreme value and goal of one's life and couldn't be divorced from whether or not one had reached his or her full human potential."

"Meaning?"

"Given those parameters, it's impossible to assess if one has lived a happy life until one's life is over."

"And?"

"And, I strongly disagree with Aristotle on this point."

It was one of the central arguments of my thesis. My position, essentially, was: What's the point of assessing happiness *after* the fact, when it's too late to do anything about it? Postscript happiness wasn't happiness at all. Maybe it was contentment. Maybe it was proof of a well-lived life. But it was not the fundamental definition of the concept.

184

Back then, when Sid and I were formulating my outline, he suggested that I first define happiness; consider how that definition was relevant to one's choices, values, and pursuits; and then compare that to what Aristotle had laid out in *Nicomachean Ethics*.

The questions I'd wanted to explore were: What is *real happiness*? "Real happiness" being the term I used to distinguish the concept from pleasure. And once I had that figured out: Is a human being *obligated* to pursue real happiness? If so, is he or she obligated to pursue it under *any* circumstance?

I thought long and hard about these questions and concluded that there were a handful of obstacles to real happiness, the two worth mentioning now being fear and a lack of freedom.

And while Sid supported my assessment, he also suggested, in his gentle Sid manner, that if I wanted my work to mean anything beyond a piece of paper, I was going to have to learn how to encode what I was writing somewhere inside of me and use it as a GPS.

"The truth is," Sid sighed, "you're very good at burying your head in your books and having intellectual conversations about all this stuff until you're blue in the face, but you don't practice what you know to be true."

He was right, but it still hurt to hear him say it. Or, rather, it hurt that he could so easily recognize this defect in me. He saw the hurt on my face too, saw me begin to retreat inside myself, but he didn't back down. He knew me too well to let me get away with that.

"You need to hear this, Joe. You happen to be unusually self-aware, and that means you have an obligation to live truthfully, specifically because you're cognizant of what the truth is. It's not too late for you, you know. Because what's the alternative? To continue like you have been and suffer the consequences? Isn't that what you've been doing? Suffering the consequences?"

There was a small stack of papers on the table, and Sid set his palm down on top of it, as if he were trying to keep it from blowing away in a breeze. He looked at me with his kind, sleepy eyes and said, "There's no such thing as inaction, Joe. There's only choice and consequence. Do I need to remind you of what you so interestingly outlined in your conclusion?"

I shrugged, hoping he would get the hint and drop it.

Pointing his finger in the direction of my heart, he said, "You concluded that happiness *is* a consequence of choice."

I mention that conversation because it speaks to where my head and heart were the morning I woke up beside October on the couch.

She was still asleep. Diego was following me around the kitchen, so I fed him and took him for a short walk on the trail behind the house. After we got back I stopped at my apartment; the dog stayed on my heels, dropping with a thud to the floor outside my bathroom, where he waited while I took a shower.

By the time Diego and I returned to the house, October had moved from the couch to the bed, and I crept into her room to see if she was awake.

She heard me come in, rolled over, and, through half-closed eyes, smiled and said, "Yay. You're back."

My chest swelled with it then. *Real happiness.* And it feels important to make this distinction: I'm not talking about pleasure or desire, or romantic love disguised as happiness. Though I felt those things too. But there was something bigger, deeper, and truer swathing everything that morning, that day, and for the majority of the weeks preceding Cal's return. A state of grace often foreign to me. *Happiness as a consequence of choice.*

Don't get me wrong, I was still scared shitless. But the fear wasn't holding me back. I wasn't dwelling on the past, I was worried only moderately about the future, and most of all I wasn't numbly trudging half-awake through some mediocre semblance of a life. I was present, and not just as a bystander but as a passionate participant.

"Joe," October said groggily. "I need me some Joe."

I straddled her on the bed but she pushed and slapped at my chest. "No. I need a *cup* of Joe, not a cup of *Joe*." She laughed at her joke and playfully demanded I go make her a cappuccino.

I leaned down close to her face and said, "You're not the boss of me." Then I laughed at *my* joke, adding, "Oh, wait. You are."

I drifted back into the kitchen to make the cappuccinos. This was a process, and I took my time with it. I had to fill the fancy Italian machine with water and wait for it to heat up. I had to grind the beans. And once the machine was hot enough, I had to pull the espresso shots individually, emptying and refilling the portafilter each time and waiting in between each shot for the machine to heat up again.

I pulled four shots, poured two into one mug and two into another. Next I steamed the milk, poured that into the mugs, and carefully spooned the foam on top like I used to do at Caffe Strada.

The whole time I was making the cappuccinos, I could feel myself grinning, and I remember thinking: This is art. This is love. It's simple and I get it. I can do this. And way back in a usually quiescent part of my mind, I heard a voice say: *You gave up so much for so long. You're not going to do that anymore.*

Not even the guilt I had over what I was doing behind Cal's back daunted me then. I had reasoned it all out in my head to justify the situation. Cal will be fine, I decided. He has women at his beck and call. He doesn't need a life here with October, because he has everything he's ever wanted.

Let me have this one thing, I thought.

The rest of that day remains lodged in my mind like an indelible song. Each moment is a note, and if I conjure up the first one, the whole tune comes back to me: what the day looked like, what it tasted like, what it smelled like, what it felt like. My skin was alive, and it transcribed every feeling in a way that went deeper than memory. Memories are fragments. Unreliable. This was an experience that seemed to exist inside of me before it happened, and it remained inside of me when it was over. In my heart and behind my eyes I can still see it, not as bits and pieces, but as a whole composition.

Here's another important distinction: I felt entirely myself that day. And I don't mean my best self. I don't mean I was pretending to be some ideal version of Joe Harper so that October wouldn't change her mind. I was the same awkward, insecure, overly sensitive Joe Harper that I've been for as long as I can remember. But the other Joe showed up too. The man who can be thoughtful, witty, and charming when he gets his head out of his ass.

I kicked off my sneakers, and October and I sat against the headboard drinking our cappuccinos. The window was open, and a light breeze was blowing into the room. Our legs were parallel, my right one touching

October's left as we watched a gray warbler foraging on a branch outside. The bird's little head moved in quick, jerky tics like the second hand on an old watch, its beak a tiny jackhammer.

"Do you think he's looking for breakfast?" October whispered, as if her voice might scare the creature off.

"He is a she," I told her. "The males have black throats. See how hers is a whitish gray?"

October dipped her head toward me and smirked. "It turns me on when you talk like the Audubon Society."

I smiled. Bob Harper was good for something.

The late-morning sun was starting to flood the room, and even though the breeze was cool, I felt warm and content, the scene calling to mind an old Johnny Cash quote I'd read somewhere online. Johnny had been asked to describe his idea of paradise. He'd pointed to his wife, June, and said, "This morning. With her. Having coffee."

This is simple, and I get it, I thought again. Then I put my hand on October's thigh and left it there for as long as it took for her to get it too.

Eventually she set her mug on the bedside table, spun her body sideways, and rested her head in my lap.

"I want to tell you something," she said quietly. There was a pause, like she was searching for the words. "I want you to know why I'm so drawn to you. And why I think this is important enough to go through what we're going to have to go through to be together."

I slid my hand into hers and said, "OK."

"It's something I feel when I'm with you, that I don't feel with anyone else. Chris says I'm always so busy noticing everyone else's feelings that I ignore my own, and maybe he's right. I don't have a lot of friends that I confide in, and it's never been easy for me to get close to people. But I wanted to be close to you the moment we met. I feel all this deep, creative energy when I'm with you, and it makes me want to explore things and express things that I've never had the courage to explore or express. Am I making sense?"

As usual, her words at once softened and baffled me. "Yes."

"In a way, I guess what I'm saying is that you inspire me. And you feel like home."

I let go of her hand, stroked her hair, and she whispered, "*Cafuné.*"

She picked at the frayed hem of my cargo shorts. The warbler outside the window was singing now, her song full of sweet, buzzy "Z" notes.

"There's a magnitude to all of this," October said. "That's what you're feeling. The magnitude of moving through life without any idea how or when this is going to end but embracing it anyway."

I let her words sink in. "Are you saying you think this is going to end?"

She flipped onto her back and looked up at me. "I'm saying that I'm scared too. But we're here now, and that's all that matters. And I'll tell you something else." She put her index finger to my chest and drew what I'm pretty sure was a heart. "I think that love lives in a space inside of us that never ends. That's why it's the ultimate art project. Because while a book, a painting, a song, a piece of pottery, a tree can outlive us, none of those things will exist forever. But love is an energy. It's infinite. So, no. Regardless of where you and I end up, I don't think this is ever going to end."

We didn't do anything out of the ordinary that day. After we finished our coffee we made love, and it was slow and intense. I melted into October, she clung to me, we whispered and laughed, and it was as if our closeness, not the act itself, was where our pleasure came from. I almost never had sex like that. So out of my head. So present.

When we got out of bed we were hungry, and October wanted to have a picnic, but the contents of her fridge were meager. She had milk, bread, cheese, anchovies, and Luxardo cherries. All I had was beer, chocolate milk, and tequila.

We went to the farmers' market in San Rafael and got two big bags of groceries. Predictably, once we got home, October wouldn't let me help her cook. But she did give me the task of scrubbing a bag of red potatoes and washing the lettuce. Though when she saw me rinsing the heads under the faucet, she laughed and said that wasn't the best way to wash lettuce; she showed me how to break the leaves apart and swish them around in big bowls of water until all the bugs and grit sank to the bottom.

I opened a bottle of Pinot Noir and we drank it over the course of the afternoon while October poached the potatoes, sous-vided chicken thighs, and made a salad.

At some point I found a Truth or Dare game in the junk drawer in the kitchen. The game looked like a deck of cards, but one side of each card had a truth question on it and the other side a dare. I told October that if she wasn't going to let me cook, she had to play the game with me. I shuffled the cards, picked one, and said, "Truth or dare?"

"Truth." She was working on the salad dressing, using a marble mortar and pestle to mash garlic and anchovies.

I flipped to the truth side of the card. "Name a memory from childhood that you're ashamed of."

"Ugh. Sissy Brown," she said instantly. "Sissy lived on my street in eighth grade. We were the same age and rode the bus to school together. And when I tell you Sissy was mean, I mean she bullied everyone. There was a handicapped boy in our class named Ricardo whom she called Retardo. She made fun of my best friend Delia's mom for being overweight. And she'd dubbed me Demon Girl, for obvious reasons. Anyway, she always sat in the back of the bus, and Delia and I sat a few rows in front. One day after school, Delia and I are sharing a Kit-Kat just as the bus is approaching Sissy's stop. Sissy walks up the aisle, sees the Kit-Kat in Delia's hand, and says, 'You're going to be as fat as your mom.' Then she leans over me and makes an *oink-oink* sound in Delia's face." October paused to crack an egg, separate the yolk, and toss the eggshell into the compost bin on her counter. "Something in me snapped, and as Sissy was walking by I put my leg out and tripped her. She went down with a thud, and all the stuff in her book bag spilled all over the floor—pens, papers, notebooks, and gum went everywhere. The entire bus cheered while Sissy scrambled to pick up her things. And at first I felt cool and justified. But then Sissy stood up and looked back at me. She was crying, her face was all red and wet, and her hair was sticking to the tears on her cheeks. We made eye contact and I felt—I don't know—her insides, I guess—the part of her life I didn't know anything about. A barrage of sadness, loneliness, and neglect; I immediately understood why she wasn't nice to anyone. Because nobody was nice to her."

"Don't tell me you befriended her and turned her life around."

She shook her head. "She moved away a couple of months later and I never saw her again. But that was over twenty years ago, and I still feel horrible about tripping her, and for never telling her I was sorry."

I ate a strawberry from one of the cartons we bought at the market. "If it makes you feel better, I was a lonely, neglected kid, and I wasn't mean."

October wiped her hands on a dishtowel, took a sip of her wine, and pecked me on the nose. "You have a good heart, Joe. I know you don't always think so, but you do."

She whisked olive oil into the egg yolk, and I picked another card. "Truth or dare?"

"Truth," she said again.

"Excluding your current occupation, what's the longest you've ever held a job?"

"For three years I worked as a massage therapist in college. But it's my turn to ask you."

I shook my head. "Nope. If I can't cook, you can't ask questions. Hold on, though. You were a massage therapist? How?"

She gave me a look. "What do you mean? With my hands."

"No, I mean, how could you touch people all day, with, you know, your gift?"

"That's why I did it. To hone my gift. I used to ask my clients to fill out a questionnaire about their emotional state before I worked on them, and once I finished the massage I would read their responses, to see how close I was. That's how I got good at it."

"This is very enlightening." I picked another card, October once again chose truth, and I huffed. "The whole reason I'm playing is so I can make you eat a dog biscuit or force you to prank call Rae and ask her if her refrigerator is running. Come on. Pick 'dare.'"

"I happen to think it's more daring to tell the truth than it is to eat a dog biscuit."

"Of course you do," I said. "And I'll let you off the hook, but only because I want to know the answer to this next question." I ate another strawberry and said, "Name a nonsexual act that you find erotic."

"That's easy. Painting my lover's toenails."

Intrigued, I raised my brow and tried to imagine if that would turn me on. "No one has ever painted my toenails."

"Duly noted."

She put the chicken, potatoes, and salad in individual glass containers; stacked them in a picnic basket with plates, cloth napkins, and cutlery; and asked me to take it all outside and set it up while she got dressed. She was wearing jeans and a T-shirt, and I didn't know why she had to change, but she said, "This is not proper picnic attire."

I took the basket to the small patch of lawn in the yard. Then I went and got the camping blanket from my bed and spread it out. I also brought an extra blanket, a pillow, a couple books, and my guitar.

October came out in a floral-patterned sundress, the flowers on it reminding me of the starry mariposa lilies that Bob, Sam, and I used to go looking for on Ring Mountain in Tiburon, the only place in the world where they grow.

She walked over, surveyed my setup, and said, "Nicely done, sir." Diego came loping out, and she made him lie down on the side of the blanket opposite the food.

We spent the rest of the day there, not doing much of anything. October read to me from Patti Smith's *Just Kids* while I lay on my back, petted the dog, and watched clouds rolling by. We talked about our plans for the holidays. I told October I normally spent Christmas in Dallas with Ingrid and her husband, Jim. October said she would be spending Thanksgiving in Rochester with her parents and asked if I would consider coming along. When it started to get dark, she wrapped herself in the extra blanket, and I played Dylan songs until my fingers got too cold to move.

Back inside, we sipped tequila and ate strawberries while October meticulously, flawlessly painted tiny animals on my four biggest toes: a blue bird, a pink rabbit, a black spider, and a red ladybug.

Being the recipient of October's unremitting focus, and the sensation of the paintbrush on my toes, did indeed turn me on. "So, this is how you seduce men?" I said. "You paint their toenails?"

"Yep," she laughed. "Works every time."

Once her work was complete, she moved the paint and brushes aside, rose up onto her knees, gently splayed my legs apart, and kissed me with her eyes open. "Whatever you do," she whispered, "don't move your feet until the paint dries."

She unbuttoned my jeans and pulled them to my calves, making sure to roll them up at the hems so they were out of harm's way of my toes. Then she went down on me, and almost immediately I started laughing. I don't even know why. I guess, looking back, I was just so happy. I felt like everything in the universe was miraculously in alignment, and the only way I knew how to acknowledge the full epic-ness of that perfection was to laugh.

October laughed too, like she could feel what I was feeling, and the vibrations coming from her throat added another layer of joy to my joy. When I came, it was like an explosion of that joy surged upward from my cock to my heart.

After she finished, she pulled my jeans back up, wiped her mouth with the back of her hand, and said, "Told you. Works every time."

Lightly, she touched all four of my painted toes in the order that she'd painted them and, surmising that they were sufficiently dry, sprayed them with a varnish that smelled like the stain I used to apply to exterior wood when I built houses. It ended up keeping the minuscule masterpieces on for so long, I eventually had to go to a nail salon in Whitefish and have them professionally removed because it became too heartbreaking to keep looking at them.

I was buzzed when I got into October's bed that night, and I tend to think too much when I'm buzzed. The closet door was open, and from where I lay I could see Cal's clothes hanging on the left side, his jeans color-coordinated from dark to light, his shirts on matching mahogany hangers, and for the first time all day I felt the weight of fear and guilt like bricks on my chest.

October walked into the closet, slipped out of her dress, and got into bed facing me. To avoid thinking of Cal, I told her about the mariposa lilies in Tiburon, how rare and beautiful they are, and how I thought it would be cool to use them in a selfie when they bloomed in the spring.

And in fact, she ended up doing just that. Months after I left California, she went to Tiburon and filmed a selfie in the little field up on Ring Mountain where the lilies grow. In the clip, she's wrapped in the camping blanket from my bed, holding an empty bottle of tequila in which she'd inserted a mariposa lily.

The clip ends with her setting the bottle in the dirt, dousing it with lighter fluid, then dropping a match and watching the little flower burn.

We'd only been in bed for a minute or so when October said, "Something's bothering you."

The day had been golden, and I didn't want it to end with a conversation about Cal or my shitty self-doubt. I shook my head and said, "It's nothing." Then I repeated what she'd said to me earlier: "We're here now, and that's all that matters."

I remember the exact expression on her face then. An openness so wide and filled with so much faith, it seemed more like blinding recklessness.

The woman believed too much in me.

She believed too much in everything.

TWENTY-ONE.

IT RAINED THE DAY before Cal's show at the Greek Theater. I remember because October and I were out on the Coastal Trail at Lands End, a park set along the craggy coastline in San Francisco with stunning postcard views of the Pacific Ocean to the west and the Golden Gate Bridge to the east.

We were location scouting for a selfie we intended to shoot the following week. It had been sunny when we left Mill Valley, and I hadn't anticipated so drastic a change in the weather, but thick, spongy clouds quickly moved in; the drizzle and wind cut right through the flannel shirt I had on, and within minutes I was damp and cold.

The plan as October had explained it was for me to film her as she walked naked through the labyrinth out on Eagle's Point. She was going to have sharp maces hanging from ropes tied around each of her wrists like macabre, medieval bracelets, dangling and slicing up her legs as she moved.

I hated the idea and tried to talk her out of it. When that didn't work, I asked her what the motivation was.

"I'm about to hurt someone very badly," she said. "I want to hurt too."

We figured we would get one take before someone called the cops to report a naked, bloody woman in the labyrinth, so we needed to plan the shot carefully. I was mapping out the camera's path when my phone rang.

I pulled it from my pocket and raindrops misted the screen as if from a spray bottle, blurring Cal's name.

I told October I'd be back and stepped off the trail to take the call.

"Yo," Cal said.

"Hey."

He was calling to say he would be landing at Oakland Airport the following morning and wanted to know if I would pick him up and take him to the venue.

"This way we can hang out all day," he reasoned.

I paused, guarded, unsure of how to respond, and Cal said, "Harp, you still there?" as if maybe the phone had cut out.

I turned around and watched October picking things up in the center of the labyrinth—talismans, rocks, crystals, notes people had left there. She was looking at me, holding up a folded piece of paper, pointing to it, but I was too far away to see what it was.

"Harp?" Cal repeated.

"Sorry, yeah. We're over at Eagle's Point. I can barely hear you."

I wasn't sure I was going to be able to act normal around Cal, and I knew it was a betrayal on top of an already inexcusable betrayal to agree to spend the day with him, given that I'd been having an affair with his girlfriend for the last month. But here's the rub: I wanted to spend the day with him. I wanted to pretend, for twenty-four more hours, that he and I were still best friends and brothers. I wanted to see what his life was like on tour. And more than anything, I wanted to watch him perform in front of eighty-five hundred people.

"Text me your flight info," I said.

Before we hung up, I asked Cal if he expected me to bring October. He sighed and said, "Nah, bro. I need to talk through some stuff before I see her. I need to pick your brain. She's going to come over later with Rae."

Earlier that year a strong winter storm had toppled half a dozen redwoods in Muir Woods, and a group of rangers had set up audio recording equipment in and around the park to capture the sounds. Imagine a distinct, cacophonous creaking, like a giant door to the sky with a squeaky hinge, and then a loud, sweeping crash, the final thud actually a symphony of thudding, because a skyscraper tree doesn't fall in isolation. It catches other branches and trees, often dragging down whatever its weight can raze.

That's the soundtrack I heard in my head throughout my last day in California. I was a rotten redwood, weak enough for the wind to knock me over. But instead of falling by myself, I was going to take my friends—the ones whose roots were helping to keep me stable—down too.

The night before the show I slept in my apartment. It was the first time I'd stayed there in weeks, but I had an asinine notion that if I didn't, Cal would be able to smell the bed, his pillow, his girlfriend on me, and I wanted to delay the inevitable for as long as I could.

Before I left that morning, I stopped by the house to see October. I made cappuccinos, and we drank them in heavy silence. I couldn't look at her, and she wouldn't stop looking at me. She didn't think it was a good idea for me to pick up Cal, but I told her it was important to me, and she let it go.

I was rinsing out my mug when she said, "I forgot to show you something yesterday." She handed me her phone, open to a photo album. "It didn't seem right to take it from the dirt, but I snapped a few shots."

The pictures were of the folded piece of paper she'd found in the middle of the labyrinth, the one she'd been pointing out to me. On the front, someone had written: *READ THIS*. The note inside said: *I miss you more than you know, my brother. But every day I feel your energy and hope you feel mine. I love you and do my best to help. One day you'll find the strength to make right all that you've wronged. One day you'll understand.*

"What the fuck," I mumbled, shaken.

"Maybe it's a sign."

Of course it was a sign. But if I've learned anything from Sam, it's that signs are only helpful if you have the guts to follow them.

October tried to put her arms around me, but I stepped away and said, "I have to go."

As I turned to leave, she said, "Joe, everything's going to be all right."

I nodded, but by then I was already starting to doubt it.

I got to the airport absurdly early and had to wait in the cell phone lot for more than thirty minutes before Cal texted to say he was walking off the plane. Much like the day before, the weather was cool, damp, and gray, and as I pulled up to the curb I had to turn on my wipers in order to spot Cal when he came out.

He exited through the sliding glass doors carrying a small leather duffle bag with shiny silver hardware, and he made a beeline for my truck, ducking into the passenger's seat headfirst like a linebacker about to make a tackle. Right away he thanked me for picking him up, his face dewy from the few seconds he'd been outside.

"That's all the luggage you have? You've been gone for months."

"Most of my stuff is on the bus. Band and crew drove up from San Diego after last night's show."

As I headed toward the freeway, I could feel Cal peering at the side of my face. He shook his head, laughed, and said, "It still trips me out to see you all grown up."

I tried to think of something to say, but my head was a clogged drain, all my words clumps of hair in the pipes, and I thought, *I was mute when Cal and I started our friendship, and it looks like I'll be mute the day it ends.*

Cal was in a talkative mood and didn't notice. And he had October on the brain. He reclined his seat, rubbed his face, and said, "It's been a long month, bro. She and I have barely spoken. I call her and instead of calling back she *texts.* It's bullshit. I mean where is she that she can't *talk* to me?"

It wasn't a rhetorical question. He looked to me for an answer.

"I don't know what to tell you, Cal."

"Fuck. I know." He fiddled with the radio, couldn't find anything he wanted to listen to, and shut it off with a smack. "Has she said *anything* about what's going on with us?" But then he waved me off. "Forget it. It's not like she's going to tell *you.* She knows where your loyalty lies."

Stupidly, guiltily, I mumbled, "I think she's looking forward to the show tonight."

"Yeah, well, I'm more worried about after the show," he said. "I finally got her on the phone last night, but she wouldn't answer any of my questions and I lost my shit with her. Outright asked her if she was seeing someone, and you know what she said?"

My body stiffened. I knew October had spoken to Cal the night before, but she'd gone outside to talk, and when she came back in, I didn't ask her what they'd talked about.

I kept my eyes on the back of the Tesla in front of me. Its license plate read "0PECL0L."

"She said, 'We'll discuss everything after the show.' That was it. No denial, no protests, no calling me crazy or paranoid. I didn't even get a lecture about our stupid fucking free love." He turned the radio back on. "I know she can be private as fuck, but you see her almost every day. Have you noticed *anything* that might be worth mentioning?"

My mouth felt like it was stuffed with newspaper. I shook my head. "Sorry."

"Don't be sorry. It's not your fault. It's *my* fault. Trust me, I've been thinking about this *a lot*, and I'm ready for whatever she's going to throw at me tonight." He turned his torso and head my way. "The thing is, all the issues October has with me, with our relationship, she's *right*."

I looked at him for a second. His resolve seemed inexorable.

"I can't expect her to sit around waiting for me while I'm gallivanting all over the world, doing whatever I want to do, with whoever I want to do it with. Did you know that when she and I first started dating, she toured Europe with me for three months?"

I did not know that.

"She turned it into one of her art projects. Photographed the empty venues during soundcheck, in every city we went to, and then she hand-sewed song lyrics onto the photographs. Showed the work at a gallery in London. It was a big hit. Back then she wanted to work *and* be with me. She was committed to it. To us. And you know what? I've never reciprocated that." Cal started opening and shutting the AC register on his side of the truck. "It was the best three months of our relationship. But have I ever been there for her? No. *Obviously* she's going to get bored and lonely. How can I blame her for that? I have no right to be mad at her if she *is* seeing someone. I just want it to stop. I want to move forward. I want another chance."

"What are you saying? That you're going to give up your career so she doesn't break up with you?"

"Of course not. And she wouldn't want that. But I've been on the road more often than not for a decade. It would do me good to chill for a while." Cal took off his jacket and moved his hands around like a conductor while he talked. "This is my plan. I'm going to vow to take a year off. I'm going to end this free love nonsense. Really commit to this relationship. And I'm going to participate in her life. I'm going to *do* shit with her. Shit *she* likes to do, like hiking and going to museums and the farmers' market—she always wants me to go to the fucking farmers' market with her, and I never do. You know, even when I took her to Big Sur I was on the phone most of the time, working. And how about taking her out for a romantic dinner once in a while? How hard does that sound? It sounds like fucking heaven, and I don't know why I haven't been doing it. I'm an asshole." Cal turned the AC on low. "So yeah, that's my plan. I'm going to show up and give her what she needs, and she's going to forget about whatever fucking fuckhead she's messing around with, because whoever he is, he can't give her what I can give her. That much I know." Cal nodded like he had it all figured out. "I'm not going to screw this up."

He stared at me, waiting.

"What?" I mumbled.

"Do you think I'll be able to convince her to give me another chance?"

This much *I* knew: Cal has a way of talking that makes people believe him. His confidence and resolve are so solid that if he told me he was going to steal a planet from the sky and leave it on October's doorstep the next morning, I would have expected to see Jupiter waiting for her when she woke up.

"Earth to Harp?"

I was watching the road but not really seeing it. "Yeah," I said with heartbroken honesty. "I think it's entirely possible you will."

Per Cal's instructions, once I got to the Greek Theater I followed the signs to the Foothill parking lot directly above the venue. A young kid in a yellow UC Berkeley rain jacket was standing guard, making sure no unauthorized vehicles pulled in. He checked my name off a list, gave me a parking pass, and told me to make sure it was visible on my dashboard.

Cal's tour manager, Wyatt, was waiting for us in the lot. He handed me a laminated All Access pass on a lanyard and gave Cal a rundown of the day's schedule. Soundcheck at 3. Doors at 6:30. Opener at 7:30. Callahan at 9. And an end-of-tour party after the show. I wondered how that was going to fit into October's plan to come clean with Cal.

Wyatt was a jovial, teddy bear of a guy in a Seattle Seahawks jersey and, despite the iffy weather, flip-flops. His long, dark gray hair was pulled back into a coarse ponytail that looked like steel wool. And instead of shaking my hand he gave me a big, back-cracking hug and said, "Any brother of Chris's is a brother of mine."

Walking into the venue from the top of the hill, we could see the Bay Bridge and the cityscape of San Francisco in the distance. And just behind the theater was Campanile, the bell tower on campus, looming above all the other buildings in Berkeley. The window of Sid's old office was visible a few streets away, as was the dorm where I'd lived freshman year.

I pointed out the dorm to Cal, and he wanted to know what it had been like to live there, as if it were an exotic experience compared to his adventures in New York. He listened while I gave him the dull rundown, and he asked specific, funny questions: *Was there a cafeteria in the building? Were the bathrooms coed? Did you have a curfew? Did you sleep with a lot of girls?* Then he wondered aloud why the massive gap in our friendship didn't make us strangers, but before I had a chance to ponder that, he said, "Because we aren't strangers. We're brothers."

"You know, for as long as I lived in Berkeley," I told him, "I've never been to the Greek Theater."

"Me neither."

We walked through the gate together, and the rush of tenderness I felt for him in that moment was suffocating, like a hand over my mouth.

Wyatt escorted us in through the back so that Cal could see the stage from the farthest point. The theater, built in the Greek Revival architectural style, is a near replica of the one in Epidaurus, and it feels historic and holy, like an ancient ruin in the middle of a city, the kind of place where Aristotle might have given lectures about how to live up to one's potential as a human.

"It's gonna sound epic in here tonight," Wyatt said.

We walked down the steep cement bleachers and climbed onto the stage. A couple of roadies had just unrolled a big Persian rug, and another was setting up the drum kit. Cal stopped to introduce me to his guitar tech, a good-looking African-American kid, Justin, who was so skinny he looked flat from the side, like a piece of paper, his thick, sphere-shaped afro the only dimension noticeable.

I turned around and scanned the empty venue. "What does it feel like? Standing up here during a show, knowing all the people out there are here to see you?"

Cal didn't answer. He just gave me a wily grin and shrugged.

Wyatt walked us backstage, where big oak trees were strung with bright blue strands of lights, colored paper lanterns hung from wires that dangled over couches and chairs, and a big bar was being set up in the corner.

We followed Wyatt down a flight of stairs and into a long hallway that ran underneath the stage. He pointed out the bathrooms and showers, the band's green room, and a separate room that said "CHRIS/PRIVATE" on the door. That room had a couch, a wall-mounted TV, and a minifridge filled with snacks and drinks.

Wyatt told us the catering was ready and took us to a large rec room where a copious buffet was set up.

Cal and I got in line and filled our plates with poached salmon, steak, mashed potatoes, and salad. I grabbed a beer, Cal grabbed a bottle of water, and we sat at a round table with the sound engineer, a British guy named Simon, who looked like a young Steven Spielberg and showed us pictures of his two miniature schnauzers while we ate.

After lunch we went back to Cal's private room to hang out until it was time for him to soundcheck.

"I have something for you," Cal said, rummaging through his duffle bag.

He pulled out a moleskin notebook and shuffled through it until he located a photo stuck between the pages. "Found it when I was in Brooklyn a couple weeks ago." He handed me the photo. "In a box of stuff my mom saved from high school."

It was the two of us, taken during an open mic performance at the old Sweetwater. Cal and I were sitting on stools, sort of turned toward each other, guitars in our laps and smiles on our faces. On the back, Terry had written: *Blood Brothers July 1996.*

For a moment I was transported back to that performance, to a time when Brooklyn was still a possibility and *what could have been* wasn't as concrete as the cinderblock walls of the room we were in.

"Wonderwall," I mumbled.

"Right! That was the night we played 'Wonderwall'!"

"Bonnie Raitt was there. Remember?"

Cal nodded, smiling. "She told you that you played guitar like a boss, and your face was red for an hour."

I felt like I was blushing again just thinking about it. "She was hot. I couldn't even say thank you to her."

"Yo, I saw her at the Whole Foods on Miller last year. She's almost seventy, and she's still hot."

I sat on the couch and stared at the photo. "Jesus. We look like babies."

"We were babies." Cal grabbed a bottle of unopened whiskey from the minibar and sat down beside me. "I don't normally imbibe before shows, but this is a special occasion." He took a drink right from the bottle, handed it to me, and we passed it back and forth a few times.

"Harp," he said, once we were both on the verge of being buzzed. "I need to say something to you." He turned slightly toward me, and I dreaded whatever he was about to reveal. "I want you to know that *I* know I wouldn't be playing here tonight if it wasn't for you."

"What?" I shook my head. "That's ridiculous."

"No, it's not." His eyes were trained on my face, full of sincere effulgence. "You were the *only* person besides my mom who believed in me. From day one." He rubbed the stubble on his chin, bit the inside of his cheek. "I was a stupid kid with no father, no friends, and a bad haircut, but for some reason you thought I was cool, and that made all the difference."

"You were cool. You didn't need me for that."

"Actually, I did." Cal's brow rose and I noticed three sharp wrinkles in his forehead, saw the small scar under his eye from where I'd caught him with the fishing hook. "I don't think you ever realized how alone I was back then. You came along and made me part of your family, dysfunctional as it was. And after that I didn't have to give a fuck about anyone else, because I knew you had my back. That was a fucking gift." He leaned forward and set his elbows on his knees. "Harp, I wouldn't be playing here tonight if I hadn't run into you on the trail that day. I know that for a fact. And I guess I just want to say thank you. I've missed having you in my life. And I'm really glad you're here."

Cal stood up quickly, grabbed his wallet from his duffle bag. "One more thing and then I'll shut up." He slipped a piece of paper out from the billfold and handed it to me. "It's obviously not the original. I made a copy for you."

The paper had been folded in half twice, but as soon as I had it partway opened I knew what it was. I recognized Cal's handwriting and could see my fourteen-year-old-kid signature alongside his at the bottom.

I felt myself getting choked up. "I can't believe you still have this."

It was the contract he'd written up the day we met.

To who it may concern. This agreement herebye states that Cal Callahan and Joseph Harper are band mates and best friends for life. Our band will be called _____ (to be determine). We will be the bosses of it and no body will ever tell us what to do or what kind of music to make. We promise to practice every day. We promise the band will always come first. Girls second. We promise never to do anything to screw up the band or our friendship. As soon as we sign this nothing will break this bond NOTHING. Forever in truth and music.

x *Joseph Robert Harper*   x *Christopher J Callahan*

I sat on that couch in the Greek Theater, holding the contract, looking up at Cal and thinking, *I can't do it. I can't.*

TWENTY-TWO.

WHEN I THINK about the Whitefish Community Library, the first thing that comes to mind is the color green. The tables are green, the chairs are green, the air ducts in the ceiling are green. And more often than not, Patty the librarian's pants were green too.

I often spent Monday afternoons at the library, not only to check my e-mail but also to work on weekly writing assignments. Sid offers a free writing workshop for veterans at the community center in town—he believes in using creative writing to help men and women heal from PTSD—and even though I wasn't a vet, or much of a writer, he'd insisted I sign up for the workshop. To process my shit.

"Do it as a favor to me," he'd suggested, once it was clear I wasn't leaving Montana anytime soon. "And if that doesn't work, we'll call it your rent."

Sid said everyone is fighting his or her own personal war, and he thought that if I put my thoughts to paper I might learn something crucial about myself and find the courage I needed to go back to California.

Every week we were given a theme and encouraged to explore that theme any way we saw fit—essays, poems, stories, you name it. There was a woman in the class who could draw cartoons really well, and she turned the themes into comic strips. Another guy was obsessed with cartography, and all of his assignments looked like treasure maps.

During REGRET week, I decided to write about the night of Cal's show at the Greek Theater.

It was early summer in Whitefish, late in the day, but the sun was still saturating my little corner of the library, casting a bright yellow light over all the green in the room, the colors echoing the canola fields that pop up all over the Flathead Valley in June.

I'd been sitting in my usual chair, with my usual book about trees as my desk, trying to capture the details of that night before Patty the librarian, in her peach-colored cardigan and camo pants, came over and said, "Wrap it up, Mr. Harper. We're closing in ten minutes."

But I didn't know how to wrap it up. Was it enough to say I was a coward and I walked away? Or did I need to include all the gory details?

When I thought about how that night unfolded, my chest was vibratile in its reminiscence, as if the cilia in my airways were clinging to the memories of that night, trying to hold them back, to sweep them away from my lungs, to keep them from reaching my heart.

October and Rae had shown up during soundcheck. I was on the platform in the middle of the theater, at the sound booth, watching Simon dialing everything in while Cal rehearsed with the UC Berkeley Jazz Choir. Cal ended all his shows with a song called "Turn the Lights Out," the big hit from his most recent album, and he brought a local choir onstage to perform it with him every night.

I saw Wyatt escort October to the left side of the stage. She was wearing a fisherman's sweater over jeans and green rain boots, and her hands were clinging to their opposite shoulders like she was cold. I watched her look around and then take out her phone. Seconds later I got a text from her that said WHERE ARE YOU? but I didn't write back because I didn't know what the fuck to say.

Cal was finishing up with the choir when he spotted her. He handed his guitar to Justin, rushed over, and swept October up in his arms. When he put her down, he whispered something in her ear; she shook her head and touched the side of his face. Then he took her hand and they walked backstage together.

"There you are," Rae said, suddenly beside me.

She had a small red box of raisins in her hand and big tortoiseshell sunglasses on, even though it was overcast and drizzly.

For the past month, Rae and I had maintained a copasetic, if not affable, relationship. I'd won points with her for the birdcage, and we'd bonded over the fact that we were both fans of the experimental post-rock band Godspeed You! Black Emperor. Meanwhile, I made sure to leave October's house earlier than necessary every morning so that Rae didn't catch me there and go back to considering me the enemy.

"You're coming backstage, yeah? October's looking for you."

"I'll be there in a few minutes."

Rae gave me a suit-yourself shrug and walked away.

I wasn't ready to be in the same room with Cal and October, and I went back to my truck to kill some time. A sharp rage was scratching at my insides. Usually my rage was silent, heavy and immobile, but that afternoon it was a panther pacing around a cage.

I took the friendship contract out of my pocket and read it again. *Forever in truth and music.*

The way I saw it, I was going to break a promise that night, and I had a choice. I could break the one I'd made to Cal or the one I'd made to October. When I finally got out of my truck and headed back into the theater, I honestly didn't know which way it was going to go.

The doors had opened by then, and people were everywhere. At the north entrance I heard someone call my name and was relieved when I turned to see Thomas and Mr. P behind me. They looked out of place in their fancy suits and slick overcoats. I told them to follow me, and I escorted them backstage. I felt safer walking in with them.

When we entered the room, Cal was pouring whiskey into little Dixie cups and passing them out. "There you are!" he said cheerily, handing me one.

The room had filled up with people clamoring for face time with Cal, and he was gregarious and hospitable to all of them. As I walked by, he whispered, "Bear with me while I shake some hands and kiss some babies," as if this was all part of his job.

October was alone on the couch, and she looked as uncomfortable as I felt. But when she saw me she smiled with hopeful eyes, like she still believed everything was going to be all right. She gestured for me to sit beside her, but I went to the corner and kept to myself.

The opening band was onstage by then, and before their set was over Wyatt came in and told everyone to follow him to the section of seats he'd reserved for Cal's guests. I got in the line behind Thomas, but Wyatt put his arm out to stop me and said, "You can stay."

Wyatt shut the door on his way out, and then it was the three of us, and I was so anxious my skin itched from the inside. Fortunately, Cal was too preoccupied to pick up on the energy in the room. He concentrated on his vocal warm-ups, singing them just like Mr. Collins had taught us, while I sat on the arm of the couch, as far away from October as I could get, and scrolled through the Redwood National Park Instagram page, because I thought looking at trees might calm me down.

When Wyatt came back, he told me and October that he'd cleared a space on the left side of the stage for us to watch the show away from any other people, and then he told Cal it was time to go.

Cal took October's head in his hands and kissed her forehead. Then he grabbed me by the shoulders, caught me with his pointy eyes, and said, "This one's for you, brother."

Most of the music Cal and I listened to when we were kids was what Bob Harper used to call the music of whiners and wallowers. But Cal doesn't whine or wallow—neither in life nor in music. His voice is like smoke at a campfire, but his presence on stage is energetic, affable, and charming. Watching him perform is like watching someone palpably releasing tension. The sonic counterpart to cracking your knuckles or jacking off. Nothing he does is showy or over the top. It's simply good. Cal is a star, but for people who don't like stars.

Nevertheless, watching the show was a roller-coaster ride. The culmination of everything Cal had done and everything I had not, each moment was a forensic study, viewed through a microscope, of Cal's successes and my failures, his bravery and my fear.

Emotions dipped and swelled inside of me as if they were dancing to the beat of the drums. I experienced everything from respect to resentment, jealousy to pride, anger to overwhelming affection, with a steady stream of *saudade* and desiderium above it all.

The most crushing moment came after I spent an entire song studying the guy playing lead guitar. While he wasn't dog shit, he was hardly remarkable, and for the first time in my life I knew for a fact that it really could have been me up there, and the despair that overtook me then made me sick to my stomach.

I still hadn't spoken to October. By then, I'd convinced myself that our relationship had been a mistake. I was going to call the whole thing off. I didn't want her. I didn't care.

And she could feel me crashing, I was sure of it, because she took my hand—to comfort me, to glean information, or both—not minding that Cal was just a few feet from us.

I pulled away with a sharp jolt and hissed something unkind at her. And for a long time afterward it wrecked me that I couldn't remember what had come out of my mouth, because it was the last thing I'd said to her before I left.

The drizzle was picking up, and although we were under cover of the stage, sheltered from the rain, it was cold enough that when October spoke I could see her breath in the air.

"Let's go back downstairs and talk."

I crossed my arms in front of my chest and pretended I hadn't heard her.

In other words, my destiny had come full circle.

I'd reverted back to the shithead I was when our story began.

For the first half of the show, Cal had a four-piece band backing him. About an hour in they left, and he played a solo set. Three songs later he thanked the audience and exited the stage.

Wyatt scuttled up beside me, animated, as we waited for Cal's encore. "Chris tells me you're quite a guitar player. Favorite acoustic—Martin or Gibson?"

I gave Wyatt what Cal would have called a *guitarded* answer—his made-up, politically incorrect term for when we geeked out on guitars. "Most Gibsons are more brittle sounding to me; I grew up playing a Martin, so they hold a special place in my heart. My Martin grabs every note I touch and hands it to me like a gift."

Wyatt shook his head. "You can't be sloppy on a Martin."

"Oh, sure you can. Have you seen Mr. Callahan play one?" I laughed. "That's his intent though. His is the warmest slop there is."

The crowd was chanting Cal's name, and he walked back onto the stage with a bottle of water in his hand. He set the water down on the drum riser, went to the mic, and said, "I'll keep playing as long as you guys don't mind hanging out in the rain."

Another eruption of applause. Behind Cal, two crewmembers were setting up stools and guitar stands. Justin the guitar tech ran over to Wyatt, they spoke briefly, and Justin ran off again.

Cal wiped his face with the bottom of his T-shirt and extended his arm out to the side, in the direction of where October, Wyatt, and I were standing. "Got a special treat for you tonight. That is, if I can convince my buddy to come out and play with me."

Cal started waving me over, and I felt myself retreating backward, shaking my head.

Wyatt said, "Don't be shy," and dragged me toward Cal, and before I knew it I was standing in the middle of the stage.

Justin came over with Cal's stunning 1964 Gibson Dove and a beautifully battered 1949 Martin D-13 I'd never seen. He placed them on the stands beside the stools.

"Say hello to my brother from another mother," Cal shouted. "Joe Harper, ladies and gentlemen."

Eighty-five hundred people cheered, and I didn't dare look over to see if October was one of them.

While Justin adjusted the mic stands in front of the stools, I turned to Cal and said, "I can't do this."

Cal put his arm around my shoulder and said, "Harp, you could do this upside down in a tub full of molasses, and you know it."

He grabbed the Gibson, sat down, and motioned for me to sit. And God knows what the expression on my face was, because Cal looked at me and burst out laughing. That made me laugh too, because when Cal gut-laughed he looked like the kid in the photo he'd shown me earlier, and for a brief moment it was as though I'd stepped back in time, to 1996, to open mic night at The Sweetwater.

Before I sat down I took out my phone and snapped a couple photos for Ingrid—one of the crowd, and a quick selfie of me and Cal, because I knew it would mean something to her to see me up there beside him, for what I guessed was going to be the first and last time.

I thought of my brother then. I searched for his presence in the sky, in the rain, in the roar of the crowd, and I really and truly felt it. Then I wondered what Bob would have made of me up on that stage, and I knew in my bones that I had something to prove. To my father or to myself, I wasn't sure.

"Let's do this," I said to Cal.

I pulled off my shoes and socks and took a moment to feel the cool, damp softness of the rug beneath my feet. Then I sat down and picked up the Martin. And I felt Sam there too. Inside the guitar. In the strings. In my hands. In my fingertips. In my heart.

I looked at Cal and said, "The usual?"

He nodded, grinning.

I counted to four and we both hit our D chords in unison.

The rest of the performance is a blur. I have no recollection of whether it sounded good or bad. I only know it felt like magic. And repatriation. And when we put down our guitars and stood up, the clapping and cheering surged through my bloodstream like a drug.

Cal took my hand and held it up in the air as if I'd just won a boxing match. "One more time, give it up for Joe Harper."

I glanced at October then. Her palms were pressed together underneath her chin, frozen in mid-clap, and her face was blank, as if she was unable to find an existing expression for what she'd just witnessed.

Behind us, Wyatt was ushering the choir onto the stage for the last song. Another crewmember dashed over and picked up the acoustic guitars. Justin walked out and handed Cal his 1966 Olympic white Jazzmaster.

I remember Cal smiling at me, lofty, proud, and emotional, like he thought we'd just accomplished something momentous together. Justin nodded for me to follow him off the stage, and I bent down to grab my shoes and socks. As I stood back up, I saw something shifting in Cal. He was focused on the ground, and the joy was draining from his face, his features seeming to absorb it like butter melting into a piece of warm bread.

At first Cal only seemed confused. Then I saw something click.

I looked back down at the ground, trying to identify what had triggered him. That's when I realized he wasn't looking at the ground. He was staring at my feet. My toes. The little animals October had painted on them.

The rest of the band had returned, and Justin was now pulling me by the arm, trying to get me out of the way before the last song began.

Cal's hands began to shake. His jaw pulsed, and his eyes darted back and forth from my feet to my face, searching for something that might suggest he'd come to the wrong conclusion.

A long line of lights went on above us, so bright they illuminated the rain. I swore I could make out every drop, and I remember having a strange, momentary insight that raindrops weren't drops at all, they were sharp, vertical lines, like little knives of water falling from the sky.

Cal's hawk eyes locked on mine. His face was like a piece of petrified wood.

"You," he said, with a disappointment violent enough to feel like a punch.

And then the blue robes of the choir overtook me like a flight of western scrub jays. Justin had me by the shoulders now, and he dragged me and didn't let me go until we'd made it to the outdoor lounge, where the afterparty was already in full swing.

I didn't know where October was, but I suspected she was still standing where I'd left her, oblivious to what had just happened.

My body was cold and numb, my mind empty, void of feeling, void of language except for one word: *Run*.

But I didn't run. I put my head down, pulled my collar up, and walked slowly but deliberately toward the nearest exit while behind me a chorus of voices chanted "Turn the Lights Out" in three-part harmony.

I bumped into Rae as I was heading up the stairs. She was coming out of the restroom and asked me where I was going.

"The party's that way, yeah?" she said, pointing back toward the stage.

"I'm sorry," I muttered. "I can't."

"Huh?"

I met Rae's eyes and held her shoulders to make sure she was listening. "Tell October this: Tell her I said I'm sorry, but I can't."

TWENTY-THREE.

THERE WAS A GUY in Sid's writing workshop, an ex-Marine named Santiago, who was working on a novel about a soldier from the future who returns to America in 2017 to assassinate the president and save the human race. It sounds worse than it was. Santiago was a solid writer with a strong voice. He was also an expert marksman and had served two tours in Afghanistan before his twenty-fifth birthday. He said that when he came back, his head was on backwards, and he'd been trying to turn it around for the better part of a decade. Writing helped. Booze didn't.

Santiago was built like a gorilla: wide as a doorframe, hirsute, with long arms and a rounded posture that made him look like he was knuckle-walking when he moved. He and I were workshop partners for a session. That meant we had to read each other's assignments and offer feedback, and every Wednesday night for eight weeks we met at the IHOP out on Highway 93 because Santiago was in AA and said it wasn't healthy for him to be around anything stronger than coffee.

During ABANDONMENT week, I wrote a poem about how I'd left October without saying goodbye. Almost all of my assignments focused on Cal or October, with the occasional bit about Sam or Bob thrown in for good measure. At any rate, Santiago knew a good portion of the backstory from conversations we'd had over pancakes, and at the end of the poem he'd scribbled two notes. The first one said: *Loving a woman who can break you is the bravest thing a man can do*. The second note said: *Go back, you spineless motherfucker. The clock is ticking*.

It wasn't like I'd intended to stay in Montana forever. My original plan had been to head back to California after the dust settled. The night I left, I'd only grabbed what I could load up in a hurry, which amounted to a duffle bag full of clothes, a couple of books, some camping gear, my guitar, and my laptop. I'd fed Diego the leftovers in my fridge, hopped in my truck, and headed north, assuming I would drive around for a week or so, talk to some trees, and end up back where I started, ready to face the consequences. But the longer I was gone, the more distance I created between myself and the mess I'd made. And the more distance I created, the more it seemed like a good idea to stay away.

For a while I was peripatetic, pulling off in parks whenever I got tired of driving. I stopped near Yreka the first day and car camped in the Klamath National Forest surrounded by white firs and incense cedars. From there I went to Crater Lake, Bend, and then up toward Hood River.

What I'm about to admit might be the stupidest thing I've ever copped to, and that's saying a lot, but as I was hiking through an old-growth forest near Indian Mountain in Oregon, thinking about Cal and October—they were all I could think about back then—I found myself wondering why they hadn't tried to contact me.

I guess I'd assumed they would have a lot to say, and I wanted them to say it. And I decided that as soon as one of them reached out—to curse me, call me a liar, a promise-breaker, a coward, the biggest fucking fuckhead on the planet—I would go back.

Neither of them did.

I wandered around in the woods for a couple more weeks, staying in cheap, dreary motels when I couldn't find a decent campsite. I drank a lot of coffee, alternated between reading *Trees of the Pacific Northwest* and *Shantaram*—the two books I had with me—and played a lot of guitar. And I suppose it would have been something of a romantic existence had I not been so empty inside.

I made my way to Spokane and considered staying there for a bit, to get a feel for where Bob had come from, to see if it provided me with any clues about who he was. But while the outskirts of Spokane were green and beautiful, the city itself was a lot of strip malls and fast-food restaurants, and that kind of banal homogenization only intensified my despair.

The loneliness I felt in those first few weeks was like a famine inside of me. Every day a vicious, gnawing hunger ate away at my flesh and made me feel like a carcass the coyotes were picking clean. It got so bad I started to contemplate hurting myself. Driving off a cliff. Buying a gun. Pills. I knew I needed a friend, but the two friends I needed the most were the ones I didn't have the courage to call. Then I remembered Sid was less than a day's drive away. I rang him up, told him I was in a bad way, and asked him if I could stop in for a visit. He has a ten-acre spread not far from downtown Whitefish, right in the middle of a ponderosa pine forest.

"Come," he said. "There's an empty caretaker's cabin on the property. It's not fancy, but it's yours if you want it."

My intention was to stay a month or two, but winter hit northwestern Montana like an invading army, and I decided to wait it out. I got a job giving guitar lessons at a small music store in Kalispell and then supplemented that income by picking up construction work here and there. By summer I'd joined the writing workshop, and Sid's house desperately needed a new roof, a project I gladly took on as a thank-you to him for putting me up. Before I knew it a year had passed; there had been no word from Cal or October, and Mill Valley got farther and farther from the end of my telescope.

Cal and October had managed to stay together for a couple of months after I left. Or maybe that was just how long it took the internet to find out about their breakup. I browsed the web regularly to check on them. When they officially called it quits, Cal moved back to Brooklyn. About a year later he started dating a woman that, according to an online celebrity gossip site, he met through mutual friends. Her name is Nicole and she makes documentaries on animals facing extinction.

I had a harder time gleaning information about October's private life, but it was probably better that way. I had her work to keep me company, and I knew that was more intimate and telling than anything else the internet had to offer.

Once the entire catalog of *365 Selfies* was available on the website, I went through phases where I visited it obsessively, watching different clips like they were episodes of my favorite TV show. Then I would swear it off like a drug habit I was trying to kick, vowing never to look at it again, avoiding it for days, sometimes weeks.

Those were the times I convinced myself I was over October. But then I would cave and start watching again. There was one particular clip that always set me back and made me wonder about things I knew it was unhealthy for me to wonder about. Number 361 of 365. One of the last selfies posted. In it, October is sitting on the same bed in the same cottage where we'd stayed in Miranda. Her eyes are wide and wild like they were the night we'd spent there, and it's obvious to me that she's eaten mushrooms again, though she doesn't mention it. She has her big sketchbook on her lap, a pencil between her fingers, and she's talking in a hyper-focused ramble as she draws.

The selfie, titled *Portrait #2*, is the only one in which she speaks directly *to* someone. And knowing all I know, I don't think it's presumptuous to assume she's talking to me.

We didn't do the second portrait that night, remember? It was the reason we'd come, and we fell asleep before we could finish what we'd started. Tonight I'm going to finish what I started. And then I'm going to put this in my rearview mirror where it belongs.

Here's what I don't understand though. Here's what I've been trying to figure out for a long time. How do you let go of something that lives inside of you? How do you remove something that feels attached to your ribcage and wrapped around your heart? How do you cut that out without losing a piece of yourself in the process?

Art?

Maybe.

That's how our story began.

With art.

Mine, not yours.

Or was it?

The first thing I asked you was how you felt about art, and do you remember what you said? You said it was a way to tell the truth. And right away I knew. Not because I liked your face—though I did. Not because I was looking for a lover—I was not. But because something about you felt like home.

You inspired me.

And isn't that where all great art starts?

Isn't inspiration born in those imaginary moments that incite riots and recognition in our spirits?

Most people think of inspiration as a kind of mystical influence that stirs the mind or the soul, but the verb "to inspire" also means "to draw in." Specifically, it's the drawing of air into the lungs. Think about that. Inspiration is how we breathe. It's how we stay alive.

I told you this once before. We were watching a bird outside the window, and I told you there was something about your energy, in its almost comical melancholy, that inspired me in ways I still don't know how to explain. But the words coming to me now are these: You reminded me of who and what I am. That is, an artist. Oh, I know, I was an artist long before you strolled into my studio, and I am an artist without you now. But you know as well as I do that artists often feel like hacks. We exist in vacuums for long periods of time and need someone or something that reflects our work back to us in a way that allows us to see it in a different light. To see ourselves in a different light.

You did that for me. You got me out of my head and back into my heart. And that meant something to me. It meant something to you too. I know it did.

At this point in the clip, October puts her sketchbook and pencil down and paces around the room. The camera follows her to the painting above the recliner, the one of the wave crashing onto the beach. She reaches out and touches it, and she laughs, and I know with complete certainty that she's remembering the night we were there together, and how we thought the water was going to spill out over the chair.

She's still looking at the painting when she says: *After you left, Chris asked me if perhaps I thought I could save you, if that had been the appeal. But I never saw you as someone who needed saving. I saw you as someone who needed to be understood.*

She goes back to the bed, picks up the pad, and studies what she's drawn for forty-seven seconds. Then she says: *You know what I missed after you left? I missed your forearms.* (She laughs again.) *I missed the way we would curl up on the couch at night, drink a little wine, and play each other songs on my computer, and you'd let me trace constellations in the freckles on your forearms. Remember the night I drew them with a Sharpie? You had Lyra and Orion inked on your skin for days.*

For a while after you left, I would go outside at night and look for Lyra and Orion in the sky, and if I couldn't find them, I would tell myself it was because you were holding them ransom in the little connect-the-dots galaxy on your arm.

She uses her fingers to shade a bit and then resumes drawing.

I'm not going to lie. I've considered the possibility that I had been wrong about you. I've wondered if my intuition had been off. If my senses had completely failed me. (She purses her lips as if she's still pondering the likelihood of this and then shakes her head.) *Whenever I try to convince myself of that, one specific memory comes back to me. That time we went to Inverness for dinner. I was driving up Highway 1 and all of a sudden you started pointing to the left, out my window, saying, "Look over there. Do you see that? It's a Swainson's hawk. Up in that eucalyptus." Then you went on about how rare they are in Marin and how they're sometimes called grasshopper hawks because that's their favorite food and blah blah blah; I can't remember the rest. I hadn't actually gotten a look at the bird, and when we got to the restaurant I asked you to pull up a photo on your phone so I could see what I'd missed. After some hemming and hawing you admitted that you'd made the whole thing up.* (She imitates my voice by dropping hers an octave and mumbling.) *"There was no hawk." That's what you said. I asked you why you'd lied, and you got all bashful and said there'd been a dead dog lying on the other side of the road, that it looked like it had been hit by a car.* (Her eyes get teary and she looks up at the ceiling then back down into the camera.) *You didn't want me to see it.* (She wipes her eyes, tilts her head to the side.) *You knew it would hurt me and you didn't want—* (She exhales.) *Ironic, I know.*

Anyway.

As I was saying.

How do you let go of something that lives inside of you?

How do you discard something that feels attached to your ribcage and wrapped around your heart?

How do you cut it out without losing a piece of yourself in the process?

You know what you are to me?

A phantom limb.

I can still feel it.

And I don't just mean I can still feel you. I mean that I know you can feel me too.

There's another pause. Another big sigh. Then she says: *I hope you're happy. That's the truth. Wherever you are and whatever you're doing, I hope, more than anything, that you're happy.*

She examines the drawing for a time and eventually nods decisively, though the camera never pans around to her POV, and we never see the portrait.

A moment later she rips the drawing from her sketchbook, rips the portrait in half, rips those halves in half, and keeps ripping until the portrait is in hundreds of tiny pieces. Then she tosses what's left of me into the trash bin near the kitchen table.

Done, she says.

I'd already been gone for two years by the time that clip was released. And though I dated in Montana—mostly women I met at the Great Northern, women who were as lost as I was, and too broken to give me any more than I could give them—not a day went by that a dozen things didn't remind me of October. My whole world had become redolent with her point of view and passions, her commitment to life and to art, no matter how far away I was.

TWENTY-FOUR.

FOUR MONTHS BEFORE the debut of *Sorrow: This Is Art*, I got word that Bob had suffered a heart attack on a flight from Cabo San Lucas to Denver and had died in a hospital a few days later. His wife of two years, Maureen, sent me an e-mail explaining what had happened, but the e-mail sat in my inbox for over a week before I got around to opening it.

When I finally spoke to Maureen, she was tearful and apologetic, as if it were somehow her fault that I'd missed my father's memorial service. Then she gave me the name and number of Bob's lawyer and instructed me to contact him regarding my inheritance.

When I called Ingrid and told her that Bob was dead, she cried and said, "Oh, Joey, I'm so sorry. I can't imagine how hard this is for you."

I didn't tell Sid and Maggie about Bob's death. I don't know why, except to say that I'm a weirdo, and I didn't want them to make a fuss.

And anyway, Bob's death wasn't hard for me. He'd been gone from my life for a long time. The only difference was that now it was final.

When I contacted Bob's lawyer, he told me that they were still dividing up the assets, but that when all was said and done, I would be left with enough money to live modestly for the rest of my life. I would never again have to take a job I didn't want. I would be able to travel more. Maybe buy a house.

I didn't foresee the money changing much else. Money can't buy guts. It can't sew up the broken pieces inside of you. And it certainly can't make amends or substitute for love.

I wanted to mourn Bob. I wanted to feel the loss of whatever relationship he and I had missed out on. But for a long time, I didn't feel anything at all.

And then one Monday night, a few days after the money came through, I left the library, stopped at the Great Northern for a drink, and had a few too many.

On my walk home from the bar, I broke down and called Bob's cell phone, which still went to his voicemail. I left him a long, blubbering message about how sorry I was that we hadn't mended fences. I told him how gorgeous Glacier National Park was. I told him about October and what I'd done to her. I told him about the birdcage I'd built and the cabin I was living in, and everything else I could think of that I'd kept bottled up inside for the last twenty years.

Then I did something even more stupid.

I texted Cal.

BOB DIED, I wrote. HEART ATTACK.

He didn't write back.

TWENTY-FIVE.

ONLY TWO PEOPLE ever showed up at my cabin uninvited: Sid and his teenage daughter, Maggie, usually to coax me over for dinner or out to a movie.

It was mid-September, early evening, still warm, and dry enough that the mosquitoes were all but gone for the season. Bob had died four months earlier, and October's big *Sorrow* exhibit at SFMoMA was a couple of weeks away. I was in the kitchen about to make coffee when I heard knocking.

I opened the door without thinking, expecting Sid or Maggie.

It was Cal. In a slim-fitted, denim button-down shirt with a distinctive, Western-style yoke and stitching, like he'd thought to dress for Montana.

Stunned, I stuttered his name, not quite sure he was real.

The look on his face was very real, however, and unambiguous. His mouth was taut and severe, his left hand in the air, index finger pointing to an invisible thought bubble above his head. He had something to say and had come to say it. But before he said a word, his face cracked like a windshield hit by a stone, and he hauled off and punched me, his fist hitting my right cheekbone, eye, and nose in one sliding blow.

I heard my teeth rattle inside my head like Tic Tacs in a packet, and I cupped my hand around my nose to catch the blood I could already taste in the back of my throat.

"What the *fuck*," I spat.

A second later Cal hit me again, this time in the gut. He knocked the wind out of me, and I doubled over, gasping for air.

"Goddamn it, Harp," he said, immediately helping me stand back up. "I *did not* come here to do that."

He walked me to the couch and I sat down, dizzy and nauseous.

"Fuck," I said again, coughing.

"I mean it. I don't know what came over me." He rubbed his knuckles, shook out his hand. "I've never punched anyone before. It hurts."

Blood dripped down my face, and I wiped it off with the bottom of my T-shirt. It was warm and sticky. "I've never been punched before. That hurts too."

Cal walked to my kitchen, wrapped a bunch of ice in a dishtowel, and handed it to me. He told me to press it to my cheek and I did. The right side of my face throbbed, and I felt like I was going to throw up.

Cal sat in the armchair diagonal from me, glowering in my direction with his head tilted back and to the side, arms crossed over his chest like a hip-hop star in repose.

I was still struggling to get a full breath, and the pain in my face made my eyes water. Blood continued to drip down my throat, and it tasted like I was sucking on a guitar string. I leaned my head against the couch to stop the room from spinning, and when I sat back up, Cal's beady eyes were trained hard on me.

We looked at each other for a long time without saying anything.

The right side of my face was burning cold, and I took the ice away. I fingered my nose and Cal said, "Is it broken?"

"I don't think so."

"Your eye is pretty swollen. Gonna have a nice shiner there."

My cheek started to ache again, and I put the ice back.

Cal was sitting on the edge of the chair now, legs spread, left elbow on left knee, chin in his palm. It could have been an album cover: *Callahan Goes Country.*

"That first punch was for fucking my girlfriend," he said. "The second one was for generally being the biggest pussy I've ever met."

I couldn't argue with him on either count, and I didn't.

I moved my jaw back and forth and heard more Tic-Tac noises.

"You have nothing to say to that?" Cal asked abrasively.

I sighed. "How did you find me?"

He threw his head back and laughed with disdain. "Seriously? Why are you such an asshat? Have you ever heard of the internet? Anyone can find anyone. We both know you're here." My face must have betrayed something when he said *we*, because he rolled his eyes and said, "Yes, Harp. October knows where you are. People on Yelp have reviewed your guitar lessons. It's not rocket science."

Part of me wished Cal would hit me again, knock me unconscious.

"Why are you looking at me like that?" he said. "Did you expect her to come knocking on your door? You're the last person she wants to see. And she's the last person you deserve."

Again, I couldn't argue with him.

"Cal, why are you here?"

He stood up and strode around the room like he was looking for something. His eyes paused on the corner where I kept my Martin, and the old Silvertone I'd recently acquired from a pawnshop in Columbia Falls. It came in a case that was also an amp, and Cal looked at it mawkishly, probably because he'd had an almost identical one when we were kids.

"Got anything stronger than water in this place?"

I nodded toward the kitchen. "Cabinet to the left of the sink."

Cal walked into the kitchen, grabbed the tequila from the shelf, opened a few more cabinets, and came back with the bottle and two mugs that said "Cowgirl Coffee" on them. He poured generous shots.

I took the ice away from my face again, pulled two cubes from the dishtowel, and dropped them into my drink.

"Why am I here?" Cal repeated. "I was asking myself that same question on the cab ride over from the airport." He downed his drink in one swallow and made a face. *Paper-belly*, I thought, and my heart ached.

I downed my drink too, and it was soothing at first, but once it settled into my gut, I swore it magnified the pain in my face.

As Cal refilled our mugs, declarations of contrition spun around my head, but I thought it best to let Cal do the talking. He was squinting up at the ceiling light, and I wondered if he noticed it was the same fake-bronze, flush-mounted fixture I'd had in my room as a kid, a frosted semicircle with a little knob in the center that looked like a nipple. Cal and I used to call it the boob light.

"I'm here because I'm a fucking sap, that's why." He stared down into his drink, ran his thumb around the rim of the mug, and I could tell by the way he was stretching his mouth from side to side that he was getting emotional. "I'm going to tell you something," he said. "And I want you to think about this. Even during all those years that we'd lost touch, whenever I imagined myself old and gray, retired to some big old house, maybe over on Muir Beach or up in Bolinas, I always imagined you there, the two of us still playing the Tam High setlist, still talking about, I don't know, guitars and girls, I guess." He chuckled a little. "And that time I beat the crap out of you in Montana."

I chuckled too, but tears filled my eyes.

"You're my family, you fuckhead. Literally the only family member I have. And what you did—" He shook his head. "I confided in you. I *trusted* you. And the whole time you were—" He stopped, covered his mouth with his palm, rubbed his chin. "I shouldn't have found out like that." He met my eyes fiercely, and I stayed with him. "You should have told me, Harp. At the very least, you should have fucking told me."

"I know. I'm sorry." I set my mug on the table without finishing my drink. "I also know the word 'sorry' is meaningless. It doesn't sum up even 1 percent of my remorse." I rubbed my eyes despite the pain in my face. "I would do anything to make things right with you, Cal."

He moved to pour me more tequila, but I covered my mug with my hand, feeling the need to be at least semi-lucid for the rest of the conversation.

"I need to ask you something," Cal said. "And I need you to tell me the truth." He ran his hand through his hair, brushing it back off his face. It was longer than the last time I'd seen him. More like the way he used to wear it when we were kids. "Did you actually care about her? Or were you just trying to fuck with me?"

I sat up and shook my head like crazy. It had never occurred to me that Cal might think I'd gotten involved with October out of spite.

"I would never do anything to intentionally hurt you, Cal."

He waited to see if I was going to add anything to that. Then he smirked and said, "I asked you two questions. You only answered one."

My heart pounded. It was at once terrifying and a relief to be able to say the words to Cal.

"I loved her." I felt my face flush. My eyebrows rose, but the rest of my body slackened, resigned to the sad truth. "I still love her."

Cal shot me a look of staggering exasperation that under any other circumstance would have been comical in its histrionics. "Well, that just reinforces my theory that you're the biggest pussy I've ever met." He squinted at me. "Which one of us were you running away from that night? Me or her?"

"Her. I just used you as the excuse."

"For Christ's sake, Harp. Help me understand this. Seriously. I need you to explain to me where bailing on her got you, because I don't get it."

I noticed the smell of smoke and meat and remembered that Sid said he was going to throw some steaks on the grill. Maggie was making cornbread and a big salad. I was supposed to bring beer and ice cream.

"Well?" Cal pressed.

After a long, laden sigh, I said, "Why have I run away from anything I've ever run away from? I was terrified. Terrified of my feelings. Terrified I wasn't good enough for her. Terrified I couldn't be what she needed. Terrified of her eventual rejection. And on top of all that, I'd made a mess with you that I didn't know how to clean up." The ice cubes in the dishtowel collapsed onto the coffee table as they melted, making a small racket. "The worst part is I never told her how I felt. I pretended she knew. You know, like when she touched me, it was clear to her or something. And on some level, I believe it was. But that's not the same thing as having the guts to look someone in the eye and voice it out loud. Of all the regrets I have—and there are many—that's the biggest one. That I felt so much more for her than I ever let on."

Cal got up and walked to the sliding glass door across the room. Vertical vinyl blinds hung in front of it. He yanked on the bead chain to open the blinds and they clattered against each other before settling back into silence at the end of the track.

I watched him stare out across the yard, through the pines, the lights of Sid's backyard visible in the approaching dusk.

"It's nice here," he said. "Peaceful."

"Can I ask *you* something?"

He turned toward me, accidentally elbowing the blinds and causing another little commotion. When he grabbed for them to stop them from clanging, it only made them clang more. Once they settled down, he raised his eyes in anticipation of my question.

"How much do you know about me and October. What did she tell you?"

"As soon as we realized you were gone, we had a long conversation about it. I believe I was given the relevant details. Nothing more, nothing less, if you know what I mean."

He came back over and sat down, and this time he relaxed into the chair. "I saw her on Friday."

My heart dropped. It was Sunday. He'd seen her two days ago. "Where?"

"San Francisco. I had a meeting in Cupertino, and we met up for dinner in the city later that night."

I immediately felt anxious. "You two still talk? You hang out?"

"We do now. Took a while." He gave me one of those subtle-but-swaggering Cal shrugs. "The truth is, she was right. We didn't belong together. She'd known it for a while, and once I realized it, we were able to become friends again. She's actually the one who introduced me to Nicole, my fiancée."

"You're getting married?" Either I'd been slacking in the online stalking department or this news hadn't yet hit the internet. "Congratulations, man."

He smiled wholly for the first time since he'd arrived. "Gonna do it right this time. No more messing around. This one's the real deal."

"I couldn't be happier for you. I mean it."

"See, this is thing about being happy, Harp. It really puts the past into perspective." Cal moved to the edge of the chair and leaned in toward me. "I mean there I was, sitting at a quiet little table in Octavia with October, and we're sharing this incredible dish of crab pappardelle, and we're talking about my wedding, and the big performance she has coming up, and it dawned on me that I have absolutely no hard feelings toward her anymore. None. Now, if you would have told me on the day she and I broke up that I would one day be able to sit across from her and share pasta, I would have bet you a lot of money otherwise."

I noticed the buttons on Cal's shirt were shiny, pearlescent snaps. The fanciest Western shirt I'd ever seen.

"During dessert something else occurred to me. I had a realization. And I looked at October and said, 'You know what? If I can forgive you, I should be able to forgive him too, right?'"

My anxiety morphed into alarm. "You spoke to her about me?"

"I'm going to be straight with you. She wasn't too thrilled about that. As soon as I mentioned you, she clammed up and stared at her crème brûlée. So, I said, 'You don't think I should forgive him?' and she said, 'Chris, I know how much he means to you, and I think you should do whatever feels right. I just don't want to talk about him.'"

Cal's words sunk into my chest like a pickax. "She hates me. Why wouldn't she? I hate me too." I picked up my mug and tossed back what was left of the tequila while Cal watched. Just as he was about to speak, I put my hand up and said, "Don't bother telling me how much I deserve her hate; I know."

Cal shook his head. "Don't underestimate her. October's above hate. She feels things hard and then channels those feelings into her fucking art. Even after you left, when *I* hated you, you know what she told me? She told me the most important thing to do when your heart's been broken is to *keep* it open." Cal rolled his eyes. "'Nurture the tenderness, Chris. Hold on to the love. Turn it into something beautiful.' Those were her exact words. And when I asked her why she wasn't furious with you, she said, 'I understand Joe too well to be angry with him. I'm just sad.'"

That crushed me. I'd take anger over sadness any day. Moreover, it's always been hard for me to accept the idea that someone could love me. But for someone to *understand* me and *still* love me? Well, that took a level of character and compassion I couldn't even begin to comprehend.

Cal was still shaking his head. "No, she didn't hate you, Harp. She was just super fucking bummed. You broke her heart. *And* you left her without an assistant."

I rubbed my eyes again. The pain was deeper and duller now. "How is she? Honestly. Is she happy?"

"I think so. She's mad excited about this MoMA thing."

Against my better judgment, I said, "Is she seeing anybody?"

Cal shrugged. "Some twenty-four-year-old muralist from L.A. He wears ironic sweaters and makes craft beer in his spare time. It's nothing. *Casual summer fling* was the phrase she used."

He nodded toward the guitars in the corner, and in what I took to be a deliberate, subject-changing non sequitur, he said, "Remember that time we had the concert in Old Mill Park? Charged a buck for admission and played Who songs until the cops shut us down. And you smashed my Silvertone at the end of the show."

I chuckled. "I was very in the moment that day. Didn't think that move through."

"Stalled the electric side of the band for a bit, as I recall." Cal snapped his finger. "But Bob came through for us that time! He got us a new one, remember?"

"Wrong." I shook my head. "You told him the guitar had been stolen."

Cal laughed hard at the memory. "Right! Someone broke into his car at the dock, and I lied and told him the guitar had been in the back seat."

"He didn't get us a new one. His insurance did."

We both laughed, but then Cal stopped, remembered. "Shit, Harp. I'm sorry about Bob. I thought about calling you after I got your text. I wanted to. I wasn't ready."

"I hadn't spoken to him in years. Missed his service too. You think I'm a bad friend? I'm an even worse son."

Cal shook his head. "Part of that onus was on him." He exhaled wistfully. "Weird to think we'll never see that fucker again, huh?"

He looked up and stared at the ceiling for a while, the way he does when he's contemplating. Then he said, "Tell me something: If you'd known Bob was going to die, would you have reached out to him?"

I'd considered that question more than once since Bob's death. "Yeah," I said sadly. "I can't tell you how many letters I wrote to him over the years. I just never sent any of them."

"What if it was me?" Cal asked.

I rolled my eyes.

"I mean it. What if you'd found out yesterday that I had a month to live, what would you have done?"

"I assure you I would have called. I would have come to see you. Begged for your forgiveness. Sat with you while you took your dying breath. I don't know. Something."

Cal dipped his chin down, and it made the corners of his eyes look sharp and pointy, like little arrows going in opposite directions. "What if I said I came here today to tell you October was dying?" He must have seen the alarm on my face, because he put his hands up and said, "Calm down. She's fine. But what if she wasn't? What if you found out *she* only had a month to live? What would you do?"

The question stifled me. "I don't know."

There was a hard edge to Cal's voice when he said, "You don't know?"

I huffed. "I would obviously want to see her. I would want to talk to her. And yes, I would be drowning in regrets. That's what you're getting at, right? That's what you want me to say? It's not that simple."

"But it really fucking is," he said, all riled up. "You *make* it complicated. You've always made *everything* more complicated than it actually is. Let me spell this out for you: She *is* dying. *I'm* dying. *You're* dying. We're *all* dying. Every single day, each one of us is one step closer to no longer existing. *Think* about that. Think about how you really want to be spending your days. And with whom."

I thought of Santiago and the note he'd written at the end of my assignment. *Go back, you spineless motherfucker. The clock is ticking.*

"There are no more chances once someone's gone," Cal said. "But until then, there's nothing *but* chances. Why don't you get that?"

"I get it. Believe me. Awareness is not my problem."

"Then what is?"

"Paralysis? Failure to act? Or, well, how did you put it? Generally being the biggest pussy you've ever met?"

Blood and snot had dried on my face, and I could feel it cracking and pulling at my skin. I walked to the kitchen, splashed my face with water and washed it with hand soap and a paper towel. Then I grabbed a clean T-shirt from my bedroom and changed into it. On my way back to the couch, Cal said, "How much more of your life can you waste moping around like this?"

"Fuck you. I'm fine here."

"Bullshit," he said. "This isn't where you belong, and you know it." Cal crossed his legs and leaned back. "Earlier you said you'd do anything to make things right with me. Here's how to do that: Go back and make things right for yourself. Make things right with her. Tell her all the things you want to tell her. At the very least, tell her you're sorry. Because what's at stake? Literally nothing. You've already lost what you were afraid of losing."

"Why do you care if I make things right with her or not?"

"I don't care. *You* care."

"Besides, she'd just tell me to go fuck myself."

"You're missing the point. This isn't about her. It's about you. There's got to be a reckoning, Harp. It doesn't matter if she tells you to go jump off the top of the Salesforce Tower with your fist up your ass. That's irrelevant. What is relevant is that you don't die with all this stuff stuck inside of you, tearing you to pieces, making you less and less until there's nothing left. And let me be blunt, if you think I wanna be hanging out at my big beach house when I'm eighty, shooting the shit and playing the Tam High setlist with a bitter old fool who's still brooding over a girl he walked away from forty years earlier, you've got another thing coming."

Our conversation was interrupted by Maggie shouting "Dinner!" and knocking on the door until I opened it.

She shrieked when she saw my face. "Yikes! What the heck happened to you?"

Maggie was sixteen and looked like a human version of the lanky coast lilies that pop up perennially on the Point Reyes Peninsula in West

Marin. Imagine a bright orange flower with little brown dots, its petals curled backward like Maggie's hair when she pulled it into a ponytail.

"I happened to him," Cal announced from behind us.

I told Maggie to come in while I went to grab the beer and ice cream from the fridge. A second later she shrieked again.

I looked over my shoulder. Her eyes were wide, facing Cal. "Wait . . . You're . . ."

"Chris Callahan," he said, shaking her hand. "And you are?"

"Margaret Elizabeth Toltz," she answered formally. "I like your shirt. Where'd you get it?"

"Saint Laurent," he told her, ironing the front of it with his hands.

I liked Maggie a lot. Her favorite pastimes were chopping firewood and driving the snowplow in winter. Over the summer she worked as a camp counselor in Glacier and tipped me off to all the good trails. In return, I was teaching her how to play power chords.

Maggie looked at me, hand on her hip, hip jutted out to the side. "Joe, why is Chris Callahan in your house? And why did he beat you up?"

"Long story," I mumbled.

I walked back over with the ice cream and beer. Cal tossed his arm playfully around Maggie's shoulder and said, "But it's a good story. I'll tell you about it over dinner."

Maggie looked up at him. *"You're staying for dinner?"*

"My flight doesn't leave until 6:00 a.m. tomorrow. So, yeah, I'm staying."

A few days before it came to pass, I dreamed I was having dinner with Cal, Sid, and Maggie on Sid's porch. I didn't recall the dream until I was at the table, and then it hit me as hard as Cal's fist in my face. Specifically, I remembered Cal sitting across from me with a bottle of Big Sky IPA in his hand, leaning back so far in the wrought-iron chair he was on that its two front legs were a foot off the ground, and I worried he was going to tumble backward. I remembered Sid cutting his steak into unusually small pieces like he always did, chewing slowly as he told Cal about the writing workshop, and Cal pointing at me with his beer, saying, "I better be a hot topic in this class, or we're breaking up for good." And before it happened, I knew Maggie was going to ask Cal to take a photo with her so that her friends would believe he was really there. But that's where real life strayed from the dream, because instead of posing for a picture, Cal took Maggie's phone, switched it from camera to video, and serenaded her with the entire first verse of Rod Stewart's "Maggie Mae" while she giggled and blushed.

"Congratulations," he said after he handed the phone back to her. "You just won Instagram for the day."

After dinner we had huckleberry ice cream and played a board game called Taboo. The object was to get your teammate to guess a word on a card within a limited amount of time, but there were five other words on the card you couldn't say to trigger them to guess the main word. Cal and I played against Sid and Maggie, and our ability to finish each other's sentences, coupled with all the inside jokes we shared, made us unbeatable. For example, during the first round, Cal pulled the word "tofu." He couldn't say "meat," "bean," "curd," "Japanese," or "healthy." He didn't have to. Sophomore year there had been a kid in our class who played bass like a boss, and we let him join our band for three days. Everyone in school called him Tofu because his family was vegan, which theoretically wasn't an issue for me or Cal. But after Tofu lectured us on the hazards of dairy products while I was making mac and cheese for dinner one night, Cal fired him, claiming that the burden of touring the world with a guy who was prejudiced against cheese would be too great to bear.

When Cal saw the card, all he had to say was "Tommy Preston," and I immediately said, "tofu."

We were playing to fifteen points, and when the score was 14 to 5 in our favor, I pulled a card, rolled my eyes, and said, "This isn't even fair." Cal looked at me and I said, "Your mom used to call us this," and he said, "Reese's Peanut Butter Cups."

Cal high-fived me and said, "*Bam!*"

Maggie said, "You guys suck."

Cal and Maggie stayed out on the porch and played with some ephemeral social media app that put animated special-effects filters on their faces and voices while Sid and I went inside to do the dishes.

Sid and I had developed a system over the years. Sid washed, and I dried and put everything away. He was old-school about it, filling the sink with water and dishwashing liquid, putting on his rubber gloves, and scrubbing everything by hand with a two-sided, yellow-and-green sponge. Something about the slow, meticulous way he worked always felt artful to me and made me think October would have appreciated his ability to be present, patient, and fully committed to the task.

Sid was elbows-deep in sudsy water, scouring the pan Maggie had used to make the cornbread, when he said, "That's a good friend you've got out there. Came a long way to extend the olive branch."

"Interesting you say that, considering what my face looks like," I joked. "I guess sometimes you have to beat your friends with the olive branch."

"You know what I mean."

I did, and I nodded. "I'm glad you got to meet him."

"I like him very much. He's quite a character."

Sid turned on the water, rinsed the soap off the pan, and handed it to me. "Who's going to help me with the dishes when you leave?" He turned off the water and pulled the drain stop out of the sink. "Certainly not Maggie," he chuckled.

I dried the pan and put it back in the drawer under the stove. "What makes you think I'm leaving?"

Sid pulled off his gloves and folded them neatly over the chrome faucet. Then he glanced at me and said, "Come on. Don't make me kick you out now."

I stacked the plates that I'd already dried in the pine hutch to my right and turned my head slightly to catch Sid's expression. The rise of his mustache told me he was smiling a little; the way his lower lip quivered told me he was trying not to.

"And Joe," he said, "sooner is better than later."

It was midnight when Cal and I got back to my cabin, and we didn't see any reason to sleep, given that we had to be in the car by 4:30 to get Cal to the airport on time. I made a pot of coffee, and we went for the guitars. Naturally, I picked the Martin and Cal grabbed the Silvertone. He told me he'd been struggling for months with a song and wanted me to help him figure it out. Though when we got down to it, it came to light that it wasn't yet a song. It was a vibe. A feeling. A sonic conversation Cal said he could hear in his head like a foreign language he didn't understand.

"I need a translator," he told me.

I asked him to give me a few adjectives to describe the sound he was looking for, and I laughed as he paced around the room in that swanky Western shirt, black sparkle guitar hanging like a rifle over his shoulder, Cowgirl Coffee mug in hand.

He turned to me and rubbed his left thumb and index finger together as if he were crushing the essence of what he was trying to convey. "Romantic homesickness? Nostalgia?" He narrowed his eyes, looked sideways at me. "But not so broad. Not so vague."

"*Saudade*," I mumbled.

"Sa-u-what?"

"*A deep emotional state of nostalgic or profound melancholic longing for an absent something or someone that one loves.*"

His eyes widened as if he'd just watched me do a magic trick. "*Yes. That.* But. Imagine it . . . *evolving* . . . a big, swelling bridge. . . . It's the longing, and then the *afterparty* of that longing . . . like, if we start out with this feeling of loss, of that word you just said—"

"*Saudade*," I repeated, and was instantly back at October's kitchen table, so sure of myself as I read her the list of words on my phone, her warm breath causing the hair on my neck to stand up. "It's Portuguese."

"So, we capture that Portuguese feeling . . ." He laughed and then got rightly serious again. "But the song crescendos to the sound of the thing being found. And the realization that it was never lost at all, that it'd been there all along. Make sense?"

"Absolute and total."

Cal smiled with pride. "I knew you'd get it." He moved his weight from his left to right foot. "Can you play it?"

I started off doing something bluesy, a lot of minor thirds and sevenths, but that turned out to be nothing, a warm-up for my fingers, a tilling of the emotive soil inside. And then I imagined myself a cryptographer, searching for a code to express something only I could express.

From there I started a strumming pattern focused on two chords— Asus and Dsus—and I fretted it in a way that left the high E string open throughout, so it rang and rang, and no other chords were necessary.

Cal said it sounded like my guitar was accompanying itself, and he plugged in and started playing along, singing non-words, trying to come up with a vocal melody that wrapped around what I was doing in a compelling way.

I threw in a weird key change during the bridge, and Cal practically lost his mind over that, spinning around the room like a whirling dervish, snapping his fingers and howling, "That's it! That's it!"

We slogged over the song for a while, experimenting and refining it, but eventually I was too bleary-eyed to keep going. Cal asked me to play it once more so he could record it on his phone and work on the lyrics when he got home, and I did. After that he took a shower, and I took a ten-minute nap on the couch.

The woods next to my cabin were alive at night. As we headed out to the truck, I could hear rustling in the bushes, probably a fox or a coyote, or the family of bandit raccoons that ransacked my garbage on a regular basis. A couple of night birds were singing a duet in one of the trees, and the katydids sounded like they were furiously typing on tiny little insect typewriters all around us.

It wasn't particularly cold out, but it was chilly inside the truck, and we sat in the cab for a couple of minutes while it warmed up. There, Cal told me he was planning on recording a new album in the spring. He asked me if I would play on it.

"At the very least you have to play on the Portuguese song."

I told him I would, and it became real as soon as I said it. Almost as if agreeing to play on Cal's record was a premonition or a vision. Not only could I foresee it coming true, I knew for a fact it was going to happen.

A worn-out silence rested between us on the drive to the airport. Downtown Whitefish was dormant at that hour, but the streetlamps were so bright they gave one the impression of being on a soundstage, on the set of a movie that takes place in a small mountain town. Once we headed south on US 93, however, the giant cabochon sky sparkled with constellations all around us.

Cal rolled down his window, and the crisp air blew his hair back. He stuck his head out and marveled at the stars.

"Big sky country living up to its name," he said.

Glacier Park International is about thirteen miles southeast of Sid's property, and despite its overreaching tag, it's a small municipal airport, the kind of place where you can still roll up to the curb, shut off your engine, and wait without being chased away by security.

I parked behind the only other car at the terminal, a dusty Subaru from which an older couple was pulling blue vinyl suitcases out of the hatchback. The woman was in a bathrobe and slippers, and I surmised she wasn't the one traveling.

I shut off the engine and turned slightly to face Cal, feeling compelled to say things before he left.

"Listen . . ." I began.

But Cal threw up his hands and said, "Oh, no. Don't get all sentimental on me now, Harp. I'm fucking knackered."

I must have looked dejected, because Cal scoffed at me, but it wasa good-humored scoff, as if he found me amusing. "What?" he said. "I punched you, you wrote me a dope-as-fuck song. We're square."

I laughed unreasonably hard at that, and my stomach hurt from where Cal had landed the second punch. At the same time, I felt an overwhelming, plaintive rush of gratitude toward him, and to the loyalty he had to our friendship, our brotherhood. "Can I at least thank you for coming? Can I acknowledge that I owe you more than I could ever put into words?"

"Fine, fine. Consider it acknowledged." He leaned on the dashboard, looked sideways at me. "Now tell me you're going back, and my work here is done."

I didn't respond one way or the other, but right then I knew I would go. And Cal knew it too, because he said, "And then what?"

"One day at a time. Let me get there first."

He accepted my answer with a single nod, and his mouth fell open like he wanted to say one more thing. Then he shut his mouth. Then he almost spoke again. Finally, he spun his whole torso in my direction, leaned in, seemed to drop his voice an octave and said, "Confession: I left something out earlier. When I was telling you about my conversation with October."

The air coming in through Cal's open window didn't feel especially cold, but I began to shiver.

"I wasn't going to mention it because I have no idea what it means and I don't want to get your hopes up, but it strikes me as pertinent at this juncture." He scratched at the stubble on his chin. "Remember when I told you how I asked her if she thought I should forgive you?"

I nodded and tried to swallow, but my mouth felt like it was coated in breadcrumbs.

"Well, after she got all weird and quiet and said she didn't want to talk about you, I pressed her on it. I said, 'You mean to tell me you *never* think about him?' and I swear over my life, Harp, this is what she said—and I quote: 'Chris, I think about him every day. For a long time, he was the first thought I had when I woke up and the last one I had before I closed my eyes, and it almost destroyed me. I poured all of that into my work. I processed it and moved on. I don't need to talk about it.'"

Cal waited for me to react, but I didn't know how to interpret October's words any more than he did, and I sat there in something of an emotional coma, watching the lady in the slippers. She was standing on the curb, holding the top of her robe together with one hand, waving to the man dragging the blue suitcases with the other. She kept waving, even as he turned his back and walked into the terminal, and something about that made me want to drown myself in Flathead Lake.

Cal checked the time on his phone and said, "I gotta go."

He got out of the truck, shut the door, but stuck his head back through the window. "I almost forgot. Wedding's gonna be in Maui on New Year's Eve. Just a few close friends and family. And since you're the only family I have, you better fucking show up."

October once asked me if redwoods were my only tree obsession and I showed her a photo of a big banyan in Lahaina. One of the largest in the world, the tree is only about sixty feet high—tiny in relation to a redwood— but it spans outward over two hundred feet, a forest unto itself, its graceful branches stretching in wild, sweeping directions like a dancer's limbs in motion.

I remember telling October that I wanted to have lunch beside that tree before I died and she'd said, "Me too. Let's have lunch there together someday."

"Harp," Cal said.

I got out of the truck, walked around to the curb and hugged him as hard as I could.

"I'll be there," I told him.

I stayed at the airport until I saw Cal's plane taxiing toward the runway. It was still pretty dark—the sun wouldn't rise for another hour—and I felt a harboring silence inside the truck, even though a handful of cars and shuttles from local lodges were coming and going, dropping off travelers for the morning flights out of town, one to Salt Lake City, and the one Cal was on to Minneapolis, where he had a short layover on his way back to New York.

I was thinking about how I, too, often woke up with October on my mind and went to sleep hoping she'd show up in my dreams. Which she did. Often.

When I pulled out of the airport and headed back toward Whitefish, the sun was just starting to highlight the peaks to the east, and I could feel my heart—I was going to say *beating*—but it wasn't a beat I felt that morning, it was a *flow*, as if my heart were an hourglass with sand trickling through it.

I had a vision then. And for the next twelve miles I formulated and designed, in my head, an art piece I was determined to build after I got back to California. The piece would be based on that hourglass feeling, and it would serve to remind me of something October had said to me the day after we ate the mushrooms.

You live like someone who doesn't understand how fast the sand moves through the hourglass, Joe.

I stopped at the Cowgirl Coffee hut for a cappuccino, and then I hurried back to my cabin, suddenly feeling the restless anticipation of having someplace to be.

At first a voice inside my head tried to correct me. *You don't have anywhere to be*, it said.

But right away I thought *No, I do*.

I thought, *I have to go home.*

TWENTY-SIX.

THE MORNING I STARTED my drive back to California, Cal emailed me an article about a border collie from Orlando named Ace who had disappeared while on vacation with his family in Hilton Head, South Carolina. The dog took off down the beach one morning while his humans were out boogie boarding and didn't come back. The family stayed for three extra days searching for him. They put up posters, promised a generous reward, and regularly checked the local animal hospitals and shelters. Nothing. Heartbroken, they went home without him. Three years later, Ace showed up on their front porch, the prodigal canine. No one knew where the dog had been or how he'd found his way home, but there he was.

There was a photo in the article, taken moments after Ace was discovered at the door. He was all skin and bones, mangy and full of scabs, but he looked happy to be back.

"Ace is your spirit animal," Cal wrote, adding two lines of laughing-face-with-tears emojis. "Good luck."

I left Whitefish as soon as I could. But I hadn't wanted to abandon my commitments the way I had before, and it took me a few weeks to wrap up my life there. I finished out the month with my guitar students and attended the last two writing workshops of the session. In the meantime, I painted the walls and refinished the floors in the cabin—my parting gift to Sid, to thank him for his profuse hospitality.

By the time I hit the road, October was already well into her monthlong stint at SFMoMA. And because I'd decided—or rather, Cal had convinced me—that visiting the exhibit was the safest way for me to reunite with her—"In a setting that forces *you* to talk and *her* to listen. Where she has no choice but to hold your hands and absorb your *Eeyore-ness*."—I didn't have time to lag on my drive.

I made it to Bend the first day and spent the night at the Rainbow Motel, a whitewashed, flowery little motor court that three years earlier I'd deemed too bright and cheerful for my state of mind. I considered it an indication of personal and spiritual growth that I chose to stay there on my return.

I left Bend before sunrise the next morning because I'd set up appointments to see three apartments later that afternoon, all within walking distance of downtown Mill Valley. For the first time in my adult life, I could afford a decent place to live in my hometown, and I ended up taking the second apartment I saw: a furnished, one-bedroom in-law unit in a well-built, contemporary craftsman-style house. The apartment had its own entrance, off-street parking, and offered a month-to-month lease, which appealed to me, because eventually I wanted to buy a place of my own.

Cal told me October was staying at the St. Regis—a hotel across the street from the museum—for the duration of the exhibit. The good news was I could get settled in Mill Valley without worrying about accidentally running into her at Whole Foods. The bad news was I couldn't accidentally run into her at Whole Foods.

It should be said that I harbored no false hopes of reconciliation. I didn't expect October to be pleased that I'd returned, and I didn't expect she'd want to see me. But I knew that in order for my hoped-for growth to be real, for it to count, I needed to face her, I needed to tell her the truth, and I needed to apologize.

One noteworthy piece of information regarding the apartment I rented: It was, coincidentally, up on Blithedale Ridge, high enough that I had a clear and direct view of Casa Diez on the opposite knoll. And while I did find it comforting to be able to see the lights of October's kitchen from my bedroom, it pained me to stand on the deck at night, look out, and think, *If I hadn't been such a pussy, I'd live over there right now.*

I drove to SFMoMA on Sunday, October 21, and arrived fifteen minutes before the museum opened. By the time I turned onto Third Street, I could see the line for *Sorrow*. It started at the Howard Street entrance, rounded the corner, ran the length of the building, and ended at the intersection of Third and Minna.

The popularity of the exhibit was something I hadn't considered, and after doing some quick math in my head, I didn't bother to park. October sat from 10:00 a.m. to 5:00 p.m. and each visitor was allowed up to five minutes with her. She was seeing, on average, twelve people an hour. That's only eighty-four per day, and there were well over a hundred already in line. With only three performances left, I was going to have to get there a lot earlier the following day, or my chances of getting in would be nil.

Monday morning, I crossed the Golden Gate well before the sun started to crack thin interstices of flame-colored light into the sky over the East Bay. When I got to SFMoMA, I counted fifty-six people already in line. At number fifty-seven, I felt confident I would see October before the day ended.

The front-facing walls of the Roberts Family Gallery where *Sorrow* was being held are all glass, on the ground floor of the museum, and visible from the street. Huge shades, white but opaque, descended from the interior ceiling, preventing anyone from seeing the exhibit until it opened. Outside, the word "SORROW" was written across the shades in a font I recognized as October's handwriting. Even that small hint of her presence packed a punch, and I braced myself for the day.

In line, I picked up on a sense of camaraderie among the people there, as if we were all connected to one another by the mere fact that we'd shown up and would, for hours, be taking small steps forward together. This was something else I hadn't considered: the lengths to which October's fans would go to see her.

Number fifty-five in line was Eli Murray, a British journalist covering *Sorrow* for the *Times*. A few years older than I, Eli lived in San Francisco's Mission District. He hadn't missed a day of the exhibit, and when I asked him why he kept coming back, he said, "Stare into an empath's eyes for five minutes, you're going to learn something about yourself every time. You'll see."

The young girl directly in front of me had come all the way from Beijing to experience *Sorrow*. She was nineteen and dreamed of being a performance artist herself. In her hand she held a piece of paper on which she'd written what she planned to say to October. She asked me if I would read it and let her know if it sounded all right. I found the note so touching, I asked her for permission to take a picture of it with my phone. She said I could, and this is what it said:

> *Hello. I be follow your career since I was small girl. Before I learn your work I am very sad like wanting to die. I think about to end me. My life is much tediousness in China. Less of art. Then I see I can make my sad beautiful. I can make my everything beautiful. Thank you for teach me this. I am Yanmei Liu from Beijing*

"You understand?" Yanmei asked me. "To make sad beautiful?"

I nodded and told her October had taught me the same thing.

The guy behind me was a ridiculously tall, bristly art student from a college in the city. His name was Jessie; he was wearing eyeliner, reeked of body odor, and talked about himself without pause. I pegged him as puerile, and most likely on some bad drugs, but listening to him yammer about his life distracted me, so I let him go. When Jessie finally asked me a question— namely, why I was there—it caught me off guard and I answered him with a shrug toward the sidewalk. After that he seemed to suss out some weakness in me; he made almost pathological eye contact as he gave me an unsolicited account of what drew him to *Sorrow*, explaining that he had a thing for older women due to the lasting impact of his first girlfriend, a sadistic, forty-two-year-old socialite whose name was also Jesse. "But without the 'i'," he clarified.

This was Jessie's second time visiting *Sorrow*. He'd been there the day before and admitted that the reason he came back was because holding October's hands and staring into her eyes had turned him on. As soon as his time was up, he planned on going to the restroom to jack off, just like he'd done the previous afternoon.

"Dude I described my cock to her in great detail yesterday no kidding I told her how I'd use it on her too if she'd let me I'm pretty sure she was as turned on as I was."

I was pretty sure she wasn't, and I almost got into it with Jessie, but I yawned and he didn't yawn back, and according to an article I'd recently read, that meant he was a psychopath, so I refrained from starting any kind of heated exchange with him.

I told Jessie I needed to center myself before I went in to the museum, and I turned around, put in my earbuds, and listened to a playlist October had made me back when we first started hanging out.

In 2013 SFMoMA had closed for an extensive renovation. It reopened three years later with three times more exhibit space, including the ground-floor galleries now accessible via the new entrance at Schwab Hall, allowing visitors into the adjacent Roberts Family Gallery without having to go through the main lobby.

At 9:56 a guard unlocked the double doors, while the mechanical shades rose at a laboriously slow speed and disappeared into the ceiling. One at a time, the people at the front of the line advanced through a metal detector and into the building. I advanced halfway to the entrance, and from there I could see bronze stanchions with blush-colored ropes demarcating the queue that snaked toward the structure in the middle of the room.

She's in there, I remember thinking, a wave of anticipation dousing my heart. But despite my anxiety, I felt grounded and eager. I believed I was where I was supposed to be. And I kept reminding myself of something Cal had said in Montana: I'd already lost what I was afraid of losing. There was nothing at stake here.

Not surprisingly, the structure was a work of art too. A 10 x 10 roofless form made of asymmetrical bronze frames, edging thick pieces of glass with just the slightest tint, as if the glassmaker had blown a thin stream of rose-colored smoke into them before they set. There was an open doorframe at the front of the glass house and one on the opposite side in the back. Each had a security guard standing by.

But the most visually compelling feature of the structure was the glass itself. All the panes looked like someone had taken a chisel to them, causing artfully crafted cracks to extend out from random points. I could barely see beyond the fractures, but even through the landscape of a thousand jagged lines, I recognized the figure of the woman seated at the table inside.

At exactly 10:00 a.m. the first person in line, a young African-American girl wearing a lot of colorful necklaces and a big backpack, was ushered up to the glass house and invited to enter.

One of the security guards took the pack from the girl before she went in. And as I advanced a few feet, I could make out October's hands on the table. I saw the girl sit down and set her hands directly on top of October's.

It was impossible for me to know if the girl spoke or not. Five minutes later she walked out wiping her eyes and smiling.

Upon entering the museum, I took out my earbuds and put away my phone.

The Roberts Family Gallery was a huge space, and the glass house was in the center of it. At the back of the room, a wide, stunning maple staircase led to the main lobby of the museum, and also provided bleacher-like seating for visitors who wished to sit and observe what was going on in the gallery below.

After Yanmei and I both made it through the metal detector and were standing inside the building, she turned around and gave me a sweet, gawky, double thumbs-up. I was about to give her at least one proper thumbs-up in return, but a familiar voice coming from the staircase froze my heart.

"*Oh, no you don't,*" she said, the tone like bullets being shot in my direction.

I looked up and saw Rae racing down the steps, dwarfed in a long black blazer over a black oblong skirt and heavy black boots. She was heading right for me, seething. There were no snacks in her hand, and her hair was back to what I guessed was its natural color, black and shiny like wet tar. She had a museum staff nametag clipped to her lapel.

"Absolutely not," she said, her hand reaching toward my chest, halting me. "You're not going in there."

Yanmei's eyes widened and she looked back and forth between Rae and me. Jessie stepped to the side so he could see what was happening.

"Nice to see you too," I mumbled sarcastically.

"I'm not kidding, Joe. What do you think you're doing?"

"Waiting my turn like everybody else."

"You know, I honestly didn't think you'd be stupid enough to show up here, but since you are, consider yourself banned. No need to make a scene. Just turn around and go back to wherever you came from, yeah?"

Yanmei looked worried. Jessie seemed to have a newfound respect for me. "Dude you're *banned*? I talked about my cock and didn't get banned; what the hell did you do?"

"You can't keep me from going in, Rae."

"I can and I will." She pulled a device from her pocket. It looked like an old flip phone but wasn't. A museum walkie-talkie, maybe? "I'll call Security and tell them you're a threat to the artist, which you are."

"Please don't do that."

I did not want this altercation to happen in public, but I couldn't step out of the line. I'd been standing for almost four hours already, and if I left I'd lose my place and have to start all over the next day.

"Please," I said again. "I need to see her."

Rae laughed with condescension. "Oh, *you* need to see *her*? Is that so? That's nice for you, yeah? And are you really insensitive enough to think that *she* needs to see *you*?"

It was a fair and cutting question, one I hadn't contemplated, and I lost my breath thinking about it.

Jessie said, "Dude are you a Danko stalker or something?"

Rae took her eyes off of me to address Jessie. "Sir, I need you to step back and mind your own business or I'll have you escorted out too."

Jessie raised his hands and backed away. "Whoa OK just chill lady."

"Rae . . ." I sighed.

"No, Joe. Don't 'Rae' me. You weren't there. You'd conveniently disappeared, yeah? *I* was there. *I* saw what she went through. She couldn't eat. She couldn't sleep. All she did was draw weird pictures of forest fires and listen to The fucking National. For a while I wasn't even sure she was going to finish the selfies project. Meanwhile, you were off doing what? Gawking at trees in Wyoming."

"Montana."

"Excuse me?"

"I was in Montana, not Wyoming."

"Whatever. You were gone. Didn't give a fuck. So I don't care if *you* need to see her, she does *not* need to see *you*. Got it?"

I tried to tell myself her words were not chipping away at my resolve, but when I said, "I give a fuck, Rae," my voice sounded feeble.

I thought about screaming October's name and wondered if she would hear me, if she would recognize my voice, if she would care.

Rae again raised her phone thing. After taking a closer look, I decided it resembled a pager from the nineties.

"I'm giving you ten seconds to turn around and walk out the door," she said. And then she started counting backwards.

And I almost did it. I almost aborted the mission. But I thought about how Cal believed this was a good idea, and I trusted that. Not to mention that if I left, if I failed to speak to October, Cal would assume I'd chickened out, and I was better than that now. I had to be.

Rae was down to 2.

"*Wait.*" I was trying to think of the right words, the right tone to sway her. "Listen. The thing is. You're right. You are." I put my hand on her hand, the one holding the phone pager thing, and said, "But are you *sure*?"

She recoiled from my touch, and I felt awkward about having touched her. "Am I sure about what?"

I chose my words carefully and spoke as if I were asking for Rae's advice, not disputing her. Because despite Rae's valid disdain for me, I knew she could be reasonable. She cared about October, and I had to trust that her decision would ultimately be based on that.

"Are you sure about what October would want you to do?" I asked. "It's highly possible you know better than I do what she wants now. But please be honest about it. If you can say with complete certainty that she would want you to kick me out of this line and send me on my way, I'll go." My voice was shaky, my mouth dry. I needed water. Most of the people in line had water with them. I was an amateur art aficionado. I cleared my throat and continued. "But if you think there's even a small chance she might not want you to do that, then you have to let me in, and you know it."

I could see her weighing my logic alongside her aversion.

Yanmei's hands were tiny, like October's, and she was pressing them, palms down, to her chest, one on top of the other like a lowercase "x." I think she recognized my good intentions and was rooting for me.

Jessie mumbled, "I vote to let the guy in."

Rae shot him another shut-up-or-die look and then glared at me with scathing hostility. And she mulled over my appeal for so long the line had to move on without me. Jessie walked by and I became number fifty-eight. The two women behind him apologized and did the same. Fifty-nine. Sixty.

Rae's face was a swarm of bees, buzzing, ready to attack.

"Rae . . ."

She gripped her hips, her elbows pointing out at sharp angles, even through her jacket. Her clothes were so boxy she looked like a child puppet about to break into a dance.

A little guy in a Chicago Cubs jacket walked around me. Sixty-one.

"*Rae . . .*" I begged one last time.

She exhaled with fury. Then she spun on all points of her feet and stomped back up the stairs in her big black boots, fuming and mumbling to herself.

It wasn't until she was gone that I heard the music playing in the room, the volume so low it was scarcely perceptible. I hadn't noticed it amid all the drama, but there it was. The same song, on a loop.

I don't wanna get over you—

TWENTY-SEVEN.

I SQUINTED AT the shattered glass house with Yanmei inside, trying to make out how the experience was going for her. All I could see were blurry, broken up shapes at a table.

I had a hunch that October was going to feel a real connection to Yanmei, and I was right, because when Yanmei's time was up, October stood and hugged the girl. She hadn't done that with anyone else all day, and Susan, the woman behind me now—a seventy-one-year-old art-loving grandmother of seven, on her third visit to the exhibit—said she hadn't seen anything like that the first two times.

Yanmei's smile was so big when she exited the glass house, I thought it might lift her off the ground. I was hoping she was going to make eye contact with me so I could check in and give her that thumbs-up I'd missed out on earlier, but the security guard at the back door ushered her to the rear of the gallery, where she had the option to exit the museum or to go up the steps into the main lobby; Yanmei headed up the steps.

When I was second in line to enter, I noticed the computer screen to my left, positioned on a bronze base at the end of the queue, framed much

246

like the house itself, only without the broken glass. It displayed instructions pertaining to the performance:

> SFMoMA and October Danko, in association with the Thomas Frasier Gallery, welcome you to Sorrow: This is Art. Please follow these directions to insure a pleasant and meaningful experience for all participants:
>
> Be seated immediately upon entering the exhibit.
>
> Once you are seated you may take the artist's hands. You may speak to her if you wish but are not required to do so.
>
> The artist will remain silent throughout the performance.
>
> At no time during the performance are you permitted to use any electronic devices. Photography, video and audio recording are strictly prohibited, and failure to abide by this rule will result in your immediate removal.
>
> It is not mandatory that you participate in the performance for the full five minutes and may leave at any time.
>
> If you chose to remain inside for the duration of your segment, a chime will sound when your time is up.
>
> When you hear the chime, please leave the room swiftly and quietly through the exit.
>
> Thank you for your cooperation.

I broke one of the rules. Before I went in, I opened the voice memo app on my phone and pushed record. I wasn't trying to be subversive, I just didn't think I would remember what I said if I didn't record it, and I wanted to remember.

The daylong wait had felt interminable, but when the guard finally nodded for me to go in, my turn seemed to come too soon. I hesitated at the door. Panicked about what I was going to say. Forgot to breathe. Wiped my sweaty palms on my jeans. Wished I'd brought a flask. Had the urge to bolt.

But I didn't bolt.

I took one step forward.

And another.

And there she was.

Her eyes were closed when I approached the table. Eli, the *Times* writer who hadn't missed a day, had prepared me for this. "Her eyes will be closed when you walk in. She keeps them closed until you take her hands and she gets a feel for you."

I felt glad for it. It gave me a chance to take her in without seeing the scorn and disappointment I was expecting.

She was wearing a ruffly, dusty rose–colored satin gown, the top half of it a dainty camisole. Her arms were thin and pale like the branches of an aspen in winter, her collarbones prominent and graceful underneath the shoulder ties of the dress. She wore no makeup, no jewelry, no shoes, and her hair was pulled back into a knot, though the layers in front hung like wispy fringe around her face. She looked radiantly tired, the way someone carrying burdens is tired. And she was even lovelier than I remembered.

The inside of the house surprised me. When I think of museums, I think architectural austerity, but that's not October's style. The chairs were covered in supple white leather, so plush it looked like whipped cream. The table was polished redwood, and I tried not to attach any meaning to that. There was a thick, shaggy carpet underneath the table, and the subtle tint in the glass walls cast a delicate, rubicund glow over everything.

I sat down slowly, moved to the edge of the seat, and slid my palms underneath October's hands. I was nervous, though my composure remained intact as I felt her gently grip my fingers.

In a matter of seconds, I heard her breath catch somewhere in her chest. A tiny, cognizant gasp.

She recognized me.

My heart pounded against my chest like a fist against a door while I waited for her to open her eyes, but she kept them closed for so long I worried she wasn't going to open them at all.

"October," I said. "Look at me."

Her face was a blank canvas as she raised her chin and adjusted her posture. Then she took another deep breath and braced herself.

When she finally opened her eyes, a noise escaped my throat. A laugh or a cry, it was hard to tell. I began to sob, but I was smiling too. A stupid, blubbering grin. I couldn't help it. I was happy to see her.

I pulled myself together as best I could and said, "Hey."

Her face stayed as neutral as Switzerland, but her eyes were wide and shiny, and a few thick, elegant tears dripped down her cheeks.

I searched her face, trying to figure out if those tears were hers, or echoes of mine, but she was too focused, too committed to her role to reveal her internal world to me. She wasn't there to give, only to take, to hold, and to release. I felt warmth in her neutrality though. Not the rejection I had expected and deserved, but tenderness, and the wide-open heart I'd always known her to have.

I leaned forward and tried to peer deeper into her. She and I have uncannily similar eyes. The same gray circles around the same redwood-brown irises. Maybe that was part of our connection, I thought. We saw ourselves in each other. Two sides of the same moon. The light and the dark.

I watched her take me in and wondered how I looked to her. I was in gray cords and a green flannel over an old T-shirt. I wished I'd dressed better and gotten a haircut. My nose was running from the crying and I wanted to wipe it on my sleeve, but no way was I going to let go of her hands.

For weeks I'd been imagining what I was going to say, entertaining the inane notion that I would be able to speed-explain the last three years of my life: where I'd been, what I'd been doing, why I'd come back. There was no place for that. The space felt too sacred to be filled up with banal specifics. I wanted to be poetic, not prosaic. Though what I ended up expressing was mostly just a series of apologetic tangents.

"I guess I should start by stating the obvious. I fucked up, and I'm sorry." I thought of Cal, of what a looming presence he was in my life, of how his ability to forgive me gave me strength, and I got choked up again. "Fucking up is what I do. Or, what I *did*. Past tense." October was listening with so much concentration and attention it stunned me and made me tremble. "I've spent a lot of my life taking the wrong turns off the right roads. I feel it when it's happening, and I regret it every time it does." I desperately needed to wipe my nose, but all I could do was sniffle. "There's no excuse for what I did to you. I know that. I'm not here to make excuses. I'm here to acknowledge what a coward I was. I'm here to say I'm sorry. If I had more than five minutes, I'd say it a thousand times." I ran my thumbs over her knuckles, caressed the tops of her hands. "I hope you can find it in your heart to hear these words and accept them as my truth and my sorrow. If I've learned anything in the last three years—and I have, I swear—it's that I'll never be any greater than the sum of my missed opportunities unless I stop missing them." I shook my head, struggled to express exactly what I was feeling, and then collapsed into it. "Fuck, October. I tried so hard to let you go. All this time I tried to stop loving you. But it just dawned on

me that I don't want to stop loving you. I just want to stop missing you."
My affection for her overwhelmed me, and it was all I could do not to dive
across the table and pull her into my arms. "Every day I think about what
I did to you. I live with that every day. I miss you every day. And the worst
part? You were my friend, first and foremost, and I hurt you."

I started shivering, and seconds later I saw goose bumps all over
October's arms.

"I know that in the grand scheme of things, we spent so little time
together, this might not mean anything to you anymore, but it means a lot to
me. It always has. Even when I didn't know how to say it. The way you used
to look at me. The way you saw me for exactly who I was but never asked
me to be anyone else. You believed in me. You changed me. You *inspired* me.
And if I died tomorrow, I'd want you to know that."

I figured my time was almost up, and I said, "Listen, I can't *not* do
things anymore. I can't *not* try. So I'm going to ask you something I have
no right to ask, but when this is all over, when you get home, do you think
I could call you? I'm back in Mill Valley for good, and I'd really like to call
you. Just to talk. Could we do that? Could we have coffee or go for a hike
or something?"

She didn't respond. She couldn't. Or wouldn't.

"How about this," I suggested. "Blink once for Yes and twice for No.
Yes, I can call you; No, you want me to leave you alone."

She held her eyes open and didn't flinch. And then the chime went off.

"OK. I get it." I nodded. "I understand."

The security guard looked at me from the doorway.

October let go before I did.

She hadn't blinked.

I went back the next day. Actually, what happened was I couldn't sleep, and
I drove to the museum at 3:00 a.m., this time with a backpack carrying two
breakfast sandwiches from an all-night diner on Lombard, a thermos full
of coffee, and drawings of the art project I'd been working on for the past
month, the one that came to me in a vision after I dropped Cal off at the
airport.

My original concept had been a sculptural, working hourglass filled with as
much sand as it would take to flow continuously from the top bulb into the
bottom until my life was over. I estimated forty years' worth of material as a
safe bet, the thought being that every day I'd literally be able to see my time
running out, and that would be a quotidian impetus for me to stop wasting
it.

I ran the idea by an architect I used to work with at Harper & Sons, and while he agreed it would be possible to build such an edifice, he concluded that the amount of sand needed, and the structural engineering it would take to hold the weight of that sand, would necessitate a sculpture the size of a small building. But I wanted something I could look at on my wall or, at the very least, in my backyard.

After further consideration, I reimagined the sculpture as a light installation made up of 14,600 tiny lights—the estimated amount of days I had left. The lights would spell the words "The Clock Is Ticking," and every day one light would go out until all 14,600 lights had gone out and, most likely, so had I. Hopefully with fewer regrets.

I'd consulted my old buddy Len, electrician extraordinaire, on the optimal way to ensure the sculpture would last for forty years, and he suggested I make the tiny lights out of hollow, colored glass, not filament. Sort of like an elaborate Lite-Brite, with a back panel that uses two separate light sources, one active and one as backup. When the active one burns out, the backup will kick in while the other is being replaced, and so on and so forth, enabling continuous illumination for the duration of my life.

For over an hour that morning, Eli and I were the only two people in line, and we passed the time talking about a trip he'd taken to Sweden over the summer. He'd been on assignment in Fulufjället National Park and stopped to see a Norway spruce known as Old Tjikko, a tree that's allegedly been growing since the Neolithic period.

Eli showed me photos of the tree with the kind of dorky zeal I assume I exhibit when I'm talking about redwoods and guitars.

"This guy was born around the time humans learned to cultivate wheat," Eli said. "That makes him older than bread. Remarkable, huh?"

It was. And at roughly sixteen feet tall, with skeletal branches that sag downward, Old Tjikko looks more like a sad Charlie Brown Christmas tree than the oldest known *Picea abies* on the planet.

"It's actually the root system that dates back ninety-five hundred years," Eli explained. "The trunk and branches have died and been reborn multiple times."

I wondered aloud if I'd been identifying with the wrong tree all my life. And without thinking, I said, "You should tell October about Old Tjikko when you see her today. She likes trees too."

Eli had been nearby during my altercation with Rae the day before, but he'd refrained from asking me any questions. Now he knit his brow, spoke softly. "You two have some kind of history, I gather."

I liked Eli. He was interesting and thoughtful. We'd exchanged phone numbers, and he'd invited me to go sailing with him the following weekend, so I didn't feel right about making anything up. But I also knew I would need a few beers in me before I could give him the real scoop.

"October and I used to work together." My body stiffened, a reminder that everything about that woman still lived inside of it. "We were close. It didn't end well. I guess I'm trying to rectify that."

The sun rose at 7:24 a.m., and by then the line was around the block and past the parking garage. The crowd was feisty that morning, undoubtedly because it was the last day of the exhibit and everyone who hadn't made it in yet had shown up expecting entry before it closed. There was a lot of pushing and shoving. People tried to cut the line. One guy offered Eli two grand for his spot. A girl in Birkenstocks and thick wool socks offered me sex for mine.

About an hour before the doors opened, a museum representative named Tamisha came out, counted off the first one hundred people by marking them with little yellow stickers, and announced that anyone who didn't have a sticker would be turned away. However, she assured those one hundred people that they would all get in to see October, even if it ran beyond the 5:00 p.m. cutoff time.

The 103rd person in line was a man who claimed he'd come all the way from Croatia to participate in *Sorrow*, to which Tamisha replied, "You should have come sooner."

In protest, the man tore off his clothes, curled up in a ball on the sidewalk, and screamed like someone auditioning for a role in a horror film until Security came and took him away.

All the commotion set a tone that Eli called "unbefitting for the last day of such a beautiful experience." He asked me to hold his spot, wandered off for a bit, and came back with five big boxes of doughnuts that he passed out to everyone in line.

At first I didn't take one because I didn't want my fingers to be sticky when I held October's hands, but Eli had anticipated that problem and also had a bag of little, individually wrapped moist towelettes. He passed those out too.

I was as nervous walking in on the second day as I had been on the first. Maybe even more so, because I was second in line behind Eli and had much less time to mentally prepare. In fact, I was already standing beside the computer screen rereading the rules when the massive shades fully disappeared into the ceiling.

Eli was still in with October when I opened my voice memo app and once again pushed record. What can I say? I'm a rebel.

I approached the door as soon as I saw Eli exit, then I waited for Security to wave me in, and I entered the room.

October was wearing the same dress she'd had on the day before, except in a different color. This one was a light, shimmery blue, and the tint in the shattered panes seemed to match the dress, though I was fairly certain it had been a pinkish rose color twenty hours earlier. Her hair was down this time, and she had a tiny gold beetle on a chain around her neck.

I slid quietly into the chair and took a mental photograph of October's expression so I would be able to notice if anything changed once she realized I had returned.

My hands were cold from standing outside, and I rubbed them together to warm them up before I touched her. Then I did what I'd done the day before. I slid my palms underneath her palms and closed my fingers around her fingers. And something did change. I saw it. The flash of a smirk, so scarcely perceptible, so minuscule a stranger would have never noticed it. But I wasn't a stranger. I knew the subtle nuances of her face, and in that half an instant I saw it sneak up on her, and I saw her immediately pull it down.

She opened her eyes right away, and while the imperturbable facade was still visible, there was something underneath it, something I strove to name, but the only word that came close to what I observed was "amusement," and that might as well have been an emoji. I had no idea how to interpret it.

I'd come with a pipedream plan: I was going to tell October about my art project, and she was going to think it was brilliant and want to work on it with me. But once I was in the chair, that topic didn't seem right.

"You wanna know something?" I said, adlibbing. "I still keep a list of words on my phone." I readjusted my hands so that I had a better hold. "Whenever I stumble across a good one, I add it to my file. There's over a hundred now. And every time I add one, I think, *I wish I could share this with October.*" It happened again. A subtle shift. This time in the grip she had on my fingers. Her skin was alive. It felt everything. "It's true. Whenever I'm trying to decide how I feel about something, I think of you. I try to see it through your eyes. I do it with songs, with art, with coffee shops and cheeseburgers and current events. You're my filter and compass for everything. Anyway, I added a word this morning when I was talking to Eli, and it seems relevant. "Heliotropism." It's the tendency of plants to turn or lean toward the light in order to grow. I'm convinced the concept applies to humans too."

I recalled something Cal had texted me the night before. A meme that said if you stare into someone's eyes long enough, your heart rates will synch up, and I decided to test that. I wanted to sit with October, to be with her without talking, the way we used to do at work. I refocused my gaze and didn't say another word, and October stayed with me, our twin eyes in sync, our chests aligned. I breathed when she breathed, and I imagined that her breath was filling my lungs and mine was filling hers. It was exciting. Intimate. And when the chime went off a few minutes later, I let go of her hands but didn't let go of her eyes, not until I stood to leave.

I exited the exhibit, walked up the maple steps and into the main lobby. Then I wandered out the front door and back to my truck, all the while *thump thump thumping* my hand against my chest, to keep the rhythm going, so as not to lose the beat of her heart.

TWENTY-EIGHT.

I'D STOPPED HAVING conversations with Sam during my time in Montana. I can't say why for certain, but I guessed it was because I had no references for him in that environment, no memories. I couldn't feel him there at all. Likewise, I was a catastrophe when I got to Whitefish, and it's hard to look for, let alone see, magic in the world when you're broken inside. Beyond that, I allowed for the possibility that Sam was so disappointed in my pusillanimity, he'd thrown in the towel.

However, once I was back in Mill Valley, Sam returned. It was coming up on the twenty-fifth anniversary of his death, and I promised Ingrid I would do something special to honor his memory. Ingrid and I had observed the day annually for a while when I was young, but Bob had given us a hard time about it, chastising us for "celebrating" Sam's death, accusing us of dwelling on the past, and eventually we stopped.

Nevertheless, twenty-five years felt like a long time, and I decided to go to Armstrong Redwoods State Natural Reserve in Guerneville to pay tribute to my brother. Bob, Ingrid, Sam, and I had spent Sam's sixteenth and last birthday there, hiking and making hot dogs on the grill in the picnic area near Colonel Armstrong.

Colonel Armstrong was the oldest redwood in the grove and Sam's all-time favorite tree. Incidentally, Colonel Armstrong would have been my favorite as well, but when we were kids and I told Sam I liked Colonel the best too, he said, "I called it first, Joey." That meant I had to come up with my own original answer or he'd deem me a copycat, and I went with Giant Tree.

Guerneville is a little over sixty-five miles northwest of Mill Valley. Allowing for some traffic, it would take me about an hour and fifteen minutes to get there. My plan was to drive up that morning, hike around a bit, have my memorial for Sam, play a little guitar, and be home by dinnertime.

Before I headed out, I wrote a list of all the things I missed about Sam on a Glacier National Park postcard I found in my backpack. I'd purchased the card before Bob died, thinking I might send it to him, but of course I never did.

At first I imagined leaving the postcard at the foot of Colonel Armstrong, but for all intents and purposes, that was littering, and I resolved to burn it instead. I shoved it between the pages of the book I was reading and headed out to my truck, lugging my Martin, my backpack, and my coffee thermos, which I was going to fill up at Equator when I stopped to grab breakfast on my way out of town.

Over a month had passed since *Sorrow* ended, and I had neither seen nor heard from October. And not for lack of trying. I wandered around Marin more than necessary, frequenting all the places I knew she visited. I went to the farmers' market in San Rafael three Sundays in a row. I hiked the fire road behind Casa Diez a couple times a week. I even drove to YogaWorks one Monday night, right about the time the 6:00 class she used to go to was letting out, even though there was nothing around YogaWorks I could pretend I was doing if I did run into her.

My last attempt at contact had been to mail her a manila envelope containing copies of the drawings I'd done of my light sculpture, with a short note explaining the piece.

She didn't respond.

The weather app on my phone said the high temperature in Guerneville was fifty-three degrees, and before I left I threw on my fleece pullover, overkill in Mill Valley, which was unusually balmy that morning, but it would be necessary under the shade of the redwoods.

When I got down to town, I parked in the lot behind Mill Valley Market and ran in to get matches, a newspaper, and some wood to start a proper fire at the picnic site. I had some incense too, and planned on burning it with the postcard as an offering to Sam.

I took the bag of supplies back to my truck, dropped it on the seat, grabbed my thermos and the book I was reading—a weird memoir about a man who had moved from Manhattan to the Rocky Mountains to follow his lifelong dream of raising alpacas—and walked the two blocks to Equator.

The notoriously slow-moving line was long, and I considered going to Peet's Coffee across the street instead, but I wanted breakfast, and Peet's didn't serve good breakfast, so I stood there and read about alpacas while I waited. Besides, there was an old Pearl Jam song playing over the speakers in Equator. Pearl Jam had been Sam's favorite band at the time of his death, and since it was a Sam-themed day, that felt like a sign for me to stay.

I didn't see her until I was about to place my order. She was sitting on the bench all the way to the right, against the wall of windows, drawing in a small sketchbook. A coffee cup sat beside her pencil case on the tiny round table in front of her. She was wearing flared jeans that looked like they were from the 1970s, a rainbow-striped sweater, and sandals that she'd kicked off onto the floor. Her legs were crisscrossed underneath her.

My hand shook as I handed my thermos to the girl in the gothy purple lipstick behind the counter. I vaguely heard the girl ask me if I wanted the single origin or the Equator blend, and I'm pretty sure I said single origin. I wasn't completely out of my head though, because I had intended to grab one of the prepackaged cups of yogurt for breakfast, but I asked for an egg sandwich instead; because that would be made to order, it would take a while, and I'd have to stand directly in front of October's table to wait for it.

I dropped my change into the tip jar, approached the table, and stood there hoping October would feel my presence and look up, but she was too engrossed in what she was doing. From upside down it looked like she was drawing a leopard, but it also could have been a skyscraper.

"Hey," I said.

Her head rose quickly, her eyes wide, her look askance. I watched her closely, to catalog any emotions she might choose to reveal, but she went Switzerland on me again.

"Hey yourself."

My throat felt dry and chalky. I took a sip from my thermos and the coffee in it was so hot it scalded my mouth.

Silence swirled like smoke in the space between us, and I knew it was up to me to diffuse it.

"How are things?" I said stupidly.

She had been biting on the end of her pencil, but she took it out of her mouth and twirled it around in her fingers like a little baton. "Things are good."

I cocked my head to the side, to get a better look at what she was drawing. "What are you working on?"

"Nothing." She shut the sketchbook and set the pencil on top of it. "I'm literally not working on anything."

"It looks like you're drawing."

"Doodling." She wiped eraser crumbs from the table, and when she spoke again there was a restrained tone to her voice. "I was pretty worn out after *Sorrow*. I'm taking a few months off to recharge."

I couldn't imagine October not working for that long, and I said, "What are you going to do all day? If you're not working, I mean?"

"We'll see," she said. "I've been traveling a lot. After the exhibit ended, I rented a cabin in Joshua Tree for a couple weeks. And I went to Rochester for Thanksgiving. I guess now I'll just be doodling and drinking coffee."

That explained why I couldn't find her in town. She hadn't been there.

"I've always wanted to go to Joshua Tree," I said. I thought better of asking the next question, but I asked it anyway. "Did you go by yourself?"

She made a face indicating that was none of my business. Nevertheless, she said, "No." There was a pause, and I was certain it was for effect. "I drove down with Diego. And I didn't talk to a single human for ten days. It was a dream."

"I'll bet."

She stretched out her legs and set her bare feet on the floor. Then she picked up her cup and held it in her palm. It was almost empty, and she stared into it as if it were full of secrets. She pulled her legs back up underneath her. Put the cup down. Ran her nail across a scratch in the table. Looked around the cafe. She seemed nervous too.

I looked at the book in my hand and thought of something I'd just read. "Did you know that alpacas can die of loneliness?"

She digested that fact and laughed. And it was a genuine October laugh. The one that used to be followed by her telling me I was funny or cute.

"Good thing you're not an alpaca," she said.

I laughed too, though there was something tragic about the joke, something that hurt my heart. And when I met October's eyes, I recognized the same nostalgic sentiment there, a desire to make all the tacit conversations explicit.

"Did you get the envelope I sent you?"

"The light sculpture," she said. "I did."

"And?"

"I like it."

"You do?"

She nodded. "Very much."

"I'm going to build it."

"Good."

She readjusted her position on the bench so that only one foot was underneath her, the other on the floor. Then she looked me up and down and said, "Why are you dressed like it's about to snow?"

The fleece jacket. No wonder I was so warm. "I'm on my way to Guerneville. To visit Colonel Armstrong. It's supposed to be chilly up there today."

"Who's Colonel Armstrong?"

"He's a redwood. Over fourteen hundred years old. And 308 feet tall."

There it was again. That smile.

A guy I recognized as someone I used to work with at FarmHouse called my name from behind the counter and handed me my breakfast sandwich. It was all wrapped up to go, and I had no reason to linger any longer.

I turned back toward October's table, and for another long, subtext-filled moment we looked at each other without saying anything.

"Well. I guess I should get going." I hoped she would ask me to stay, but she didn't. "It was really nice to see you. To talk to you."

All of a sudden she looked profoundly sad. "You too, Joe."

"Well," I said again. "I guess I'll see you around."

She nodded. "See you around."

I had parked under a big, shady oak tree, and when I got back to my truck, it felt like dusk inside the cab. I sat there without turning on the engine, without moving, crippled by a desperate longing. *Saudade. Desiderium.* There was a lump of regret in my throat, thick and hot like a ball of wax, and a familiar hunger in my belly so gnawing, so dire, it felt as though it were eating me from the inside out.

No, I thought, my breath short and quick. *Not again.*

I dropped my head back and let out a deep, rage-filled roar.

Fourteen thousand six hundred days.

I wouldn't make it. Not like this.

I thought about a question I'd asked October back when things were good between us, when I believed we had a future. "If we'd never gotten together, if I hadn't been willing, I mean, do you think it would have haunted you?"

I remember her looking at me like I was crazy. "Why would it haunt *me?*" she'd asked. "I said yes to us. What more could I have done than that?"

I got out of the truck and sprinted back to the cafe, stopping outside the entrance to catch my breath before I went in.

She was still there. Not drawing, just sitting with her elbow on the table, her chin in her palm, watching the barista pour hot water in slow, concentric circles over coffee grounds in a filter above a Chemex.

"Hey."

She turned toward me, her eyes dancing all around my face.

I slid onto the bench beside her and leaned in. *Heliotropism.* Bending, turning, reaching toward the light.

Fourteen thousand six hundred days, I thought.

"I was just wondering . . ." I said. "Do you want to come with me? To see Colonel Armstrong, I mean. I think you'd like him."

There was an aura of calm around her now. It radiated like heat on a sidewalk, blurring everything in the background.

She reached over and rested her hand on top of mine, and I could feel the electricity in her fingertips, prickling through my skin, digging down for my truth.

Her eyes were wide and sharp, her breath long and steady, and she titled her head slightly to the right, examining me as if she were in her studio, in front of a canvas, contemplating the next brushstroke.

We were inside of this. Both of us. A work in progress. A living exhibit. The ultimate art project, for which there was no ending. And I wasn't certain if it was my vision or hers.

"Yes," she said. "As a matter of fact, I do."

Acknowledgements

First and foremost, I want to thank my agent, Albert Zuckerman. The wisdom and love with which he guided and championed this book is one of the greatest gifts anyone has ever given me, and I am forever in his debt.

Everyone at Woodhall Press, especially Colin Hosten, for believing in this story, and for being willing to take a chance on it; Matthew Winkler, for his thoughtful editorial notes; and Paulette Baker for her precise attention to detail.

I am full of gratitude to Genevieve Gagne-Hawes for her insightful notes on early drafts of this manuscript.

Much thanks and love to my incomparable guitar consultants, Kyle Nicolaides and Don Miggs, and to my trusted construction authority, Jeff Jungsten. And a special shout-out to Tad Buchanan, for introducing me to a beautiful book about redwoods that inadvertently unlocked secrets to this story and its characters.

Big love and thanks to Tim Sandlin, for being a cherished reader, writer, and friend.

Lots of love and thanks to my extraordinary assistant Cielle Taaffe-Spurgeon, for her boundless creativity and support.

This book would quite literally not exist without the friendship and encouragement of Tarryn Fisher and Colleen Hoover. I love you both to bits.

I would be remiss if I didn't acknowledge the work of artist Marina Abramovic as an inspiration to *Sorrow: This is Art*.

Extra special indebted gratitude goes to The National, a band whose music planted seeds in my head and heart that grew like a redwood into this novel.

And while we're on the subject of music, a heartfelt thank you, as always, to U2. Decades ago, their music opened a door for me, leading me into a world where love never ends, and where sonic landscapes are the portals to that love. Forty years later those landscapes still live inside of me and continue to inspire so much of my work.

Unconditional and eternal love to my family: Candy, Eddie, Lisa, Nikki, Asher, Milo, Jasper, Don and Chad. I'd do anything for you people.

To JP. With love and gratitude x infinity. Because what is true is never lost.

And to Scott. For all the hours you listened to me talk about this story. For all the drafts you were kind enough to read. For all the notes you were smart enough to give. But most of all, for being the spiritual warrior that you are, walking so bravely beside me on this magnificent journey. I love you truly, madly, deeply, and eternally.

About the Author

[Photo credit: Jenny Jacklin Stratton]

TIFFANIE DEBARTOLO IS THE AUTHOR of the novels *God-Shaped Hole* and *How To Kill a Rockstar*, as well as the graphic novel *Grace: Based on the Jeff Buckley Story*. She is the co-founder and Chief Executive Super Goddess of Bright Antenna Records, the co-founder of the ShineMaker foundation, and also wrote and directed the film *Dream For An Insomniac*. She lives in Mill Valley, California.

Check out these other titles from Woodhall Press:

The Astronaut's Son by Tom Seigel

A finalist for the 2019 Connecticut Book of the Year, this fast-paced novel follow's Jonathan Stein's relentless pursuit of the truth about his father's death—leading to disturbing revelations about the Nazis who worked for NASA. Come along for the ride as Tom Seigel takes us into the murky past and toward a thrilling future.

Songs from a Voice by Baron Wormser

No one can speak for Bob Dylan except Bob Dylan. Fiction, however, has other thoughts. In *Songs from a Voice* Baron Wormser has created a narrator who offers a first-person take on the years that begin in the spaces of the upper Midwest and wind up in the streets of Greenwich Village. Baron Wormser's eighteenth book is a genre-bending novel that explores creativity through poetry, prose, and American music history. Songs from a Voice is a homage, investigation, sly nod and, ultimately, an affirmation of the strength of one man's imagination.

Man in the (Rearview) Mirror
by LaRue Cook

A finalist for the 2019 Georgia Author of the Year Award, this essay collection has been hailed by Pulitzer winner Eli Saslow as "a work of vivid reporting about this fractious American moment." LaRue Cook explores a deeply personal journey through love, loss, and self-discovery, using the lens of a physical journey across the United States, and abroad, by a former corporate sports-editor-turned-Uber driver. Part voyeuristic, part inspirational, sometimes hilarious, always thoughtful and probing, *Man in the (Rearview) Mirror* is a book about learning to love yourself (and others) at a time in America when it is often too easy to hate

WITHDRAWN FROM LIBRARY

CPSIA information can be obtained
at www.ICGtesting.com
Printed in the USA
LVHW090826201020
669177LV00013B/908